JUST NAUGHTY ENOUGH

Gil took her whispered words as a benediction, his kiss ravenous. Need pounded through him like a runaway train. He'd always prided himself on his ability to please a lady, but with Josie his control seemed nonexistent.

"I want to stoke the fire in you, sweetheart. Touch you all over."

She set off sparks in him that he'd never felt before, sending his intentions to take it slow and easy up in smoke. "Yes."

He longed to rip their clothes off. But something about laying here half-dressed in the dark felt just naughty enough to be nice.

Also by Janette Kenny

ONE REAL COWBOY

Published by Zebra Books

ONE REAL MAN

JANETTE KENNY

ZEBRA BOOKS
Kensington Publishing Corp.
www.kensingtonbooks.com

ZEBRA BOOKS are published by

Kensington Publishing Corp.
850 Third Avenue
New York, NY 10022

All Kensington titles, imprints, and distributed lines are available at special quantity discounts for bulk purchases for sales
promotion, premiums, fund-raising, educational, or institu-
tional use.

Special book excerpts or customized printings can also be created to fit specific needs. For details, write or phone the office
of the Kensington Special Sales Manager: Attn. Special Sales
Department. Kensington Publishing Corp., 850 Third Avenue,
New York, NY 10022. Phone: 1-800-221-2647.

Zebra and the Z logo Reg. U.S. Pat. & TM Off.

ISBN-13: 978-0-8217-8147-0
ISBN-10: 0-8217-8147-2

First Printing: April 2008
10 9 8 7 6 5 4 3 2 1

Printed in the United States of America

Acknowledgments

To Bill Burleigh at Laramie River Ranch in Jelm, Wyoming, for answering my long list of questions about working and dude ranches. Much thanks, Bill!

To Gene Sikora, for challenging me to get half of this story outlined "in case" an editor wanted to buy it. She did, and I was ready.

To Sharon Long, who honestly told me what worked, what didn't, and why. To Amy Knupp, for reading this manuscript in the eleventh hour, even though she had a deadline facing her. The help you both gave me was priceless.

To Mom, who continued to have faith in me when my own faltered.

Chapter 1

Gil Yancy leaned against the porch post and gave Rocky Point Ranch a long, hard gander.

His old friend's idea of a thriving cattle ranch and Gil's sure as hell weren't the same. Oh, the clapboard house was right nice, but the weathered outbuildings and cabins could use a good whitewashing. Hell, if not for the curtains fluttering at the windows or the string of horses milling in the corral, he'd swear the place was deserted.

To think he'd nearly thrown his shoulder out patting himself on the back for buying up a third of Rocky Point Ranch for a song. To think he'd finally stopped dodging that Pinkerton detective and had it out with him in Maverick.

Gil blew out a weary breath. Even if he wanted to, he couldn't walk away now and come out with a winning hand. Nope, he'd make his stand right here on this ranch.

He was fixing to mosey down to the barn when a

woman stepped from a cabin nearest the swaybacked bunkhouse. She stopped on the stoop and tossed a bucket of water on the ground, then wiped her brow and pressed a hand to the small of her back, like it ached her. A kerchief held her hair off her face, and the wind set her skirt and apron dancing a wild jig.

Though he couldn't see her face, she looked fairly young. Mighty shapely too. The woman picked up the bucket and slipped back inside the cabin.

Since Everett Andrews was older than dirt, this bit of muslin must be the housekeeper. Yep, his old friend probably hired the woman to help his missus with the chores and tend the cabins for this guest venture Mrs. Andrews had cooked up.

Gil's boot heels kicked up dust and his spurs chink-chinked as he headed across the parched ground. At least he'd found someone who could tell him where to find Everett.

The three cabins looked new and about the size of line shacks. Guests' quarters, he reckoned.

He stepped up to the open cabin door. The woman was on her hands and knees, her faded calico skirt spread around her as she scrubbed the pine floor-boards. Her rounded bottom gyrated like a silent invitation to come have a feel.

A twinge of lust caught him off guard and got him thinking about other chores this woman might take on here. *Get your mind off diddling, Yancy.* Hell, the woman was probably married to one of the ranch hands.

He rolled his shoulders to work out the tension knotting him and stepped through the slice of sunlight filtering through the lone window. "Morning, ma'am."

She looked up, but instead of the smile he usually

received from the gentler sex, she gawked at him like he was the devil come calling.

Dammit! He hadn't meant to put a fright in her. "I'm looking for Everett Andrews."

"No," she said.

If that wasn't the craziest fool thing to say. The woman got to her feet and backed up, clutching that rag to her chest and looking scared to death.

That's when recognition slapped Gil upside the head so hard his Stetson damned near went tumbling onto the newly scrubbed floor. He blinked to make sure his eyes weren't playing tricks on him.

Nope. It was her, all right.

The odds had to be a million to one he'd find her again. As for the rewards—Hell, they couldn't come at a better time.

"I reckoned our paths would cross one of these days."

He stepped inside and heeled the door shut, casting a long shadow that swallowed her up. Her eyes took on a wild, skittish look, but instead of cowering, she jabbed a finger at the door.

"Get out of here."

So the feisty little filly found her tongue. "Afraid I can't do that, even if I had a mind to."

Gil smiled and stepped around the bucket. She'd filled out right nice and lost that hungry look that had haunted him. But she still had that wealth of black hair that had felt like silk gliding through his fingers. Still had a pouty bottom his hands itched to fondle.

Seeing her again was better than his memory. Without all that paint women of her ilk put on their faces, she appeared younger than she had twelve years ago, writhing beneath him in a Kansas bordello.

But it was her. Make no mistake about it. This time she wasn't going to get away from him.

No, sirree. This sweet little thief owed him plenty and he meant to collect every red cent with interest.

The woman sidled to the wall, looking as wary as a rabbit cornered by a coyote. She was trapped in more ways than one and knew it.

Good. Gil wasn't a violent man, but after what she'd done to him, she had reason to be shaking in her unmentionables. He'd never given up hope he'd catch up to the thieving shady lady one day. And when he did—

"What are you doing here?"

"That's none of your business." He reached for her.

She yelped, threw the scrub rag at his head and ran toward the door.

Gil dodged the sopping rag and grabbed her. He pressed her to the wall and planted his palms beside her stiff body, corralling her. He caught a faint whiff of vanilla that was at complete odds with his spicy memory of her.

"Let me go."

"In due time. I want the money you stole from me."

She swallowed hard and seemed to shrink in on herself, feeling tiny and vulnerable in his grip. Gil snorted. He'd fallen for that act once before and ended up the big loser. He damn sure wouldn't be that gullible a second time.

"How did you find me?"

Pure dumb luck. Not that he'd tell her that. Let her think he'd been tracking her all this time. Let her squirm.

"Don't see as that makes a bit of difference now, does it? I'm here and I want my money."

"I'm sure you do, but I don't have it."

"You don't have it right now, but a lady as talented as yourself knows how to come by it."

She jerked her head to one side as if wounded by the truth.

Guilt bulldogged Gil for being crude, leaving a slow burn across his nape. Though she was a calico queen, and not some lady he had to mind his manners around, he'd never talked vulgar or laid a mean hand on any woman. But after treating him to the best ride he'd ever had in his life, this shady lady had coldcocked him and robbed him blind.

"You don't understand."

He scrubbed a hand over his mouth. "Then explain it to me, 'cause I know how much money I've squandered on shady ladies like yourself."

If looks could kill, his carcass would be fertilizing a field. "Men like you soiled the doves in the first place."

"It wasn't my fault you chose to make a living whoring. What do you do for Everett Andrews?"

"Whatever I damn well want."

He glanced at her red, chapped hands and realized they belonged to a hard-working woman, not a sporting one. "Everett and his missus know you made your living on your back before they hired you as a domestic? That you weren't beyond stealing a cowpoke blind?"

"Do they know?" She pressed her lips together as if trying hard not to snicker, then laughed and laughed until tears streaked down her pale cheeks.

He frowned. The woman was either half-pixilated

or thought it was sidesplittingly funny that she'd gotten the best of him.

"Ain't nothing amusing about what you did and I doubt the Andrewses will think so either."

Her laughter died, but her pale blue eyes failed to reflect one iota of remorse. "How do you know Everett?"

"We go way back. Been good friends a right long time."

"Is that a fact? I suppose you're good friends with his wife as well?"

"Can't say I've had the pleasure to make her acquaintance yet, but I reckon me and Mrs. Andrews will get along right fine."

"Don't hold your breath," she said. "Now get off Rocky Point Ranch."

"I ain't going nowhere. I own a piece of this spread."

"You what?"

"Last fall, I agreed to be Everett's trail guide. Maybe you don't know, but his missus and him are starting up a guest ranch venture and Everett cut me in on it. So you ain't getting rid of me."

"That's where you're wrong, cowboy." She twisted free and ran toward the old Henry rifle propped in the corner.

Hell's bells! She aimed to plug him.

Gil lunged after her, snatched the rifle from her hands and held it out of her reach. He spun her around and corralled her between the potbellied stove and him.

Instead of the scrawny body he'd remembered, she was all soft, womanly curves. But still was as wild as a broom-tail, kicking and bucking and hollering at the top of her lungs.

"Let me go!"

"So you can shoot me? Forget it. I'm hanging on to you until I talk to Everett."

She stopped struggling and looked up at him. "You don't— Oh, my."

He waited for her to go on. Watched surprise and worry play over her face. Then her eyelids drifted down a mite and her mouth went all dewy and soft. Inviting lips.

He swallowed hard, almost tasting them. Dammit all, she was fixing to seduce him. Wouldn't you know his pecker thought that was a fine idea. Good thing his mind was stronger than his cravings. Or would be once he reined in his lust.

"Where's Everett?"

"Gone," she whispered, her fists uncurling to graze his sides as she pressed her breasts against his chest, firing him up for a fare-thee-well.

Yep, a bolt of heat burned through his shirt and arrowed to his crotch. The fact they were alone wasn't lost on him.

This spitfire was offering herself, and he was mighty hungry for a woman's touch. He shoved thoughts of Everett from his mind and lowered his head toward her.

Out of the corner of his eye, he saw her swing something at him. A heartbeat later, pain exploded in his noggin and licked over his scalp faster and hotter than a prairie fire.

His vision blurred. The last thing on his mind before his knees buckled and he crashed to the floor was that for the second time in his life, the shady lady had clobbered him a good one.

Josephine Andrews clutched the small, round stove lid to her heaving chest and scrambled away from the man she'd hoped she'd never lay eyes on again. He sprawled still as death, but the rise and fall of his broad chest proved he was alive. Just like before.

And the same as way back then, she shook like a leaf caught in the wind. She could scarce draw a breath. Fear kicked her heart into a flat-out gallop. Mercy, she still didn't know who he was, or what she was going to do with him.

One thing was mighty clear: he'd be madder than a rabid dog when he came to.

She gnawed her lip and glanced at the rifle propped against the sideboard. One bullet would get rid of this cowboy forever. But she hadn't been able to shoot him years ago, and she sure couldn't do it now.

Josie pressed her back against the wall and rubbed her aching temples. She didn't see any easy way out of this fix Everett left her in. Willing or not, this man from her past was her new trail guide. He now owned part of Rocky Point. Or was this snake lying?

That's what she had to find out. But how? The bill of sale Maverick Land and Security made up for Everett was how. Her husband's copy was in the lock-box hidden under the kitchen floor, along with the will that Everett had drawn up that left everything he owned to Josie and Sarah Ann.

Maybe this man had the title on him. What did Everett say his name was? Will Clancy? No, no. Yancy? Yes, that was it. Gil Yancy.

Josie set the lid back on the stove and knelt beside the cowboy. She slid her hand into a vest pocket.

Touching this big man had her face burning something fierce. And the flood of memories—

He was as big and warm as she recalled, and with his eyes closed, just as vulnerable as she'd left him. Yes, she'd taken all his money, and a part of him with her. More nights than she cared to recall since then, she'd lain in bed wondering what had happened to the handsome cowboy.

She pushed those thoughts from her mind and checked his other pocket. Her fingers grazed cool metal. She tugged out a gold pocket watch. Her heart sank as she read the name engraved on the cover— Gil Yancy.

Josie slipped the watch back in his pocket and kept on searching. Finally, she tugged a folded paper out of his pocket.

She read it slowly, her heart sinking as she recognized Everett's mark. The cowboy wasn't joshing her. Gil Yancy was her new trail guide.

Oh, Everett, do you have any idea the fix you left me in?

Her stomach heaved. Maybe she should shoot Yancy dead anyway. She sure couldn't give back what she'd stolen from him, though that lusty gleam in his eyes proved she'd have a devil of a time having a respectable partnership with this man.

Like Reid Barclay, her neighbor to the north. Reid wanted one thing from her, and he hadn't hesitated to proposition her a month after Everett passed on. He was willing to pay handsomely for her charms.

Josie stared at the man sprawled at her feet. He'd be more apt to trick her into his bed. Or worse— force her there to keep her past a secret from the townsfolk. And what about her daughter?

She heard a scuffling at the door and looked up.

Sarah Ann stared at the man, and Josie's heart gave an odd thump. Thank God she didn't favor the cowboy.

But judging by that frown, Josie figured her daughter had seen more than she should have. Had she heard them arguing, too?

Sarah Ann smacked her straw hat on one leg of her britches, sending dust flying everywhere. "Who's he?"

"Gil Yancy, our new trail guide. I cleaned up in here, so don't be making a mess."

"Sorry, Ma." Sarah Ann ventured closer, looking and sounding more like a young cowpoke than an eleven-year-old girl. "You sure walloped him a good one."

Her shoulders drooped. So Sarah Ann had seen. "I didn't mean to hit him so hard, but he walked right in and scared the dickens out of me."

She hated to lie to her daughter. But she didn't have any choice. At least not one she could live with.

Sarah Ann nudged one of his boots with her own. "Is he dead?"

"No, he's knocked out cold."

Josie draped an arm around Sarah Ann's narrow shoulders and urged her away from the cowboy and the past that had haunted Josie for so long. Her daughter meant the world to her. God knew she'd do anything to protect her. She'd already done the unthinkable long ago. What more would she be forced to do to keep this child she loved safe?

"Go fetch Hiram," Josie said.

Sarah Ann looked like she'd balk; then she ran toward the barn. Josie hugged herself and stepped back inside the cabin. Gil Yancy gave her a mountain of new worries.

As her advertisements boasted, for the handsome

price of two dollars a day, folks could take their meals, ride the range and enjoy the pleasant company of a genteel ranch family while they "experienced the true wonders of the West."

Her future and Sarah Ann's depended on her having the image of a respectable businesswoman. Even with Everett's passing, she'd managed to hold on to her dream. And now the one cowboy who could ruin it all was smack dab in the middle of her life again.

Mercy sakes! If a whiff of her unsavory past got out, those upstanding ladies she hoped to coax out here would turn up their noses and her dream would die. Decent folk in Maverick would shun her, making her an outcast in the only place she'd ever called home. Worse, Sarah Ann would suffer.

Josie pursed her lips and stared at Yancy. Her stomach lurched, but she had no choice. She'd have to honor their agreement and trust he'd keep her secret. And if he refused? If he blackmailed her into doing more?

She rubbed her forehead and closed her eyes. Instead of coming up with a way out of this mess, she trembled at the memory of this cowboy seducing the bloomers off her.

Damnation! She might have to shoot him after all.

The heavy clomp of boots jerked Josie from her morbid thoughts of silencing Gil Yancy for good. She drew a ragged breath and turned to the door.

Hiram towered in the opening, his ebony features taut with worry. "Miz Sarah says you need my help."

"Actually, our new trail guide does."

Hiram ambled over to Yancy and stared down at the big man for a tense moment. "What happened to him?"

"I hit him."

"With what?"

She pointed to the stove lid, drawing a whistle from Hiram. "Mr. Yancy and I had a misunderstanding and one thing led to another. He's going to have a big egg on his head."

"That he will, but I reckon he won't notice right off with the pain it'll cause him."

Josie rubbed her brow, but the headache born from Gil Yancy's arrival tormented her—like she feared he aimed to do to her from here on out.

Hiram gave the downed man another long, hard look and shook his head. "You sure you want the likes of him around here?"

Not one bit, but getting rid of Yancy for good would bring trouble on her—one way or the other. "He's the man Everett trusted, and I feel obliged to respect his wishes." *For now.*

"What you want me to do with him?"

"Put him in bed. It's best Mr. Yancy recuperate in his own cabin." Far from her house.

"Reckon so."

Hiram grabbed one of Yancy's arms and pulled the man to a sitting position. Without breaking a sweat, he hefted Yancy over one broad shoulder as if he was picking up nothing heavier than a sack of flour.

Yancy's hat tumbled off, and Josie stared at his light brown hair thickly woven with gold. Soft curls. Soft hair.

Another jolt of remembrance shot through her. Twelve years ago, the room had been so dark that she couldn't tell the color of his hair, but she remembered how it had felt brushing against her bare skin, curling around her fingers.

Clamping an arm over Yancy's legs, Hiram pivoted and stomped to the bed Josie had made up. The ropes groaned as Yancy hit the mattress and sprawled on his back, arms spread and features relaxed.

She stared at the dust motes dancing in the shafts of light spilling in from the open door and lone window. As she'd learned long ago, all the scrubbing in the world wouldn't stop dust from seeping into the ranch buildings.

It was something you learned to live with. Like the wind. Like a checkered past.

Still, she'd wanted her new partner to feel right at home, so she'd spent a week fixing up this cabin. She'd aired the feather mattress and whitewashed the log walls. She'd put a rag rug on the floor, spread an old but serviceable quilt on the bed and hung calico curtains at the window.

Now as she stared at the cowboy, she wished she hadn't lifted a finger to make it nice. She had a notion his kind wouldn't appreciate her efforts to make him welcome. Nope, he'd be more inclined to use that against her, too.

"Reckon I'd best tend his horse," Hiram said.

"Please do. No sense in that animal waiting for him to wake up and see to him." Josie hooked Gil Yancy's hat on the peg by the door, then grabbed her cleaning supplies and headed for the house.

The bite in the air did little to cool her anger. Though she needed to come to some agreement with Yancy, she couldn't waste time waiting for him to rouse. She had chores to do and not much time to get them done before her first guests arrived at the ranch.

She still couldn't believe her good fortune. After months waiting for a reply to her advertisements, a telegram arrived from Philadelphia three days past.

The lady wanted to come to Rocky Point as soon as possible and had wired the deposit.

Josie had hurried into Maverick and sent a telegram right back, inviting Mrs. Hastings and her party to come ahead. By the time she finished getting supplies at Stanley's Mercantile, she'd had a reply from the lady.

Now Josie expected to see her visitors, and a portion of the money, within the week. Good thing too, because they were down to their last dollar. Again.

Sarah Ann sat on the porch steps, picking cockleburs from Deuce's tangled coat. The old hound slept on, oblivious to the less-than-gentle grooming he was getting.

"Pa would've been madder than a grizzly if he'd heard that man say he aimed to hold on to you." Sarah Ann looked up at her, all innocent curiosity. "Is that why you clobbered him?"

"Yes, it is." Good Lord, Sarah Ann had heard them. "But I don't think he meant me harm." *Liar, liar.*

"I don't like him none."

Josie didn't care one wit for Yancy either, but she kept her reasons why to herself. "We don't have to like him. Just tolerate him."

"For how long?"

"I don't know." As far as Josie was concerned, Gil Yancy had already worn out his welcome.

Chapter 2

Gil forced his eyes open and damned the stampede going on in his head. He squinted at his surroundings but he had a hard time focusing. Didn't help that his thoughts swirled like a dust devil.

He eyed the cabin. Someone had taken pains fancying up this place. A woman, judging from the curtains and the hint of vanilla wafting in the air. That brought it all galloping back to him.

Gil swung his legs off the bed and sat up, then wished he hadn't moved so fast. He held his pounding head and took deep breaths until the bed stopped twirling like a wild bronco.

Anger pelted him like an icy downpour. Twice she'd gotten the best of him. If she robbed him blind again, God help her.

A quick check proved his Colt .45 Peacemaker was in its holster on his hip and the coins he had on him were in his pocket. His hat hung on the wall peg above a ladder-back chair with one slat missing. His saddlebags rested on the lone chair by a scarred dresser that held a chipped washbowl and pitcher.

Gil gritted his teeth. He hadn't brought his gear in, which meant she'd done it.

He strode to his saddlebags and dug to the bottom. His breath sawed fast and hard as he pulled out the small poke and looked inside. Yep, his stash was still there, every damn cent of it.

He shoved the sack in its hiding place and crossed to the washstand. Though every bone in his body ached to rest, he didn't aim to get comfortable until he talked to Everett.

Gil poured water into the chipped bowl and bent to splash water in his face. The cabin door creaked open a smidgeon.

He glared that direction, half expecting the shady lady to be standing there with a rifle aimed at his brisket. Instead, a wiry boy stood in the wedge of light. He kept his head down so all Gil saw was the top of his battered straw hat.

"You stay away from my mama." The boy's voice strained on the high side, confirming he was a young sprout far from manhood.

"I aim to do that."

Gil grimaced and splashed cold water on his face. He'd only met one woman today—the shady lady. Dammit all, this boy garbed in a plaid shirt and snug buckskins must be her son.

Taking out in trade what a soiled dove owed him was one thing. But a man sure as hell couldn't parlay a woman with a kid into warming his bed. Not and be able to live with himself when it was all said and done.

He dried his face on a towel, surprised the boy was still standing there gawking at him. "You know where I can find Everett Andrews?"

The kid tucked his hands in his armpits and

straightened, and Gil realized the boy was taller than he'd thought. "He's up on the hill behind the house."

"Thank you kindly. What's your name, boy?"

"Sarah." The kid took off, slamming the door shut behind her.

Gil winced as that explosive bang tore through his head. Everett and his missus must be saints to put up with the tomboy and her mama with the checkered past.

'Course, the shady lady might've lassoed her a cowboy. Nothing saying she wasn't an honest woman and had a kid or maybe more. If so, Gil could forget getting his money back.

He set his hat on real easy and stepped out the door. The sun squatted right overhead, burning away all shadows and making his eyes throb something fierce. He must've been dead to the world for a good couple of hours.

Gil looked around for his horse and spotted Rhubarb in the corral amid the remuda. Someone had unsaddled his gelding and turned him out. Everett?

He reckoned he'd know soon enough.

According to the tomboy, Everett was on the hill behind the house. Gil set off that way, hoping it wasn't a long hike to the top. His new boots were making his dogs howl.

A fancy surrey was parked in front of the ranch house, and a dude wearing what he'd swear was livery tended the fine horse standing in the traces. He reckoned Mrs. Andrews had company—highbrow folks by the looks of it.

Gil brushed two fingers over his brim at the groom and angled around the house, no longer irked that he'd missed out on the chance to own a fancy ranch and stable of horses back in Kansas. Yep, Everett had cut him a damn sight better deal here in Wyoming. Not only did Gil hold title to a third of this ranch, he had Everett's promise he'd sell Gil more of it.

That'd take a spell as Gil aimed to buy cattle with the cash he had. Since he'd sworn off gambling, he could forget recouping his losses that way. That left saving his wages and trying to get his money out of the former sporting girl turned ranch housekeeper.

Everett couldn't be paying the little thief much more than a cowpoke would make. Maybe not even that much. And why in the hell didn't he remember her name?

He'd never asked her back then or today, that's why.

Formalities had been the last thing on his mind that night, which wasn't like him because he always made a point of calling the calico queens by their names instead of some endearment. Yep, those words of affection were best saved for a lady he was sweet on.

Dammit, he had to talk with Everett. Did his old friend and his missus know about the ladybird's past?

Gil reckoned he'd have that answer soon enough. He took his time climbing the hill behind the house to the dry plains above, careful to avoid loose rocks.

Metal sawed metal in the wind, the sound as plaintive as a lone wolf mourning its mate. What was Everett up to?

A hot, dry wind slammed into him the second he reached the plateau. His vest plastered against his chest and his chaps flapped like crazed birds.

Scrub and sage dotted the high plains. A mile-high sun punished the already baked ground and glinted off the fenced-in area some fifty feet from him.

He scanned the high plains for Everett, vexed by

that old ache gnawing at his gut. Nothing or nobody
up here but a cemetery. There were two headstones
in it.

Ah, hell.

His gut commenced knotting as Gil strode toward
the walk gate that creaked back and forth in the
wind. A handful of wildflowers lay on each grave,
their stems held down with rocks to keep them from
blowing away.

He stood before the larger headstone, knowing
before he read it who rested there.

Everett Andrews
Beloved husband and father
Born July 22, 1842
Died April 12, 1894

Gil squatted by the grave and took his hat off, holding it before him. His old friend hadn't mentioned
having children.

"What the hell happened to you, Everett?"

Wind tore at Gil's hair and grit pelted his face. He
thought back to meeting up with Everett in Laramie
last fall, trying to remember the things he'd taken for
granted.

Everett had looked a mite puny, but Gil attributed
it to a grueling roundup and days in the saddle. Now
he wondered as bits and pieces of their conversation
drifted back to him.

"I need a man I can trust around my missus,"
Everett had said. "This guest ranching venture is all
her idea, so you'll be working close with her."

Gil had nodded, well aware of how some men took advantage of a woman. "What're you wanting me to do?"

"Map out trails to take these here ranch guests on. Find good places for 'em to camp," Everett had said. "Then go along with them so they don't get themselves killed."

"Yep, it's smart to keep an eye on these rich men while they're out hunting. Ones I've seen are usually mighty anxious to squeeze off a shot without looking."

"That they are." Everett had looked him straight on then, and Gil clearly recalled the worry on the older man's face. "When I ain't around, I want a man I trust to watch over my family."

"You can count on me," Gil had said and meant it.

He might drink a bit much and had tended to gamble away his last cent, but when he gave his word, by damn he stuck to it.

"Rest easy, Everett. Nobody will hurt your kin while I'm around."

He rose and moved to the other tombstone, half expecting it to be the resting place of a child. He read the name and dates on the weathered stone. "Lillian Ballard, beloved sister. Born January 31, 1862, died August 2, 1882."

Gil slid his hat on, wondering if she was Everett's kin or his wife's sister. He left the cemetery, closing the gate behind him. His friend's passing changed things a mite.

First off, he had to give his condolences to Everett's widow. Then he had to see if she planned to go on with this guest ranching venture. It wouldn't be easy for a woman to run it alone, even if he was here to help her out.

Gil stood atop the ridge that rimmed the ranch proper. Envy stirred within him, bitter and ballsy in turn. For years, he'd dreamed of owning a big spread like this. But cowboying didn't pay worth a damn. Didn't help he'd squandered a good deal of the money he'd earned on the turn of a card.

Last year, when he rode out of Kansas, he'd sworn off gambling. He'd squirreled away what winnings he'd held on to, and added his wages over the winter to it. Good thing he had.

When Everett had tracked him down in Laramie and offered to sell him a third of his land, Gil had jumped at the offer. Now his ol' partner was gone, leaving a widow who may not be far behind.

Mrs. Andrews was bound to be up there in years. If Gil played his cards right, he might be able to talk her into selling him more of the ranch now. Hell, she could stay on in her house as far as he was concerned for as long as she lived.

He let his gaze drift over the high plains, and his chest puffed with pride. Rocky Point Ranch wasn't fancy, but the land was ideal for grazing and went on for miles.

You'll never amount to a tinker's damn, his father had said.

"I'm going to prove you wrong old man," Gil said.

Soon as the trains were running, Gil expected a visit from his father. Yep, Gil would confront his father right here on the ranch that would one day make him a rich man.

Gil skidded down the hillside, dodging clumps of sage and wind-twisted pines hanging on to the rocky soil. If Mrs. Andrews's company was gone, he'd talk to her now.

If not— Well, he'd go looking for the shady lady. She owed him and he damned sure was going to nag her until she promised to pay him back.

* * *

Josie shifted on the settee, wishing she would've had time to wash up and put on clean clothes before Twila MacInnes came calling. It was bad enough the Scottish lady made Josie feel like a pauper, but after a morning spent scrubbing their new trail guide's cabin—and her run-in with her past—she looked and felt like a beggar.

"Sarah has the talent to be an exemplary equestrian." Twila smiled, looking as proud of Sarah Ann as if she were hers. "I tell you truly, I am quite impressed with her abilities."

"She's good with horses."

That was putting it mildly. Sarah Ann was as good as any man when it came to riding and roping.

"I would love to see her compete in the National Horse Show at Madison Square Garden."

Josie sighed. They'd had this conversation before and Josie hadn't changed her mind. She wasn't about to let Sarah Ann traipse off to New York with Dugan and Twila MacInnes.

"Maybe she will one day, but right now she's too young to venture away from home."

"I understand your concerns, Josephine. Truly I do. But surely you realize this is a momentous opportunity for Sarah. You do want her to have a better life."

"Of course I do. When she's of age, she can do what she wants. Until then, I'm not about to send her clear across the country with strangers."

Twila's mouth puckered up like she'd eaten a sour ball from Stanley's Mercantile. "I would hardly refer to us as strangers. My husband has owned this land since the early eighteen-eighties and was well acquainted with Everett."

That didn't change the fact that Dugan MacInnes was a snob through and through. Why, the brusque Scotsman barely spoke to Josie all the years she'd lived here. As for Twila— The woman was an interfering pain in the backside.

Twila fussed with her gloves. "It cannot be easy for you managing this ranch while you're in mourning."

That made the third time Twila remarked about Josie being in mourning. Since Josie hadn't worn black once and neither had Sarah Ann, Twila probably thought they were being disrespectful to Everett.

Their uppity neighbor didn't know Everett had made Josie promise she wouldn't wear widow's weeds, nor dress Sarah Ann in black crepe. Call her pigheaded, but Josie wasn't about to enlighten the woman.

"We're getting by just fine, Twila." Or were, until Josie's past claimed squatter's rights.

"I'm sure you are." Twila's tone said the opposite.

Twila was a highbrow and Josie never would be. Yet ever since the woman laid eyes on Sarah Ann racing with the cowboys this spring, she'd started nagging Josie to hand her daughter over into Twila's care.

The very idea annoyed the stuffing out of Josie. She'd never give up Sarah Ann.

But Twila MacInnes was as stubborn as a horsefly. And since Sarah Ann was horse crazy and the MacInneses had a herd of blooded stock, Sarah Ann had taken to sneaking over there. Mercy, her daughter was playing right into Twila's hand.

"May I be blunt?" Twila asked.

Like she hadn't been already? "Be my guest."

"Sarah is on the cusp of womanhood. Do you want

her to attain that stage of life with grace and dignity, or do you intend to let her grow up wild as a weed?"

"She's eleven."

"Indeed, time to squash any rash tendencies before they take root. She comports herself like a young boy, and those buckskin breeches she wears are absolutely scandalous. Do you know she aspires to be like Annie Oakley?" Twila wrinkled her haughty nose.

"Sarah Ann is impressed with the fancy clothes and what all in the Wild West shows." *Like she had been at that age, and look where that had gotten her.*

"It won't be long before men will start paying attention to Sarah. Think about that. How she comports herself in the near future will determine the type of man she attracts."

A time Josie dreaded. Not that she'd admit that to Twila.

"Just because a man is well dressed and well mannered doesn't make him a gentleman," Josie said. "In fact, most of the cowboys I've met have regarded women far better than those upper-crust men."

Especially one young cowboy who'd treated Josie with a tenderness she'd never known before then. Who still haunted her dreams. Who'd shown up at the ranch, madder than a just-cut bull and demanding his due.

"I suppose there is truth in that there are bad sorts in every walk of life." Twila rose and gave her taffeta skirt a shake to right the folds. "Do think about my offer, Josephine. My husband and I can give Sarah the chance to have a much better life than she'd have living here, or if she aligned herself in one of these traveling shows married to a poor cowboy."

Josie didn't know which was worse—Sarah Ann

running off to be in a Wild West show, or letting Twila MacInnes sponsor her in these highfalutin horse shows back east.

"I won't change my mind."

"We shall see." Twila walked to the door. "Good day, Josephine."

"Same to you, Twila." *Don't let the screen door smack you in your big bustle on the way out.*

Josie closed the door with a click, pressed her back to the wall and buried her face in her hands. Dang that woman! As long as she kept coming around here pulling at Sarah Ann with her grand notions, Josie wasn't going to have any peace.

The screen door screeched open and three solid raps echoed off the front door. Josie didn't know or care what the woman forgot to tell her. In fact, she was of a mind to ignore Twila MacInnes.

Josie wanted to change out of her soiled work clothes and get dinner started. But another three smacks on the door changed her mind. She jerked open the door, but the greeting she was fixing to force out stuck in her throat.

Gil Yancy scowled down at her, filling the doorway with his tense form and her heart with dread. "I should've reckoned you'd skedaddled up to the house."

"I have work to do."

He thumbed his hat back. "I saw Mrs. Andrews had company, so I held off stopping by until the lady left."

"That's right good of you." And a surprise. "But I'm mighty busy right now."

She started to close the door. He grabbed the panel and put his weight against it, forcing Josie to step back.

"Tell Mrs. Andrews I need to talk to her."

Josie rolled her eyes. "About what?"

"That's between me and Everett's widow."

So he knew. "Can't it wait until later?"

"Nope. I paid my respects to Everett and now I want to extend my condolences to his missus."

She hadn't expected that. But then she hadn't expected that the trusted friend of Everett's was this cowboy. Mercy sakes, could things get any worse?

"Come on in the parlor." Josie frowned at his fine boots, wishing she had the money he'd spent on them. "But no spurs in the house."

Gil bobbed his head and set to shucking his spurs, determined to make a good impression on Everett's widow. When he looked up, the shady lady was gone. He reckoned she went to fetch Mrs. Andrews.

He left his spurs on the porch and wiped his boots on the rag rug inside the door to knock the dust off. After hooking his Stetson on the ornate hat stand, he took a gander in the mirror.

Damn wavy hair of his had a mind of its own. He licked his fingers, smoothed his hair down the best he could and then moseyed into the parlor. Nothing fancy, but the room was in good order and smelled like flowers.

Gil settled on a big Morris chair that looked sturdy and comfortable. A lacy, black shawl was draped over the back of an armless chair. He imagined a frail older woman wrapped up in it, whiling away her hours knitting or doing some such handiwork.

A minute soon turned into fifteen. Dammit to hell and back! Had the shady lady bothered to tell

Everett's widow he'd come calling and was down here waiting for her?

He was about to go looking for the old gal when he heard footsteps on the stairs. He settled back in the chair, both anxious and dreading this first meeting with Mrs. Andrews. Couldn't be easy on the old gal to be alone.

A woman stepped into the parlor doorway, and Gil's jaw damned near hit the shiny pine floor. Instead of Everett's widow, the shady lady had returned.

She'd changed out of her dirty dress into a clean one that hugged her in all the places a man longed to touch. She'd pinned her dark hair up, but a few curls fell to her shoulders.

The sweet little thief looked pretty and wholesome. Smug as all get out, too.

"Now what is it you want to talk about?" she asked.

The skin on his nape crawled. Uh-uh, naw, the idea that was going through his head couldn't be true. His ol' partner wouldn't have married a shady lady.

"What I have to say is between me and Mrs. Andrews."

"Of course." She walked to the armless chair angled next to his and sat down, drawing the shawl around her narrow shoulders. "We have a problem, Mr. Yancy."

"How do you know my name?"

"Everett told me."

Ah, hell— "Did he now?"

She smoothed her skirt to cover her trim ankles, the jerky movement hinting she was more nervous than she looked. "Yes, he did. My husband kept no secrets from me."

"Husband!"

Gil pinched his eyes shut, finding no pleasure that

his hunch proved out. The shady lady who'd robbed him blind was Everett's wife. This had to be the damnedest fix he'd ever landed in.

"I can't believe you married Everett."

"Believe it, Mr. Yancy. I've been Josephine Andrews for twelve years."

Gil frowned, thinking it odd that he had met her that same year. "Have you now?"

"Yes." She fussed with her skirt again. "I know you think the worst of me, but the fact remains we are partners of a sort. The question is whether we can find a way to work together amiably."

Gil had a mind to tell her to forget it and walk out. Wouldn't that please the hell out of her?

Nope, he wasn't going anywhere. He owned a third of this spread. If he took off now, he'd live up to his old man's low expectations of him.

Besides that, Gil had a hunch Josie's story had more holes in it than his old winter union suit. She sure hadn't been married to Everett when she'd been working at the Gilded Garter. Hell, Everett had been living here on this ranch. So how did a shady lady from Kansas end up married to a Wyoming rancher?

Gil scrubbed his knuckles along his jaw, vexed as another question dug its rowels into his conscience. How old was that tomboy of hers?

"Reckon how we get on depends on a couple of things," he said.

"Such as?"

"First off, I want what you stole from me."

Her sigh was shaky. "Once the ranch starts making a profit, I will pay you back in time. What's the other thing?"

"Who is Sarah's pa?"

Chapter 3

"Everett, of course." Josie smiled, grateful her husband had taught her how to hold a poker face. "Sarah Ann was our only child, and Everett was such a wonderful papa. He spoiled her rotten, though."

"How old is she?"

"Eleven. If you have something on your mind, say it."

"Being as Everett was ranching in Wyoming, and you were working in Caldwell at the time, I'm wondering how you met him. Wondering too how long it was from when I visited you that night at the Gilded Garter to when you roped him into marriage?"

"You ask an awful lot of questions."

"I'm the curious sort. You were about to tell me how you went from working in a whorehouse to being Everett's missus."

"We don't mention that place or others like it where young ears can overhear. Nor do we talk like we're in a saloon. Do I make myself clear, Mr. Yancy?"

His neck and face turned a wind-burned red. "Yes'm. I'll mind my words. Gotta say it was right nice of Everett to do right by you."

If he only knew the truth. Josie jumped to her feet. "You listen to me, Gil Yancy. You're surely entitled to your low opinion of me, but Everett was an honest rancher, a faithful husband and a loving father. How we met is none of your business. I'm a widowed rancher now with a daughter to raise. That's all you need to know. And I warn you right now, if you fill Sarah Ann's head with lies or vulgarities, or lay one hand on her in anger or lust, I'll shoot you dead."

He stood and matched her glare. "What kind of low-life cur do you think I am? I'd never hurt that child. Never! Hell, I gave Everett my word I'd look after his family."

"Forgive me if I don't believe you."

Josie walked to the front window and admired the only home she'd ever had. Though she'd missed the green, rolling hills of Kansas, the raw, open beauty of Wyoming agreed with her. She couldn't imagine ever leaving it. But if the truth ever came out, she could lose everything she loved.

"I'll prove myself to you, but know I'm only doing it because of Everett," he said. "He was a damned good friend."

She turned to Gil Yancy. He was big, but not as intimidating as she'd recalled. But then she'd been scared to death that night at the Gilded Garter. Scared and desperate.

Everett trusted this cowboy. But could she? No, but right now she needed Gil Yancy's help.

"I received a telegram a few days ago from our first ranch guests," she said. "They should arrive this week, so we have a lot to get done before then."

"Everett said something about marking trails."

"Our advertisement promised two trails that guests

could use anytime, and one two-night campout on the high plains," she said. "We supply their needs, and while you oversee the trail ride, Dwight will go ahead and set up camp. Everett told me you were real good with horses."

His mouth pulled to one side, and that glimpse of arrogant pride took her breath away. "I get the job done."

"Good. Some of the guests might not be used to riding much, so you'll have to make the trail fairly easy."

"Most men can handle themselves fine in the saddle, even city dudes. With summer nigh on us, I reckon they'll want to hunt antelope. Maybe bear."

"Actually neither. Our first guests aren't interested in hunting or fishing."

"They why are they coming?" A look of pure horror marred his handsome face. "Don't tell me these rich men aim to play cowboy."

He looked plumb thunderstruck by the notion of watching over dime-store cowboys. She opened her mouth to correct his misconception, but burst out laughing.

"Ain't nothing funny about wet nursing a bunch of damned greenhorns," he said.

"Trust me, Mr. Yancy. Cowboying is the furthest thing from their mind. Our guests are coming to relax and relish the wonders of the West."

"What the hell does that mean?"

"Our women guests simply want to enjoy God's country."

"Women! You're joshing me."

Dear Lord, the man looked poleaxed. "I'm serious, Mr. Yancy. Didn't Everett explain all of this to you?"

"He said he was starting up a guest ranch that was sure to turn a tidy profit." He squinted at her. "Said it was his missus's idea."

"It was. I posted advertisements in several Eastern newspapers, stating that we welcome groups of women in need of mental recuperation and spiritual renewal. The fact a party of women have jumped at the chance to visit is a good sign for our success."

"I don't believe it. Where did you come up with this idea?"

"Experience and a good dose of common sense. Men go off hunting and such. Why shouldn't women have the opportunity to get away from life's drudgery? Here, they can bask in the beauty of nature while partaking of true Western fare and hospitality."

He shook his head. "That's got to be the craziest thing I'd ever heard. Now you stop giving me that look that says I ain't long on smarts."

"I suppose you're plenty smart enough when it comes to ranching and horses. Mark my words. Women need a safe haven—a retreat solely for them. Rocky Point Ranch is just that place."

"I can't believe I bought into this venture. After this last depression, money is tighter than a fat woman's corset. Hell, until this railroad strike ends, you ain't going to get folks from the East out here."

"Women are resourceful. Why, Mrs. Hastings noted that she and her party were en route by stage and would arrive as planned."

"From where?"

"Pennsylvania."

He mumbled something—probably a curse—and picked up the book she'd been reading. "That's a long haul for women to undertake. Don't be surprised if they don't show up." He looked from the book to her. "You aiming to travel to the Adirondacks?"

"I am using that as a guide for our guest venture." She took her coveted copy of *Adventures in the Wilderness* from him and put it back on the table.

"You do realize there's a world of difference between camping out in New York and roughing it in Wyoming?"

"The principles are the same."

"Your guests may not agree with you."

"I made no overt promises."

"After this Hastings party leaves Rocky Point, when are the next guests due to arrive?" he asked.

"I've had inquiries from a group in Chicago, but they haven't made arrangements yet."

He scraped his knuckles along his lean jaw that needed shaving. "That's it? Just one batch of women forked over money to stay here?"

"Yes, but our business is new."

"We're gonna lose our shirts."

Not if Josie could help it. "If you don't care to partake in this venture, then pack up and leave now. I can arrange to buy you out over time."

"I'm staying, Josephine."

Josie was afraid of that. "Very well, but call me Josie."

"Only if you call me Gil. That mister stuff gets old."

"That it does. Now if you'll excuse me, I have work to do. Supper is served at five. Come on up to the back door when the bell clangs."

Josie hoped Gil couldn't hear her knees knocking as she passed him and headed into the kitchen. All the questions about when she married Everett and Sarah Ann's age had her insides twisting something fierce.

If Gil knew the truth, there was the equal chance he'd run from responsibility, or she'd never get rid of him. But the fact remained he didn't know, and he couldn't prove he had a claim to her daughter even if he suspected the truth. Josie sure wasn't about to tell him.

Gil stepped out onto the porch, pulled the front door closed behind him and settled his hat on. Though the wind was still ripping, it wasn't as brisk outside as it'd been in the parlor with Everett's widow, Josephine.

Nope, she wanted to be called Josie.

The abbreviated form of her name conjured up thoughts of picnics and sunshine, not at all fitting the shady lady he'd never forgotten. Oh, he'd told himself she'd stuck in his head because she'd gotten the best of him that night in more ways than one, but truth of the matter was he'd not had such a sweet lover before or since.

As for her daughter— Well, he'd figured it in his head twice, and the tomboy was likely Everett's. That was a relief. Gil sure didn't need or want a half-grown daughter to fret over right now.

Gil strapped on his spurs. Working with Josie wasn't going to be easy, but like he'd told her, he wasn't pulling freight and leaving. Besides, when no other women jumped at the chance to pick cockleburs out of their bloomers, she'd see the right of it and open the ranch to men hankering to hunt game.

He headed to the barn. If he set out now, he could get a feel for the lay of the land. Seeing as he was going to get stuck with womenfolk on the trail, he'd best make sure he laid out gentle ones.

Gil found his saddle in the tack room that smelled

of leather and saddle soap. Someone had done a fine job caring for the older saddles.

"You fixing to hit the trail?"

Gil looked at the newcomer. He'd seen plenty of Negro cowboys, but he'd never met one as big and black as this man.

"Aimed to saddle up and take a gander at the ranch and my share." Gil thrust his hand out. "Gil Yancy, trail guide for Rocky Point Ranch and new neighbor."

The black man stared at him a long time before he uncrossed his thick arms and shook Gil's extended hand. "Hiram Tucker, foreman. So you're the cowboy who bought a third of Rocky Point."

"Yep. Aim to take a look at my land."

"Ain't any different than what you're seeing now. It's all fenced as one spread, and from what Everett told me, he hoped you'd keep it that way. Even mentioned it'd be best if the trails wound over his land and yours."

"Reckon that won't be a problem." Though he had thought of buying registered cattle latter on, and he sure wouldn't want his prize bull servicing Josie's stock. "How long have you been Everett's right-hand man?"

"Nigh on thirteen years."

"Then you remember when he married Josie?"

"Sure do. Was right before the first snow in '82."

A good six months after Gil's run-in with her. "You know how Everett met her?"

"Nope, and I never asked."

Gil had a hunch Hiram knew, but wouldn't say out of loyalty to Everett and respect for Josie. That left Gil with a passel of questions. Had any of Gil's money gone into Rocky Point Ranch? Did Everett know what his wife had done? Was that why he'd looked Gil up in Laramie last fall?

"The boss was a good man," Hiram said. "Damned shame he took sick and all."

"Must've been fast. What happened?"

"Doc Neely said it was cancer."

"Damn. Wish he'd have told me."

"If you'd have known the boss was dying, would you have bought the land and gave your word to lend a hand to Miz Josie's undertaking?"

Gil didn't have to think about it. "Yep, reckon I would've."

Hiram edged a bit closer than Gil liked. "Everett liked you and trusted you or he'd never have offered you a third of the ranch. But I'm telling you now, you hurt Miz Josie and I'll string you up."

Gil didn't doubt the big man would do it too. "Fair enough."

That earned him a toothy smile. "Where you from, Gil Yancy?"

"Spent a good deal of my life in Kansas." That was all he aimed to say about his past. "Everett claimed this land he sold me is good for grazing and has a cabin and water nearby. I'd be much obliged if you'd point out how to get to it."

"Saddle up and we'll head out."

Five minutes later, Gil and Hiram rode up onto the ridge that curved around the homestead and out on to the high gray-green plains. In the distance, Gil could see snow clinging to the high peaks along the Laramie Range. The sun had burned off the nip in the air, leaving it right nice.

"That creek over there"—Hiram pointed to the left where a long line of willows prospered along the meandering water's edge for as far as Gil could see—"it divides Rocky Point from Dugan MacInnes's spread to the west. Your land runs along the creek to the foothills up north. Some of that ain't fit for nothing 'cept rattlers."

"This MacInnes. What's he like?"

"Tighter than scrub pine growing in rock. Got him a title of some sort that makes no never mind to me. Has a castle in Scotland."

What were the odds he'd end up neighbor to another wealthy foreigner? Gil wondered if this one had a stubborn daughter half the territory was sniffing after, too.

"MacInnes holds title to a mighty big spread," Hiram said. "But the blizzard of '86 took most his herd."

"Aberdeen-Angus?"

"Yup, and fancy sheep. Imported both all the way from his family's estate. Last week or so his woolies have been dropping lambs." Hiram made a face. "All that bleating gets a damned sight annoying."

"You ask me, everything about sheep is right aggravating."

Hiram chuckled, the sound deeper than the gouged arroyos to Gil's left. "Last couple of years MacInnes has been breeding thoroughbreds and shipping them east."

Gil shook his head at the strangeness of running sheep, cattle and blooded horses on the same land. "Big outfit."

"He runs a tight one. Don't hold with no tomfoolery. Hires hay men when needed, but he keeps on a handful of cowpunchers and sheepherders." Hiram scowled. "When he sees something he wants, he goes after it."

"Can't blame a man for that, unless he's got his eye on this spread."

"Ain't the land he wants."

"Then what's he after?"

"Miz Sarah. Come on and I'll show you what he's up to." Hiram reined his big gray mount south and set off at a trot.

Gil heeled Rhubarb and rode beside the big black man. His thoughts tripped over themselves in his head. Foremost was why would these foreigners want Everett and Josie's daughter?

They crossed the creek a mile or so downstream where the bank leveled out some, then loped across the short grass plains toward another creek that looked wider and deeper than the first one. The temperature dropped as they crossed a narrow wooden bridge and rode under a canopy of cottonwoods, their big leaves rustling in the wind.

Hiram urged the big gray up a slope, then reined in at a clump of poplars and pointed down at the ranch below them. "See all them fences in that field?"

"Sure do." Gil had watched the Englishmen back in Kansas urge their horses over those obstacles when they went foxhunting. "I've never seen any gates that high before."

"I ain't either. They're teaching Miz Sarah how to jump, 'cept they're making her use a sidesaddle. Wouldn't have known if I hadn't been trailing a stray calf yesterday. Saw her fly over one of them stone fences with my own eyes." Hiram wet his lips. "Scared the shit out of me."

Gil could well imagine. "Damn risky pushing a horse

over those jumps when you're forking a saddle. I hate to guess how hard it'd be to keep your seat using a sidesaddle."

"Yup. That girl could break her neck."

The thought made Gil want to puke. "Josie shouldn't let her to do it."

"She didn't. That girl's been sneaking over to the Diamond M when her mama told her not to." Leather creaked as Hiram shifted in the saddle. "Reckon I'll tell Miz Josie tonight after supper."

"Good idea."

Gil turned his attention to the short man leading a saddled horse from the stable toward a tall, dignified man. "That big man. He MacInnes?"

"Yup."

MacInnes climbed onto the horse and took off at a trot toward the field. The sorrel had a right smart gait, and his lines were in keeping with fine thoroughbreds.

Horse and rider circled the field half a dozen times. On the seventh round, MacInnes urged the horse toward the series of jumps. The sorrel sailed over the first fence and took the next without breaking stride.

"Quite a horse he's got there."

Hiram snorted. "MacInnes bought him last fall. Heard he planned to use him for stud, but the papers weren't right. He got so pissed off he had the stallion gelded."

"Of all the damn dumb things to do. He could've used him and produced some fine horses."

"Yup, but MacInnes wouldn't be able to prove they were blooded. That tell you what kind of man he is?"

"A high and mighty one. Why's he letting Sarah jump his horses?"

"Man's up to no good, I'm thinking."

"He has designs on the girl?"

Hiram shrugged and turned his horse back toward the creek. Gil did the same, troubled that the Scotsman had his eye on an eleven-year-old girl.

"MacInnes never gave Miz Sarah the time of day while Everett was alive," Hiram said, "but right after he passed on, MacInnes and his missus started in with all this talk of Miz Sarah performing at some garden in New York City."

"Madison Square Garden?"

"That's it. MacInnes wants to give Miz Sarah one of their horses and take her there this fall."

Gil doubted MacInnes was offering this chance to Sarah out of the goodness of his heart. Nope, he didn't like the sounds of this one damn bit.

"What did Josie say about them taking Sarah away?" Gil asked after they rode across the creek and headed north.

"She was riled. Told MacInnes she wouldn't allow it, and told Miz Sarah to stay away from the Diamond M."

"But the girl hasn't."

"Getting to ride those fine horses is mighty tempting to Miz Sarah."

"Reckon she wants to ride in the Garden."

"Miz Sarah wants to be like Annie Oakley. Hell, she's always talking about how Everett aimed to teach her to shoot and such." Hiram reined up near an outcropping, and Gil came up beside him. "What worries me is that girl misses her pa something awful. MacInnes is using her grief to get his way."

The weight of his promise to Everett settled on

Gil's shoulders. He couldn't sit by and do nothing, especially if Everett's daughter could end up getting hurt.

"If MacInnes is trying to lure Sarah to run off with him, I say we'd best keep a close eye on her."

"You reckon they'd take off with Miz Sarah?" Hiram asked.

"They might, but with the trains deadlocked, they can't move out of here fast. They damn sure won't give her a horse and leave it behind."

"Be right nice if we could get Miz Sarah's mind off riding in this fancy New York garden."

"That it would. You say Sarah has a mind to shoot?"

"Yup. Everett aimed to teach her this summer."

Everett wasn't a sharpshooter, but Gil was. Since horse-crazy Sarah had dreams of being Annie Oakley, who better to teach her than himself?

Gil pointed to a spot up the hill. "There's a broken limb on the scrub pine about fifty yards up. Keep your eye on it."

"What're you fixing to do?"

Gil drew his Winchester rifle from the scabbard, figuring it was easier to show him. He aimed and fired. Before the echo died, the pine limb snapped off.

"Damn fine shooting," Hiram said.

"Reckon that'll impress Sarah?"

A slow smile spread across Hiram's face. "Oh, it'll get her attention, all right. But convincing Miz Josie to let you teach that girl how to shoot ain't gonna be easy."

Gil smiled. "I'll handle Josie."

Hiram burst out laughing. "That'll be the day. Where'd you learn to shoot like that?"

"From an old cowpoke. He had me plugging a

dozen holes in tossed cards and shooting out matches like Annie Oakley does today."

"You a gunslinger?" Hiram asked.

"Nope, learned a few tricks to amuse the ladies and earn a few dollars."

"I bet you did. Let's get a move on and see this land you bought while the day's young."

They set off at an easy pace riding north. Gil filled his gaze with the vast openness of the high plains and the sky that looked so close he could reach up and stick his finger in a cloud, the color as clear as Josie's eyes.

The willow-lined creek to his left angled westward. So did the bluff on his right, creating a narrow plat between the two. Smack dab in the middle squatted a shack.

Hiram reined his mount in. "Your land starts here, running east from the creek, over these foothills, and sloping straight down on the other side. Beyond this pass, the land widens out and rises to the high plains."

"Good range land, but that lean-to ain't much to look at."

"Last time that line shack was used was when this was all open range. Come on. There's a good-sized cabin on the other side of the hills."

Hiram's big gray whinnied and shied at the same time Gil heard a bone-chilling rattle. Followed by another. And another.

"Pit vipers." Hiram backed his horse up till he was beside Gil's nervous gelding.

Gil scanned the area, spotting one snake slithering backward from a big clump of greasewood with its business end ready to strike. Another one coiled between two large bushes between the shack and the bluff. Damn if he didn't spy a four-foot-long rattler sunning on a rocky shelf.

"Bet they got a den back in those rocks."

"Yup. Like I said, some of the land ain't fit for nothing 'cept pit rattlers." Hiram headed out.

Gil kept his eyes peeled for more prairie rattlers as they hugged the foothills and angled north. The ground rose slowly, and the sage and greasewood thinned out, giving way to short grass.

When the high plains leveled out, he could see for miles. He caught a glimpse of the railroad tracks in the distance.

"As I recall from the land description, those tracks are my northern border."

"Yup," Hiram said. "The rails separate your land from Reid Barclay's spread. He's been angling to get a spur built along here."

"What's he run on his ranch?"

"Durham cattle and thoroughbred horses."

They rode south along the bluff for a good twenty minutes. The old homestead Everett had told Gil about backed up to the ridge, giving it natural protection from harsh winter winds.

As for the cabin, the walls appeared straight but half the tin was gone off the roof. He'd have to put new poles on the corral fence, and replace a few boards on the barn.

But the place had potential, and a good hundred yards down the sloping trail ran a deep creek. Water and shelter. It was enough for now.

Gil heard the thunder of hooves before the sleek chestnut stallion galloped into view on the trail below. The rider leaned forward, urging the horse to go faster. In moments, he was out of sight.

"Fine-looking horse."

Hiram made a face. "Barclay and his prize stallion. Everett always said he had the devil's luck to end up owning land between two foreigners. Barclay is the worst of the two."

"How so?"

"He never hid the fact that he had his eye on Miz Josie. You'd best keep that in mind."

Gil did that as they rode back to Rocky Point. The land was better than what he'd hoped for, but he wanted more. He wanted all of Rocky Point.

Getting it was the problem. He didn't have enough to buy the rest of the ranch, not that Josie seemed apt to sell out. Then there was the problem of Barclay sniffing after her.

Dammit! Gil had sat on his butt before and let another man steal the woman and the ranch out from under him. He damn sure wasn't going to come up the loser this time.

Chapter 4

Sarah Ann stomped into the kitchen, looking like a hay hand and smelling like one, too. Josie wiped her hands on her apron and sighed. Her daughter knew better.

Everyone on the ranch made good use of the wash-stand on the back porch before coming to the table. But ever since Everett's passing, Sarah Ann seemed to forget good manners.

"Wash up."

Sarah Ann heaved an enormous sigh and headed back onto the porch. Water splashed into the bowl.

If Sarah Ann would just take to dressing for dinner. When their Philadelphia guests arrived, it wouldn't do to have her daughter going from sunup to sundown wearing buckskins. Or acting like she'd been born in a barn. Or smelling to high heaven.

Moments later Sarah Ann stomped back to the kitchen, face and arms scrubbed clean. Josie wrinkled her nose. A rangy odor hovered around the girl.

"Go on up to your room so you can clean up

proper," Josie said. "Why don't you put on that blue gingham dress? You look pretty in it."

Sarah Ann crossed her arms tight across her chest and slumped in a chair. "I feel silly in a dress."

"You'll get used to it. Besides, I imagine our lady guests will have fancy clothes the likes of which we've never seen."

Josie hoped that might appeal to Sarah Ann's feminine side like it'd started doing this winter, but her daughter didn't show the least bit of interest now.

She gave her biscuit dough a couple of good wallops then caught herself. Mercy, they'd be hard as rocks if she didn't use a gentle hand.

"Set the table for five tonight and then dress for dinner."

While Josie cut biscuits and placed them on a pan, Sarah Ann got plates from the cupboard and set the table as always. Well, not quite. Instead of putting the extra plate beside her own chair, she put the setting at the head of the table. Everett's place, that had remained unused since his passing.

Now what was that girl up to? Dare Josie hope her daughter was getting over her grief?

"You can't ride a horse in a stupid dress," Sarah Ann said.

Josie smiled and slid the pan of biscuits into the oven. At least her daughter wasn't flat out refusing. But what Josie wouldn't give if Sarah Ann would take an interest in something besides horses. Something feminine.

"There are special riding skirts made just for women," Josie said.

"I don't have one."

"You will before long. I'm about done stitching yours up."

"Is it going to be like Mrs. MacInnes's?" Out-and-out dread tinged her daughter's voice.

"No," Josie said. "I'm making us split skirts."

Sarah Ann's green eyes widened. "Like Annie Oakley wears?"

"Similar." Only without the fancywork that was better suited to the stage than a ranch. "Dwight got back from town a while ago with those new sidesaddles I ordered, so you'd best start practicing how to sit one. Dwight said he'd help you."

Sarah Ann crossed her arms atop the back of a chair, proof she was growing like a weed. "I don't like riding a sidesaddle."

"How do you know if you've never used one?"

She shrugged, her cheeks looking ready to burst into flames. "I like riding astride."

Her daughter was hiding something. "Though I suspect I already know, where have you used a sidesaddle?"

"What difference does it make?"

"Plenty, if you sneaked over to the Diamond M when I told you not to."

"Mrs. MacInnes is nice to me."

"She wants to take you away from here. Answer me, Sarah Ann. Did you go over there and ride?"

"Yes, Mama."

Her daughter's entire face was beet red now. Anyone who didn't know Sarah Ann might think she was embarrassed to death. But the stubborn set to her mouth was proof the girl was fuming because she'd gotten caught.

"There will be no more of you traipsing over to the

MacInnes ranch, young lady. Stay away from them. You hear?"

"Yes, Mama."

"Now ring the dinner bell, then go wash up and put on a dress. You smell of sweat and horse."

Sarah Ann stepped out on the back porch and set the bell clanging, then stomped from the room and ran up the steps, her boots thudding loud on the treads. Josie dished the beef stew in a tureen, hoping she'd gotten through to her this time. But she wouldn't hold her breath.

In the past few months, Sarah Ann's stubborn streak put a Missouri mule's to shame. Oh, she'd do as bidden now, but as sure as the sun rose tomorrow, that girl would set out to defy Josie again.

Josie took her pan of biscuits from the oven, burning a finger in the process. She sucked on the stinging digit, but the pain was nothing compared to what she'd feel if she lost Sarah Ann. And unless she could reason with her daughter, she feared that was a very real possibility.

By the time Josie set the coffee to boiling, Hiram and Dwight strode onto the porch and took turns washing up at the basin. She set the tureen on the table and then fetched the basket of biscuits that she feared were tougher than rawhide.

Hiram took the chair to the right of the head of the table like he'd always done. Dwight parked across from him.

Gil Yancy strode in the door last and looked around, no doubt wondering which of the three chairs to claim. Sarah Ann burst into the kitchen and narrowed the choice for him.

She plopped down at the head of the table in a

swirl of gingham skirt and ruffled apron. But she hadn't taken off her work boots.

Josie guessed she couldn't expect miracles right off. And then she caught the stunned look on Gil's face and went cold all over. Why was he staring at Sarah Ann so intently?

She compared Gil's chiseled features to her daughter's impish ones and saw nothing similar. Nothing.

But then the only traits Josie shared with her daughter were their dark hair and the bow of their mouths. Still, she couldn't see where that would startle Gil so. And then it dawned on her.

Her daughter was wearing a dress, looking and smelling like a young lady. Josie relaxed a bit. That had to be it.

With a dip of his chin, Gil walked around the table and took the chair next to Josie. That was too close for her peace of mind, but she couldn't very well run him off.

"You look right pretty, Miz Sarah," Hiram said.

Dwight's handlebar mustache curved upward. "You surely do, missy."

Sarah Anne eyed Josie before smiling at the hands. "Mama said I had to dress up for dinner from now on."

"That's to be expected anyway." Gil filled his bowl with stew, looking as jittery as a treed raccoon. "My sisters always dressed for supper."

"Why'd they do that?" Sarah Anne asked.

"It's how gentle ladies do," Gil said. "They wouldn't have dreamed of coming to the table any other way, and if they had showed up wearing something improper, my father would've sent them packing to their rooms."

"My pa wouldn't have done that to me."

Josie took a biscuit from the basket and winced, embarrassed she'd served up sinkers. "Your pa let you do as you wanted, whether it was good for you or not."

"It didn't hurt me none," Sarah said.

"It didn't help you none either." Josie broke her biscuit in her bowl and ladled stew atop it. "We don't want our first guests thinking we raised you in a barn."

Gil helped himself to two biscuits and handed the basket to Sarah Ann. "Your mother is right. You don't want to give folks reason to look down on you."

"That's what Mrs. MacInnes told me," Sarah Ann said.

Josie bit back a curse. "About time Twila said something useful. Still and all, I don't want you over there visiting or riding their horses anymore."

"Yes, Mama."

Hiram nodded as he helped himself to a gigantic portion. "So you know what she's been doing then."

"Sarah told me, though I had to drag most of the story out of her," Josie said. "Any of you see her at the Diamond M Ranch, I want to know about it right away."

The men murmured agreement and then dug in. Hiram and Dwight gobbled their meal down like they were starving. She expected Gil Yancy to do the same, but he showed surprisingly good table manners for a cowboy.

Sarah Anne lapsed into moody silence and picked at her food. Josie's own appetite wasn't much better, but she couldn't allow her daughter to keep acting like a hooligan.

At least Gil had stopped gawking at Sarah Ann. Now

if Josie could just ignore the cowboy from her past, but she couldn't seem to stop stealing glances at him.

The cowboy beside her didn't fit her memory. Gil took his time eating, and never spoke with his mouth full. He didn't rest both elbows on the table like her hands did. And he hadn't just washed up on the back porch.

Gil's jeans and white cambric shirt were clean, and his damp hair proved he'd scrubbed more than his hands and face. And was that Bay Rum she smelled?

God yes, and that sharpened the memories of that night.

"Mighty fine meal." Gil helped himself to more hardtack and stew.

Against her will, she blushed at the compliment. "Thank you. Everett mentioned you were an old friend of his from Kansas. Do you hail from there, too?"

"No, ma'am."

Josie waited for Gil to go on, but he didn't offer any more. In fact he went on eating, chewing slow like he had all the time in the world.

Prying was downright rude, but Josie knew nothing about this man her husband trusted. What little she recalled about him didn't ease her mind none. It was up to her to protect her daughter and herself.

"Where do you call home?" she asked.

He didn't answer for the longest time, but she noted his subtle stiffening. "East of the Mississippi."

Josie stared at his bent head. She'd swear the man was hedging on purpose, though she couldn't imagine why. Unless he'd done something he wasn't proud of. Or he was on the run. Good grief, could Gil Yancy be an outlaw?

She filled their cups with coffee, and caught Gil

watching her every move. No, that wasn't right. He'd stared at her behind the longest time, let his gaze drift up to her bosom, which had never been much to ogle over, and then looked her straight in her eyes.

Him staring at her was the most indecent thing to do, though it appeared nobody but her noticed it. Mercy, her husband had never looked at her that way, though their relationship hadn't been a normal marriage.

In fact, Josie had plumb forgotten what it had felt like to be the object of a man's lust until Reid Barclay started paying her visits this spring. But where Reid's frank stare made her spitting mad, the heated look Gil slid her way had her heart pounding so hard she feared it would beat right out of her skin.

She set the coffeepot back on the stove, damning the way her hand shook. Of all the cowboys out there, why was Gil Yancy the one who'd bought a third of Rocky Point Ranch?

"May I be excused?" Sarah Ann asked, proving she did have manners.

"For now, but stay in the house. After supper, I want you to try on that split skirt," Josie said.

"I'd just as soon wear my buckskins."

Gil Yancy scowled. A dull flush climbed Dwight's thick neck. Hard to tell Hiram's reaction, but Josie imagined it was the same as hers and Twila MacInnes's.

"You're not wearing britches around here anymore unless it's under one of your old dresses."

"Why?"

"Because I said so."

Josie should've told her daughter weeks ago that those womanly curves she was getting looked inde-cent in tight britches, but she hadn't taken time to give her *that* talk. Why oh why did Sarah Ann have to grow up so fast?

"But Pa bought those buckskins for me." Sarah Ann was close to tears now.

"It doesn't matter. You're getting too old for them." She hoped that put an end to it because she did not want to have this conversation in front of the men.

"It matters to me," her daughter said.

"Stop your sniffling and mind your mother," Gil said.

Josie opened her mouth to tell Gil he had no right to spout orders to Sarah Ann, but her daughter beat her to it.

"You ain't my pa and I don't have to do what you say!"

If only the first part of that were true, Josie thought as Sarah Ann bolted from the kitchen.

"Now see what you've done!" Josie flung down her napkin and took out after her troubled daughter.

Gil hoped his gut would stop gyrating like a sunfisher fixing to toss his rider. He'd tried telling himself his eyes were playing tricks on him, but he knew they weren't.

Sitting across from Sarah Ann was like sitting across from his little sister. Oh, Sarah's hair was dark like Josie's and she had that pout to her mouth like her mama's, but those clear green eyes were dead ringers for Abby's.

Cooper eyes, his father had called them.

Only one way that could've happened. Gil had gotten a child on the shady lady twelve years ago at the Gilded Garter.

He gulped down his coffee, mulling over his last set-to with Josie. She hadn't denied she'd robbed him, but she'd looked him straight in the eye and swore Sarah was Everett's.

Considering her former profession, he reckoned Josie didn't know who'd knocked her up. For some reason the thought of her servicing men night after night pissed him off. That made no sense at all because he sure as hell wasn't jealous.

Nope, the more Gil thought about it, the more he figured Josie wasn't lying to him about Sarah. Unless she'd met his father or Abby, Josie would never know her daughter had inherited those Cooper green eyes.

But Gil knew. Question was, what did he aim to do about being a father?

Pride, shock and out-and-out fear bounced around in Gil like tumbleweeds. On one hand, he had the urge to stake his claim and raise the girl right. On the other, he thought it best he let things ride as they were. Leastwise for now.

True, Josie and Everett had let Sarah grow up wild as the prickly pear cactus on the high plains. The flowers were pretty to look at, but a fellow got stuck bad if he got too close. But in the West that wasn't such a bad thing.

Far as Gil could see, nothing would be gained by owning up to his responsibility. Hell, bringing all this up now would likely confuse the girl and cause her harm.

'Course, he might not have a choice.

If that Pinkerton detective Gil had confronted in Maverick delivered Gil's message to his father, the old man would likely show up here without warning. Soon as Gil's father set eyes on Sarah, he'd know the truth and be convinced he'd been right from the start. That Gil was irresponsible. That he'd never amount to a bucket of slop.

Dammit to hell and back! Gil wasn't sure whether to 'fess up or shut up. But he'd best decide because the only thing he'd get out of fence straddling were splinters in his crotch.

A long, mournful howl sliced through the silence, dragging Gil away from his troubles. The old hound he'd stepped over on the back porch let out a couple of wheezing barks which wouldn't scare off a mouse.

"That coyote is mighty close," Gil said.

Hiram nodded. "We herded a heifer due to drop a calf into the pen out back. Coyotes must've scented her."

"I heard 'em howling and yipping last night," Dwight said. "Reckon they're whelping and hankering for an easy meal."

"Best get that heifer in the barn for the night. Coyotes took down a couple of MacInnes's ewes last week." Hiram grabbed his hat and went out the back door with Dwight trailing him.

"I'll bring her in," Dwight said.

Gil tossed a look at the dishes cluttering the table and the meal Josie didn't eat. Guilt dragged its rowels over his conscience. He reckoned he should apologize for getting on his high horse around Sarah, but he damn sure wasn't about to tell Josie why he'd acted the way he had.

He jammed his hat on and caught up to the two cowpokes moseying toward the barn. "We had more than our share of coyotes back in Kansas. Always sent the hands out in the winter to find the dens. Easier to track in snow."

"That they are," Hiram said. "We used to do the

same, but what with Everett falling sick this winter, it didn't get done. Now we'll have to watch the stock."

"You need help?" Gil asked as they neared his cabin.

"Naw, won't take long to settle that heifer inside. I'll be back before the coffee is ready." Dwight headed toward the barn, now draped in deep shadows.

Hiram stopped. "If you're up for a game of poker, come on down to the bunkhouse. Three is better than two for a game."

"Thanks, but I ain't a gambling man." *Least he wasn't one any more.*

"Don't know if it makes a difference, but we ain't playing for money." Hiram's teeth gleamed. "Me and Dwight's been working for room and board long before Everett's passing."

"He was that hard up?"

"Yup, down to nothing 'cept hope that this venture of Miz Josie's would pan out."

Gil tossed a look to his lonely cabin. There couldn't be any harm in a friendly game where all he stood to win or lose was matches or some such.

"Reckon you can deal me in then."

A silver-slipper moon helped light their way to the bunkhouse. Hiram lit the kerosene lamp and set to making a pot of coffee. Gil took a chair at the scarred table and dug his makings from his pocket, taking in the crude surroundings.

Nothing on the table except the coal-oil lamp, a box of matches and a dog-eared deck of cards.

The room was fair-sized, yet there were only two bunks nailed to the walls opposite one another. The others had been removed and not too long back, judging from the markings on the wall. He wouldn't be surprised if they'd burned the wood to keep from freezing last winter.

At least Gil had his own cabin and could chop his own wood. He wouldn't have to smell the other cow-pokes' feet and butts, or trip over the riggings they left lying around.

Gil rolled a cigarette, struck a match and puffed his smoke to life. He'd lived the cowboy life for so long he rarely thought of the one he'd been born into. But looking into Sarah's green eyes had brought it all back to him.

The pain of betrayal cut to the bone.

Dwight ambled inside and the hound lumbered behind him. "That coffee ready yet?"

"Just is." Hiram poured the steaming black brew into tin cups, then straddled a chair and started shuf-fling the deck, but the snap and whoosh of cards mixing together failed to fire Gil's gambling fever. "Five card draw."

Dwight divided the matches among them, wallow-ing a large chew from one side of his mouth to the other. "Ante up."

They all tossed five matchsticks in the center of the table, then Hiram dealt the cards.

Dwight scooped his up and eyed them. "I'll go five." He tossed his bet on the pile.

"I'll see you." Hiram shoved five matchsticks into the pot and glanced at Gil. "What'll it be?"

Damned sorry-assed hand, but he'd won on less. "I'm in."

"I'll take two good ones," Dwight said, discarding two from his hand and laying them facedown.

Hiram slid a pair his way and faced Gil. "Whatcha need?"

Gil held on to the ten and king of spades. "Give me three."

Before Gil picked up his cards, he knew Lady Luck was dumping a load on him. He fanned them out. Damn hand like a foot.

"Dealer takes one," Hiram said.

"I'm kicking in ten." Dwight tossed his matchsticks on the pile.

"I'm out." Gil laid his cards down, unable to concentrate and unwilling to try. "Been a long day. Past time I hit the sack."

"See you in the morning," Hiram said.

Gil walked to his cabin, enjoying the chill bite in the air. He shucked his duds and stretched out on his cot, but instead of drifting off to sleep, he kept thinking about Sarah.

She was a split-tail filly, all piss and vinegar. Her eyes sparkled with life and Cooper confidence.

Gil frowned into the dark, needled by a new worry. What besides a kissable mouth and wealth of dark hair had his daughter inherited from her mother?

Chapter 5

The next morning, Josie sloshed fresh coffee in their cups, proof she was nervous. No wonder, since she'd spent a good part of last night lying awake, mulling over whether to go through with her idea.

It'd been a very long time since she'd put her talents to use. Thinking about doing it again brought back a wave of bad memories. But for her plan to work, everyone on the ranch had to do what they were best at.

Josie stole a glance at Gil Yancy. She half expected him to balk at her new decision, not that it'd do him a lick of good. She'd made up her mind on how to draw a paying crowd to the ranch and her two-thirds ownership gave her final say.

"What are you fixing to do today?" she asked Gil.

Gil took a sip of coffee, then swiped his tongue over his lips as if savoring every drop. Heat washed over Josie, searing her with memories of his mouth on hers, soft and gentle, nipping her ear, her neck, then sliding lower—

"Reckon I'll lay out two riding trails for your gentle guests," Gil said.

"That'll take up most of your day." She turned to Hiram and Dwight, hoping her face wasn't as flushed as her insides. "What about you two?"

"There're two more heifers ready to drop calves," Dwight said. "Reckon I'd best pen 'em up like I did the one last night. Coyotes are thicker than the fleece on MacInnes's woolies, so I'd best go hunting after I bring them heifers in."

"That's a good idea," Josie said. "I don't care to explain the necessity of hunting down coyotes to our guests."

"You wouldn't have to worry about that if you'd turn this venture into a hunting camp for men," Gil said.

Josie curved her fingers around the warm china, feeling suddenly chilled. The thought of catering to a bunch of rich men made her stomach knot. Why, she wouldn't get a wink of sleep for fretting over those strangers on the ranch, willing to pay anything to satisfy their wants.

"If I did that," she said, "I'd have to worry about some city slicker killing one of our cows or the neighbors' stock."

Gil nodded. "Reckon there's some truth to that. But if your guests aren't used to the saddle, we'll have our work cut out for us on the trail rides."

"Speaking of that, looks like we got an outlaw in that string of horses you bought," Hiram said.

Josie swore under her breath. "We can't afford to spend money on a bad mount. Are you sure he can't be broke?"

"Yes, ma'am. I climbed on that grulla stallion yesterday morning and my backside bit the dust before I knew it," Hiram said. "Bronco busting is all he's good for."

Just the opening she needed. "I've been thinking of a means to entertain our guests and give them a taste of real ranch life. The best way would be to put on an exhibition right here on Rocky Point, and that would surely draw a paying crowd from town and the outlying area."

Josie caught Gil staring at her. Was that genuine interest in his eyes?

Hiram winced. "I don't mind some bronco riding, but I ain't getting on that kidney-scrambler again."

"Reckon we could get the ranch duded up in a day or two." Dwight sawed a finger under his nose. "I could sure put on a bulldogging show."

"Miz Sarah is of an age to partake of it," Hiram said, then canted his head Gil's way.

Josie glanced at Gil, but he stared into his cup. Now what was that about?

"I thought Sarah Ann could show off her roping tricks," Josie said.

"Do you mean it, Mama?"

"I most certainly do. But you'll have to practice every day before the guests arrive."

Sarah Ann wiped her mouth on the napkin and tossed it beside her plate. "Can I start after school?"

"I don't see why not."

Josie smiled as her daughter bounded out the door. Encouraging her to practice roping here would keep her away from the MacInnes spread.

She faced Gil, and his frown swiped the smile off her face. "What about you?"

"I'll think on it."

"Surely you have talents that folks would enjoy watching," she said.

Gil's mouth kicked up in a grin, but the heat in his eyes promised a skill best suited to the bedroom. She swallowed hard and fought the urge to squirm. Damn the man for making her ache for something she couldn't afford to feel right now.

Hiram cleared his throat. "Gil is mighty good with a gun. Bet he could do some fancy shooting tricks."

"I'm sure whatever he chooses to do," Josie said, "will prove entertaining to the ladies."

That knocked the cocky grin off Gil's face.

"You got any fancy tricks you can do for your paying guests?" Gil asked.

The innuendo wasn't lost on Josie. Anger stepped right in and gave those unwanted, lusty thoughts the boot.

"I do a fair job cracking a whip," she said.

Dwight erupted in a coughing fit. Hiram pinched his eyes shut and let out a deep chuckle. Gil frowned, looking confused or disbelieving. She couldn't decide which, and really didn't care.

Josie got to her feet and gathered the dishes. Yes sirree. Let Gil Yancy wonder what she could do.

It was well past noon when Gil finished laying out one easy trail for their guests that wound over the sage-dotted plain, crossed a creek, then hugged the foothills before turning back toward the ranch. The entire route took about two hours, and folks would get a good view of the high plains as well as the mountains ringing the valley to the west and east.

The whole time he worked, he wondered what

Josie had up her sleeve. That is, when he wasn't calling himself ten kinds of a dumb-ass for spouting off his mouth in front of the hands.

Since he'd managed to embarrass Josie and put a burr under Hiram this morning, he decided it best to spend the afternoon on his land today. God knew he didn't seem fit for gentle company.

After satisfying the gnawing in his belly with biscuits and jerky, Gil removed the poke tied to his saddle and commenced setting up targets. Though he'd impressed Hiram with his shooting skills yesterday, it'd been luck he'd hit his mark.

He couldn't remember the last time he'd tried any fancy stuff. Might as well get in some practice and blow off steam at the same time.

A good thirty minutes later, Gil had shot so many holes in the cans he brought along that they looked like tin lace. He reckoned it'd take a couple of days practice to get his timing perfected again.

The hair on his neck stood up as he slid his Winchester back into its scabbard. He'd been so intent on shooting he'd lost his edge and let someone sneak up on him.

He turned, ready to draw his Peacemaker if his company turned out to be trouble. Less than ten feet from him, Sarah sat on her horse.

"That's fine shooting," Sarah said.

"It'll do."

Gil thumbed his hat back at stared up at her. His breath hitched. In the sunlight, her green eyes sparkled with excitement like Abby's. And that nubbin of a nose. It was the same shape as his little sister's.

"How long you been watching?"

"Not long," she said. "I haven't ever seen fancy shooting like that before."

"Takes practice."

"If I could shoot like you do, I'd join a Wild West show."

Gil scrubbed his knuckles along his jaw, dumbfounded. He'd said the same thing years back, but he damn sure didn't want his daughter to take up that life.

"You ever shoot before?"

"Some. Pa started teaching me last fall, but he took sick right after." Tears glittered in Sarah's eyes, and Gil's heart squeezed painfully. "And then he died."

That catch in her throat was all it took for Gil's conscience to gallop over his gut. The girl was grieving for Everett—the man who'd trusted Gil to look after his family.

His ol' partner believed Sarah was his. A promise was a promise, and Gil intended to keep his end of the bargain.

Gil fished two bits from his pocket and tossed the quarter to Sarah. "Catch."

She grabbed the coin midair, proving she had good reflexes.

"Throw it straight up as hard as you can."

She stared at him a second, then tossed the quarter as he'd told her. The sun glinted off the silver coin as it flipped end over end and reached its zenith.

Gil drew his Peacemaker, aimed and fired. The coin rocketed back up in the air, then dropped to the ground some twenty feet away.

"See if you can find it," he said. "Be careful if you do. It'll be hot."

Sarah jumped off her horse and went looking for

the coin. After a good deal of searching, she picked something up and jostled it in her palm. Gil knew he'd hit his mark when she faced him, smiling from ear to ear.

"Wow, you put a hole clean through it," she said.

"Anybody can do the same with practice." A lie, but he was betting Sarah had a good eye like him.

She stared from the coin to Gil. "Can you teach me to shoot like that?"

"Your ma may not like it."

Sarah kicked a dirt clod, showing that rebellious streak that mirrored his. "If you taught me some fancy shooting tricks, I could do them when our guests came. It'd be a good surprise for Mama."

Gil wasn't so sure Josie would feel the same, but he didn't see how teaching Sarah would hurt her either. Besides, she was his. What harm would there be in Gil spending a bit of time around the girl, getting to know her?

"All right, but we'll have to practice every day."

Excitement two-stepped in her eyes. "School lets out at one. It takes me about twenty minutes to ride home. We could practice after that."

"It's settled then. We'll meet here every day at half past one." Gil held up a hand when she squealed. "But you got to promise you'll do as your ma wants and wear that split skirt she's making for you. You hear?"

"I promise." Sarah swung up into the saddle. "I reckon if Mama ain't going to wear britches anymore, I won't either."

He watched Sarah trot off, but the image he saw in his mind was Josie in tight britches. Or better yet, Josie wearing nothing but a smile and lacy stockings.

Gil fished his makings out of his pocket and rolled a cigarette, feeling like he was all thumbs. A heavy ache settled in his belly and his pecker stiffened.

Different men had different longings. He was a butt man, pure and simple. He liked to cup a woman's bare bottom in his hands. Knead the lush fullness.

In fact, getting two handfuls of Josie's firm behind as he sunk into her and took them to the promised land was the last thing he remembered about that night at the Gilded Garter. He'd be lying if he said he didn't ache to bed Josie and relive every delicious moment of it.

It sure as hell would beat the memory of Gil waking up to his partner dragging him out of bed amid a cloud of choking smoke, having a headache the size of Texas. Of staggering outside with the saddlebags only to realize that the shady lady had robbed him blind.

Yep, Gil had been stomping mad at Josie that night, but he'd never lost his desire for her. According to Hiram, he wasn't the only man packing a hard-on for the little lady.

Gil climbed on his gelding and reined the roan north. It was high time he paid Reid Barclay a visit and found out what type man he was going up against.

The lay of the land altered drastically when Gil rode onto Barclay's land. An iron gate spanned the road, proclaiming this was the Crown Seven Ranch.

The sweet grass looked thicker and the deep streams were wider. In the near distance, he could make out the roof of a big, stone house.

A lone rider raced toward Gil. He recognized him as the man who'd barreled past Gil's land the other day.

Barclay reined up his chestnut stallion. "State your business."

"Name's Gil Yancy. Everett Andrews sold me the land running parallel to your spread. Thought I'd best make your acquaintance."

"So he actually did sell some of Rocky Point." A muscle pounded in Barclay's lean cheek. "Good luck with it."

Gil recognized that unspoken invitation to get the hell gone, but he ignored it. Barclay appeared to be the type who was used to getting what he wanted, and if he had his mind set on having Josie, Gil aimed to let him know he was wasting his time.

He thumbed his hat back and forced a smile. "Me and Everett go way back, but I've known Josie a good spell as well. She insisted I stay at Rocky Point. That cabin of mine is mighty rough, and since I'm acting as trail guide for her guest ranch venture, it's best I stay close to her."

Barclay's lips twitched, and for a moment Gil thought the man would laugh. "What's your point?"

"Everett asked me to watch over Josie and Sarah. I aim to make sure nobody tries to wheedle the ranch from them."

"How bloody commendable," Barclay said.

"I'm a man of my word."

"No doubt you believe you are, but in this case I wager you are more interested in the ranch than you are the woman and her child."

Gil forced a smile—let him think what he will. "Keep in mind that my land is between the Crown Seven and Rocky Point."

"Are you insinuating that you're the wall between me and the lady in question?"

"Take it any way you want."

Barclay leaned forward and crossed his hands atop the saddle horn. "Know this, Mr. Yancy. Unless you marry Josephine, you have no say in how she lives her life or with whom she agrees to share it."

A truth Gil didn't like looking too long or hard at. "You saying you want to marry Josie?"

"I would enjoy entering into a relationship with her and have offered her such an arrangement that would be mutually beneficial to her and myself."

"Son of a bitch! You asked her to be your mistress?"

"Does that shock you?"

It did, which made no sense considering Josie had been a sporting girl in her youth. "What about Sarah?"

"I would gladly pay for the girl's education at a private boarding school."

Not if Gil had his way. His dislike for Barclay kicked up another notch. "I should've figured you'd ship Sarah off to get her out of your hair, not that Josie would let you do that."

"No doubt you are right, but one never knows what one will do when one is in a pinch." Challenge played over Barclay's hard mouth. "Good day to you, Mr. Yancy. May the best man triumph."

He heeled his horse's flanks and rode off, leaving Gil steaming over his veiled threat. *Arrogant son of a bitch.*

Barclay wasn't going to give up on making Josie his mistress, and once Barclay got in her bed, he'd no doubt have a say in how Rocky Point was run. Hell, Gil wouldn't be surprised if Barclay ended up marrying her.

And where would that leave Gil then? A cow pie in the middle of Reid Barclay's spread.

"Dammit all!" Gil wasn't about to end up on the losing end this time.

At the sound of an approaching horse, Josie put her sewing aside and looked out the front window. Dugan MacInnes climbed off his sorrel gelding and tied the lines to the hitching post.

A sense of dread washed over her. She could count on one hand the times he'd come over here to see Everett. He'd barely acknowledged her then. So what brought him here now?

Heavy boot falls thudded on the porch, then her front door rattled from four hard raps. Guess she'd soon find out.

Josie smoothed her skirt and went to the door. Her welcoming smile faltered when she looked up into his tense face.

"Good afternoon, Mr. MacInnes. What brings you by?"

"Business, Mrs. Andrews." MacInnes's burr was as thick as his bulging middle. "There's a matter of grave importance we need to discuss in private."

She hoped he wasn't going to harp on taking Sarah Ann away again. Dealing with Twila MacInnes was more than enough for anyone to bear.

"Do come in." She stepped back and motioned him into her parlor. "Can I get you something to drink?"

"Nothing, thank you." Dugan MacInnes marched into the room and eased into Everett's chair by the now cold stove. "Were you aware of the promissory note I extended to your husband?"

"I remember it." She'd been against borrowing

from Dugan MacInnes from the start, but the bank wouldn't lend them money at the time and Everett wouldn't ask Reid Barclay for a cup of water. "As I recall, Everett paid you back as soon as he sold off our cattle."

MacInnes bobbed his shaggy head and withdrew a paper from his pocket. "That he did. He paid off the loan, and I acknowledged receipt of the amount. Unfortunately it didn't satisfy the interest he had accrued."

"Excuse me?"

He unfolded the paper. "I loaned money to your husband in good faith. But as a bank would operate, I expected to be recompensed for my inconvenience."

She shook her head, unable to grasp what he was getting at. "Everett paid you more than he borrowed, like he'd have done if the bank in Laramie had extended him a loan."

"That he did, but I'm not a bank." MacInnes handed her the paper. "As you can see by this, I required a bit more than a modest rate of interest. It's all here in the loan document, signed and dated by your husband and myself. My groom witnessed the transaction."

Josie's hands shook as she took the paper and stared at MacInnes's handwriting. It was as tight as the man standing before her.

The more she read, the madder she became. When she got to the total amount she owed him, she was tempted to shoot Dugan MacInnes dead and nail his hide to the barn.

Not only was the interest double what they would've paid a bank, but this Scots son of a bitch worded the loan to confound a person. She would bet that Everett, with his limited book learning, hadn't realized he'd owed MacInnes interest that long-ago day last winter when he'd paid him, or that every day piled more debt on them.

But Everett had put his mark on the loan, not saying a word to her about compound interest, even though she was more book smart than him. And MacInnes had let it ride all this time until she now owed her neighbor seven hundred dollars. It might as well be seven thousand.

She waved the agreement in his face. "This is a dirty scheming trick and you know it."

"'Tis business, Mrs. Andrews. With this depression following so close to two disastrous winters, I've found myself in a financial dilemma and need to call in the note."

Damn him. "I can pay you a third of it now, Mr. MacInnes." All she'd earned off the Hastings party plus the little she had saved for an emergency.

"That's a drop in the bucket, and don't offer to sell me any of your land. I'm land poor as it is." MacInnes stood and tugged his vest over his gut. "I'll give you a day to settle the debt before I sell your loan to the bank."

Meaning she'd owe double what she did now. "My God, if I can't pay the bank, they'd foreclose. I'll lose everything Everett and I worked for."

"Aye, 'tis a shame to see that happen." MacInnes stared down at her, his smile as shallow as her breathing. "There is one way I'd be willing to set your debt aside for good."

Ice congealed in Josie's veins. "What is it you want, Mr. MacInnes?"

"Sarah. 'Tis no secret my wife and I were unable to

have children. Sarah is a wonderful young lady. So talented. She could have a wonderful life."

Josie stared at him through a swirling, red haze. "You can't be serious?"

"I am," he said. "If you allow us to adopt Sarah, I'll tear up the loan papers."

"No!" Sarah Ann shouted. "I won't live with you!"

Josie whirled to see her daughter standing in the doorway, a look of hurt and confusion marring her face. Damn this man for doing this to her and Sarah.

MacInnes's coarse features softened. "Sarah, dear. You must know we'd give you a better life than you'd have here on this ranch."

Tears streamed from Sarah Ann's eyes. She shook her head so hard her dark hair looked like a thundercloud.

"You have no right assuming that," Josie said. "Get out of my house and don't ever set foot on my land again."

"As you wish. The choice is yours, Mrs. Andrews. Either be prepared to sign adoption papers, or pay what you owe me in full tomorrow."

Chapter 6

Gil's ill temper hadn't sweetened one bit by the time he returned to Rocky Point. He'd bought into this ranch because Everett promised he'd sell him more land later on. Now it appeared he'd have to fight and finagle to stop Barclay from destroying his dream.

He ground-reined Rhubarb and headed for the house to have a word with Josie. On the ride he'd come up with a surefire plan to give him equal say in Rocky Point, but he wasn't sure if the bargaining chip he had on Josie was enough to bend her to his way of thinking.

Gil reached the porch as Dugan MacInnes stormed out the front door with Josie's curses dogging his steps. Sarah's crying inside joined the fray.

"What the hell's going on?" Gil asked MacInnes.

"I am not in the habit of answering to hired help." The big Scotsman climbed on his sorrel gelding and galloped off.

Gil had a mind to go after him, but the caterwauling in the house demanded his attention. He yanked open the front door and stormed inside, following the wailing to the parlor. Josie sat on the settee beside Sarah, arms wrapped around the sobbing girl.

"What's all the ruckus about?"

"Everett borrowed money from MacInnes last fall to see us through," Josie said. "Though my husband paid back the debt, he wasn't aware he owed MacInnes additional interest. Outrageous interest, I might add. Now MacInnes demands payment in full."

Gil had a hunch he knew the problem, but he asked anyway. "Do you have the money?"

"I'm five hundred dollars short."

Sarah looked up, and the tears filling her big, green eyes hurt him worse than any gut-punch he'd ever taken. "Mr. MacInnes wants me instead or we'll lose the ranch."

"He told you that?" he asked.

Josie nodded and patted her daughter's back. "Dugan MacInnes and his wife want to adopt Sarah Ann. He said if I didn't pay the debt now or sign adoption papers, he'll sell my loan to the bank."

Barclay sniffing after Josie to get the ranch pissed Gil off, but MacInnes forcing Josie to choose between the ranch or her daughter had Gil seeing red. Damned interfering foreigners sure threw a kink in his plans.

"That's blackmail."

"I know. If I can't pay the bank, they'll foreclose and we'll lose Rocky Point." Josie hiked up her chin. "I'll risk that before I'll let them have Sarah Ann."

Sarah sniffed loudly and swiped her flushed face. "Maybe if I get good enough at trick shooting, I could join a Wild West show and help pay off the bank."

"No," Josie and Gil said at the same time.

Josie glared at him. He shrugged and jammed his thumbs under his belt.

Sarah sniffled. "But I want to help."

"I know you do, and I appreciate it." Josie's smile was shaky as she smoothed Sarah's hair back. "Go wash up. I need to talk to Gil in private."

Sarah flicked another look his way, then got up and clomped out of the room. Gil watched her go, feeling her helplessness in every weary step.

Josie cleared her throat. "Seeing that I earn ten dollars for every guest, and that I can comfortably accommodate six people, it will take me nine days to earn the money I need. As time is short, I'd like to offer you a proposition, one I believe you'd be hard-pressed to refuse."

Gil rubbed his knuckles along his jaw, torn between hearing her out or laying his own cards on the table. Fact was he couldn't bear the thought of his daughter's mama selling her wares.

"If you'd just agree—"

"Whoa, Josie. Your idea tempts me—don't get me wrong—but there's a better way to pay off MacInnes than by selling yourself to me."

"Why you arrogant, no-account drifter." She jumped to her feet, every sweet inch of her spitting fire. "What makes you think I was offering myself to you?"

"You said you aimed to proposition me."

Josie's face flamed. "If you could pay off MacInnes, I'd have made you a partner in the guest ranch, but I've changed my mind. If I can't sell of a sixth of Rocky Point in Maverick, I'll pay a visit to my near neighbor."

Son of a bitch! "Like Barclay?"

"Yes." She barreled past him.

Gil grabbed her arm and pulled her back. "Now hold up here. I made an honest mistake, given your past profession and all."

"Let. Me. Go."

"Hear me out first."

"Why should I give you that courtesy?"

Damn good question. Again he'd managed to get his boots and spurs in his mouth. Getting them out without drawing blood wasn't going to be easy or painless, but he had to stop her. Any way he could.

"I'm sorry I jumped to the wrong conclusion. Forgive me?"

The fire left her eyes, and her body relaxed some. "I don't know. I'd have to be crazy to even consider it."

He smiled, sidling closer and dropping his voice to a husky whisper. "Come on, Josie. You don't want some stranger owning part of Rocky Point, putting up a house, barn and fences wherever they damn well please."

She chewed her bottom lip, and he felt her softening toward him. "Are you saying that won't happen if I sell part of my share to you?"

"Your share?"

"Sarah Ann and I own the ranch equally, though title won't revert to her until she's of age. The land Everett sold you was his third of Rocky Point. He set it up that way long ago so we'd always have a home. You didn't know?"

Gil wasn't sure whether to laugh or cuss a blue streak. Ol' Everett conned him real good, promising Gil he'd sell him more land later on—land that belonged to Josie and Sarah. Why'd Everett come to him, made him the offer and lie? Was he handpicking the man to ride herd over this spread? To protect Josie and Sarah from MacInnes and Reid Barclay?

Whatever the reason, it didn't much matter if Josie lost hers and Sarah's shares. "How much do you owe MacInnes?"

"Seven hundred dollars," she said. "I need five hundred."

Damn near every red cent Gil had left to his name. He'd aimed to use it to buy cattle, but he sure wasn't about to pass up the chance to own more of the ranch.

Gil bent his head to hers and her vanilla scent swirled around him. "I've got that much. Reckon that ought to give me title to half of your share."

Instead of seeing relief light her eyes, her pretty mouth puckered into a knot. "Damn you. That only comes to five dollars an acre."

"We're in a depression, Josie. Money's tight."

"Seems you are, too. Everett said the land was worth thirty-five dollars an acre. Maybe more."

He hadn't figured she could cipher so fast, or have that much sense about land values. "Would you rather let the bank hold your loan on the entire ranch?"

"I'd just as soon not be in this fix."

The way she worried her mouth plumped her full lips, making it mighty hard for him to concentrate on money. He had a sudden hankering to kiss her.

"I'll sell you a third of my share, plus make you a partner in the guest ranch," she said.

"Half your share, Josie. If you can pay me back in six months, you keep the title and I'll continue on as your equal partner in the guest ranch."

She stared at him for the longest time, and Gil wondered what all was going on in that pretty head of hers. If she found him as eye-catching as he found her. If the thought of being partners stirred another longing in her that they'd shared once.

"All right, then. We'll go to town tomorrow and have an agreement drawn up with Maverick Land and Security."

"I say we draft it here and be done with it."

She pulled away from him, frowning. "Why? Are you trying to swindle me?"

"No, ma'am. I'm keeping our deal between us. You want everyone in Maverick knowing you're in a financial bind?"

"No."

Josie fetched a paper from her desk and wrote out a simple agreement between them. She signed it, her smile tense. Gil added his name below hers, wanting to send up a whoop of delight for getting his hands on more land, but for some strange reason he couldn't muster up the energy.

"I'll stow this in Everett's lockbox and fetch what money I have." She was back in no time, clutching a stack of greenbacks. "Here's two hundred dollars."

He took it and shoved it in his vest pocket. "I'll add mine to it and head over to the Diamond M." But he couldn't get his feet to budge.

"Why are you looking at me like that again?"

Dammit all. It was mighty hard to fool a woman who knew so much about men, and that reminder spurred his ego.

"Many a man has sealed a deal on a handshake and his word."

She blinked. "Are you saying you want to shake hands?"

"Seeing as we know each other so well, I thought

we'd improvise." He winked, certain she'd catch his meaning.

"For the love of Pete, I should've shot you when I had the chance."

"Now, Josie, you took my meaning wrong again. Instead of a handshake, I was thinking we could seal our deal with a kiss."

She didn't pull away or look like she wanted to bash him again, giving him hope he was wearing down her defenses. In fact, her eyes darkened to a smoky blue.

"That's what you want? A kiss?"

"Yep, all I want is one." *A long kiss with plenty of tongue.*

She licked her lips, and his pecker jolted something fierce. Damnation, why was he torturing himself this way?

"All right. But I don't want Sarah Ann knowing I've had to sell off more of the ranch. And only one, you hear?"

"Yes'm." He aimed to kiss her until he was forced to come up for air.

Gil lowered his head slowly, taking in the widening of her eyes, the slight opening of her mouth. Hot damn, but she had that innocent act down pat. A shame he'd gone too long without her to play with.

His mouth settled over hers, hungry and demanding. Hers trembled against his the slightest bit, but he couldn't bring himself to pull away.

Gil eased the pressure though, wrapping an arm around her and fitting her against his length. He swallowed her gasp and soaked up her shivers, aching to melt her restraint.

Her womanly curves pressed into him, fitting

perfectly like she was made for him. She felt small and fragile in his arms and he wanted to protect her. But the knot on his head was a reminder that Josie Andrews wasn't frail or helpless.

He deepened the kiss. Except for the softness of those lips against his and the subtle taste of peppermint on her tongue, he might as well be kissing a picture of her.

Dammit, there was fire in her. He'd felt it once all the way to his toes. If he could just stoke it to life again.

Gil slid one hand up her arm, damning the roughness of his skin against hers. He wondered if the rest of her felt as firm with muscle as he deepened the kiss, letting his hands roam.

Her fingers dug into his arms, like she was holding on for dear life. Then she finally did it. Her tongue did a bit of exploring, though it was so fast he almost missed it.

He coaxed her to try again, and those tentative flicks of her tongue sent a bolt of heat straight to his pecker. His hands moved up and down the curve of her spine, lingering on her rounded behind. She let out some odd sound and lurched closer to him. *'Atta girl.* He filled his hands with her sweet ass.

His ears buzzed so he barely heard the scuff of boots or the muffled, "No."

Josie jerked free of him like she'd been scalded, leaving him standing there puckered up and hurting like the dickens. She stared past him, eyes wide and cheeks blotchy from passion and what he supposed was embarrassment at getting caught swapping spit with him.

Gil turned around, having a good idea who stood behind him. He took no pleasure in being right.

Sarah stood in the doorway staring at Josie and him in turn, mouth hanging open and eyes bugging out of her head. He felt his own cheeks burn at getting caught fooling around with the mother of his child.

Josie stepped around him and went to Sarah. "That was a friendly kiss, nothing more."

Bull. It was exactly what it looked like. If Sarah had come in a tad later, Gil would've had Josie's skirts up. He sure didn't want Sarah to see that.

Damn! He scrubbed a hand over his face, wondering if he could manage to kick his own ass.

"Gil has agreed to help me pay off Dugan MacInnes, and be an equal partner in the guest ranch." Josie slid him a smile that bordered on frosty. "Isn't that right?"

"Yes'm."

She turned back to Sarah. "Once our next guests pay me, I'll reimburse Gil for his trouble."

Sarah took her time giving him a long once-over, proving she wasn't easily fooled. He hoped she couldn't tell how Josie's kiss physically affected him.

"Why are you helping us?" Sarah asked.

Because it earned him what he wanted most—land. "Because your pa was my friend, and I promised him I'd look after you and your ma."

"Everett really asked you to do that?" Josie asked.

"Yep. Made of point of it."

Josie shook her head, and Gil could only wonder what she must think of Everett for tracking Gil down and bringing him here. Just like that, twelve years of hiding were erased.

"When are you going to pay Mr. MacInnes?" Sarah asked.

"I aim to see to it now."

No getting around the fact that worry was lining her young face. Gil didn't blame the girl none.

MacInnes's threat of selling Josie's loan unless she gave him Sarah was real. Damned low-down and mean. Ruthless.

The successful man is ruthless in business, his father had told Gil time and again.

Yep, his old man hadn't stopped at nothing to get what he wanted. He'd even double-crossed his own son.

Gil tipped his hat to the ladies and walked out, certain the deal he'd struck with Josie was fair for her and him. Just because he aimed to own the entire ranch in due time didn't make him ruthless. Nope, he'd never screw Josie out of the land.

That's why he'd given her a chance to recoup her shares, and give himself a say in the ranch. Yep, this worked out damn fine and proved again to Gil that he wasn't cut from the same cloth as his father.

Josie sent Sarah Ann an apologetic smile then hurried out the door. "Gil, wait. I—" She broke off, not knowing what to say, not wanting to admit why she'd run after the man she'd sworn she'd skedaddle from should their paths cross again.

He stopped by the hitching post and faced her, and the heat in his eyes melted something inside her right then and there, something warm and wanting that she hadn't felt in twelve long years. "Something you need?"

She wrapped her hands around the rough boards on the porch post and leaned into it. Up until a few minutes ago, she hadn't thought she'd need anything from this cowboy. And now—*Don't think those thoughts.*

"Thank you," she said.

He dipped his chin, turned and walked on.

Josie dropped her forehead against the post and listened to the chink-chink of his spurs until he disappeared into the barn. She should feel relieved Gil hadn't demanded more of her, but instead she quivered with an odd ache.

"You like him, don't you?" Sarah Ann asked.

Did she? Josie didn't know. She'd never forgotten his gentle kisses or his bone-melting touch, though she'd been too consumed by fear to allow herself true pleasure. And now? Now it may be too late for that.

"Your pa thought a lot of Gil."

Sarah Ann sat on the porch rail and leaned her back against the middle post, watching Gil ride out. "I never saw you kiss Pa like that."

Truth be told, Gil was the only man she'd ever kissed. As for her marriage, she wasn't about to explain to her daughter or anyone else what she and Everett shared. Their relationship had been more father and daughter. Why, he'd never laid a hand on her in anger, or in lust.

"Your Pa wasn't one for spooning and neither was I."

Sarah Ann was silent for so long Josie thought she'd satisfied her curiosity. She should've known better.

"What's it feel like?" Sarah Ann asked.

Josie's stomach fluttered from the memory of that kiss and what the question meant. She'd hoped she wouldn't have to have this conversation for a few more years. But the fact remained that Sarah Ann was growing up fast, and before long boys—and men—would notice her.

She'd have to tell her about the birds and bees.

But not today. Not after that kiss that left her tingling with want.

"Don't tell me you're starting to think more about boys than horses?"

Sarah Ann blushed. "I don't want boys kissing on me. It's just I was curious, is all."

Josie couldn't hold back her smile. Her daughter was still a child in so many ways.

"If you're smart, you'll stay curious about boys for another eight years or so," Josie said. "How about helping me fix dinner?"

"As long as I don't have to peel potatoes."

"I tell you what. You fetch carrots and onions from the root cellar and I'll tend to the potatoes."

"You got a deal." As if she feared Josie would change her mind, Sarah Ann tore into the house.

Josie turned to go inside when the thunder of hooves caught her attention. She looked up the lane, expecting to see Gil coming back.

Instead of spying the cowboy she couldn't get off her mind, she recognized Virgil Keegan. What in the world brought the sheriff galloping out here again?

He reined up by the porch and brushed two fingers over the hat brim shading his long thin face. "Afternoon, Josie."

"Same to you, Virgil. I hope good news brought you to these parts in a hurry."

"Can't rightly say." He fished in his vest and removed a letter. "Telegram came in for you. Big Dan at the depot said it was urgent."

"Oh, my. Thank you for bringing it out." She took the telegram and broke the seal, dreading bad news. "Would you care to come in and have a cup of coffee?"

"Some other time. I've got to get back to town directly."

Yet he didn't make any move to leave. In fact, the way he kept stealing looks at her had her nerves snapping like wet wash on the line. Could he tell something was different about her? That she'd recently been kissed senseless and was aching for more?

"Are the trains running yet?" she asked.

"Nope. Pullman strike still has 'em shut down, 'cept for the U.S. Mail cars." He shifted in the saddle and glanced around. "How're you getting on with that new trail guide? What's his name again? Yancy?"

"Just fine." Thank goodness her voice didn't quiver like her insides. "Gil's mapped out a couple of easy riding trails and he plans to mark a longer one so our guests can camp out a night or so in the wild."

He shook his head. "I can't figure why rich folks want to sleep on the ground if they ain't coming out here to hunt."

Josie could. For years, the only peace she got at night was sleeping outside, away from the raucous hell going on in the brothel, night after night.

"It's all part of getting close to nature, something I suppose they don't do much of where they live."

Virgil's bushy mustache twitched, like he'd gotten a whiff of fresh manure. "A highfalutin Pinkerton detective rode into town last week. Said he was from Chicago. Didn't come to me straight off. Nosed around the saloons and such. By the time he looked me up, I didn't much care to oblige him."

"Did he say who he was looking for?"

"Sure did. He had a picture of your trail guide and wanted to know if folks had seen him."

She pressed a hand to her throat. "Please tell me it wasn't a wanted poster."

"Nothing of the kind. It was an old daguerreotype. Fact is I was hard pressed to match the young dude in the picture with the cowpoke that rode into Maverick the day before."

"You sure it was Gil Yancy?"

"I'd say. About an hour after this detective tracked Yancy down at Maverick Livery, the two had a set-to." Virgil shook his head. "Whatever your trail guide said to that detective sent him packing, though old Dan at the depot told me that Pinkerton sent a telegram before lighting out on the evening stage for Laramie."

"Maybe the detective mistook Gil for someone else."

"I don't think so. This detective claimed Yancy was Harrison G. Cooper the Third." Virgil crossed his hands over the saddle horn and leaned forward. "I got a hunch your trail guide ran away from home a long time back and changed his name. Reckon his kin are wondering if he's still with the living."

How Josie wished she'd had kin that would've taken her and her sister in. "Some folks have good reason to leave home."

"Yep. Reckon most folks came west to escape something or someone."

Josie hugged her waist, well remembering how it felt to skedaddle in the dark of the night and never look back. To start over with a new name and new life. To put a bad life and an even worse man far behind.

For years she'd feared her past would one day catch up with her. Now part of it had. Was it possible she and Gil shared something in common?

"For a week afterward," Virgil said, "Yancy hung

around town, checking with Dan a couple of times a
day to see if a telegram had come for him. Then
Yancy packed up and left town."

And he headed straight to Rocky Point Ranch. She
pressed a hand to her fluttering stomach, guessing
how let down he must've felt if he'd expected word
from kin, and never got it.

She smiled at Virgil. "Thanks for bringing my
telegram, and for telling me about the Pinkerton man."

"That's my job, watching over folks. You need anything, you send Hiram or Dwight into town, you
hear?"

"I'll do that."

As soon as Virgil rode off, Josie opened the telegram and read the short message.

DEAR MISSUS ANDREWS [STOP] MY FAMILY
AND I HAVE FINALLY ARRIVED IN OMAHA
[STOP] WE SHALL LEAVE SHORTLY BY STAGE
AND EXPECT TO REACH MAVERICK IN TWO
DAYS [STOP] IF YOU ARE ABLE TO MEET AND
WELCOME US TO ROCKY POINT THREE DAYS
EARLIER THAN PLANNED I WILL GLADLY PAY
FOR ANY INCONVENIENCE [STOP] PLEASE
LEAVE WORD AT THE TELEGRAPH OFFICE
AS I WILL CHECK FOR NEWS FROM YOU ON
HOW WE SHOULD PROCEED WHEN WE
REACH MAVERICK [STOP] CORDIALLY ELIZA
HASTINGS [STOP]

Josie folded the telegram and slid it into her
pocket, intending to send Dwight into town tomorrow with a reply for Mrs. Hastings. Her first guests.

Relief swirled around her like a Chinook wind. In three days she'd have money to start paying Gil back.

She gazed up at the ridge that'd protected this homestead from harsh winters and her past from prying eyes for years. Everett had trusted her, and Gil as well, or he wouldn't own a part of this ranch now.

Like Everett, Gil was privy to her troubled past. Would he protect her as well?

It was a chance Josie had to take.

Chapter 7

Gil tethered Rhubarb to the iron post and squinted at MacInnes's fine house. It put to mind those grand old mansions back in Philadelphia. Like the one he'd grown up in where he'd learned the true meaning of undying love, and gut-twisting betrayal.

His already prickly mood soured. He headed to the front door, spurs jingling and nerves twisting tighter than the dally line on a half-crazed bull.

He'd taken an intense dislike to the Scotsman who had an eye for Sarah. This last stunt to take the girl from Josie had him stomping mad. He twisted the brass ringer on the door, then rapped his fist on the oval etched glass for orneriness.

Gil saw a shadow pass before the door. It opened, and he stared eye to eye with a gaunt old gentleman wearing a fine gray suit. Not a flicker of emotion showed in the man's puckered face as he gave Gil a mile-long once-over.

"Good afternoon, sir," the gent said, a slight burr shadowing his clipped English accent. "May I inquire who is calling, and the nature of your business?"

"Gil Yancy from Rocky Point Ranch. I'm here to speak with Dugan MacInnes."

"One moment, if you please." The older man pushed the door closed, but Gil put his weight against the heavy panel and elbowed his way inside.

"I'll wait here."

The butler glared at him. Gil answered in kind and jabbed his thumbs under his gunbelt.

With a huff, the butler tottered down a long hall nigh as wide as Gil's cabin. One look told him Dugan MacInnes had money. Old money, from the looks of this house. Hell, the marble-topped table holding a silver server for calling cards was probably worth more than he'd earned cowboying last year.

An uneasy silence drifted around Gil. The pocket doors opening to the parlor were open, so he bode his time taking in the stiff, formal furnishings and opulent paintings.

At one time, he wouldn't have given the blue cameo wallpaper with dark red roses a second glance, but it looked garish to him now. Odd how he learned to appreciate bunkhouses papered with cattle breeding charts, newspaper and flyers. Or how relaxed he felt in Josie's house with walls papered with pale clusters of flowers and lacy curtains that let in light.

A door down the hallway closed with a soft click. The butler trudged toward Gil, looking bored as all get out.

"Laird MacInnes will see you. May I take your hat?"

"Hell, no." But Gil did remove his Stetson and finger comb his hair, not that it did a lick of good to try and tame his thick mop.

"Very well. Follow me."

He wiped his feet and trailed the butler down the hall. The servant opened the heavily paneled door and stepped aside to let Gil pass.

Gil strode into the room, anxious to get this over with and get gone. If it weren't for the animal trophy heads hanging on the walls, he'd swear he'd stepped into his father's study in the Cooper mansion.

The heavy drapes were pulled back from the two big windows and let in a good deal of light, but the dark wood wall panels made the room feel cold and inhospitable. So did the big man with the red mustache and spade beard holding court behind his monstrous desk.

"That is all, Dowd." Before the old gent slipped out of the room, MacInnes said, "So, Mr. Yancy. What brings you to the Diamond M?"

"I'm here to settle what Everett and Josephine Andrews owe you." Gil tugged his stash of greenbacks from his vest pocket and tossed them on the desk. "Seven hundred bucks there. I want a receipt that their loan and interest are paid in full."

MacInnes scooped up the bills and counted them out, piling them in a neat stack like a gambler tallying up his take for the night. The Scotsman leaned back in his chair and regarded him with shrewd eyes that grated on Gil's patience.

"Most cowboys of my acquaintance couldn't satisfy half the amount of this debt, yet you managed to come forth with the entire amount so soon after buying a third of Rocky Point from Everett Andrews. I find that quite extraordinary, Mr. Yancy."

"I've been saving up for a spell." Since last year when he'd lost twenty-five thousand in a poker game. "I want proof of payment."

MacInnes took a sheet of paper from his desk and proceeded to write on it. When he was done, he replaced his pen in the holder, waved a hand over the wet ink and then slid the paper toward Gil.

"There you are, Mr. Yancy. I trust that is satisfactory."

Gil read the wording, but didn't make a move to take it. "Call in someone who can read and write. I want a witness to verify Andrews's debt is paid in full, and that we all signed and dated this document."

"Dowd!" MacInnes reared back in his chair and an amused smile played over his thin lips. "You've a good head on your shoulders, Mr. Yancy."

"I get by."

MacInnes chuckled. "You do more than that I suspect. I've lived in this rugged country for well over a decade, and I've met few cowboys with any business savvy."

"Reckon there's some truth in that."

Dowd trudged in. "Yes, Laird MacInnes."

"Mr. Yancy and I have concluded a financial matter of import. He requested a witness to the fact I have accepted this money as payment in full"—MacInnes patted the stack of greenbacks—"and that we have affixed our signatures. Yours is required as witness."

"Very well," Dowd said.

MacInnes scrawled his name, then angled the pen and ink toward Gil. He read the receipt again to make sure he hadn't missed any angle that could come back to Josie at a later date. Once Gil was satisfied, he signed his name and date beneath Dugan MacInnes's scrawl.

Dowd took the pen and signed his name with a flourish, adding "witness" afterward. "Would there be anything else?"

"A glass of whiskey," MacInnes said. "Will you join me in a celebratory toast, Mr. Yancy?"

"Reckon I can spare the time." Satisfy his curiosity to boot.

Gil dropped into the chair before MacInnes's desk,

crossed his leg and balanced his hat on his knee. He took the heavy glass of whiskey Dowd handed him and imbibed. Smooth as a woman's skin and almost as satisfying on the tongue.

"That sorrel I saw in your corral. He's got fine lines."

"Aye, that he does." MacInnes scowled and drank deeply of his whiskey. "I bought the horse last year and I should have suspected I was being gulled by one of the best."

"How so?"

"The Irishman sat in on a high-stakes game in Laramie of which I partook. Myself and three others folded early, but the Irishman and another man were locked in a standoff." MacInnes snorted. "The Irishman offered the stallion to cover his bet, but his opponent refused, so he offered to sell me the horse."

"Sounds like you got a good deal."

"I'd seen the stallion, and there was no doubt he was a thoroughbred, so I accepted. But his papers were completely fraudulent, like the cheating Irishman who vanished. The entire matter so enraged me, I had the animal gelded this winter, symbolic of what I wanted to do with the Irishman should I ever be so lucky to catch him."

Gil sipped his whiskey. "You realize that horse was probably stolen."

"Aye. I contacted the sheriff in Maverick, and he assured me he'd look into the matter. But he hasn't come across any posters on a horse matching that description yet."

Gil ironed the glass over his hat brim resting on his leg, smoothing the felt and gathering his thoughts. "Tell me something, MacInnes. Why didn't you let that stallion you bought stand at stud? You'd have made money off his colts."

MacInnes scowled. "There are enough men breeding all manner of horses for the army and ranches. The real money is in blooded stock with papers."

"Then why'd you keep this one?"

"As a reminder, Mr. Yancy." MacInnes tossed back his whiskey and set the heavy crystal down with a thunk. "I try not to ever make the same error twice."

Gil finished off his booze and eased the glass onto the desk. "This Irishman that palmed the sorrel off on you. What was his name?"

"Boyd Rowney. At least that's the name he was using in Laramie. I suspect it was as bogus as the stallion's papers."

Gil had never heard the name before. He tucked the receipt in his vest pocket and stood.

"Thank you for the whiskey."

"My pleasure. Do you gamble, Mr. Yancy?"

"Nope." Though if he had more than two bucks to his name, he'd be tempted to chuck his promise and try his luck again, maybe recoup some of his losses. "One more thing. If Sarah Andrews comes by here, send her on home."

MacInnes bushy eyebrows bunched up. "What's this? Are you taking on the responsibility of the Andrews women now?"

"You might say that."

"Is Mrs. Andrews aware of your new status?"

"I'm here, ain't I?"

MacInnes smiled. "That you are."

"I'll let myself out."

He strode across the room, feeling hemmed in by old memories of squaring off against Harrison Cooper. When Gil built his house, there'd be plenty of windows and not a stick of dark wood in the whole damned place.

"Mr. Yancy," MacInnes said, and Gil stopped in the doorway. "Bear in mind my wife pines for a child. If Sarah Andrews wants to live with us, I'll do all in my power to make her ours."

"Save yourself time and money, MacInnes. Sarah might've enjoyed riding your horses and all, but she doesn't want to leave her mama or Rocky Point."

"You sound sure of that."

"I am."

Gil left the affluent house and slid his hat on. Like MacInnes, he'd do all in *his* power to make sure Sarah wanted to stay in Wyoming.

Josie put the last pin in the hem of the split skirt and managed not to stick her finger this time. She'd spent the past fifteen minutes telling Sarah Ann all about the birds and bees, and so far her daughter hadn't said one word.

Maybe she was too blunt about it, but mercy, she hadn't wanted her to be terrified and ignorant like Josie had been. Which was beyond peculiar since she'd lived in a brothel from the time she turned ten, but her older sister had kept Josie away from the sporting girls and their men callers.

Then Ross Parnell decided Josie was ripe for his picking.

Josie shook off those horribly painful memories and eyed her daughter. "Is there anything you don't understand?"

Sarah Ann chewed her lower lip. "When this bleeding comes, can I still ride my horse?"

"Yes, but you might not feel like it. Anything else you want to ask me?"

"Will men know that it's happening?"

Dark memories jolted through Josie, but she pushed them back into a corner of her memory. "Some will, but a gentleman would never say a word about it. They know all women have their time to endure."

Sarah Ann exhaled. "As long as Hiram, Dwight and Gil don't josh me about it, then it won't be so bad."

When had Gil become important to Sarah Ann? Maybe she thought highly of him because he was an old friend of Everett's. Maybe it was because he'd lent them a hand financially when they needed it most. Maybe she was drawn to Gil like any woman must surely be, Josie included.

"There, now." Josie stood back to gauge the fit of Sarah Ann's new garment. "You look so grown up."

"I do?"

"Oh, yes. I can't believe how tall you've gotten."

Or how much she'd blossomed. One day she'd be a woman grown and leave here. And then what would Josie do?

Don't think about it. "It'll be easy for you to ride in this get-up."

Sarah Ann held out the wide legs, her expression more curious than repulsed. "It's kind of nice, though it's not as soft as my buckskins."

"I know, but a lady doesn't wear such conforming clothes around men." Not without suffering dire consequences, as Josie well knew.

"Can I ride my horse now?" Sarah Ann asked.

"*May* you ride her." Josie shook her head, wondering again if the new, young schoolmarm teaching over at Chalmers' Ranch knew a lick. "Take off your skirt so I can put in the hem. If you promise to stay right here on Rocky Point, you can wear your buckskins today."

"I promise," Sarah Ann said.

Josie bit back a laugh as Sarah Ann shucked her new skirt in favor of her beloved buckskins. In no time she was out the door and running toward the barn like a hooligan.

"What would I have done without you, Everett?" Josie asked.

The better question was what was she going to do now that he was gone and Gil Yancy had moved in.

He made her feel things that scared her. No, that wasn't true. He made her feel things she'd longed to feel, and that scared her.

Many a sleepless night she'd wondered what it would be like to have a young husband. Longed for a lover's touch. Ached to bear his children. To get lost in his dreams and love a man like there was no tomorrow. To grow old together.

Last night she'd had that dream again, only this time Gil's face loomed above hers. He coaxed her to give her all to him, and she wanted to. Oh, how badly she'd wanted to. But fear held her back.

Fear of giving over control to a man. Fear of giving her feelings free rein.

In her heart, she was drawn to Gil Yancy. But something about him didn't add up.

Oh, he looked no different than any other cowboy she'd known, talking the talk and walking the walk. But even without knowing his true name, she knew Harrison G. Cooper the Third wasn't a run-of-the-mill cowpoke.

He was smart. She'd bet he'd had more schooling than most folks she'd ever met. And there was her curiosity about the Pinkerton detective from Chicago. Why had Gil changed his name? What had he run from?

Josie put the questions from her mind for now and

picked up the curtains she'd made last week. She headed for the first cabin. Her guests were due in two days and she had to ready their living quarters.

Three ladies from Pennsylvania coming here. She could hardly wait.

If they had a pleasant stay, they'd spread the word and more folks would want to come to Rocky Point. And if things soured? *Don't think that way.*

Gil cut across his own property on his way back from the Diamond M ranch. He reined up near his cabin and gave it another look. It was a shack, but, dammit, all of it was his. Same with the land.

This spread was more than he'd thought he'd ever own. Some was tillable, but the bulk was good grazing land. Now he held the lien on half of Josie's land.

If she couldn't pay up, he'd own more of Rocky Point. And where would that leave Josie?

Gil tugged his makings from his pocket, lit his cigarette and drew the smoke deep into his lungs. As much as he hankered to own this ranch, he couldn't stop thinking about kissing Josie. The little woman was damn good at firing his blood. Why wouldn't she be, considering what she'd done to earn a buck?

Yet Josie had ended up here, married to a man old enough to be her father.

Gil frowned into the distance, irked that the past always found a way to barge in.

His old man had taken a young wife. One promised to another. One who'd broken her vows.

Though the numbing sense of betrayal had eased with time, the lesson stuck. Only a fool gave his heart or trust to a woman completely. He'd be damned if he ever gave a woman that much power over him again.

Gil heard the pounding of hooves coming closer. Rhubarb blew and stamped a hoof, no doubt sensing another horse was bearing down on them.

He squinted to get a clear look at the rider. A black-and-white-spotted horse tore around the bluff. The slight rider stretched forward, gripping the reins in one hand and giving the horse its head.

Sarah, riding without fear. Riding with the wind. Riding straight toward him.

He ground out his smoke, hoping trouble hadn't visited the ranch. Had something happened to one of the men or Josie?

A tinny sound carried on the wind, like a drummer's wagon gone loco. What the hell?

She reined up less than five feet from him, kicking up a cloud of grit. Her smile relaxed him some.

"I was hoping you'd be here." She untied the poke from around the saddle horn. "I found a bunch of old cans behind the cook shack. I thought we could use them for targets."

Her shooting lessons. He'd forgotten all about his promise to meet her here.

Gil started to tell her they'd have to put it off till tomorrow, but the excitement glowing on her face stopped him. He could visit Barclay's spread later.

"Cans will do fine."

He took the sack from her. Way he figured, they had an hour or so before dinner. That ought to be plenty of time to start teaching her.

"You tether the horses by the trees and I'll set up the targets over by that rocky ledge."

She slid off her piebald mare and gathered Rhubarb's line before Gil dismounted. He smiled and walked across the uneven ground to the natural shelf some hundred feet away, wondering if he'd ever been that excited at that age.

After setting up two triangles of stacked cans, he walked back to Sarah. He felt an odd catch in his chest. She looked so much like his little sister that he had to shake his head once to make sure he wasn't dreaming.

For damn sure, Sarah was a Cooper. But where she was at home on a horse, neither of his sisters would be caught dead on a Wyoming cattle ranch, much less be anxious to hold a gun.

Gil slid his Peacemaker from the holster and checked the cartridges. "We'll practice with my six-shooter today. Once you get used to handling it, we'll try the rifle."

"Like Annie Oakley uses."

"Yep, except I ain't about to put a cigarette in my mouth and let you shoot it in half."

Her eyes rounded. "Can she really do that?"

"That and a whole lot more. Come on."

Gil stood Sarah about twenty-five yards from the targets and handed her his revolver. "Grip it with both hands." He positioned her small hands on the gun. "Now you point at what you're looking at and squeeze the trigger real easy like."

The Peacemaker wobbled up and down in her hand, proving it was too damned heavy for her. Gil was about to take it from her and suggest they forget this fool idea when her arms steadied and the barrel barked lead.

None of the targets fell, but she flushed out a jackrabbit hiding beneath a big clump of sage. Probably scared the critter half to death.

"Dang, I missed."

"That's okay. Didn't expect you to be perfect the first time out. Try again."

He stood behind her so he could sight along her

arm. If she'd learn to control her hold, she'd be right on target.

Gil grabbed her upper arms. "Bend your elbows a bit. There. Try it again."

"This gun is sure heavy."

"That Winchester rifle weighs more, so if you can't master this, there's no sense even trying to teach you to shoot it."

That seemed to put the starch in her. She heaved a sigh and lifted the revolver. Her stance was damn near perfect and her arms barely quivered.

She fired one shot, jerking the Colt to the left as she did. The top can went flying off the pile.

"I hit it!" She whirled around, gun wobbling in her hand.

Gil grabbed his Peacemaker and pointed the barking end straight up. "That's real fine shooting, but rule number one: never point a gun at something you don't aim to kill."

She flushed. "Sorry. Can I try again?"

"Have at it. We've got another thirty minutes to kill."

Sarah didn't hesitate. She whirled, aimed and fired. Again and again. Each time she got better. And faster.

He smiled, feeling mighty proud of this girl's natural talent. Damn, Annie Oakley had best watch her back.

Chapter 8

Josie cleaned up the kitchen after dinner while Sarah Ann stored plates in the sideboard. Anxiety plucked at Josie's nerves. Hiram and Dwight had taken their leave but Gil dawdled over his spice cake and coffee.

Sarah Ann stored the plates, then laid the box of dominoes on the table. "You want to play a game?"

"Sure, why not?" Gil said, surprising Josie.

She could think of plenty reasons why a man wouldn't want to play dominoes with a child. So why had he agreed to hang around?

Memories of their kiss heated her blood. Had Gil tarried on the chance of getting her alone again?

If he did, she shouldn't let him kiss her. Make no mistake, she enjoyed it, but getting cozy with this cowboy could hurt her in the long run.

No, it was better to think he stayed because Sarah Ann had turned those big green eyes on him. Because the two of them seemed to be closer today.

She noticed that Gil had taken an interest in Sarah

Ann the past few days. An interest that her daughter rushed to embrace.

Josie knew Sarah Ann sorely missed Everett's attention, but was Gil's interest in the girl fatherly? Until she knew for certain, she couldn't be completely at ease with their closeness.

It was as if Gil and her daughter shared a secret. And secrets between a man and young woman brought back ugly memories for Josie.

"One game." Josie took up her sewing and settled in her chair. "It's already seven o'clock and Sarah Ann has to get up early for school tomorrow."

"Yes'm," Gil said.

Sarah Ann dumped the dominoes on the dining table and turned them face down. "You draw first."

Gil took his time selecting seven tiles, tossing Josie a sly glance that jumbled her thoughts. "Go on and dip into the boneyard."

In no time, Sarah Ann chose her tiles. "I got a double five." Sarah placed hers crosswise.

"*Have* a double five," Josie corrected.

Sarah Ann scowled as she tallied her score. "What difference does it make?"

"The difference between sounding like a smart young lady or a hick from the sticks."

"It's a fact ladies don't talk like field hands." Gil plunked a domino on the table.

They played in silence for a round or two. Josie tried to keep her attention on her sewing instead of Gil's boyish smile.

"Lookee there," Gil said after Sarah Ann's last play. "I happen to have a boxcar."

"Dang, you got eighteen points."

Josie put her sewing down. "Sarah Ann, I told you to stop saying that word."

"Sorry, Mama, it slipped out."

No doubt it did that many times throughout the day. Josie sighed and resumed putting in the hem while the game went on. Teaching her daughter to talk and act like a gently bred lady wasn't going to be easy.

"Fourteen points for me."

"You're two up on me total, but not for long." Gil winked at Josie.

A peculiar warmth flowed through her like a lazy river, heating her cheeks and making her squirm. Mercy, the man was flirting with her. And in front of her daughter.

No, their daughter.

The impropriety of it all should have doused these strange, needy feelings bubbling in her, but in all honesty she'd never felt so wanted. So alive as a woman.

Josie focused on her sewing and blew out a breath, hoping that it would cool her flushed face. The only way she'd get the hem in and not stick herself was to avoid looking at him. She couldn't let herself get swept up in his charm.

The steady plunk of ivory on wood told her the game progressed at a good pace. Faster than what she and Everett played, but then they'd never been in any hurry to finish one game and start another. It was like their days. One was like the rest.

Josie tied off her thread as Sarah Ann let out a loud huff. She looked up. Judging by the pooch of her daughter's lower lip, Sarah Ann must have lost.

"Game over?" she asked.

"Yep." Gil bent over the paper, pencil in hand. "Appears I won by fifteen points."

"You were lucky and I wasn't," Sarah Ann said. "Guess I used it up shooting."

A shiver passed over Josie when her daughter flushed a guilty red. Gil looked a mite dumbfounded himself.

"G'night." Sarah Ann jumped off the chair and skedaddled toward the stairs.

"Stop right there, young lady." Josie's stomach knotted as she looked from Gil scratching a furrow in his nape to her daughter's face. "What is going on?"

"Nothing," Sarah Ann said.

"I know when you're fibbing," Josie said. "Now what's this about shooting?"

Gil grimaced and cleared his throat. "I was teaching Sarah how to shoot today. She's real good."

"You what?" Josie could scarcely draw a breath.

That explained all the noise she'd heard this afternoon. And the relaxed way Gil and Sarah Ann got on.

Sarah Ann jutted out her chin, finding her backbone. "He's teaching me to shoot like Annie Oakley."

So she could perform? My God, Josie had traveled that road and knew it led through hell.

She willed her hand not to shake and pointed to the hall. "Go up to your room."

"But Mama—"

"We'll talk in the morning, Sarah Ann."

"You don't understand." With a huff, Sarah Ann tromped up the steps like she was going to her own hanging.

"Reckon I'd best find my bed, too." Gil pushed to his feet.

"Not so fast, Mr. Yancy."

Josie tossed her sewing down and stormed over to the table. She planted her hands on the smooth surface, scattering the dominoes.

"I don't know why you got it into your head to teach my daughter to shoot, but I don't appreciate you doing it behind my back. Especially something as dangerous as trick shooting."

Gil scrubbed a hand on his ruddy neck. "I thought if I got her interested in something here at the ranch, she'd stay away from the Diamond M. Ain't no harm—"

"Yes, there is. You're encouraging her to run off."

"Like hell I am."

"Sarah Ann has turned a deaf ear to the cold truth about living by your charms and talents, and has glamorized Annie Oakley's life in a Wild West show." Josie straightened, mindful to keep her voice down. "I know the pitfalls that lie in wait for a young woman on her own."

"Reckon you do, at that. But you can't keep her on this ranch forever unless she wants to stay. One day she's going to grow up and have a life of her own. Whether she's married to a rancher, a farmer, or a cowboy riding from circuit show to circuit show, it's her life to live."

"I know that, but I won't have you helping her to take up a life like that."

"Save me from a stubborn woman." He pressed his fists on the table and leaned toward her this time. "You mentioned the other day you wanted to put on an exhibition of sorts for your guests. You know what Sarah was of a mind to do?"

Heat burned her face again. "Probably do some

roping or racing, since she's got horse on the brain most of the time."

"She was thinking about jumping fences like they do over at the Diamond M. They've let her try her luck, and I'm here to tell you a person can break their neck jumping over those damned obstacles," he said. "Saw it happen once to a man from England who'd been jumping most his life."

"How'd you know she's doing that?"

"Hiram saw her. Hell, we thought Sarah told you about it the other night before dinner."

"She 'fessed up to using a sidesaddle, but she conveniently left out she'd been jumping those fences." And Josie had never thought to press her daughter for details. "Damn them for luring her over there. For putting her in danger."

"I told MacInnes if she came around, he'd best send her on home, but to make sure he does, I thought I'd meet Sarah on her way home from school," Gil said. "That's when we planned to practice shooting."

"About that."

"Don't say it," he said. "If you take that away from her, the girl will rebel."

He was right, damn him. Josie drummed her fingers on the table, staring at the few pieces that remained of the game her daughter and Gil had spent a pleasant evening playing. How odd that Sarah had more fun with her real father than she had with Everett, the man who'd loved and raised her.

She didn't so much mind Gil teaching Sarah Ann to use a gun. But she wouldn't hold with him correcting her daughter, or taking it on himself to bend her to his liking.

"All right. You can teach her to shoot." Josie looked him square in the eye. "But I'm going to be there watching you from now on."

"Suit yourself. In fact, if you don't know how to use a gun, I'd be obliged to teach you, too."

"I can shoot." But she didn't like to.

Besides, she had another means to protect herself and was damned good at it. If Gil Yancy made one wrong move on Sarah Ann, he'd soon feel the sting of what she did best.

"One other thing," she said as Gil turned to leave. "You hold a lien on the land, but the guest ranch is my business. I give the orders."

"I'll keep that in mind, but remember this. When I take your guests on these trail rides, I'm the boss."

A role he naturally assumed, she thought as he walked out.

She had to be very careful around him or she'd lose control over the ranch. And her wary heart as well.

The next day, Josie had hung the last of her white wash on the line when Virgil Keegan rode up. What brought him out here this time?

"Afternoon, Josie. Got a letter for you."

She wiped her hands on her apron, hoping this was in answer to one of her many advertisements. "Thank you for bringing it out. Would you care for a cup of coffee?"

"Don't mind if I do. You here by yourself?"

"Hiram's putting new rails on the corral. Sarah Ann went to school. Dwight and Gil lit out early, saying they aimed to finish clearing the camping area for our guests today."

Which was fine by her since Mrs. Hastings and her party would be here tomorrow. Or at least Josie hoped they would.

Vigil tethered his horse to the iron ring out front and trailed her into the kitchen. He eased onto a chair, his smile almost bashful.

"Reckon you'll be mighty busy when those folks get here, what with cooking and tending to them and all."

"I imagine I will be." She set his coffee and a plate of sugar cookies before him. "Is the stage running on time?"

"'Pears to be. Good thing since the railroad is still deadlocked, 'cept for the mail train." Virgil shoved a cookie in his mouth.

Josie glanced at the address on the letter and smiled. St. Louis, Missouri. She'd posted an advertisement in their paper a month past. Hopefully this was an inquiry about her guest ranch.

She tore it open and read.

Dear Josie,
We have unfinished business. Don't think the sheriff will help you once he hears what you did to me. Don't try to run. By the time you get this, I'll be in Wyoming at your guest ranch, watching you.
R. Parnell

Josie froze, hardly able to draw air into her lungs. My God, this couldn't be happening. He couldn't have found her.

"Something wrong?" Virgil asked.

"Nothing at all."

Josie folded the letter and slipped it in her pocket, shaking like it was twenty below. She'd always feared she'd bring Parnell to Everett's door, but her husband had told her not to fret. He and the hands would take care of her and Sarah Ann. They'd protect her.

But as the years passed, and Parnell never showed his face, she'd thought he'd forgotten her. She'd even convinced herself lately that he might be dead.

She should've known better. The devil never died.

Her blood ran cold. God knew she'd given Parnell plenty to resent her for, just as he'd left her with countless reasons to hate him. Now he was likely nearby, watching, waiting for the chance to strike back at her.

"Those are mighty fine cookies, Josie. No wonder Everett sang your praises in the kitchen."

"He was a hearty eater and not the least bit picky."

Dare she risk telling Virgil? No, not yet. That'd only raise more questions about the past she'd tried to hide.

"Got to be hard on a woman as young as yourself to be without a husband and all," Virgil said.

"There are sad times, but I'm managing."

"That's good." He nodded until she thought his head would fall off. "I was thinking maybe you wouldn't mind me calling on you one day."

Talk about horrible timing. "I'm not ready for that."

"Guess it is soon. I figured since you didn't hold with a traditional mourning period—"

The crack of a rifle put an end to Virgil's rambling. Less than a second later another shot rang out.

Virgil frowned. "Dwight hunting?"

"I imagine that's Gil and Sarah Ann. He's teaching her to shoot and I promised her I'd come watch."

She stood, eyeing his empty cup. "Thanks for bringing the letter."

"Just part of my job." Virgil got to his feet and slid his hat on. "I'll hold off calling on you for a month or so."

"Thank you."

Not that the wait would make a difference, she thought as the sheriff saddled up and rode off.

Virgil was a fine man, comfortable as an old shoe. But with Parnell's threat hanging over her, she couldn't entertain thoughts of welcoming any man into her life.

No, after she killed Ross Parnell, the only thing the sheriff of Maverick would have to do with her was lock her in jail. And she had no doubt that killing Parnell was the only way she could stop that worthless excuse of a man from ruining her life and Sarah Ann's.

She ran upstairs and fetched Everett's old Navy Colt, making sure to grab cartridges. It weighed heavy in her pocket, but was nothing compared to her worry over Sarah Ann. Mercy, she'd have to have the hands keep watch on her daughter all the time because if Parnell got his hands on her—

The hatred and fear that Josie had been shackled with for years twisted in her as she saddled her paint mare and headed over to Gil's. She topped the rise and reined up. Her daughter stood a good fifty yards away, seeming at ease with the rifle she held.

Over by the ridge, Gil set up a stack of five cans, pyramid style. It was the simplest of targets, and in a way she hoped Sarah Ann would never progress beyond that point. But the fact remained it was in her blood to perform. And her daughter may need to use a gun to save her life.

Gil strode back to Sarah Ann, pride radiating in every slow step. She imagined his muscles bunching under his jeans and cambric shirt, imagined gliding her hands over his bare, hot skin. Imagined she could watch this man move for the rest of her life and still be captivated by him.

She imagined Parnell ruining her life again.

Gil stopped beside her daughter, turned and looked across the short expanse. The heat in his eyes burned Josie all the way to her toes.

Josie squirmed in the saddle. Did he know the effect he had on her? Is that why he was smiling?

Gil turned back to Sarah Ann and nodded. Her daughter took aim and fired.

In rapid succession, the cans from the top flew off one by one. Five shots and Sarah Ann didn't miss once.

Josie said a silent prayer that her daughter could defend herself, then said another one, begging that Sarah Ann would never get the fever to perform and join a Wild West show. Or worse, that she'd end up in a fix like what happened to Josie.

Sarah Ann put the rifle down, let out a squeal and ran to Gil. Josie watched in stunned silence as her daughter launched herself at the tall cowboy. Gil grabbed Sarah Ann up and hugged her, their mingled laughter clear and clean as the sky.

The fact they were father and daughter was lost on Josie as dark memories swirled around her like smoke, thick and choking out the sensual haze she'd been hiding behind. She heeled her mare, galloping toward the pair.

Sarah Ann pulled away from Gil and smiled up at her. "Did you see me shoot, Mama?"

"I saw. You did real good."

Gil thumbed up his hat brim, his grin boyish. "She's a natural with a gun."

He seemed pleased by that fact, and that troubled her even more. "I can see that."

"Can I shoot some more?" Sarah Ann asked.

Gil slid the Winchester into the scabbard. "Nope, that's it for today. You don't feel the pull in your arm and shoulder now, but you will tomorrow."

Instead of kicking up a fuss, Sarah Ann surprised her by gathering the cans and dumping them in a burlap bag. It all seemed natural and innocent. Was she overreacting?

"Thought you'd forgotten about Sarah's shooting lessons," he said.

"I remembered them." *Belatedly.*

"Something bothering you?"

"The sheriff came by earlier. He said there was an outlaw in the area," she said, unable to tell him the truth. "From now on, I don't want Sarah Ann going off riding by herself. Same with our guests, especially with them being ladies and all."

"What about you?"

"I've got Everett's sidearm."

Still, worry that Parnell would strike without warning dogged Josie all the way back to the ranch. She found Hiram in the tack room.

"Remember when Everett had you and Dwight keeping watch in case Ross Parnell tracked me here?"

"I remember."

"I got a letter from him today, warning me he's here."

"You tell the sheriff?"

She shook her head. "He'd need to know why Parnell was after me. I'm worried about Sarah Ann."

Hiram's features turned stony. "We'll watch her. Make sure she gets to school and home safe. Gil has to know."

"I told him the sheriff said there was an outlaw in the area."

"That'll do. For now."

She nodded in agreement, but she dreaded having that conversation for it would only spark more questions.

Supper was quiet and tense. The men excused themselves after eating.

Sarah Ann went to bed early, plumb worn out from all that shooting. No doubt her daughter would dream of firing that rifle, and Gil Yancy's smile.

If only her dreams would be that fanciful, but she feared the devil from her past would fill her with living nightmares.

After cleaning the kitchen, Josie doused the lights and climbed the stairs to her lonely bedroom. She put on her nightdress, but instead of going straight to bed, she opened the trunk at the foot of it.

She lit the lamp and dug to the very bottom. Her fingertips danced over the braided rawhide coil before her hand closed over the cold, silver handle.

A tremor streaked through her and she licked her dry lips, damning the excitement that had never died. It'd always been like that.

At one time she'd been the star of the stage, delighting in showing off her talents to the crowd. For four years she'd loved every minute of it.

Then Josie turned fourteen, and Ross Parnell decided it was time she offered his customers more than a stage show.

Josie lifted the bullwhip from the chest, moved

away from the bed and gave the rawhide a snap. The long coil unfurled with a soft hiss.

She hadn't touched the thing since she'd stowed it here the day Sarah Ann was born. Everett had told Josie to pitch it, she wouldn't need the whip for show or protection anymore, but Josie wanted it near as a reminder to never let down her guard around a man again.

Her ability with this whip had saved her life and her sister's one dark night. Now it appeared she might need it again for the same reason.

It'd been so long. Could she still wield it?

She eyed the bonnet hanging on the doorknob and flicked her wrist. The rawhide sang through the air and yanked her hairbrush off her dresser and sent it flying onto the bed.

She frowned. Maybe she'd been standing in the wrong place.

Josie paced before the window, stretching her arms overhead, then shaking them at her sides to relax. She took a stance near the window and tried for the bonnet again.

The tip of the whip sailed out, but instead of lifting her target, it caught the fringe on her dresser scarf. Faster than she could blink, the whip yanked everything atop her dresser on to the floor. Dang it, how could her aim be so far off?

Bare feet pounded down the hall. "You all right, Mama?"

Double damn. "Yes, just a bit of a mishap."

Josie dropped her whip in the corner as her bedroom door burst open. Sarah Ann looked from the mess on the floor to Josie.

"What happened?"

"I guess I caught the scarf when I was walking by."

Josie knelt to pick up her possessions, more angry that she'd lied to Sarah Ann again than the fact she'd broken her hairpin case. "Go on back to bed."

Sarah Ann stood there awhile longer, probably trying to decide whether to believe Josie's whopper. Finally, the door closed.

Josie downed her head, torn between calling her back and telling her the truth, or letting her go. She should tell Sarah Ann what she'd been doing, but right now she wasn't ready to own up to her ability with the whip. If in fact she still had any knack for cracking ten feet of leather. God knew she'd been way off target tonight.

Besides, if she told Sarah Ann she'd been practicing with the whip, her daughter would want to know how she'd learned to handle the thing and why she'd never messed with it all these years. She sure wasn't about to ever tell her the truth, even a whitewashed version. Sarah Ann showed too much interest in the Wild West shows as it was.

So how would she explain her talent? Another lie?

Why not? She'd lived a lie for so long she'd almost forgotten all the ugly truths.

A coyote's yelp was soon joined by another. Josie walked back to the open window, welcoming the rush of cool air to her heated face. She stared out into the dark night toward the barn. Her breath hitched and an odd warmth stole over her.

The faint red glow she saw near the last cabin could be only one thing. Gil Yancy having a cigarette, giving him full view of the house and especially her bedroom. Was he watching out for her? Or just watching her?

Chapter 9

The clang of metal jarred Gil awake. He cracked an eye. Hell, the sun wasn't even up yet.

Stamping hooves mingled with the racket. Was that harness rings he was hearing? Had to be.

He rolled out of bed and opened his door. Sure enough, he spied Dwight before the barn hitching a dapple gray to a two-seater spring wagon. Over by the corral, Hiram hunched on the buckboard's seat, holding the lines to a big bay mare.

A surrey for the lady guests, and the wagon for all their baggage. Knowing womenfolk, the wagon would be stacked high with all manner of trunks and whatnot.

Gil scratched his chest and yawned. If the stage was on time, Hiram and Dwight should be back from Maverick with the guests by early afternoon.

Soon as their stay here was over, he aimed to get to work readying the cabin on his land. He wanted it livable before the first snow.

Sooner if possible. If he was on the other side of the ridge, he wouldn't be tempted to stare at Josie's bedroom half the night, hoping to catch a peek of her in her in a nightdress that didn't leave anything to his imagination.

Damn, she'd looked like an angel last night. An angel that knew how to take a man to heaven.

Gil shook his head. He didn't know what kind of dance she'd been doing, but the light had silhouetted her body just right, emphasizing her curves. The memory had tormented his dreams all night and left him semi-aroused.

He started to close his door when he caught sight of Josie rushing toward the buckboard. The wind plastered her calico blouse to her breasts and tore at her skirt.

She handed Hiram an enamel pail. Her smile brightened the dawn, and Gil caught himself wondering how it'd feel if she'd favor him with a cheery welcome.

Reckon that wasn't going to happen.

Out of the corner of his eye, he saw Sarah heading toward the spring wagon with another enamel pail. Josie must've fixed breakfast for her hands, another thing he hadn't expected from the former shady lady.

Gil toed the door shut and padded to the washbasin. He splashed cold water on his face, then he worked up a lather and scraped off his whiskers. Thoughts of Josie gyrating in her room last night pushed into his mind.

Was she teasing him, reminding him what he'd tasted once? Or was she making the first move?

"Reckon I'll know soon enough."

Gil dressed and headed up to the house. He let himself in the back door and walked into the kitchen that smelled of bacon, coffee and home sweet home. That got him thinking about the Josie he didn't know. Wife to his old partner. Mother to his own child.

Gil helped himself to a cup of coffee and eased into a chair. He hadn't expected Josie to be such a fine cook, a good mama, or a damned hard worker.

Since he'd been here he'd never seen her rest. Nope, her chapped hands were never idle.

The door opened and Josie rushed into the kitchen, rocking to a stop when she saw him. Her face flushed as she hurried past him. He wondered if the bloom in her cheeks was excitement of seeing him or windburn.

She slid him an odd smile. "I didn't think this day would ever get here."

Did that mean what he thought it did? He shifted on the chair, wondering when he'd become such a randy goat.

"I had my doubts."

"So did I, which I guess is understandable since we got off to such a rocky start. Hope you like flapjacks."

"Yes'm, I sure do."

Josie picked up a bowl off the sideboard, stirring the contents as she walked to the stove. She spooned batter onto an iron griddle. The round flapjacks sizzled and his stomach growled, thankfully waking a different hunger.

Still, as Gil sipped his coffee, he couldn't help but admire the sway of her hips as she worked at the stove. Dammit, he had to stop thinking about sex.

"Sheriff say who this outlaw is?"

"Yes, but I don't recall the name." Josie set a plate filled with flapjacks, eggs and bacon before him, seeming mighty edgy.

"He say what this hombre is wanted for?"

"No." Josie fixed herself a plate and took a seat across from him, but she picked at the food.

Gil dug in with gusto, trying to figure out her angle. But he had trouble keeping his mind focused.

He was into his second helping of flapjacks when it dawned on him they were alone. "Where's Sarah?"

"Dwight took her to Chalmers' Ranch."

"She has school on Saturday?"

"No, but she forgot to take some things to her teacher yesterday. When Dwight gets back from town, he'll fetch her home."

Hot damn he'd been right. She'd teased him last night by moonlight and sent Sarah off this morning.

"What are your plans for this afternoon?" she asked.

"Suppose you tell me, sweetheart?"

She frowned at him, her cheeks reddening. He was a mite flushed himself, surprised that endearment had popped out. 'Course, now that it had, it seemed natural.

"Why did you call me that?"

"Reckon it's fitting since you"—he wiggled his eyebrows—"arranged for us to be alone and all."

"Whatever gave you that fool idea?"

"Last night you danced in front of your window when you knew damn well I could see you, and this morning you sent Sarah off so we'd be alone." He frowned, confusion giving way to irritation. "The way I saw it, you was inviting me to your bed."

"That was last thing on my mind."

"So you were teasing me?"

"Of course not! Why were you watching my window?"

"Hard not to, Josie."

She jumped to her feet and carried her plate to the sink, looking guilty as all get out. But was it because he'd caught her trying her hand at seducing him from afar, or because she'd lost her nerve to go through with it?

"Much obliged for breakfast."

"You're entirely welcome," she said. "Speaking of meals, I'll be busy getting last-minute things done today for my guests, so if you want lunch, help yourself to the biscuits, jerky and pie left over from last night."

He came close to telling her to forget it, but she made the lightest biscuits he'd ever eaten, and her pie was pure heaven itself. No sense punishing his gut because he was irked at her and himself for jumping to the wrong conclusion.

"Yes'm, I'll do that." He filled the basket she handed him with food, then grabbed his hat off the peg and headed to the door.

"What do you plan to do today?"

Gil glanced at her, noting the tightness of her shoulders and worry in her eyes. "Aimed to repair my saddle. You need me, you holler."

Her smile was brief. "I will."

He headed out the door, his grip of desire replaced by confusion. If he lived to be a hundred, he'd never understand how a woman's mind worked.

As soon Gil disappeared into the barn, Josie ran to her room and fetched her bullwhip. She figured she'd have an hour or so to practice before Gil finished what he was doing in the barn.

Everett's last words came back to her. *Before long you're gonna find a man who'll love you proper.*

Josie didn't believe it any more than she had six months back. "You brought Gil here because you trusted him. But I can't bring myself to do that."

Though down deep she wanted to. Something about Gil Yancy drew her like a bee to a purple pasque flower. And that same fascination scared her to death.

That tingling went through Josie as she picked up

her whip. She grimaced. Her daughter had inherited this longing to perform.

Josie wasn't about to let her traipse off and join a Wild West show. She had to get Sarah Ann interested in the guest ranch. Putting on an exhibition here should do just that.

Nothing cowboys liked better than to show off their talents. That trickled down to the cowgirls, too.

If folks traveled miles to partake of a rodeo and barbeque, wouldn't her guests find it entertaining too? Only instead of having one or two shows a year, she'd host one every month during good weather. They could put on mother and daughter shows. They could make enough money to pay off Gil and maybe build more guest cabins.

A good dose of nerves beset Josie as she picked up her bullwhip and flicked her wrist. Yes, she'd do her part in the exhibition. And she'd be ready to fight off Parnell again.

Gil finished repairing his saddle and had rubbed down the new sidesaddles long before noon. To keep from thinking about Josie and what she might be doing, he thought on the house he aimed to build one day. Didn't have to be grand like Reid Barclay's.

He'd be right happy with a place the size of Scotty Donnelly's ranch house back in Kansas. Or Josie's simple home with the big front porch.

Problem was he couldn't build it himself. Nope, he hadn't honed a lick of carpentry skills over the years in the saddle. Leastwise nothing that'd suit for building a nice house.

He'd have to hire the work done. That'd cost him, and all he had to his name was two silver dollars.

Gil wasn't fool enough to think Josie's guest ranch venture was going to bring in much money anytime soon. Nope, it'd be a year before she could pay him back, and by then he'd own more land and be as poor as he was now.

He had to do something to earn money fast. Gambling came to mind right off. He'd vowed he wouldn't squander another cent on the turn of a card and aimed to stick to it. But there were other ways a man could bet and win big.

The exhibition they planned to put on for the Rocky Point guests was his chance to get ahead. For a fact, cowboys loved to gamble. No reason he couldn't run a side bet on himself. Hell, he could triple his money in no time.

A loud crack split the air, followed by another. Were those gunshots? Had the outlaw found his way here?

Gil drew his revolver and slipped out of the barn, unsure what the hell he'd find. He spotted Josie in front of the house and his mouth went dry.

A kerchief caught her mass of hair and held it back. She'd pulled her skirt between her legs and tucked the hem in her waistband in front, giving him a tempting look at her long legs covered in serviceable black stockings.

Josie held a bullwhip in her right hand and stared intently at the rags tied to the porch. In one smooth movement, she cracked the whip overhead and plucked the rags off the railing, like those fancy show people did.

Gil holstered his Peacemaker and headed toward her. "Where in the hell did you learn to do that?"

Josie whirled, the whip curling around her ankles like a snake. She'd been so intent on practicing that she hadn't seen or heard Gil sneak up on her. Her heart felt too big for her chest, pounding and carrying on like it always did when she stared into Gil's eyes.

He motioned to her whip. "Well?"

"Ross Parnell taught me how to use it when I was around Sarah Ann's age. Do you remember him?"

He frowned. "He the man that owned the Gilded Garter?"

"That's him."

"You were that young when he got hold of you?"

She backed up the steps, not about to talk about that part of her life. Why, she'd never gotten up the courage to tell Everett all of the ugliness, and she owed her and Sarah Ann's life to her husband.

"He held a contract on all his girls, but even if he hadn't, I loved doing tricks before all those folks." Until she grew up and realized the true depravity of Parnell and what he had in store for her when her little girl charm faded.

"What about your folks?"

"They were dead."

"You didn't have any family?"

"A sister." Her laugh was as raw as the memories. "She was one of Parnell's queens, and he promised Lillian that as long as she paid our way, he'd never force me to whore."

"That who's buried up on the ridge?"

"Yes."

His shook his head, eyes narrowed. "That why Parnell sent you to my room that night, 'cause your sister stopped paying your way?"

"Parnell gave me a choice."

"I just bet that son of a bitch did."

Gil moved closer, pressing her back until her spine slammed into the house. She fought off the sensation of being trapped by this man.

"Why'd you coldcock me and rob me blind?"

"If I hadn't, Ross would've killed my sister. She was bad sick, and he kept pushing men on her."

"You should've told me the truth that night in Caldwell. I'd have helped you and your sister."

She laughed, a hollow sound that mocked the anxiety boiling in her. "I'd have been crazy to put my life and Lillian's in a drunken cowboy's promise."

"Well, you sure as hell lit up the town when you left. Last I heard folks were still talking about the night the Gilded Garter burnt to the ground."

"It did?"

"Yep. Heard Parnell got in a fight in the back room of the saloon and they upended a lamp. Fire spread fast, even though the Gilded Garter watered down their whiskey."

"Are you sure?"

"Damn right, I am. If Cord Tanner hadn't dragged my ass out of that room, I'd be dead."

Mercy, Parnell had caught Josie and Lillian in the back room, moments from escaping. Josie had pressed the money bags in her sister's hand and shoved her out the door. Then she'd uncoiled her whip and confronted Parnell.

The rest happened so fast Josie barely remembered it. The whir of the rawhide slicing through the air. The muffled hiss as the tip sliced through flesh. Parnell's roar of agony.

Josie had fled into the night and hadn't looked

back. Had Parnell set his bordello on fire? Is that why he hadn't come after her right away?

"Did everyone get out?" she asked.

"Far as I know." His hand cupped her cheek, startling her with its warmth and tenderness. "I'd have gotten you away from him, Josie."

She smiled. Everett had tried, and failed. Could Gil have gotten her and Lillian out of that hell? Maybe, but at what cost?

"Parnell would've killed you if you'd taken us," Josie said, answering her own question.

"He'd have been welcome to try his luck."

Instead of jerking away, she found herself leaning into Gil's warmth and strength. She'd fought and run and looked over her shoulder for so long.

His mouth closed over hers. She'd expected him to be demanding, taking what he wanted. Selfish even. But his kiss was as slow and gentle as a warm summer breeze whispering over her tingling skin.

Her resolve crumbled to dust, leaving her trembling with an intense need she'd never felt before. Never wanted. Or never thought she'd crave. As if he knew her knees were turning weak, he pressed his body against hers.

The fear of having hard, cold clapboards bite her backside and a firm, hot cowboy hem her in lasted less than a heartbeat. It was the kisses that comforted her. Undid her.

He carefully took her in his arms, holding her close like she was something precious. Like she wasn't someone he'd paid to abuse, but someone he ached to love. Like she was his sweetheart.

All her old terrors of men and their brutality vanished with the wind, laying bare feelings Josie had denied yet secretly harbored all her life. She glided her hands up his arms, emboldened by his low, rumbling moan. Or did that sound come from her?

This cowboy could charm a lady into shucking her morals. Any woman could drown in his arms, and Josie felt herself slipping under the warm, lazy waters of longing again.

Why, she even heard bells. Bells? No, that was harness rings. Lord a mercy!

Josie's eyes popped open, but it took her a spell to focus on the blurry images in her front yard. Gil jerked his head to the sound as well, his expression fierce, his body so taut she thought a rock was holding her against the house.

She blinked and stared at Dwight sitting on the spring wagon before the house, gaping at her. The three ladies he had with him in the wagon wore fancy straw hats and shocked looks.

Her ranch guests! What must they think of her?

Josie pushed Gil from her, batted down the skirt she'd tucked up earlier, and rushed to the porch railing on legs that trembled. "Welcome to Rocky Point Ranch. I hope you had a pleasant journey."

She didn't get so much as a howdy-do from her guests. In fact, all three women looked right past her as if she wasn't there to the cowboy she felt standing way too close behind her.

Dwight's mouth closed with a clack of teeth. He jumped off the wagon and gave a hand to help the women down.

Josie elbowed Gil. "It wouldn't hurt you to help."

He didn't budge or say one blame word.

She glanced back at him and wished she hadn't.

He stared at their guests like they were something to be feared.

A big old wall of dread smacked into Josie as she faced her guests. She had the feeling Gil would act the same even if she wasn't here. Even if these fine ladies hadn't caught them spooning.

The woman in the blue serge traveling suit rushed toward the porch, her gaze fixed on Gil. "Gilbert? Is it truly you?"

Behind Josie, Gil grumbled something that sounded like a curse. "Hello, Eliza."

"Oh, my God!" The woman ran up the stairs and launched herself into Gil's arms.

He stood like a statue, then muttered another curse and hugged the sobbing woman. Josie hadn't expected him to be on a first name basis with one of her guests. But it was clear he knew this woman real well.

A girlish squeal had Josie whirling around. Another woman wearing a mauve dress and a smile bigger and brighter than the sun bounded across the yard and onto the porch.

"Oh, mercy me, Gilbert! We feared we'd never live to see the day." She threw herself on Gil and the other woman. "You rascal, where have you been all these years?"

"Here and there," he said.

Josie looked from Gil's flushed face to the two women. Both of them had stubborn chins and lips that quirked in smiles, but it was the younger woman's green eyes that stole the breath from Josie.

Merciful sakes alive! The younger woman's eyes looked exactly like Sarah Ann's.

Chapter 10

What the hell? Gil glanced to the two wagons weighed down with Saratoga trunks and carpetbags. He'd been expecting a visit from his father—not Eliza and Abby. But having his sisters hang onto him like cockleburs did warm his heart and remind him how much he missed them.

Josie staggered back against the house like she was hit with a nor'wester. But it wasn't because a strong wind whipped down off the mountain. Nope, Josie had gotten a good look at Abby.

He'd caught Josie in a bald-faced lie. Two whoppers. Sarah and his little sister had those same Cooper green eyes and nubbin of a nose. But the truth he'd gotten a child on Josie hobbled him just the same.

Gil couldn't blurt out where or how he and Josie got tangled up without sullying Sarah's name. He'd never do that. But once Eliza saw his daughter, he and Josie would have some fast explaining to do.

Hell, judging by his older sister's pleased smile, she already had him and Josie heading toward the altar. Damnation, why did she have to be the one to catch them swapping spit?

"Please excuse my rudeness." Eliza pulled away from Gil and smiled at Josie. "You must be Mrs. Josephine Andrews, owner of this guest ranch."

"Yes, ma'am. But please call me Josie."

"I shall. As you have probably surmised, I am Eliza Hastings, but I prefer we eliminate the formalities."

"Hastings, is it?" Gil asked.

"My husband's surname." Eliza tugged off her gloves, revealing a wide, gold wedding band. "Stuart and I have been married for seven years."

"You a mama now?"

"We have two sons."

He'd had no idea. His choice. But still and all—

"I wasn't aware you all knew each other," Josie said.

"Eliza and Abby are my sisters." He looked from one Cooper woman to another. "I can't believe the old man let the two of you travel out here alone."

"Father wasn't pleased," Eliza said as Dwight helped the third woman alight from the spring wagon.

Gil's insides coiled into a hard old knot as his sisters' traveling companion walked toward the house, her posture poised and her bearing refined. Though a veil covered her face, every nerve in his body recognized her.

She stepped onto the porch, but kept a practiced distance from everyone. "How nice to see you again, Gilbert."

"Ivy." He inclined his head, refusing to utter some nicety he didn't feel. *Could this get any worse?*

"This is Ivy Cooper," Eliza said to Josie. "Our stepmother."

Josie's mouth dropped open, no doubt surprised their stepmother was so young. Damn strange reaction though, considering Josie had married a man old enough to be her father.

"A pleasure to make your acquaintance," Josie said.

"The same to you." Ivy gave the ranch a passing glance. "I did not realize this place would be so rustic."

"It's a working ranch," Josie said.

Ivy pressed a hand to her throat. "Does that mean you have a fair amount of men working here?"

"Three cowhands. You met Hiram and Dwight, and you know Gil," Josie said.

"Maybe you'd be more comfortable taking a room in town." Gil sure as hell would rest easier if he didn't have to rub elbows with Ivy on a daily basis.

"Really, Gilbert," Eliza said.

"I am sure the suggestion was made sincerely, but I shall stay here with Eliza and Abby," Ivy said.

Gil bit off a ripe curse. More than likely Ivy had tagged along so she could watch his sisters' every move.

"The old man fixing to show his face here?" Gil asked.

Ivy pursed her lips and sent him a frosty glare that used to put him in his place. But that'd been years back, before she'd played him for a damned fool.

"Father isn't coming here," Eliza said, but the look she shared with her sister didn't convince Gil.

In Maverick, Gil had sent the Pinkerton detective back with a message for the old man—if he had anything to say to Gil, he could damn well come here to Rocky Point. They'd have it out here or not at all. His father sure wouldn't send women to do his bidding.

"Where are my manners?" Josie motioned to the front door. "Would you ladies care for a bit of refreshment while the men stow your trunks in your cabins?"

"Not I." Ivy pressed the back of her gloved hand to the high lace collar at her throat. "The journey was taxing. I would like to retire to my cabin and recuperate before we dine."

"Of course," Josie said. "I'll have Dwight fetch your

trunks while I show you to your quarters. Gil, do take your sisters inside."

"Yes'm."

Josie slid Gil one last questioning look, then escorted Ivy toward the second cabin. Guest or not, it burned his behind to see Josie fussing over Ivy Cooper.

He opened the door and ushered his sisters into the parlor. "Make yourselves at home."

Abby sashayed around the room, her wide skirts swishing from side to side, before she finally settled on an armless chair by the window. "How long have you gone by Gil Yancy?"

"Since I left Philadelphia. What'd the old man say when that Pinkerton detective gave him my message?"

Eliza took a seat on the settee and shook out her skirt. "Father doesn't know we found you. I hired the detective, Gilbert. He delivered your message to me."

Gil jabbed his thumbs under his belt and eyed his sisters. "Why?"

"I want you to be at my wedding," Abby said.

Eliza's frown said just the opposite. "Our family estrangement has gone on far too long. Abigail's impending wedding is the ideal time to mend the rift."

"There're no mending fences and you damned well know it," he said. "You must have wired Josie the minute the detective told you that I'd settled down on Rocky Point Ranch."

"I did," Eliza said. "In fact, I couldn't believe my good fortune when the Pinkerton detective informed me Josie owned a guest ranch."

Gil shook his head, not surprised at the speed at which his sister moved. She'd always been smarter than him. He was actually glad she'd found him, though once Ivy returned to Philadelphia, Gil could expect a visit from his old man in due time.

"Why the hell did you bring her along?"

"I assume you mean Ivy?" Eliza asked.

He dipped his chin in answer.

"Father wouldn't hear of me traveling to the wilds of Wyoming without an escort," Abby said.

"Likewise, Abigail's intended was violently opposed to our impromptu journey." Eliza made a face. "I feared Landon would horn in on our venture, but when Ivy heard me explain to Father that this was the perfect place for women to rest and commune with nature without a man's interference, she insisted the three of us go."

"Father never gainsays her," Abby said.

Gil wasn't surprised. He reckoned the old man would do damn near anything to please his young wife.

"Now it is my turn," Eliza said. "What is your relationship with Mrs. Andrews?"

Damned good question, but Gil had no idea how to answer it truthfully. "I'm the trail guide for Rocky Point."

Abby grinned. "You two seem very friendly for a man who recently moved here."

Gil scrubbed a hand over his face. It was getting mighty hot in here. "We go way back."

"Ooo, how romantic," Abby said.

Like hell it was.

"Please tell me she's widowed," Eliza said.

"Josie's husband died this spring, about five months after I bought land off him. Before you ask," he said to Eliza, "Everett was an old friend of mine."

"Well, you wouldn't be the first man who ended up married to his friend's widow," Abby said.

"I ain't fixing to marry Josie."

His sisters shared a look that set warning bells clanging in his head. Dammit all, they probably figured he and Josie were bed partners. Wouldn't you know the idea of crawling in the sack with Josie sent a bolt of fire to his pecker.

That kiss on the porch. He shouldn't have done it because once he got the taste of Josie on his tongue he always hankered for more.

"So you expect us to believe you're just Josie's trail guide?" Eliza asked.

"It's a long story." One he'd have to go over with Josie before his nosy sisters met Sarah.

The door opened and Josie breezed in on a breath of fresh air. She stopped at the hall mirror and fussed with her hair, and he had the sudden urge to tug the pins out and see how long it was. If it was as silky soft as he recalled.

Josie stepped into the parlor, her smile welcoming. "Now then, would you ladies care for a cup of tea?"

"I certainly would," Abby said.

"None for me, thank you," Eliza said. "I never acquired a taste for tea."

"Neither did I," Josie said. "I can fix you cocoa, and the coffee is on, though I imagine it's stronger than a man off the trail by now."

"Coffee would be fine," Eliza said.

"I made bread pudding this morning," Josie said. "Would you all care for some?"

Eliza smiled. "Please."

"Just a small piece for me," Abby said.

"I'll be right back." Josie ducked into the kitchen.

"Reckon I'll lend Josie a hand." Before either of his sisters could reply over the oddity of a cowboy helping his boss with woman's work, Gil stormed into the kitchen.

Josie looked up from placing portions of bread pudding on plates. "Is there something you need?"

"We've got to figure out what to tell my sisters."

"About what?"

"You can't deny Sarah has Cooper eyes."

"I daresay there are a lot of people with green eyes."

Stubborn woman. He grabbed her by the hand and hauled her to the doorway. "Take a good long look at Abby."

Josie pushed the door open and took a peek. The sharp breath she sucked in proved he'd gotten through to her.

"Now enough of this runaround," he said when she closed the door and turned to face him. "Sarah and Abby have the same nose and eyes. Only two ways that could be. Either you entertained my father, which I don't believe you did for a second, or I got you with child that night at the Gilded Garter."

"Everett is her—"

"Don't say it because we both know it's hogwash." He pulled her so close he could smell vanilla in her hair. "Open your eyes, Josie. Sarah is going to be a shock to my sisters and they're going to ask questions, so we'd best have some answers ready."

"In other words, you propose we concoct some story about us." Josie pushed from him and fixed tea, her hands shaky and her mouth set in a grim line.

"It's for the best."

She frowned. "I don't know."

"Use your head, Josie. My sisters saw us on the porch tongue dueling, so they know there's more going on here than me being your trail guide."

"What did you tell them about us while I was getting Mrs. Cooper settled in?"

"That you're my old friend, Everett's widow, and I knew you way back. But I know Eliza. She won't let this rest. Hell, she hired a Pinkerton detective to track me down. Wouldn't put it past her to hire one to look into your past."

Josie nearly dropped the china cup she was holding. Having the sordid details of her past hung out for the world to see was the one thing she'd feared.

At least now she knew why the Pinkerton detective had been looking for Gil. No, Harrison G. Cooper the Third.

She didn't want to believe it possible, but after coming face to face with Gil's sister Abigail, she could no longer cling to the lie she'd lived since Sarah Ann was born. No getting round the fact that Gil truly was Saran Ann's pa.

Folks were going to talk. Talk had a way of growing into something entirely different.

And somewhere out there, Ross Parnell was waiting for his chance to get back at her.

"What's it going to be, Josie?"

"I don't want Sarah Ann hurt."

"Same here, which is why it's best if we come up with some story about how I loved you and left you."

She was thankful her hands didn't shake as she put forks on the tray. "How noble of you."

"You got a better idea?"

Not a one. No man had ever romanced her, so it was as good a story as any of the ones she'd cooked up.

"Is everything all right?" Eliza asked from the doorway.

"Just fine." Josie forced a bright smile. "We'll be right out."

Eliza stared at her a tense second, then retreated into the parlor. Josie took a breath to calm her nerves and wished for a sip of Everett's whiskey.

"Well?" Gil asked.

"Carry the tray into the parlor. We'll avoid the subject for now and come up with a story when we're alone tonight."

"It's going to work out fine."

"I hope you're right."

Gil nodded, then carted the tray into the parlor.

Josie gripped the back of the chair, breathing in deeply and letting it out real slow. She had a mind to send the whole lot of them packing. But that wouldn't solve a thing.

She sighed and headed into the parlor. God help her, by tomorrow she'd have another lie to learn to live with.

"Aren't you at least going to ask how Father is?" Eliza asked Gil as she helped herself to a cup of coffee.

He shrugged, but there were hard lines around his mouth Josie had never seen before. "Seeing as Ivy isn't wearing black, I reckon he's alive."

If not for the flash of pain in Gil's eyes, Josie would think he was a heartless man. What set him and his pa at odds? And had she imagined the tension between Ivy and Gil?

"Father is Father." Abigail waved a fork above her plate. "He can be terribly despotic at times, but he had the good sense to bring Landon into my life."

Eliza sniffed. "It's quite possible our father is losing his mind."

Abigail jumped to her feet. "That is mean and uncalled for."

"Landon Baxter is an autocrat." Eliza set her plate on the side table with hands that shook ever so slightly. "Why can't you see that?"

"You're jealous because Father intends to put Landon in charge of Cooper Enterprises instead of you and Stuart. Do excuse me, I have a headache and need to lie down." Abigail set her plate aside, grabbed her bonnet and stormed out the door.

Josie thought it a shame Abigail had been allowed to carry her childish tantrums into adulthood. Lord knew she'd pretty much broken Sarah Ann of such fits long ago.

Gil jumped to his feet. "Hold up there and I'll see you to your cabin."

He stepped outside with his sister, then was back inside before Josie could take a sip of coffee. "Hiram's standing guard."

Eliza paled. "Oh, dear. Are we in danger from savages?"

A choked laugh slipped from Josie. "Not at all. An outlaw was spotted in the area and so it's best to keep a watch out."

"How unsettling." Eliza rubbed her forehead. "As you can see, Gilbert, I do not share our father's and sister's enthusiastic opinion of Landon Baxter. That's why I needed to find you. You must help me get Abigail to see reason."

Gil whistled. "The way she defended this Baxter, changing her mind ain't going to be easy."

"How well I know. Despite what she said about wanting to come here, she nearly caved in to Landon's demand that she stay in Philadelphia."

"You'd best fill me in about this Baxter," Gil said.

"He's from old money," Eliza said. "I warrant that acquiring wealth is all he truly cares about."

At the sound of hoofbeats, Josie looked out the window. Her heart galloped as Dwight and Sarah Ann rode up to the barn. Though it'd be putting off the inevitable, Josie willed her daughter to stay down there like she always did, rushing in the back door late to clean up before dinner.

China tinkled as Gil helped himself to more coffee. "Whose idea was it for Abby to marry this man?"

"Father's, of course." Eliza dabbed her mouth. "Landon is touted as the new mover and shaker. That was enough for Father, so he arranged for Landon to meet Abigail, and the man literally swept her off her feet. Though in all honesty, she would have done whatever Father asked of her."

A doormat, Josie thought. *Just like Lillian.*

Gil snorted. "What about your husband? Did the old man arrange your marriage?"

"Heavens, no. Father opposed Stuart from the start and forbade me to see him." She blushed. "He changed his mind when I told him I was with child."

Josie's head snapped up. She hadn't expected the wealthy socialite to have done such a thing, much less admit it in front of a stranger.

"You must think me crass," Eliza said to Josie. "But if I hadn't been in the family way, my father would have foisted me off on someone I didn't love."

"I admire a woman for following her heart." Josie glanced at Gil and blushed.

Eliza smiled, and Josie was struck again with how much Gil favored his older sister. "I'm afraid Landon will come here and insist on staying to ensure his fiancée is safe."

"He know how to handle a gun?" Gil asked.

"I don't know, but I imagine so." Eliza frowned. "Why do you ask?"

Gil glanced at Josie. "Wouldn't hurt to have another set of eyes watching the place."

"Who's going to keep an eye on Landon and Abby?" Eliza asked.

"Among all of us," Josie said, "we ought to be able to ensure Mr. Baxter behaves like a gentleman."

And with Parnell lurking about, having another armed man on the ranch was to their benefit. The problem was where to put the man. Unfortunately, there was only one suitable place.

"I trust you have accommodations," Eliza said.

"He can have my cabin," Gil said over the clatter of a buckboard. "I'll bunk with the hands."

Not the most comfortable quarters, but the only other choice was the house and that'd only stir more gossip.

Josie heard the creak of wagon wheels coming closer toward the house. She got to her feet and peered out the window, dreading who'd decided to call on her this late in the day. Surely Parnell wouldn't be bold enough to walk up to her front door in broad daylight.

A buckboard from Maverick Livery pulled up before the house and a stranger decked out in a fancy gray suit and bowler hat climbed down. The driver tossed a carpetbag and valise to tall, dapper man.

"I have the feeling this is Abigail's intended," Josie said.

Eliza hurried to the window. "That's him, in all his pompous glory."

Chapter 11

As soon as Josie ushered Landon Baxter into the parlor, Eliza spoke up. "How dare you infringe on our holiday."

"You convinced your husband and father that three women traveling to the West was a perfectly safe undertaking," Baxter said. "But I know there are all manner of cutthroats and scalawags looking for a vulnerable mark."

"You'll find that breed of vermin everywhere." Gil towered in the doorway, thumbs hooked on his belt.

Baxter frowned. "Who are you?"

"Our brother, Gilbert," Eliza said.

Gil strode toward Baxter, eyes narrowed and muscle pulsing in his jaw. Josie held her breath, certain he'd hit the man. From what little she'd heard she had a mind to do the same. "Like to talk with you later," Gil said.

"I look forward to it." Baxter's smile bordered on mocking. "I'm most curious to hear about the brother who deserted his family obligations."

Gil's bland expression gave no hint of his thoughts,

though Josie imagined he was stomping mad. If these two men didn't come to blows she'd be surprised.

"Where's Abigail?" Landon asked.

"Resting, which is what I intend to do after such a trying journey." Eliza smiled at Josie. "Thank you for the dessert and coffee. Both were excellent."

"You're welcome," Josie said, feeling an odd kinship bloom with Gil's sister.

"I'll see you to your cabin." With a wink to Josie that had her blushing again, Gil walked out the door with his sister.

Josie faced Landon Baxter, hoping her smile looked pleasant instead of forced, hoping he couldn't tell how being alone with a strange man jangled her nerves.

Impatience sharpened Baxter's features as he tugged a calfskin wallet from his jacket pocket. He pulled three greenbacks out of the stack.

"Forgive me for not making prior arrangements. As I understand, your rate is two dollars a day," he said, handing her the money. "I trust you have accommodations for me."

"I do." Her fingers closed around the crisp ten dollar bill. "You plan to stay five days?"

"If that long."

"Very well. It will take me a spell to ready a cabin. The one nearest the barn is yours. We take our meals together in the house. I clang the dinner bell when it's ready."

"How countrified." Baxter inclined his head. "I shall wait on the porch, Mrs. Andrews."

Josie closed the door behind him and sagged against the panel, emotionally wrung out. Her idea to open a guest ranch had seemed so sound at the time.

She'd gotten her first guests quickly and was sure it

was a matter of time before more folks booked out-
ings. But only one other group had expressed interest.
Mercy, the reason the Hastings party had come here
was because they'd found out their brother had
bought part of Rocky Point. The brother who'd run
away from home a long time ago.

Josie shook her head and headed to the kitchen.
Once she put this money in the strongbox and put
on a pot of stew for supper, she'd ready Baxter's
cabin, and then talk to Gil.

She'd shared some of her secrets with Gil. It was
high time he did the same for her.

Gil crossed his arms across the split rail fence,
watching Hiram and Dwight cull the grulla stallion
from the remuda. No doubt about it: the line-back
bronco had a belly full of fire.

The stallion could spin in a blur of motion as well.
Yep, the mustang would make a fine cutting horse.
If Gil could break him. Some horses were plain
mean, and Hiram was of a mind this one was the
devil's creation.

"He's a pretty horse," Sarah said from her seat atop
the fence. "Shame he can't be gentled."

"Don't know that for sure."

"Hiram said he was an outlaw."

He looked up at her, and felt that familiar pull in
his gut as those big green eyes locked on his. "Are you
saying Hiram is never wrong?"

"He knows horses."

Gil thumbed his hat back. "What makes you think
I don't?"

"You never gave me any reason to believe you do."

The girl wasn't one to back down or sugarcoat anything. Like Josie.

"That horse has Spanish blood in him. He'd throw some fine-looking foals."

"I want one of them," Sarah said.

"That's up to your mama." *For now, anyway.*

Yep, the more he thought on it, the more he'd like to see this animal put to good use.

Gil exhaled heavily and turned back to watching Hiram. Now all he had to do was concoct a story on how he'd left Josie high and dry with his baby swelling her belly.

Owning up to being footloose didn't bother him none, but he didn't like being called a lothario. Not that Josie had been innocent. But to protect her reputation and save Sarah from shame, he had to 'fess up to seducing a sweet young thing into his bed, then turning his back on her and taking off.

Not a soul in Philadelphia would have any trouble believing he'd done that again, even if it had been a damned lie. But his family had branded him a rogue, and they were the only ones he had to convince he hadn't changed.

"How old are you?" Sarah asked.

"I'll turn thirty-one in June."

"You're older than Mama."

"That he is," Josie said from behind, startling him. "So you were nineteen when I met you."

He faced Josie. Life on the ranch had aged her a bit faster than it would her city sisters, yet she looked mighty young to have an eleven-year-old daughter.

"On the dark side of it. How old were you, Josie?"

She stared at him a long time, and he wondered if she knew what he implied. If she'd answer.

"On the new side of fifteen." She climbed onto the fence, her smile rueful. "Seems a lifetime ago."

"Doesn't it, though."

Damn! When Gil had bedded Josie, she hadn't been much older than Sarah, too young to be forced to pleasure a man. But he'd been a drunken jackass that night and hadn't realized it.

He glanced at Sarah, and some emotion he couldn't name rammed into his heart. *His* daughter. His and Josie's.

Starting now, Gil aimed to do right by Sarah. Josie, too, if she'd let him.

"I got Baxter settled in your cabin," she said. "Thanks for moving out while he's here."

"Ain't no never mind where I sleep." A lie. If he had his druthers, he'd crawl in the sack with Josie.

They lapsed into silence as Hiram cut the stallion from the remuda. The grulla raced into the corral and reared, black legs pawing the air and black tail and mane whipping in the wind. His front hooves slammed the ground as he let out an ear-piercing bugle, no doubt catching the scent of a mare in heat.

Sarah jumped down and hurried to the other side of the corral where Dwight stood, leaving him and Josie alone. Odd, but it felt right. Not that he aimed to tell her that. But like the stallion, he'd caught her scent. A bit of vanilla, fresh air and hot promises.

"I'm thinking it best we say I courted you, maybe at a barn dance or such," Gil said. "You were young, and I took advantage of your trust and heart. Then I rode off and left you."

Her laugh surprised him. "I didn't know you were such a good storyteller."

"There's a lot you don't know about me."

She looked at him. "Are you going to tell me your secrets?"

"Not unless you're fixing to tell me yours."

Except for the grulla's snorts and drubbing of hooves, all was silent.

"This plan of yours is bound to cause us all hurt," Josie said.

"How so?"

"Your family will expect you to do the gentlemanly thing by me."

"You mean marry you."

She nodded. "I don't want a husband."

He didn't want a wife right now either. But the more he was around Josie, the more the idea appealed to him.

"It might be smart to change your way of thinking, for Sarah's sake," he said.

"What are you getting at?"

"Think about it, Josie. We have a daughter. We're partners on the ranch. I can't think of one reason why we shouldn't tie the knot and make the whole ranch one again."

"I can."

"Mind telling me what that'd be?"

She bit her bottom lip. "I won't marry for convenience's sake again."

What the hell did that mean? Surely a former shady lady knew better than to put stock in all that mushy stuff.

"Why'd you run away from home?" she asked.

"My father had a set of plans for me, and I had other ideas. Since he wouldn't bend, I took off."

"What did he want you to do?"

"Marry a woman who swore she was carrying my child."

"You're sure the baby wasn't yours?"

"Positive." He laid a hand atop hers. "She betrayed me and then lied about it. That's no way to start a marriage."

She nodded, looking everywhere but at him. "I'd best get back to the house. Supper will be ready in a bit."

Gil watched her until she slipped inside the house, then he stared at the grulla's rippling coat. Yep, he had his work cut out for him breaking the horse. And if he aimed to win Josie over, it appeared he'd have to sweet-talk her.

To Josie's surprise, Eliza was standing at the stove when she returned to the house. The bubbling stew filled the kitchen with a savory aroma that made her stomach growl.

Eliza smiled at her. "I hope you don't mind, but it's difficult for me to sit around the house and do nothing."

That surprised Josie. She expected all wealthy folks had people doing for them.

"I'm the same." Josie went to the sideboard and dumped out flour, hoping her tension wouldn't translate into rock-hard biscuits. "When my hands are idle, my mind wanders."

"Forgive me for being bold, but have you and my brother been close for long?" Eliza asked.

She wasn't sure how much to say. "I met Gil when I was real young, a year before I married my husband. Everett was a good deal older than me."

"That's not at all unusual. Look at my stepmother.

She was only seventeen when she married my father."
Eliza made a face. "He was forty-four at the time, but
unlike you and Mr. Andrews, they never had a child."

"Actually, neither did we." Josie's hands shook as
the truth poised on her tongue. "I was in the family
way when Everett and I married, but my daughter
doesn't know. I'd like to keep it that way until I can
tell her about her real pa."

Eliza's features softened in understanding. "I
would never carry tales that would cause your daughter hurt."

Josie wondered if she'd feel the same once she met
Sarah Ann. The front door opened and slammed
shut. Boot heels thundered on the wooden floor as
her daughter ran into the kitchen.

"Come quick, Mama. Gil's fixing to ride that
outlaw." Her daughter spun around in a whirl of
calico and ran back out the door.

"Oh, my God." Eliza stared, mouth agape.

Josie didn't know whether Eliza had gotten a good
look at Sarah Ann, or if she realized the risk Gil was
taking. She sure didn't have time to worry about it now.

She wiped her hands and skedaddled out the door.
Her gaze fixed on the corral.

Hiram sat astride his big gray horse. A rope
stretched taut from his saddle horn to the grulla
they'd gotten stuck with. The mustang had been saddled, but it was mighty clear he was none too happy
about it.

Sarah Ann had climbed the fence beside Dwight.
And Gil—

The handsome fool was in the corral, slowly working his way down the dally line toward the stallion.

Josie stopped running so as not to spook the already agitated horse. Her heart pounded like a smithy's hammer.

"I gather that mouse-colored horse is the outlaw," Eliza said, her voice a tad breathless.

"He is." Josie looked at Gil's sister. "And your brother is a taking a dangerous risk trying to ride him."

Eliza faced her. "Something tells me going up against a wild horse is nothing new for him."

Still, this particular mustang was an outlaw. Even Hiram was leery of him, and her foreman was considered the best in these parts for breaking horses.

"Don't let your skirt flap." Josie held hers down and inched toward the corral, her heart in her throat.

Gil had reached the stallion. The animal's eyes bugged wide and his nostrils flared.

Josie climbed up beside Dwight and hooked her arms over the top rail. Eliza joined her.

Gil ran a gloved hand over the animal's quivery coat, easing toward the grulla's left. He grabbed the horn and swung into the saddle in one fluid movement.

For a heartbeat, the stallion stood there. No doubt he was surprised a man had gotten the best of him.

Gil gathered the reins in one hand and released the dally line with the other. That must've been the signal for the grulla to come out of his stupor.

The stallion's slate-gray coat quivered, and powerful haunches bunched. His front hooves shot off the ground and slammed back down in a wink. Both back legs kicked out, pitching Gil forward.

Again and again the animal bucked. In seconds, a cloud of dust rose in the corral, nearly obliterating the stallion and the man clinging to him.

Hiram shouted a time or two, but Josie couldn't

make out a word. Muffled grunts came from Gil and she winced, hearing pain in the tone.

Seconds seemed to crawl by as horse and rider whirled like a cyclone, going so fast they were no more than a blur. But not for long.

The stallion stumbled and his front legs crumbled beneath him. In a blink the stallion rolled onto his back with Gil still in the saddle.

Eliza gasped. Josie held her breath and dug her fingernails into the fence, searching the churning dust for Gil.

All four of the stallion's legs kicked the air in turn. Before the dust cleared, the stallion rolled to his feet and commenced bucking and whirling again.

And Gil— His hat was gone and dust covered him from head to toe. But he stayed in the saddle like his behind was glued to it.

The grulla blew and whirled, and Josie was sure Gil was getting the best of the mustang. But instead of giving up the fight, the stallion lunged forward, rocked back on his haunches just as fast and spun to the left.

A dark blur flew over the horse's head. Gil. And the grulla stallion kept bucking and whirling like a demon.

Sarah Ann gasped.

"Oh, my God," Eliza said.

That was Josie's thought too. She couldn't breathe, couldn't see Gil for all the damned dust.

"Shit and sagebrush," Dwight said.

The fence shook as he jumped down and ran toward the gate. Hiram heeled his horse and charged the stallion, but the outlaw lunged again and escaped being hemmed in.

Josie finally saw Gil kneeling by the fence, head down and left hand gripping a rail. "Get up!"

She was sure he'd stand and get the hell out of the corral. But his hand slid off and he sprawled in the dust. And the stallion zipped past her and galloped straight toward Gil.

Hiram's big gray crowded the wild stallion away from the downed cowboy. But where the hell had Dwight gone?

Gil's deathly still form terrified Josie. She wished she had Everett's old Navy Colt so she could shoot the grulla. Wished Gil wouldn't have ridden the outlaw. If he died—

She'd own the entire spread again. Free and clear. She wouldn't be under any more obligations to him or any man.

And for all her protesting and fretting, losing Gil was the last thing she wanted to happen.

Chapter 12

Josie stared at the dusty heap of denim and cambric sprawled by the fence. Gil lay there like an old rag, used up and tossed away. He looked dead.

That one thought slammed into Josie and nearly dropped her to her knees. She grabbed hold of the fence, barely feeling the splinters dig into her palms.

Beside her Sarah Ann wriggled close. Her shiver sent an answering one through Josie.

That snapped her out of her daze. Josie hadn't let her daughter see Everett when he breathed his last, but she'd been helpless to keep her daughter from watching Gil take that horrible tumble off the stallion.

As Hiram wrangled the grulla into a pen, Josie hoped they wouldn't be tagging killer onto the stallion's reputation.

Don't let Gil die. Please. Not now. Not in front of his daughter. Not when he's finally gotten reunited with his kin.

Dwight yanked open the gate and ran straight toward Gil. Josie pushed from the fence and did the same. Sarah Ann and Eliza were right on her heels.

Josie dropped to her knees beside Gil, her heart

slamming in her chest as she watched Dwight check him for broken bones. She hoped Gil would wince or moan, but he didn't move. Didn't make a sound.

"That tumble snuffed his lights out good and proper," Dwight said. "I saw it happen to a feller once and he ne'er did wake up."

The coffee Josie drank earlier threatened to spew from her. She stretched a shaky hand toward Gil's face, holding her fingers near his nose. That subtle puff of air wasn't much reassurance. What if he didn't wake up?

Josie blinked back the sting of tears and rested a hand on Gil's chest, somewhat eased by the steady beat of his heart. She brushed his hair off his brow and the waves fell right back, proving his hair was as stubborn as the man.

"We need to fetch the doctor," she said.

"I'll ride into Maverick soon as we get him settled," Dwight said.

"Let's get him up to the house."

"You sure about that? He might be laid up for a spell."

"That is all the more reason for Gil to recuperate in the house." Now that Josie had made up her mind, she wouldn't back down for anything. "You and Hiram are going to be busy tending to the ranch and seeing to our guests. It'll save me steps if Gil is close by."

"Makes sense," Hiram said, standing behind her and breathing hard. "Where you want him?"

She glanced at Sarah Ann's solemn face. There was only one vacant bedroom in the house, and putting Gil there would close a door that she wasn't sure her daughter was ready to close. But there was no other logical choice.

"Put Gil in Pa's bedroom," Sarah Ann said, having eyes only for Gil.

"Yes." Josie nodded to Dwight. "Take him up to Everett's room, but be careful. We don't know how badly he's injured."

"Take his feet," Hiram said to Dwight.

They lifted Gil and started from the corral. Josie picked up Gil's hat and slapped it against her leg to knock most of the dust off.

"Run ahead and turn the covers down, then fetch a pitcher of hot water," Josie told Sarah Ann.

"Yes, Mama."

Sarah Ann ran to the house, dark curls flying behind her and boots kicking up puffs of dust. She wasn't surprised that Eliza ran after Sarah Ann, no doubt worried sick over her brother and wanting to help.

Josie trailed them all, misgivings dogging her every step. She was doing the right thing. Doing what any ranch wife would've done. Doing what Everett would've wanted.

The last was what gave her pause. Why had Everett trusted Gil Yancy?

Had he thought Gil would be a good father figure to Sarah Ann, protecting her like Everett had done? That Gil would help Josie manage the guest ranch? That in time Gil might fill that lonely place in her heart?

After what she'd lived through in Kansas, Josie had never thought she'd love a man. But as Dwight and Hiram laid Gil on her husband's bed, she could no longer deny she had feelings for this virile cowboy.

An odd tingling nipped up her arms and legs then expanded inside her as they reached the house. It shouldn't surprise her that Gil suggested they become partners—in bed and out. Even her own physical wanting for this cowboy from her past didn't stun her. But the rightness that washed over her whenever she found herself thinking of him shocked her.

That should've put a stop to these crazy thoughts going through her head. But it didn't. If anything, it made them all the more enticing, like the jars of penny candy in the mercantile she'd ached to taste when she was a kid but could never afford.

"You need me to help you?" Hiram asked after Dwight rode off to Maverick.

Josie's cheeks heated. "I can manage, but I'd appreciate it if you'd see if you can find Boyd Rowney. He promised me six horses broke to ride and I want him to make good on that grulla stallion he palmed off on us."

"I'll see what I can do." Hiram gave Gil one last look then left.

Eliza stood with Sarah Ann by the window overlooking the front of the house. "How long will it take for the doctor to get out here?"

"That depends on how quickly Dwight can get to town, and if the doctor is in," Josie said.

Eliza paled. "What will we do if the doctor isn't there?"

"The best we can."

Which is what she'd had to do when her home remedies failed and Everett took a turn for the worse. By the time the weather cleared so the doctor could get to Rocky Point, Everett was too far gone.

Not again. Please, not again.

"What can I do to help?" Eliza asked.

"Get his boots off." Josie swallowed, letting her

gaze travel up Gil's long length. "Anything else that's binding."

"Of course." Eliza tugged off his boots and set them by the wardrobe. "My goodness, look at the holes in his socks."

Josie gave them a passing glance as she unbuckled his belt. "They need darning."

"Or throwing out," Eliza said.

Holey socks weren't unusual in Josie's world, but she supposed they were unheard of for rich folks. Even when they were no longer good to wear, Josie found plenty of uses for rags around the ranch.

Eliza sniffed. "What's that awful smell?"

"Smoke. Did you put something in the oven?"

"My biscuits are burning." Eliza darted out the door in a swirl of blue organza.

Josie shook her head and tugged the belt from under Gil. Her gaze lit on Sarah Ann. Her daughter worried her lower lip the same way as she had when Everett took ill.

"He's going to be all right." Josie prayed she was right this time.

"You want me to do anything?"

Josie gave that a lot of thought. She'd prefer keeping Sarah Ann away from Gil's family until she had the chance to tell her the truth, but she didn't want her camping out beside Gil's bed either.

"Mama?" Sarah Ann asked. "Is something wrong?"

Josie went to work unbuttoning Gil's vest. "Promise me you'll stay in the house."

"You worried that outlaw is around?"

Someone far worse. Josie stared at Gil's cambric-covered chest and sighed, trying to find the words to explain.

"Yes. I don't want you or our guests going outside alone. It's up to you to make sure they understand they're to have a man with them when they leave the house or their cabin. Can you do that?"

Sarah Ann nodded. "Yes, mama."

"If you see a stranger around here, you run for Hiram or Dwight."

"Or Gil?"

"Or Gil."

Josie wet a cloth and cleaned the dust and grime off Gil's face, feeling the catch of pale whiskers. Another memory. That raspy scrape on her bare skin as he'd nuzzled her bosom had doused her fear under a blaze of desire.

The rattle of wheels snapped her back to the here and now. "Go see who's here."

Sarah Ann ran to the window. "It's Doc Neely and Dwight."

So soon? "Let the doctor in, then take your meal with our guests," Josie said. "And mind what I told you."

"I will."

Josie turned back to Gil and found him watching her. "Thank God you're awake."

He blinked, his eyes dark as molasses. "I could hear you and Sarah, I just couldn't get my eyes to open."

Doc Neely stepped into the bedroom before she could summon up a reply. "I didn't expect you'd get here this fast."

"Dwight caught me on the road." Doc stared down at Gil. "Ah, you're awake. Good. How do you feel?"

"Like I got stampeded."

Doc set his black bag on the bed, then crossed to the washbowl to scrub up. "I imagine you do.

Dwight tells me you ended up eating dust, thanks to a grulla mustang."

"Yep, took a helluva spill."

"I think he cracked his head on the fence when he was thrown," Josie said.

"I'll take a look." The doctor probed Gil's head, grunting and mumbling to himself and dragging a muffled groan from Gil. "You know your name, cowboy?"

"Gil Yancy."

"Well, Gil Yancy, you've got a good-sized egg on your noggin. Let's get your shirt off so I can see what else is busted or bruised."

In no time, Doc had Gil shucked down to his union suit. Josie stepped back by the door, torn between taking a peek and keeping a respectful distance. Not that the idea of Gil near naked conjured up any decent thoughts.

"Your ribs are battered but intact," Doc said. "They'll cause you some discomfort, but it's nothing you can't handle."

"I've had worse."

"Yes, I see the scars."

That brought Josie's head around, but the doctor blocked her view of Gil. Scars? She hadn't remembered him having any. How had he come by them? How much had he suffered?

"Not much to do for the bruised ribs except rest, not that I think you'll listen to me," Doc said.

"I'll make sure Gil takes it easy," Josie said.

Doc chuckled. "I have no doubt you'll do that, Josephine."

Gil frowned, but didn't say anything.

"All right, cowboy. Follow my finger with your eyes."

The doctor held his hand before Gil, then moved it slowly back and forth across the width of the bed.

One back and forth movement and Gil's eyes closed on a moan. "Damn."

"Room's spinning, is it?"

"Yep. Real bad."

The doctor straightened. "Like I said, there isn't anything I can do to lessen the dizziness except advise you to rest today. You can drink and take your meals, but no alcohol or patent medicine of any sort. Best you don't sleep until night comes either. You may need company to keep you awake."

"I'll stay with him," Josie said.

"Good. Well, that's all I can do with the possible suggestion you sell that horse before he does you in."

Josie couldn't agree more. "Thank you, Doc. Help yourself to dinner."

"Believe I will." The doctor paused at the door. "A young woman who claims to be your sister wants to see you. Care if I send her up?"

"Fine by me," Gil said, drawing the covers over him.

The doctor left and Josie gathered up Gil's dirty clothes. "Can I get you something to drink?"

"Yeah, whiskey."

She pressed her lips together, stifling a grin. Lord knew she could use a shot herself.

"You can have water or coffee."

His eyelids drooped. "Best bring me coffee."

Abigail burst into the room and rushed to Gil's bedside. "You poor thing. How do you feel?"

"Middling."

"Keep him awake." Josie hurried down the steps to fix a tray for Gil and check on her guests.

"Whatever were you thinking to saddle that demonic

horse?" Abby plopped onto his bed and the abrupt movement shot a bolt of pain through Gil's head.

"That's how we break horses in these parts."

Abby shivered. "I'm sure we have a better way of doing that chore in Philadelphia."

"Yep, you buy one that's ready to ride."

She favored him with a dazzling smile and fussed with her skirt. "So will you come back home with us now?"

"Hell, no."

"But there's no reason for you to stay away any longer. Surely you're over your anger at Father."

Gil's head throbbed doubly hard at the reminder. Not that he needed one.

"My life is here, Abby."

"Life? From what Landon has told me, living on a ranch is hard. You don't need to put yourself through that abuse. Come home where you belong."

"Perhaps your brother prefers the West," Baxter said, standing in the doorway.

"Don't be ridiculous, Landon."

Baxter smiled as Abby launched into a spiel about the advantages of living in Philadelphia and her eagerness to move up the social ladder.

Gil took the opportunity to study his uninvited visitor as Abby droned on. Hell, Gil had been born into that life of high finances and scheming, just like Baxter. But that was a lifetime ago. He hadn't become a real man until he'd shucked what he'd known and took up the cowboy life.

The steady thud of shoes on the stairs reached him. Who next? Eliza, maybe. Or had Ivy come to gloat.

"Excuse me," Josie said.

Baxter stepped aside and Josie bustled into the

room packing a tray laden with dishes. The aroma of stew reached him first.

"I brought your dinner." Josie set the tray on the bureau and then moved to prop Gil up in bed with pillows, teasing him with her nearness.

"Hope you brought enough for both of us."

"I did, though I'm not terribly hungry."

"Neither was I," Abby said, "which was a good thing since I'm not partial to stew or similar pot dishes. Neither is Landon."

"I thought since your sister made dinner . . ." Josie shrugged. "Perhaps I can come up with something tomorrow that's more to your liking."

"That would be most welcome," Abby said.

His little sister fussed with her skirt again, and Gil had the urge to throttle her. When had she turned into a snob?

"We should leave them to their meal," Baxter said. "Eliza has asked us to join her and the girl in a game of dominoes."

"I'm not much into games, but I suppose we have no choice." Abby leaned close and pressed a fleeting kiss on Gil's forehead. "Do think about what I said."

"I won't change my mind."

Abby wrinkled her nose and flounced out the door with Baxter sniffing behind her. Gil waited until he could no longer hear them going down the stairs.

"Don't care much for that pompous son of a bitch."

Josie set the tray before him. "Neither do I. Now eat while it's hot. The biscuits are harder than rocks, but your sister forgot all about them when you put on your show. Mercy, Gil, what were you thinking?"

"I wasn't. I lost my concentration." But damned if he could remember what had distracted him.

"You're lucky you didn't lose your life," Josie said.

"I've had worse tumbles." He dug into his stew, savoring the spiced beef. "This is mighty good."

Josie cradled a bowl and dipped a spoon into hers, eating slowly. "When I find Boyd Rowney, I will surely give him a piece of my mind for selling me that worthless stallion."

Gil stopped chewing. Rowney. Wasn't that the name of the horse thief who sold Dugan MacInnes the sorrel?

"That stallion could make you money in the long run."

She snorted. "How do you figure that?"

"Easy. I aim to turn a tidy profit with him during the exhibition."

"Oh, no. You're not riding that mustang ever again."

Gil set his bowl down. "Come again?"

"You heard me the first time. I will not let you risk your life on that horse."

Now if that didn't beat all. "Josie, you can't tell me what to do."

"And why not?"

"Because you ain't my mother, my boss or my wife." He smiled, certain that'd shut her up.

Her eyes narrowed, and he knew before she opened her mouth that he was lucky he hadn't put any money on that bet. "The horse is mine, and I'll say who rides him."

"Yes'm."

Butting heads with her only made his head pound all the more. Best to let the subject drop for now.

That grulla stallion was the means for him to earn some money. He damned sure wasn't going to let anyone or anything stand in his way.

Chapter 13

Gil shifted in the bed and groaned. "Where're my clothes? I got to relieve myself."

"Oh." Josie hadn't considered. "Lie still while I fetch the chamber pot."

"Don't. I'll use the privy out back."

"No, you won't. You will not get dressed or leave this room the rest of this day."

"Dammit, Josie."

"No arguments." She fetched the china commode from under the washstand and placed it beside the bed. "There. When you feel up to it, I'll help you."

"I don't need help."

"But—"

He tossed off the covers and swung his long legs over the side of the bed. The front of his union suit gaped open from neck to crotch, showing a sprinkling of golden hair that angled from his broad chest clear down to his—

She gulped. *Oh, my.*

"You gonna stand there and gawk?"

Josie opened her mouth, but nothing came out.

She grabbed the tray of dirty dishes and rushed from the bedroom, flushed and tingling and unable to stop grinning.

She shouldn't have stared at him like a brazen hussy. But before she knew it, he'd tossed off the bedsheet and she was curious if her memory served her right. And it did.

My, my, my, but he was still a fine-looking man—all over.

Halfway down the stairs, Abigail's words drifted up to Josie. "I don't understand why we shouldn't telegraph Father immediately."

"If your brother wanted to renew his relationship with his family, he would have done so by now," Baxter said. "You must face the fact that Gilbert has chosen this life, and a forced reunion with your father will likely send him on the run again."

"I disagree, Landon," Ivy said. "This estrangement between Harrison and Gilbert has gone on far too many years. If something horrible happened to either of them, the other would bear the burden of holding his silence and resentment forever."

Josie agreed with Gil's stepmother. But she couldn't dismiss what Baxter said either. How would Gil take to seeing his father again? Would he stand his ground? Or pull up stakes?

She wouldn't be surprised by anything a man did, especially this hardheaded cowboy. That's why she hated telling Sarah Ann the truth. She didn't know how her daughter would take losing another pa.

"I agree with Ivy," Eliza said. "Look at what happened today. If Gilbert had died and we hadn't alerted Father of his whereabouts so he could make amends, he would have never forgiven us."

"Must I remind you that if your brother had wanted to end this estrangement, he'd have done so before now?" Baxter asked.

That served to silence the women in the parlor. But Josie doubted they'd hold their tongues for long. Gil's sisters wanted their family to be reunited.

The question was, just who did they expect to apologize? Gil's pa for trying to force Gil to marry a woman who'd betrayed him? Or Gil for not caving in to his pa's demand?

Josie eased down the stairs and peeked into the parlor, but saw only saw Ivy. Like her, Ivy had married a man old enough to be her father. A marriage without children, according to Eliza. Maybe that was for the best. Ivy's way of mothering Abigail was far too smothering.

"I suggest Landon ride into Maverick tomorrow and send a telegram to Harrison," Ivy said. "Considering his health, we dare not waste anymore time."

Baxter snorted. "Which is why we shouldn't upset Harrison. A journey by stage would surely be the death of him."

"Landon has a point," Abigail said. "Gracious, what should we do?"

"I suggest we seek our beds for tonight," Eliza said. "It's been a very long day for all of us, and clearer heads should prevail in the morning."

Ivy rose and gathered a wrap around her. "I agree. As Sarah Ann has reminded us endlessly, let's prevail upon Landon to escort us to our cabins."

The front door opened and Sarah Ann clomped in. Her eyes slid from the three women walking into the hall to Josie on the stairs. Worry clouded her daughter's eyes.

Josie hurried the rest of the way down the steps. "What's wrong?"

Sarah Ann frowned. "I looked out my bedroom window and saw a man sneaking around behind the cook shack, so I came down and told Hiram."

"Did Hiram catch him?" Josie asked, fearing Parnell would make his move now that Gil was down.

"Nope, but Hiram got a good look at him. He said it was the man who sold us those horses."

"Boyd Rowney." *Thank God it wasn't Parnell.*

"Is he the outlaw?" Ivy asked, clearly shaken.

"No, he's a horse thief and swindler." Josie wanted to call those words back when Ivy Cooper's face lost its color. "Rest assured the hands are keeping a watch out for him or any other scallywag."

Ivy gathered her wrap around her. "I sincerely hope they do. Good evening."

"Good night," Josie said as her women guests filed out the door with Baxter following, his back stiff and arrogant head held high.

Josie wrinkled her nose. She'd seen his type before. Fancy and polite in public, and dirty and mean in private.

"I don't like him," Sarah Ann said.

"Neither do I. He hasn't looked at you odd has he?"

"Nope, but Mrs. Cooper and Mrs. Hastings sure did for the longest time." Sarah Ann turned her head to the side. "Do you think I look like Abigail?"

Josie nearly swallowed her tongue. Why couldn't the Coopers have had blue eyes? Or brown? And why did her daughter have to be so observant?

"Well, you both have green eyes."

Sarah Ann smiled. "I've never met anyone besides Miss Abigail who had eyes like mine."

"No doubt there's a good reason for it." One Josie would have to explain to her daughter real soon.

"Can I visit Gil before I go to bed?"

"May you visit him," she said, and Sarah Ann wrinkled her nose at being corrected. "Go on up, but knock on his door first. He might be, uh, sleeping."

"All right. Good night, Mama."

Josie kissed her daughter on the forehead, then carried the tray to the kitchen and finished cleaning her dishes. She was about to toss her wash water out the back door when she remembered the cups in the parlor.

She slipped into the dining room and gathered up her china. Her gaze lifted to the front door, and a chill feathered up her spine.

All the years she'd lived here she'd never locked her doors, but the fear that Ross Parnell could slip in without warning terrified her. She secured the front door and looked out the oval glass.

A dim light glowed in Landon Baxter's cabin, but the women's quarters were pitch-dark like the bunkhouse. Was Baxter keeping watch tonight? She couldn't imagine that. Perhaps he was one of those folks who didn't seek his bed early.

Josie returned to the kitchen and carefully cleaned and dried her china. She tossed her soapy water out the back door, then made sure the door was locked before snuffing out all the lights and heading upstairs.

She didn't need light to get to her room. She knew how many steps it took. Where to turn. Which treads creaked so she could avoid them and not awaken her daughter or ill husband.

At Everett's door, Josie stopped and listened. Soft snoring filtered to her. Good, Gil was finally resting.

She eased her door closed and donned her nightgown. As bone tired as she was, she knew she'd fall asleep as soon as her head hit the pillow.

Josie curled up in bed, and that resonant snoring that had comforted her at first made her restless. She tossed and turned, wishing sleep would come.

When it did, dreams of Gil pressing her down in the bed invaded her peace, filling her with an ache so sharp and hungry she tossed and turned the rest of the night.

Damn Gil Yancy. He roused this longing in her. And that was a dangerous feeling for her to have for that cowboy.

"I won't go through with it." Gil's silk tie felt like a garrote as he paced his father's private study.

His father sat at his desk and glared at him. "You can't be serious. The wedding is in two days."

Gil threaded both hands through his hair, trembling with fury. "She should've thought of the consequences before she let another man fuck her."

"Your crudity is uncalled for."

"Is it? Would you willingly raise another man's bastard?"

"What I would do is of no import. Ivy swears the child she carries is yours."

"She's lying."

"Too much is at stake here to walk away, Gilbert."

Gil seethed over his father's dictatorial ways, over Ivy's infidelity. Why couldn't the old man understand that Gil would be a fool to marry an unfaithful woman?

"I don't give a damn. I won't do it."

His father came around the desk and clamped his hands on Gil's shoulders. "Apparently I'm not making myself clear. You will wed Ivy."

"Like hell I will!"

He struggled to pull loose. To distance himself physically as well as emotionally from his father and all he'd known. All he'd been groomed to be.

"Let me go, dammit! Let me go!"

"Let me go!"

"Gil, wake up," Josie said. "You're having a nightmare."

His eyes popped open and he searched the darkness to get his bearings, his chest heaving as his old nightmare blurred with reality. He wasn't in his father's house—wasn't having the old confrontation that had dogged him for years.

He focused on Josie leaning over him. How much had she heard?

A sliver of moonlight illuminated her face. Her small hands cupped his shoulders, her breathing as ragged as his.

The scent of vanilla and hot woman roused the lust that had hit Gil when he'd first laid eyes on Josie. He'd gone after her without much thought to how she'd feel about a quick tumble.

She'd worked in a damned brothel. Shady ladies didn't bat an eye about crawling in the sack with a man.

But knowing now that Parnell had put Josie to work when she was just fifteen, that the son of a bitch had forced her to whore, changed everything. Oh, Gil still wanted her more than ever before, but he wouldn't push her.

Nope, if he ever gave her a tumble, it'd be because she wanted it and made the first move. Right now he was so hard up he'd settle for her wiggling her finger his way in invitation.

"Why are you staring at me like that?" she asked.

He looked away, not wanting her to know where his thoughts had veered. Moonlight reflected off the closed door.

Damn, that was her doing. They were alone. Private.

"Gil? Is something bothering you?"

"You shouldn't be in here."

"You called out and I was worried. Are you going to be all right? You sound like you're in pain."

He laughed, a raw sound. "Trust me, that ache will ease once you get back to your room."

"Ache?" she asked, her voice a mere breath. "Oh, that kind of hurting."

"Yep. Why are you whispering?" he asked, his voice pitched just as low as hers.

"I don't want to wake Sarah Ann."

Their daughter. He hadn't thought about Sarah, and that admission made him want to kick himself. Satisfying his needs was how he'd gotten a child on Josie in the first place.

He figured Josie would up and leave, but she didn't move. In fact, unless his ears were deceiving him, her breathing grew more labored.

"You're not the only one hurting, cowboy."

Then her mouth found his, and he tasted her uncertainty mingled with desire. Everything in him wanted to pound into her, but he reined in those urges and lay there like a log, letting her kiss him, giving her free reign to do whatever she felt like doing.

If she couldn't do no more than kiss him? Hell, he'd find a cold stream tomorrow and jump in.

She leaned back and her fingers moseyed over his bare chest, fired him up till he was sure they'd see smoke at the Diamond M. "Do you want me to leave you alone?"

"Hell, no. Not unless you want to, that is."

"They why aren't you grabbing at me like you did before?"

Gil winced at her frankness. Welcomed it too, even though it was another slap upside his hard head.

"Lovers don't grab, sweetheart. They caress and fondle each other, and kiss until they're so fired up they can't stop."

"Oh, I didn't realize."

Had Everett taken Josie like she was still a working girl? Maybe his old partner hadn't had any finesse.

Not that Gil had any room to talk. Every time he'd gotten her alone, he'd been picturing Josie as she'd been at the Gilded Garter, decked out in sporting clothes. Not once had he opened his eyes and seen her standing before him in her simple calico dress, face scrubbed clean and eyes brimming with hesitation.

Now that he did, Gil felt lower than a worm. Josie was a widow lady. The mother of his child.

He owed her a heap of respect.

Gil slid a hand up her bare arm and marveled at the shivers racing over her smooth skin. "I'd like to show you how good it can be between us."

"I— All right." Again, her voice was so soft and low he barely heard that stutter of uncertainty.

He smiled into the darkness as she stretched out beside him, her hand on his chest tentative and light as a butterfly. The bed creaked, and her ragged breathing joined his.

He rolled to his side and glided a hand over her

rounded hip, bunching her thin gown in his wake, surprised his hand shook. He prided himself on his prowess, but the feel of her soft-as-velvet skin beneath his palm had him sweating from want.

That near-silent moan she made deep in her throat was like throwing logs on a raging fire. His pecker was already so hard he could plow a field with it. But when she threaded her fingers through his hair and pressed up against him, he damn near popped then and there.

She trembled, and his heart commenced galloping. "What do you want me to do?"

"Whatever you want, sweetheart."

Her fingers moved ever so slowly over his bare chest, leaving him shaking like an untried boy. How the hell could she do that do him?

Not that he was complaining. This restless ache was new, and that made it all the more sweet.

Gil bent close and nipped kisses along her jaw and down her throat, and she let out the sweetest moan of pleasure.

"Oh, mercy."

He took her whispered words as a benediction, his kiss ravenous. Need pounded through him like a runaway train. He'd always prided himself on his ability to please a lady, but with Josie his control seemed nonexistent.

"I want to stoke the fire in you, sweetheart. Touch you all over."

She moaned again and raked her fingernails down his back, setting off sparks in him that he'd never felt before, sending his intentions to take it slow and easy up in smoke. "Yes."

His hand splayed over her silky-soft belly and his

fingers drove into the tight curls between her legs, his body demanding he get on with it. She arched her back and pushed against his palm, as if agreeing he'd waited long enough.

Sweat slicked his body and hers, and he longed to rip their clothes off. But something about laying here half-dressed in the dark felt just naughty enough to be nice.

He slipped a finger inside her, testing, teasing, stunned she was so tight. The blood roared in his ears as he pushed another finger inside her. If he didn't know better, he'd swear she was a virgin.

Just realizing she wasn't as used as he'd feared set his blood roaring like a swollen river. He took slow, even breaths, struggling for control.

He'd never wanted a woman so badly. Hell, he'd never wanted to pleasure one so, putting her needs above his.

Her fingers dug into his arms and she bucked against him, her hungry muscles milking his fingers. "Ohhhh, d-d-don't—"

He clenched his teeth and didn't move, fearing he'd hurt her. Dammit, for a man who'd had his share of women, he was sure screwing this up badly.

"Don't stop," she said, her voice breathy as she lifted her face to his.

His mouth closed over her soft lips as his fingers stroked her heat again. Going slow was sheer hell, but he reckoned she was a virgin at foreplay.

He aimed for her to see the fireworks behind her eyes. He wanted her to remember this night instead of that one in the Gilded Garter when he was a green buck, too full of himself and whiskey to think to ask her name. He wanted her to forget he'd taken all she had to offer and gave her nothing to remember him by but a baby swelling her belly.

Her back arched, and her fingers dug into his arms. "Yes, yes."

"That's it, Josie. Just let yourself go, sweetheart."

He kissed her deeply, rocking with her. Their tongues danced in time to his thrusting fingers. His heart slammed against his ribs with each sultry moan, each sigh, each time she dug her fingernails into his bare back.

She gave a hard shudder, and his mouth captured her cry of pleasure. He held her close to his heart, thinking that sound was the sweetest music he'd ever heard.

She wiggled close after the tremors died, like she belonged right here next to his heart. "I never knew."

Talk about a cowboy's lament— Regret gnawed at him that he hadn't taken it slow and easy with her years ago. That he hadn't had the good sense to steal her away then.

Yep, she probably thought all men were the same, taking what they wanted and then walking away. But this time was different. She was his ol' friend's widow. Gil's partner. His daughter's mama.

Gil pulled back a smidgen, not wanting Josie to feel the lodge pole between his legs and have her think that's what he expected from her again. Didn't matter that he ached to toss her nightdress off her and sink into her. He wasn't about to mar this new memory with needs of his own.

She cupped his jaw. "You're mighty quiet. Does your head pain you?"

"Some."

Both ends throbbed like a blue bitch, yet holding her felt so good. So right.

He'd never felt this odd sense of oneness before. Never dreamed a man could receive so much pleasure watching a woman come, or holding her close. Snuggling and talking.

"I need to find my own bed." The springs twanged as she set up, but again she didn't make a move to leave.

He opened his mouth to tell her to stay, then knew that was a mistake. As much as he wanted her, he'd probably end up taking her in the night with hurried passion.

"This was—nice."

"Yep, it was. 'Night, sweetheart."

"Good night." She slipped from the room and eased the door shut with a soft click.

Gil tucked his hands under his head and frowned at the ceiling. He heard her bedroom door open and close, then a deep silence settled over the house.

If somebody had told him that fondling a shady lady would be nice, he'd have laughed in their face. But what happened between them had been mighty fine. Innocent. Right.

That got him wondering how much experience Josie truly had—in the Gilded Garter, and as Everett Andrews's wife.

The next morning Josie slipped downstairs before the sun came up. She'd barely slept last night and it was all Gil Yancy's fault. But even as she said it, she admitted that it was a bald-faced lie.

The quivering and pleased smile she couldn't erase

when she'd left his bed vanished as soon as she'd reached her room. She'd always had needs she hadn't fully understood, feelings that would gnaw at her some nights when she remembered how she'd melted in Gil's arms the one time at the Gilded Garter.

Last night he'd showed her what she'd been missing, and the experience was more wondrous than she could've imagined. But the strange sense that'd come over her later worried her.

Yes, they'd shared something rare. Something she dreamed she'd never feel. But for her, she wasn't just scratching an itch, or satisfying her curiosity.

She cared for Gil more than she should. Why, when that outlaw bucked him off, she thought her heart would stop. If he'd died, a part of her would've died with him.

Josie heaved a sigh. Was what she was feeling love? She didn't know, but she wasn't about to do what she did last night again until she sorted it out in her mind.

The aroma of coffee enveloped her halfway down the stairs. She grabbed the railing, nearly missing a step.

Until Everett became bedfast, he'd always had the coffee going long before she roused from bed. In fact, she'd often wondered if her husband slept much.

Josie hurried down the steps and into the kitchen, uncertain what she'd find. She stopped in the doorway and stared at the back of Gil's dirty shirt. He stood by the stove, pouring coffee into a cup.

"You're an early riser." She fought off a wave of embarrassment as she walked to the sideboard and set to making biscuits. "How do you feel?"

"Fair to middling."

"Thank you for making coffee."

"Want some?"

She went still for a heartbeat. Such a simple question and one she'd asked guests hundreds of times. But nobody had ever asked her that. Oh, Everett made the coffee, but he always left her to pour her own.

"That would be nice."

Josie grimaced, realizing she'd said the same about his loving last night. Mercy, could she be any greener?

She dumped flour on the board and reached for the lard tin, damning the way her hands shook as she mixed the dough. She hoped if she ignored the tingling in her belly, these needy feelings would go away.

"What happened to your folks? Fever take them?"

"A twister." Josie arranged the biscuits on a tin pan and put them in the oven, relieved to change the subject even if it was to recall something sad. "Pa had a dirt farm outside Randolph, Kansas. He'd fought drought and grasshoppers and held on, but he couldn't best two tornadoes."

He let out a low whistle. "You saw it happen?"

"No. My sister and I were at school, but our two brothers were at home helping Pa plant corn. When Lillian and I got home, there was nothing left. A neighbor found my ma and pa and was burying them. The sheriff found our brothers, both drowned in the creek."

"Why didn't the neighbors take you and your sister in?"

"We weren't the only ones who lost everything that day. One family offered to take Lillian, but they were looking for help on their farm and didn't want me. Lillian promised she'd take care of me till I was old enough to help out. So we packed what we could find and took the stage to Abilene."

"Lillian. She couldn't have been very old. Where'd she find work?"

"The Lyceum Theatre. Ross Parnell was the owner, and he filled Lillian's head with promises of making her a star." Josie tried to smile as she washed her hands, but the dirt of those memories was ground in. "Two months later, he won a new place in Caldwell, so he sold the theatre and took us with him. As you know, the Gilded Garter was a saloon with a stage, and Parnell was a flesh-broker. You can figure out the rest."

He was silent a long time. "He taught you that whip act to entertain folks in the saloon, and put your sister to work upstairs."

"Yes." Josie picked up her coffee, welcoming the heat on her palms.

He frowned into his coffee, and she wondered what was going through his mind.

"I did some thinking this morning. We'll say I met you at a square dance in Caldwell. Being I was a foot-loose cowboy in town, letting off steam, I sweet-talked you into bed then took off. Nobody knew where I went. You ended up in the family way, met Everett and he—"

"Made me an honest woman?"

"That's what happened."

She laughed. "All right, Gil Yancy. We'll tell them your story for Sarah Ann's sake and add a good dose of truth. Everett said it didn't matter if I was carrying another man's child, that he'd raise him or her as his own. And don't ever forget that Sarah Ann doesn't know any different."

Gil nodded once, but his features looked a bit strained. Not that she cared. The last was the honest to God truth.

Everett hadn't batted an eye over Sarah Ann. In fact he loved her just as much as if she'd been his daughter. And in all the ways that counted, she was his.

Josie diced potatoes into one skillet and put sausage on to fry, thinking it amazing that Gil had gone to so much trouble to concoct a story. All for his family's benefit. And his ego?

Sarah Ann slipped into the kitchen, and her green eyes lit up the moment she saw Gil. "Do you feel better?"

"Sure do," he said.

To Josie's surprise, Sarah Ann set the table without being asked. "I never saw a horse and rider take a tumble like that before."

"I did once, but this is the first time I experienced it firsthand." Gil grimaced. "Once is enough."

Josie took the biscuits from the oven and put them on the table, silently agreeing. She never wanted to go through that fear again.

Hiram and Dwight trudged in from the back porch, their hands a bit wet. She put the basket of biscuits on the table, and the men dug in. As soon as the hands split their biscuits on their plates, she poured redeye gravy over them, then added good-sized servings of fried spuds.

"How you feeling?" Hiram asked Gil between bites.

"Good enough to take the women on their first trail ride this morning as planned."

"You can't be serious." Josie stared at him. "The last thing you should do is ride after taking that spill."

His mouth hiked up in a smile that melted her

insides. "I'll be fine, Josie. All I'm fixing to do is take my sisters over to my land. We won't be gone more than a couple of hours."

"Can I come?" Sarah Ann's eyes rounded.

Josie shook her head. "You have school today."

"Next time we'll go in the afternoon," Gil said.

"Can we practice shooting this afternoon?" Sarah Ann asked.

Gil stood and winced. "Let's put it off a day or so."

Sarah Ann's shoulders drooped, but she nodded.

"Any sign of Rowney?" Josie asked Hiram.

"Nope. But in case he's fixing to take back the horses, we decided to pen them up at night."

"I got half a mind to give him back that devil that pitched Gil," Dwight said. "Miserable horse nearly took a chunk out of my arm while I was hauling the saddle off him."

"He's not getting that horse unless he pays for it," Josie said.

Gil snorted. "I got a hunch this Rowney never bought a horse in his life."

"I was thinking the same thing," Hiram said.

Josie stared at Gil, her appetite gone. "Are you saying I bought horses from a horse thief?"

"I'd bet on it." Gil turned to Hiram. "Any particular brand on those horses?"

Hiram shook his head. "No two alike."

"Sarah Ann saw him snooping around last night while I was upstairs tending you," Josie said.

"We looked all over, but didn't see him." Hiram pushed his empty plate away. "Whatever he wanted couldn't have been good."

"We're watching everything that ain't nailed down,"

Dwight said, getting to his feet. "A man that'll steal horses won't stop there. We can't afford to lose cattle."

A fact she was well aware of. They hadn't needed the extra worry of Parnell, though Josie wondered if he was really here. It'd be like that snake to send her that letter to keep her jumping at shadows, running scared again.

"Best get a move on," Dwight said to Sarah Ann. "Time to head off to Chalmers' Ranch."

Her daughter grabbed her poke and headed out the door with Dwight trailing her. Hiram was a step or two behind.

"Thanks for the breakfast and the company last night." Gil winked at Josie, and she thought her face would go up in flames.

Yes, indeed, that cowboy had a wicked streak in him. One that appealed to her far too much, and could leave her heartbroken if she wasn't careful.

Chapter 14

Gil guided Rhubarb around the rocky outcropping, staying a good ten feet behind the tenderfoots Dwight was leading. He'd taken drag duty, partly because he couldn't get the touch and taste of Josie off his mind, and partly so he could keep an eye on the trio of guests.

So far, he hadn't seen any sign of an outlaw. Whoever he was had probably lit out of here days ago. Still, he kept an eye peeled, knowing trouble could pop up anytime.

Ivy sat the sidesaddle easily, but then she'd been raised around horses. His sisters hadn't and it showed.

He didn't like the fact Abby and Ivy had gotten close. There was no denying the bond between the two. He reckoned that made sense.

Eliza had never had any patience with their little sister. Fact remained Abby was mighty young when Ivy married his father.

The old rage that had stuck like a burr in him festered the longer he dwelled on that. If it'd been any other man who'd eaten the sheets out from under him he'd have forgotten about Ivy's betrayal long ago.

But the bitch had screwed his father while the old man was in mourning. So much for damned society mores.

When a man had a hard-on, damned near any hole would do. Least that's the way Gil had always looked at it. Thinking his father and Ivy had tender feelings hurt too damned much to contemplate.

"Is your land near here?" Eliza glanced back at Gil.

"We've been riding on it the past twenty minutes."

"I had no idea you owned that much," Ivy said.

"I hold title to a decent spread." Close to fifteen hundred acres.

But he wasn't about to enlighten his stepmother about the exact amount. Even if he knew she wouldn't spill her guts to his father, his business was none of hers.

"Can we rest?" Abby asked, her voice strained.

"In a bit."

Damn, Abby had grown up to be a beautiful simpering miss. Easy to see why.

Ivy coddled her. She probably encouraged Abby to do their father's bidding. Seeing the way Abby fawned over Landon Baxter made him right sick. It was as if his little sister had no mind of her own.

At the cottonwood grove, Dwight reined up and dismounted. He grabbed the martingale on Abby's chestnut mare, then snagged the lead to Eliza's dun gelding.

Gil's muscles bellowed like hell as he climbed off Rhubarb and ground-reined his roan. He helped Abby dismount first, then strode toward Eliza. But she'd already figured out how to get off the horse herself.

That didn't surprise him none. His older sister had always fended for herself, much to their father's annoyance.

"Would you give me a hand, Gilbert?" Ivy asked. "I'm a bit rusty at this."

He peered up at her and felt his neck burn. The glint in her eyes challenged him—did he have the balls to touch her?

Gil bit off a curse and plucked Ivy from the saddle, making no apology that his gloves were rough cowhide instead of smooth leather. Her back remained as stiff as her stays as he set her on her feet.

She grabbed his upper arms. A bolt of ice shot through his veins, same as it had the last time she'd touched him.

"I would like for us to be friends," Ivy said. "For your father's sake."

Bull. "In the West, a friend will back you up to hell's door and beyond, not push you through it."

"I never meant to hurt you."

"But you did anyway."

He walked off. If she aimed to apologize, it came too late. Anyway, Abby was giving Dwight what for.

"Something wrong?" Gil asked.

Tears glittered in his little sister's eyes as she held her skirt out. "It's ruined. All because he led us too close to those stinky bushes."

Gil scrubbed a hand over his face. "You were holding the reins, Abby. All you had to do was guide your mount away from the brambles."

"Nobody told me to do that." Her lower lip curled down.

"Some things ought to be obvious."

Ivy breezed past Gil. "You've had this riding habit a

good while anyway, so don't worry if it is ruined. Perhaps Mrs. Andrews can clean it for you."

That ripped it. Damn if he'd let Ivy turn Josie into a servant.

"Don't see why you two can't pick the burrs off yourself," Gil said. "Hell, she'll probably pick up more on the ride home."

Abby looked appalled by that notion. Ivy stared down her thin nose at him. Hard to believe at one time he'd thought her the most beautiful woman he'd ever met.

"I told you before we embarked on this journey you wouldn't have servants at your beck and call," Eliza said.

She and Ivy exchanged a look, and Gil knew then and there that his older sister and stepmother were used to sparring over Abby. Is that why Ivy had come along? So Eliza wouldn't get the upper hand?

Ivy turned to Dwight. "Is there someplace we can rest in relative comfort?"

Dwight pointed to the rocky slabs he'd staked out the other day. "Yes, ma'am. Right over there by that outcropping. I cleared the brush away so you wouldn't get your skirts tangled up. Give me a minute to spread a blanket for you."

"Come, Abigail." Ivy led his little sister to the spot like she was a child.

"Is she always that way?" Gil asked Eliza.

"Unfortunately. May we take a walk?"

"Reckon so."

He wasn't much for walking, but with Ivy close, he wanted to put distance between them. Like a couple of territories.

"I don't know who has been the worse influence on Abigail. Ivy or Landon."

Gil figured it was pretty much a tie. "How do Abby's intended and Ivy get on?"

"Usually they don't. Yesterday when you lost consciousness, Abigail wanted to send a telegraph to Father immediately and Ivy and I agreed, but Landon thought it unwise."

Son of a bitch. "Did you wire the old man?"

"No. Landon convinced Abigail and Ivy of the terrible jolt that would cause Father. Since you've recovered, I didn't balk." Eliza looked at him, worry evident in her eyes. "It has been that way in everything. From Abigail, to business dealings, to Father's health."

Gil stared at her. "Are you saying Baxter has a say in how Cooper Enterprises is run?"

"Of late, he has. Ivy offers no opinion concerning Father's business, and he pays no attention to my suggestions or my husband's advice."

"Sounds like the old man has chosen his successor."

Hurt flashed in Eliza's eyes. "So it seems. But my husband discovered Baxter gambles, and has lost a goodly sum of his holdings of late. If he gains control of Cooper Enterprises, he could ruin the company."

"That's the old man's problem."

"Are you so cavalier you don't care that Landon will also ruin Abigail's life?"

"Hell, no. But I don't see what we can do to stop her from marrying him."

Eliza smiled. "I do. Get her to see Landon for the wastrel he is."

Gil sighed. Best way would be draw Baxter into a high-stakes game. Unfortunately, all Gil owned was his share of Rocky Point, and he wasn't feeling all that lucky right now.

Josie set two pies on the window ledge to cool. A steady chink-chink echoed from the blacksmith's shop, confirming that Hiram was working.

She wrapped her shawl around her shoulders and stepped out on the front porch. The sweet smell of balsam poplars in bloom carried on the cool breeze, teasing the silky fringe on her shawl and coaxing her to sit a spell.

Deuce sprawled before Everett's chair. She didn't have the heart to run the old hound off, so she stepped over him and eased into her rocker.

If she closed her eyes, she could almost imagine nothing had changed on Rocky Point Ranch. That Hiram was busy shoeing horses Dwight had singled out. That Sarah Ann was at school. That Everett would hobble up to the house any minute, thin, stooped and exhausted but smiling at her like she was the only sun in his world.

In a way she supposed she was. Least ways that's what he'd claimed up until the very last when he couldn't even form words anymore.

At the sound of a rider approaching, Josie opened her eyes and her smile vanished. Landon Baxter stood on the step, his gaze focused down the lane. A shiver ripped through her. She hadn't even heard him walk up.

"It appears you have company," he said.

She squinted at the visitor. "That's Sheriff Keegan. Maybe he has news about the train strike."

"One can hope it ends soon. I don't look forward to the journey back to Philadelphia in a stagecoach."

Virgil brought his horse to a dust-choking stop before the porch, the saddle leather protesting as he dismounted. "Morning, Josie. Got a telegram for Landon Baxter."

"I'm Baxter."

He took the note and opened it. His expression hardened in a blink.

"I hope it isn't bad news," she said.

Baxter folded the telegram and shoved it in his vest pocket. "A minor problem with one of my holdings. Would you lend me a horse so I may ride into Maverick?"

"Of course. Hiram is in the blacksmith's shack down by the bunkhouse. He'll fix you up with a horse."

"Thank you." Baxter took off for his cabin, his refined pace hurried.

"That coffee I smell?" Virgil asked.

She smiled. "It is. Come on in the kitchen and I'll get you a cup."

"Much obliged." He followed her inside and took a chair at the table. "Doc Neely told me Gil took a nasty spill off a bronco yesterday. He still laid up?"

"No, he recovered quickly, and returned to the bunkhouse."

Too quickly in her opinion. She poured a cup of coffee and set it before Virgil.

"That's good," he said. "Ain't right for your trail guide staying in the house with you and Sarah Ann. A woman's got a reputation to protect."

She wanted to laugh at his defense of her honor. If he only knew the truth, that she'd ended up kissing and carousing with Gil last night in her husband's bed. That she'd thrilled to the cowboy's touch and ached for more. That she feared she'd lost her heart to him somewhere along the way.

"Any chance you're closer to that courting stage?" Virgil asked, cradling his empty coffee cup.

She looked into his sad puppy dog eyes and sighed. "I'm sorry, but I can't."

He nodded and stood. "You ever change your mind, you let me know. I'd do my best by you and Sarah Ann."

"I know that, Virgil."

"You need me for anything, you send Dwight or Hiram in."

"I will."

Josie followed Virgil outside and watched him ride out with Landon Baxter. She didn't want to hurt the sheriff. He was as nice as could be and would be a good husband. But the day she'd let him court her would never come, because she didn't love him, and she doubted that would change in time.

Inside, she grabbed her mending and settled in the chair before the front window where she had good light. She'd no more than threaded her needle when she saw a short, stocky man sneaking around Baxter's cabin.

Boyd Rowney. Now was her chance to give the horse thief a piece of her mind over selling her that outlaw stallion.

Josie tossed her mending aside, grabbed Everett's Navy Colt and hurried out the door. Rowney was nowhere in sight. Neither was Hiram.

In fact it was far too quiet.

Josie held the heavy revolver in her hands and hurried toward the bunkhouse. The chink of metal hitting metal resumed before she rounded the corner and saw her foreman at work in the smithy.

"Hiram!"

He faced her, and she waved him near. Where in tarnation had Rowney gone?

Behind her, hoofbeats drummed the ground.

Josie whirled, catching a glimpse of Boyd Rowney galloping down the lane. "What in blazes does he want?"

"Reckon anything he can steal," Hiram said. "I'd best check out the barn and tack room."

Near dusk, the clomp of hooves got Abigail running to the window. "Thank God! Landon has finally returned."

"Shame he didn't take off for parts unknown," Gil said.

Eliza chuckled. "We should be so lucky."

Josie had to agree. At least dinner had been enjoyable without Baxter's presence, though Abigail had spent a good deal of the time moping when Eliza began picking on Baxter's shortcomings.

"He would never leave Abigail in the lurch." Ivy gained a bright smile from Abigail, and a scowl from Eliza and Gil.

Baxter strolled in, clothes covered with dust and face lined with worry. "My apologies for returning late. It took longer than I'd hoped to send a telegram and receive an answer."

"Is everything in order now?" Abigail asked.

"I'm afraid not. I need to return to Philadelphia soon."

"Have a good trip," Eliza said.

A muscle pulsed in Baxter's cheek. "Considering there's an outlaw at large, I insist Abigail accompany me."

"Whatever makes you think she would do that?" Eliza asked, and for a change, Abigail didn't appear so eager to please.

Baxter smiled, but the gesture looked pained to Josie's way of thinking. "Because she realizes that I am the better judge of seeing to her needs, now and always."

His reasoning was lost on Josie, but judging by Gil's scowl, he knew what Baxter was up to.

"What drivel," Ivy said. "Abigail's reputation would be in tatters should she travel back to Philadelphia with you."

"Evidently I didn't make myself clear." Baxter took Abigail's hand in both of his. "My dear, I realize you have made elaborate plans for our wedding, but I propose we have a civil ceremony in Maverick and proceed home as husband and wife."

Abigail blinked. "I don't know."

"Come now. It's the perfect solution and, if you wish, we can go through with a formal ceremony in Philadelphia."

Oh, he was a smooth operator all right. Josie couldn't hold her tongue any longer. "I fail to see the need for a rush wedding, especially since Abigail has gone to great pains planning the ceremony."

"My thoughts exactly," Ivy said. "Harrison would resent being excluded from the wedding, civil or not. I doubt you wish to suffer ramifications from your future father-in-law."

"Quite the opposite." Baxter released Abigail's hand.

Abigail smiled, though not as brightly. "All is forgiven, Baxter. I understand if you need to leave immediately."

"Very well," Baxter said. "If you all will excuse us, I would like to escort Abigail to her cabin and have a few moments alone with her in private."

"Actually, I am ready to seek my bed as well," Ivy said.

Baxter's jaw tensed. "Abigail and I will await you on the front porch."

"Good night all." Abigail wrapped her cloak around her and let Baxter hurry her outside.

Gil snorted. "The more I'm around that man, the more he reminds me of a wolf packing a sheepskin coat."

"You are more cynical than Harrison," Ivy said.

"I learned not to believe every sob story I hear," Gil said.

Eliza jumped to her feet, clearly nervous. "It's past time for me to turn in. Supper was sumptuous, Josie."

"My pleasure," Josie said.

"Yes, thank you for a wonderful meal." Ivy slipped her wrap around her and followed Eliza to the door, then paused and looked at Gil. "Why can't you put the past behind you?"

Ivy closed the door behind her. Gil frowned, his lips pressed into a disagreeable line.

Josie stared at Gil. "What did Ivy mean by that?"

"Hell if I know." He pushed to his feet and crossed to the door. "Lock up after me."

Josie turned the key and watched Gil disappear into the darkness. What in the world had caused the animosity between Gil and his stepmother?

Chapter 15

After filling her sixth bucket with hot water, Josie realized that catering to city women was a pain in the back. And the behind. Namely hers.

To think she'd planned to do laundry today. Ivy had surely changed that idea after lunch.

"I would like to indulge in a bath," Ivy had said the moment they were alone.

Josie had anticipated such when she'd set up her guest ranch. "Help yourself. There's a bathing room at the top of the stairs. I'll heat water, and you can pull it up on the dumbwaiter."

"Oh, no. I prefer bathing in my cabin. Surely that can be arranged?"

"Only if you can soak in a tin tub."

The high-flown woman had smiled, though it looked about as thin as Josie's patience. "I can make do with that."

That was thirty minutes ago. Thirty long minutes.

Josie swiped the sweat off her brow as Hiram plodded in the back door with two empty buckets. "Please tell me it's filled to her liking."

Hiram grunted. "Miz Ivy says she needs one more pail of hot water."

"Thank God." She poured a kettle of steaming water in a pail. "Is Mrs. Cooper demanding or am I being critical?"

"The lady has a problem getting on with folks."

"How so?"

Hiram lifted the filled bucket. "Acts like she don't get out much."

The woman had spent most of her time locked in her cabin. So much for basking in the wonders of the West.

"She seems to be close to Abigail."

"Yes, ma'am. They're together now, fussing over the tub I hauled in." Hiram headed for the door. "Once I take this bucket to her, I'm heading over to the south quarter to tend the fence. Won't be back till late."

"Take your time. I'll keep a plate warm for you."

Hiram hesitated in the doorway. "If there's any left, I'd be obliged for a slice of that apple pie."

She smiled, certain Hiram was blushing. He always did when he hedged for something sweet.

"I'll make sure to keep you a big slice."

His mile-wide smile was thanks enough.

Josie went into the parlor for her sewing, hoping she could put the finishing touches to Sarah Ann's split skirt today. It was the first time since her guests arrived that she had time to herself.

Gil, Eliza and Sarah Ann had gone off riding this afternoon, supposedly over on his land again. Abigail declined, saying she'd like to rest before they all left for the camping outing tomorrow, but she was clearly helping Ivy. Landon had ridden into Maverick this morning to send another telegram and arrange for passage on the stage.

The afternoon passed in blessed quiet, broken occasionally by Dwight's hammering down behind the barn. The broken spokes on the wagon wheel were probably Boyd Rowney's doing.

Josie held up the split skirt and examined her work. The stitches were tight, even and should hold despite the roughness Sarah Ann would give the garment.

She checked the clock, stretched and headed into the kitchen. Best get supper on. Any time now she expected Gil, Eliza and Sarah Ann to return.

Josie jostled her big skillet on the cast iron grate. An odd sound drifted on the wind before the iron clanked on iron. Was that a scream she heard? Had Dwight hollered for her?

She froze, listening.

Not one sound reached her. She shook her head and checked her pantry. Dang it all. She thought she'd brought up enough carrots yesterday, but the bin was empty.

Josie slipped out the back door and headed to the springhouse. Halfway there she heard it again. Stronger this time. Recognizable.

A woman had screamed, and it came from the cabins.

Josie ran into the house to fetch Everett's sidearm. She checked to make sure it was loaded, then picked up her hem and ran out the front door.

Deuce's ears pricked, proof he'd heard the sound. He loped after her, for once not barking or growling.

An eerie silence vibrated in the air. She rushed to Abby and Eliza's cabin and opened the door. Not a soul inside.

The fear Boyd Rowney had struck again hit her as she hurried toward Ivy's cabin. She thumbed back the Colt's hammer and went inside, afraid what she'd find.

Ivy slept soundly in the bed. Alone.

Abigail. Where the dickens was she?

A faint whimper carried on the wind, and this time Josie knew it came from the last cabin. She whirled and ran, dread clutching her insides.

Josie barged inside and aimed the revolver at the man kneeling over a tangle of skirt and petticoats on the bed. "Touch her and I'll blow your balls off."

The man scrambled to his feet, fumbling to button up his trousers. He turned, and Josie stared into Landon Baxter's angry face.

"It's not what you think," he said. "But even if it were, we are engaged to be married."

"If it's not what I think, then why is Abigail in tears?"

"She is the high-strung sort."

Of all the worthless excuses—

Abigail batted her skirts down and scooted off the bed. The bruise on her cheek said it all, as did the way her lower lip quivered.

"You hit her," Josie said.

"It was an accident." Baxter moved to grab Abigail, but she sidestepped out of his reach.

"Don't doubt that I'll pull this trigger, Mr. Baxter."

He stopped dead in his tracks. "This is none of your affair, Mrs. Andrews."

"This is my ranch and Abigail is my guest. I don't hold with any man abusing an animal, woman or child." She spared Abigail a quick peek. "Go on up to the house. He won't hurt you there."

"Don't listen to her, Abigail," Baxter said.

For a moment, Josie feared Abigail would bend to his will. Like her sister had done to Parnell too many times to count.

"Eliza was right about you all along." Abigail held her torn bodice together and ran to the door.

"This is all a misunderstanding," Baxter said, and to Josie's annoyance Abigail paused in the doorway. "I care deeply for you. You know that."

"No." Abigail's voice was so faint Josie had to strain to hear it. "If that were true, you would have stopped when I asked you to. When I begged."

With that, Abigail ducked outside.

"Dwight, come quick!" Josie backed up to the door, keeping the sidearm trained on Baxter. "You, get off my ranch."

"Damn you." Baxter stormed toward her, as if daring her to shoot.

Josie's arm shook, and she knew she couldn't shoot this man. Damnation, where was Dwight? She aimed at the ceiling and squeezed the trigger, hoping the sound would bring him running.

The old Colt boomed. Baxter yelped and staggered back as splinters rained down from the ceiling.

"What the hell is going on here?" Gil asked, stepping behind Josie and easing her to the side.

"A misunderstanding," Baxter said.

Gil held his six-shooter on Baxter, and Josie didn't doubt he'd be able to kill the bastard. Dwight came running, rifle in hand.

"He tried to force himself on Abigail," Josie said.

For a minute Josie thought Gil would pull the trigger.

"I did not ravish your sister," Baxter said.

Gil spared Dwight a look. "Get some rope."

"I'll be right back." Dwight ran to the barn.

"Wait! You can't hang me," Baxter said.

Gil snorted. "The hell I can't. Don't doubt it. But since I don't want to bring trouble on my sisters or Josie, I'll hand your sorry ass over to the sheriff. What he does with you is his business."

After Abby told him what really happened, Gil wished he'd shot the son of a bitch. In fact if Abby hadn't assured him that Josie had stopped Baxter from raping her, he'd have ridden to the Maverick jail tonight and filled the no-account with lead.

As it was, his little sister admitted she was sad she'd misjudged Baxter so, but insisted this one attack wouldn't haunt her. Gil found that hard to believe.

Even Josie seemed unusually quiet and withdrawn tonight, proof her run-in with Baxter had upset her. Sarah took it all in with big, owlish eyes. As for Ivy—

He rubbed the bridge of his nose. His stepmother had eaten like a wren and enlisted Hiram to walk her to her cabin soon after. Though she'd been a bystander, seeing Baxter's dark side had shaken her up pretty badly.

"Thank you for the loan of the revolver." Eliza held Everett's Navy Colt like it was a wiggly lizard.

Josie smiled. "It's the least I can do. I feel responsible for harm befalling a guest."

"Wasn't your fault." Gil frowned at his older sister. "You sure you know how to use a gun?"

"My husband taught me."

Gil had his doubts, but despite his objections, Josie had given Eliza the revolver. "Make sure you point that barrel at the wall for the night."

"I will. Now if you'll excuse us, Abigail and I will find our beds. It's been an exhausting day."

"I'll walk to your cabin," Gil said.

Once there, Abby kissed him on the cheek. "Thank you, big brother. I always knew I could count on you."

One episode didn't near make up for the years she'd needed him and he was long gone. "Sleep tight."

Eliza looked at him, her expression troubled. "You scared me today. There was an anger in you I'd never seen before."

"I had call to be mad."

"True, but today I realized that you're not the same boy who left home. You've lived a hard life and grown into a man who knows how to fend for himself. God knows what you've seen."

More than he wanted his family to ever know. "Sometimes a man's got to be harder than a whetstone to survive."

"I imagine so. Josie is lucky to have you."

He wasn't sure Josie would agree. "You need anything, you aim that gun at the ceiling and squeeze one off. I'll come running."

Eliza nodded. "Good night, Gilbert."

"'Night."

Gil started toward his cabin, then noticed the lights on in the house. He swiped a hand over his mouth.

Josie probably couldn't sleep, or wouldn't close her eyes all night. Hell, he'd probably sleep with one eye open himself.

He walked around the house to the back, checking the windows as he went. A good thing Everett installed those new locks on all of them, though if a man wanted in, all he had to do was break the glass.

But that would cause a commotion and result in

the would-be thief looking down the barking end of Gil's Winchester. He stopped at the back porch and stuck his head inside the doorway.

"What are you doing?" Josie asked.

"Just checking the house."

"Oh." She stood in the open doorway, and the dim light behind her outlined her curves. "I have coffee left if you want some."

"Don't mind if I do."

He came inside the kitchen and took the chair nearest hers. Though the oven had cooled, the faint scent of cinnamon and vanilla hung in the air. He licked his lips, remembering the same taste had clung to Josie.

"There's one slice of pie. You want it?"

"Josie, there's one thing you never have to ask me and that's if I want a second helping of your cooking."

She laughed softly. "That's kind of you to say."

"It's the truth. You're a fine cook."

Gil caught her blush before she turned her back to him and dished up the pie. Her rounded hips swayed slightly as she moved, and his insides tightened.

He shouldn't be thinking about how much he enjoyed kissing her. Or hungered for that sweet taste that was all Josie. Or how much he just liked talking to her.

The dominos lay on the table where Sarah Ann had left them. He turned them face down and absently mixed up the boneyard to take his mind off sex.

She set the pie and coffee beside him.

"Have you practiced with that whip again?" He dug into the pie, savoring the cinnamon-laced apples.

"No. I need to be alone, and that hasn't been possible of late." She curled her small hands around her cup. "What about you?"

"I'm going to ride that outlaw."

"Are you crazy? That damn horse nearly killed you."

He shrugged. "That wouldn't have happened if I hadn't been distracted."

"Uh-huh. What caught your attention, Gil Yancy?"

Gil frowned, thinking back. The sun had glinted off something up on the ridge. Someone had been up there, watching. The outlaw? Or Boyd Rowney?

"Just what I thought," Josie said. "You didn't get sidetracked. That horse bested you."

His gaze flicked to her face. Mischief sparked in her eyes, and a smile played over her sweet lips. Was she flirting with him?

His pecker swelled at the thought. *Rein it in, Yancy.* She might be playing him for a fool again.

He swallowed the last of his pie. "Doesn't matter now. And don't try sweet-talking me out of riding that grulla because nothing you say or do will change my mind."

She shifted the dominos on the table, the scraping sound soft compared to his heavy breathing. "The first time I met you I thought you were a gambling man."

"I've been known to bet on a hand or two."

Big wagers, big losses. It was a habit he'd finally broken after the last time he'd had to start over from scratch. Once the gambling fever took over, he wouldn't stop until he was down to nothing.

"I propose we have a game of dominos," she said. "If I win, you won't ride that outlaw."

He frowned at her over the rim of his coffee cup, debating. Surely a friendly wager between them wouldn't set him off.

"If I was fool enough to get roped into a game, what would I win when you lose?"

Her smile drew him like a bee to a lupine. "I could bake you a pie."

He leaned back in his chair and laughed. "Nice try, Josie. The stakes would have to be higher than that. Let's say if I win, you have to put on a show with your whip."

"Nobody is going to want to watch me snapping bottles off a rock with my whip, and without practice, that's about all I can do."

"Then practice. Folks would sure come see fancy tricks done with a partner."

Her hands stilled on the dominos, and though the light was dim, he'd swear her face bleached of color. "Are you crazy?"

"Nope. I'll volunteer to be the prop for you. I saw a man plug a cigar from another man's mouth once."

She shivered. "That's a dangerous stunt. One miscue and I could scar you for life."

Damn, the last thing he wanted to do was chase the play out of her. "Okay, we won't try that one. Has to be some mighty fancy tricks you can do with that whip. What do you say?"

Her mouth thinned, and for a moment he was sure she wouldn't go for it. "Mix 'em up and draw seven."

He did, and after two plays he realized not only was Josie lucky, he'd misjudged her ability. Forget about cutting this little lady any slack.

She placed a double four on the board and smiled. Either she knew how to bluff, or she was holding back on him.

Gil looked at his tiles and swore, not having one he could play. He'd have to draw from the boneyard, and there were only three tiles left.

"If I can make twenty points on this next play, you owe me a boon."

"I'm afraid to ask what you have in mind."

"I was thinking of something real simple and sweet."

"You already ate the last of the pie."

"I wasn't taking about food." He smiled, and wanted to whoop when she grinned. "How about a kiss?"

She licked her lips, her smile widening. "All right. I'll kiss you if you win. What happens if you lose?"

"Then neither of us gets a kiss."

Josie looked at the tiles lined up on the table. He could almost see the wheels chugging away in her noggin and hear her figuring out the odds.

He'd have to draw a double six in order to come up with that many points, and if she had that one remaining double six, he was shit out of luck. But he had a gut feeling Lady Luck was riding with him this game.

She flicked another quick glance at his mouth, then bit her bottom lip. It wouldn't take much for him to go soft in the head over his sweet little thief.

Gil turned up his last tile. *Come on, baby. Be the one.*

A slow smile spread across his face as he laid the boxcar on the lone six.

"Pucker up, sweetheart."

Chapter 16

Josie wet her lips and stared at his mouth, certain her heart and stomach were playing hopscotch. Mercy, the anticipation.

She'd taken him up on his bet, knowing full well he probably either had that double six or would draw it. She ached to kiss him again. Ached to believe she had a chance at winning his heart.

"I never met a man who liked fooling around like you do," she said.

"You complaining?"

"No."

One side of his mouth kicked up in a grin, and she almost believed that story he'd cooked up about them was true. Heaven knew if he'd charmed her so when she was a sweet young thing, she'd have fallen into this cowboy's arms. And in love.

So this giddy feeling filled with sunshine was what Everett had wished for her. Wished for? No, her husband had sold his shares to Gil Yancy. Oh, both men claimed they were old friends, but could Everett have known Gil was Sarah Ann's pa?

No, that was too far-fetched. But she couldn't believe

it was a coincidence that Everett had brought Josie's first and only lover to Rocky Point Ranch. With Everett gone, there was no way of knowing his reasons.

Her ponderings popped like a soap bubble at Gil's soft chuckle. "Hell, Josie, if the thought of kissing me is troubling you so, forget about it. It's just a game."

"I'm not upset."

"Then why do you look like you'd just as soon paint the house with a feather than pay up?"

"I don't want Sarah Ann seeing us"—she fanned her hand, as if trying to get the word to materialize out of thin air—"being friendly."

"You're blushing."

Knowing she was had her face heating up even more. Mercy, she'd seen and done a lot in her life, but she'd never flirted with a man or had one josh with her. Never thought doing so would make her feel so good. So alive. So wanted.

"You want that kiss or not?"

"I want it, but we'll do it your way." He got up, tugged her to her feet and led her out on the back porch.

She laughed, unable to help herself. Then his mouth found hers, cutting off her words. Not that she had a thing to say.

The dark swirled around them like a velvet blanket, then his strong arms banded around her and pulled her close to his heart. Like before, one of his hands traveled south to rest on her bottom.

An old sense of dread hid in the shadow of her memory, but she kept telling herself that Gil wasn't like Parnell. That Gil wouldn't hurt her.

That's all it took to bust the dam on a river of warmth that flooded the past, leaving her awash in a wanting so keen she nearly begged him to touch her. And then his tongue did that same flicking in and out of her mouth, teasing her to follow suit, making her wonder how she'd lived so long without this cowboy in her life.

She wrapped her arms around his neck, leaned against him and kissed him for all she was worth. Putting everything she had into it.

Vaguely she heard a coyote howl. Then another.

Gil tensed a heartbeat before he pulled away from her. A rifle cracked in the night, and the bunching of his muscles broke the languid spell he'd woven around her.

"You reckon Dwight is hunting coyotes?"

"Could be. They're breeding." His warm breath feathered over her face. "I know how they feel, all tied up in knots when they catch the scent of female. She teases and they follow. Like you're doing to me."

She increased the distance between them, glad the darkness hid her face, which felt white-hot. "Is that a bad thing?"

"Hell, no. But sometimes I get the feeling you don't know how to pleasure a man, and we both know that ain't true." He trailed a finger down her burning face. "'Night, sweetheart."

And then he was gone and she bit her tongue to keep from calling him back and telling him the truth. But she couldn't tell him everything.

What Parnell had forced on Josie shamed her to her soul. She'd never even told Everett. Nope, this was one secret best left buried.

All the time Josie had lived on Rocky Point, she'd never had to ring a bell to call the hands to breakfast. Most mornings they tromped onto her back porch at dawn.

Not so for her guests. Ivy and Abigail didn't rise

until way past nine o'clock and didn't make it to the house until close to ten, which took a big chunk out of Josie's day.

This morning, Abigail made a surprise appearance. Josie had a feeling Gil's sister was afraid to be alone now. How she understood. It'd taken Josie years to be able to sleep through the night without fearing Parnell would visit her. Knowing he could be out there now robbed her of sleep again.

"Are we going to practice this afternoon?" Sarah Ann asked Gil.

His gaze locked on Josie's, and something warm and welcoming unfolded in her. "If it's all right with your mama."

"You know I don't mind." Josie focused on breakfast, but all she could think of was lying in Gil's arms, loving him and being loved in return. Such fanciful dreams.

"What are you practicing?" Abigail asked.

"I can't tell," Sarah Ann said. "It's a secret for our exhibition."

"Aha! When is this exhibition?" Eliza asked.

"This weekend," Gil said. "I want to get the word out so we can draw a good crowd."

Abigail's green eyes glittered with the same excitement as Sarah Ann's. "This sounds thrilling."

"It will be." Gil shoveled in the last of his flapjacks and turned to Dwight. "Did you bag any coyotes last night?"

"Wasn't me doing the shooting."

Josie stilled, glancing from Dwight's worried face to Gil's tense one. Was Rowney trying to spook the herd into stampeding? Or had Parnell decided to stir up trouble, a reminder that his threat was real?

Eliza set her cup down with a clatter. "Do you suppose this outlaw was bent on mischief last night?"

"Wouldn't be surprised," Gil said.

"Horses are all accounted for," Hiram told Gil. "If you're fixing to stay around this morning, I'll head out after breakfast and see what all the hullabaloo was about."

"Good idea," Gil said. "I aimed to help Josie practice her part in show this morning."

"Not a moment too soon." With trouble lurking, Josie had to be dead on target with that bullwhip.

"What are you going to do, Mama?" Sarah Ann asked.

"Let me guess," Eliza said, and Josie held her breath and wondered if her guest had seen her. "It's a surprise."

"That's right." Josie caught Gil's eye and fought a blush when he winked.

Dwight finished off his coffee, sliding a nervous look Abigail's way before pushing to his feet. "Come on, Sarah. Time I saw you to school."

Sarah Ann drank the last of her milk and hurried from the room. At least she was wearing the new split skirt Josie had made. And to think she hadn't had to fight her about it.

"You fixing to ride along, Miz Abigail?" Dwight asked.

"I'd love to." Abigail dabbed her mouth and rose.

Gil scrubbed his knuckles along his jaw, watching the threesome leave. "I'd have bet good money that Abby wouldn't have asked to go riding."

"She slept fitfully, no doubt reliving that ordeal with Landon." Eliza shook her head. "I didn't expect her to rise before noon, let alone want to leave the ranch."

"It takes time to get over something like that," Josie said before thinking. "So I've heard."

"Of course, you're right." Eliza sipped her coffee.

"Look how the morning is flying by. When and where are you going to practice your trick for the exhibition?"

"Now would be good," Gil said. "You have a place in mind, Josie?"

"Behind the cook shack is best." The wind didn't gust much there, yet Gil would have a fair view of the ranch. "Soon as I fix breakfast for Ivy and clean up the kitchen, we'll start."

"I'll cook her breakfast then set the kitchen to rights," Eliza said. "You and Gilbert go on and do what you'd planned."

"I can't let you do that," Josie said.

Gil stood. "Why not?"

"Because Eliza is a guest."

"Oh, pshaw." Eliza flicked a teasing look at Gil, then patted Josie's hand. "Ivy will likely sleep till noon, and I've nothing to do but twiddle my thumbs anyway. So you and Gilbert go on."

Gil pushed to his feet. "If you're staying in the house, lock the back door. You hear anything, you step out the front and fire that Navy Colt."

"Stop fretting," Eliza said, shooing them out the door.

"I need to get my whip and change into something more suitable for practice," Josie said at the foot of the stairs.

Gil fished his Bull Durham pouch from his pocket. "I'll wait for you on the porch."

A good twenty minutes later, Josie peeked out the front door. Gil leaned against a porch post, looking so at home and handsome her breath caught.

She stepped outside, hoping she didn't look as jittery as she felt. He turned, grinding his cigarette under his boot as his gaze inched over her, pausing at the hand holding the bag, then meandering down her new split skirt. His slow grin eased her tension and coaxed a smile from her.

It felt a mite odd to be free of petticoats and skirt. Oh, she'd worn britches a time or two on the ranch, but she'd found them too confining.

"That's like Sarah's get-up," he said.

"I made us both one."

"Yours fits you right fine, but then you've got more curves than Sarah."

Josie prayed she wouldn't blush again. That was beyond ridiculous. "Are we going to practice or are you going to stand here and talk about my clothes?"

His devilish grin was back. "Let's see what you can do with that bullwhip, sweetheart."

How was she going to concentrate with him looking at her like he wanted to kiss her from head to toe while his fingers had their wicked way with her? Thinking how incredible that felt, and how much she wanted his touch again, had her throbbing deep inside.

Josie took off toward the outbuildings, thwacking the bag against her thigh. She'd found nothing pleasurable in what went on between a man and woman in bed until Gil Yancy barged back into her life. Her dreams of them entwined had been poor imitations of the fire he'd ignited in her with just a look. She'd burned from his kisses and caresses.

Why, she'd go up in flames when he finally took her after all this time. And she admitted it was just a matter of time before she gave herself fully to him again.

She strode past the last cabin, mindful of Gil keeping pace beside her. But where she was going at a good clip, he went at an ambling pace. No surprise there.

His legs went on forever. She remembered the power in them as he'd stretched out atop her, and the little quakes and quivers that went through her, like she'd been struck by lightning.

He jerked a thumb toward the cabin. "You blew a hole in the roof."

That reminder of her set-to with Baxter made her more determined to get back her edge. Confronting him had been too similar to her last standoff with Parnell, but instead of following through on her threat to shoot, she'd froze.

Had Baxter been Parnell, he'd have gotten the upper hand before she could run for help. She couldn't let that happen.

"Aim to get it fixed this afternoon," Gil said. "Reckon you won't mind if I move back into it."

"Go right ahead."

Josie would rather Gil lived in the house, but she'd never flaunt a lover in front of Sarah Ann. As far as she knew, that's all they'd be. Partners in the ranch, and in bed.

They passed the long, squat bunkhouse to the quiet spot behind the cook shack. The wind wouldn't hinder her aim here, and she didn't have to fret over prying eyes. Well, just one devilish pair that she'd caught staring at her far too much.

Josie dropped her carpetbag at her feet, anxious to get at it. She took out her whip and held the coil in one hand. Holding it filled her with equal measures of comfort and dread.

"What tricks do you have in mind?" he asked.

"Something new."

Last night, sleep bedeviled her with dreams of Gil Yancy, so until the wee hours, Josie tried to come up with a routine that would please a crowd. Something daring.

Gil poked around in her carpetbag. "Are these red balloons?"

"Uh-huh." She dug in her bag for the small foot pump.

He whistled. "There must be a couple dozen of 'em."

"A little more than three dozen."

"Where'd you come by then?"

"Everett ordered three bags out of the Montgomery Ward catalogue for Sarah Ann, but she wasn't the least bit interested in them. That was forty cents a dozen shot to hell."

"What do you aim to do with them?"

"Blow them up, then tie the balloons on the fence to use as targets."

"You're going to be blue in the face when you get these inflated."

For a smart man, he could sure be dense about some things. She handed him the foot pump.

"Use this. It's for inflating bicycle tires."

"You have one of those, too?"

"No, but the catalogue said it was the fastest way to blow up balloons. You know how to do that?"

"Nope, but I'll figure it out."

Brow furrowed, he skinned the pump tip into a balloon and started pumping. She smiled. At first he went at it like he was stomping spiders, then he eased up and fell into a slow rhythm.

Men. Josie went about gauging the distance from the fence as well as at different angles.

"How the hell big do you want these to be?"

She gave the apple-sized balloon a passing glance and watched his behind tighten with each pump. That cowboy did have a fine body.

He stopped pumping, and she knew before he

said a word that he'd caught her staring at him this time. "Well?"

"I suppose dinner-plate size would be easiest to see."

"Easiest to hit, too."

She grimaced. It was the truth. The smaller the object, the harder the trick.

"Make them a bit bigger than an apple, then."

After being away from it for so long, she couldn't expect to hit the marks right off. Hopefully she wouldn't waste too many balloons before she got the feel for it again.

As soon as Gil inflated one balloon, Josie put a knot in its end then used twine to fasten it to the fence. When she had half a dozen in place, forming a triangle, she picked up her bullwhip and found her mark.

The red balloons bobbed in the breeze, but that made the target all the more challenging. That was part of the excitement, for her and those watching. As she'd learned long ago, if there was no challenge, folks wouldn't be impressed. If folks were bored, they wouldn't come back for another show.

"Stand far left of the targets and see if you can keep an eye on the tip of my whip," Josie said.

"Yes'm." Gil walked to the fence and stood far enough back so she didn't have to fret about hitting him.

Josie shook her whip out behind her, making sure it wasn't tangled. Her fingers flexed on the silver handle and her hand shifted until the smooth leather knot butted her heel.

When the grip felt right, she swung her arm up and over her shoulder until her elbow was pointing at her targets. The slight drag of the whip uncoiling behind her tugged on her arm.

Before the tip could snap the ground, she took a step forward and swung the whip straight toward the target. She caught a hazy image of a loop as the whip sliced the air.

The tip popped loudly before recoiling. Dang it all, she missed the balloon.

She swung her arm back but instead of making another throw, she let the tip drop to the ground. "How far off am I?"

"It went so damn fast I barely saw it, but I'd say you're a foot short of the target."

Josie took a step forward, shook both arms to ease her tension and tried again. This time right after the first loud pop, the tip cut into the balloon. It exploded in another pop and red bits of rubber flew everywhere.

Her body hummed with excitement as she brought the whip back to coil at her feet

"That's it," Gil said, smiling.

She blocked him from her thoughts and swung the whip forward, concentrating on the balloons, letting the whip be an extension of her arm. One loud pop after another, she reduced the balloons to bits of red rubber.

Josie swung the whip behind her and let it drop. Her breath came fast and her heart raced. It'd been so long since she'd used the whip and enjoyed it.

"Your aim is remarkable." Gil strode toward her, his eyes glowing with excitement. "Why don't I hold a cigarette in my mouth and—"

"No! That's too dangerous." She wouldn't risk scarring Gil's face for any show.

He stopped a good eight feet in front of her and fished his Bull Durham bag from his vest pocket. Her mouth went dry as he tapped tobacco on a paper and rolled it up tight, wetting the edges to seal it.

"We had a bet and you lost." He stuck the cigarette in his mouth and lit it, then walked to the fence and turned sideways. "Best hurry before it burns down. I'm a bit partial to my nose."

So was she, and the thought of marking him like she'd done Parnell terrified her. Josie flicked her wrist and the whip snaked out behind her in a straight line. She'd done this trick hundreds of times without missing.

"What the hell are you waiting for?"

Courage, and it sure wasn't coming. Not today.

Instead of throwing it overhead, she swung the whip in a sideways move. The thong uncoiled and reached toward Gil. A loud pop split the air before the whip wrapped around his lean waist, trapping his arms to his sides.

His cigarette tumbled from his mouth and his eyes bugged. "Damn, woman, you lassoed me."

Josie couldn't help it. She burst out laughing.

"Yep, looks like I roped myself a cowpoke."

"Whatcha gonna do with me, sweetheart?"

She tugged the whip to unbalance him. "What do you think I'll do?"

"Reckon we have the makings here for a real show-stopper."

Gil grabbed the thong and dug in his heels, keeping the line as taut as her nerves. The heat in his eyes had her flushed inside and out.

Then he smiled, and her heart did that funny thud again. Hand over hand he pulled her to him.

Josie held on, rising to the challenge, but he was too strong to best, or resist. "I'm the one who's supposed to be dragging you toward me."

He gave the thong one last jerk and she slammed against him. "We'll do it your way next time, sweetheart."

Before she could think up a rejoinder, his lips

found hers. He enveloped her with heat, and his kisses filled her with warm promises she longed to believe could be hers.

She opened to him, welcoming him with a hunger she'd denied too long. Mercy, she could stand here forever kissing this man.

A scream cut through their sensual haze. Gil and Josie jumped apart, her heart pounding.

"Must be Ivy." He tensed and scanned the area.

"I see her. She's behind the outhouse." Why, Josie could only guess. Had Ivy heard the pop of the whip and come to look, even though they'd warned her time and again to not go off alone?

"I hope she didn't run up on a rattler," she said.

Gil drew his revolver. "Damn."

They took off at a run, but Gil outdistanced Josie in no time.

"What's wrong?" he asked Ivy.

The woman shivered and pointed down the hill.

Josie looked that way and grimaced. "There's a man down there." Sprawled on the rocks below with a dark red hole in his forehead and his lifeless eyes staring upward.

Ivy pressed close to Gil and laid her head on his chest. "He's dead, isn't he?"

"I'd say." He frowned, tugging Ivy closer, like he'd done Josie. "You recognize him?"

"Boyd Rowney," Josie said.

She turned from the dead man and faced Gil. His arms were tight around Ivy, and his stepmother clung to him, her face pressed against his neck.

Josie buried her fists in her side pockets, resisting the urge to march over to the couple and pull them apart. What was wrong with her? He was comforting his terrified stepmother. His young, beautiful stepmother.

The clomp of hooves drew her attention away from Ivy clinging to Gil, but the sting of jealousy remained. "That's Sheriff Keegan. I best go see what brings him out here and tell him about Rowney."

"I'll join you directly."

Josie took off toward the house, telling herself she had no right to be jealous of Gil. Yet for some reason the way he tucked Ivy close stirred something ugly inside Josie.

The slam of a cabin door tempted her to look back, to see if Gil had escorted Ivy inside. Then the chink-chink of spurs echoed in the stillness.

Josie slowed and glanced back. Gil was coming toward her at a good clip, his features shadowed by his hat. She picked up her pace and reached Virgil a heartbeat before Gil.

"I'm mighty glad you dropped by," she said, suppressing a shiver as Gil stopped behind her, enclosing her in his long shadow.

The sheriff stared from her to Gil, his expression bordering on annoyed. "Doubt you'll feel the same when you hear what I got to say. The circuit judge heard Landon Baxter's case this morning and let him off with a fine."

Chapter 17

"I'll plug that son of a bitch if I catch him nosing around my sister again," Gil said.

"Don't think you have to worry about that dandy showing his face." Virgil folded his hands atop the saddle horn. "Soon as the judge cut him loose, Baxter boarded the stage headed east."

Or had he fooled them? Josie stole a glance at the corral, and her stomach took a tumble. Dwight's horse and another one were missing. Mercy, he and Abigail should've been back by now.

"Good riddance to him," Gil said. "Found a man back in the draw, dead. Josie said he's Boyd Rowney."

"Any idea what happened to him?" Virgil asked.

"Yep, appears he took one shot between his eyes." *But who killed him? Parnell?*

"Wonder if this Rowney came up on that outlaw you told Josie about?" Gil asked.

Virgil frowned. "What outlaw?"

"Josie?" Gil stared at her.

Dang! No way out of this except to tell the truth.

"I got a letter this week from Ross Parnell," she

said. "He said by the time I got it, he'd be here watching me."

"Why didn't you tell me?" Virgil asked.

Gil snorted. "Just what I'd like to know."

She took the easy one first and faced Virgil. "I didn't tell you because there wasn't anything you could do about it."

"Still and all, I'm the sheriff and should know if trouble is heading my way."

"I didn't think of it like that." In fact, she'd been near paralyzed with fear after she'd gotten that letter. "I told my men, and we've been keeping watch and making sure my guests and Sarah Ann are never left alone."

"'Bout all you can do. Believe I'll take a look at your dead man." Virgil heeled his horse and rode off toward the draw.

"You told Hiram and Dwight to be on the lookout for Parnell?" Gil asked.

She nodded.

"Why didn't you tell me the truth?"

"What difference would it make?"

"Plenty. An outlaw would likely be hunting easy pickings," Gil said. "Why would Parnell come looking for you after all this time?"

"It's a long story."

"Then you'd best get at it."

"Later when we're alone." She turned at the sound of hooves, and breathed easier seeing Dwight and Abigail ride up. "I'll see your sister and Ivy to the house while you and Dwight get Rowney loaded onto the buckboard."

"What's the sheriff doing?" Dwight asked.

"Ivy found a man behind the outhouse," Gil said. "He's been shot dead."

Abigail gasped. "Oh, my. Poor Ivy. Where is she?"

"Her cabin," Josie said. "I think we'd best take her to the house while the men tend to Rowney."

"I agree." Abigail started toward the cabin, but Gil stopped her.

"Abby, the sheriff rode out this morning to warn us that Baxter left on the stage."

Gil's sister sucked in a shaky breath. "Is he sure Landon is gone?"

"Looks that way, but I don't want you taking any chances." Gil cut Josie a hard look. "Baxter isn't the only no-account waiting for a chance to get a woman alone."

"Believe me, I won't leave the ranch without Dwight, or you, of course." Abigail hurried toward Ivy's cabin.

Dwight's Adam's apple bounced like one of the balloons Gil had inflated. And his face— Why, he almost looked windburned. What got him all flushed?

She followed the direction of Dwight's gaze. Abigail? Oh, dear, what had they done on that long ride this morning?

"Best get the buckboard hitched," Gil told Dwight.

"Getting on it now." Dwight led the two horses in the barn, leaving Josie alone with Gil.

"I want you to get the women in the house and keep them there," Gil said. "Dwight will stay with you until I get back."

She hugged her waist. "I'm worried about Sarah Ann."

"The Chalmers' won't let her leave alone," Gil said. "I'll ride by there on my way back from town and bring her home with me. You going to be all right?"

She nodded, but didn't feel one bit of confidence. "I need to fetch my whip."

"I'll get it. Go on and herd the women to the house."

Josie looked into his eyes once more, feeling his anger and worry to her soul. "Be careful, Gil."

He dipped his chin in answer.

She started toward Ivy's cabin.

"Josie."

She stopped and looked back at Gil.

"I'm holding you to that talk tonight."

"I expected you would."

Josie hurried to Ivy's cabin, wishing she wouldn't have put off telling Gil what had happened after she'd left his room that night. But as she knew full well, she couldn't alter the past.

Before Josie got to Ivy's door, Abigail opened it. "How's Ivy?"

"Her nerves are terribly unsettled. She's about to take a draught to calm herself."

"Tell her wait until we get to the house," Josie said, stepping inside the cabin.

Ivy huddled on the bed, looking more bleached than the bedsheets. "I prefer staying here."

"I know that," Josie said, "but it'll be easier for Dwight to keep watch if we're all together."

Abigail bobbed her head. "As you always say, Ivy, let's not dawdle."

Ivy clutched a shawl around her narrow shoulders and shivered. "Very well, but I must admit I will be glad to return to civilization."

The three women started toward the house, and Josie damned every odd sound that made her flinch. Dwight stood in the front yard, his rifle cradled in his arm. Eliza paced the porch, but came down the steps as they drew near.

"Dwight told me what happened," Eliza said.

"Good heavens, Ivy. Are you all right? Can I get you anything?"

Ivy plodded up the steps like a woman twice her age. "If Josie would allow me use of one her beds, I would like to take a draught and lie down."

"Of course." Josie held the door open for the guest she was torn between helping and resenting. "Help yourself to Everett's room at the top of the stairs."

"I'll see her up." Abigail ushered Ivy inside.

"What does Gilbert intend to do?" Eliza asked.

Josie craned her neck, catching a peek of Gil behind the cook shack. "I'm not sure, but he insisted on driving Boyd Rowney's body into town."

"If Gilbert doesn't object, I would like to accompany him." Eliza tapped her fingers on a porch post, watching as the buckboard drew near the house. "I imagine Landon will appeal to Father, so he needs to be aware Landon attacked Abigail."

"Of course." Josie leaned over the porch rail. "Dwight, tell Gil to stop here before he heads out."

"Yes, ma'am." He ambled away from the house where he could flag Gil down.

"Your daughter is a delight to be around," Eliza said.

"She can be a trial at times."

"That is a typical Cooper trait." Eliza laid a finger on Josie's arm, dragging her attention back from Gil. "Abigail has noticed the family resemblance in Sarah Ann. I'm sure Ivy has as well."

"A person would have to be blind not to," Josie said as the buckboard creaked to a stop near the house. "Please don't say anything to Sarah Ann yet. She doesn't know."

"I won't, but I suggest you should have a talk with her soon. Once Ivy tells Father about Sarah Ann, he'll likely make a nuisance of himself."

Another problem she didn't need. Josie leaned against the porch post, watching Eliza hurry to the buckboard. Dwight helped her up beside Gil.

Gil inclined his head Josie's way, and though she couldn't read his expression, she felt his worry reach out to her and her heart thudded. He handed Dwight her carpetbag and whip, then flicked the lines and the buckboard lurched forward.

Josie hugged her waist, unsure what she dreaded most. That he would be gone for hours, or that she had to figure out the best way to tell Sarah Ann that Gil was her father.

Gil walked down the boardwalk toward the telegraph office, for once anxious to get a letter off to his father. Not that he aimed to bury the hatchet with the old man.

Nope, Harrison Cooper needed to know Baxter tried to rape Abby. "I hope to hell the old man has him arrested."

"Even if he could, Father wouldn't because once word got out, the incident would disgrace Abigail."

"Ain't right that bastard can move on and try his ploy on another heiress."

Eliza shook her head and laughed. "Goodness, Gilbert. If I didn't know better, I would swear that you were born and raised in the West."

"Spent a good part of my life out here."

"You ran away, created a new identity and means of making a living, but at what cost?"

"Unlike attending Harvard, like our father insisted I do, graduating from the school of hard knocks only took a lot of sweat, blood and grit to master."

"As well as alienating yourself from your family, but then it seems you acquired one as well. The question is will you do what is right concerning Josie and Sarah Ann."

"Right, being I marry Josie?"

"That seems the logical choice. Sarah Ann admires you and needs a father. And Josie— Well, it's obvious she's quite smitten with you."

Gil bit back a laugh. If that was true, then why the hell hadn't she told him about Parnell's threat?

"Unless I have lost my flair for reading people, you're taken with her as well." Eliza paused outside the telegraph office. "Have you told her how you feel about her?"

"Josie knows I want her."

"Sometimes you are so much like Father I could scream." Eliza poked his chest with a finger. "As you well know, I'm talking about what's in your heart for Josie."

He rolled his shoulders and scrubbed a hand over his neck, checking to see if anyone nearby heard his sister. Even if he could put a name to what he felt, he damn sure wasn't about to talk about it standing outside the telegraph office.

"Time's a-wasting." He reached around Eliza and opened the door.

"Yes, it is. Don't waste your chance."

He tucked that advice away to chew on later and trailed Eliza into the telegraph office.

Josie was going through the list provided in W.H.H. Murray's *Adventures in the Wilderness* one last time when Virgil came to the back door.

"We've combed the area around Rocky Point and

couldn't pick up any trail, or find anyone who'd seen a man matching this here Ross Parnell's description." Virgil planted his hands on his hips. "Could be that letter was sent to rile you."

"I thought of that."

"Since Boyd Rowney swindled half the men in the territory, it's likely one of them tracked down Rowney and killed him."

Again, she agreed. "So that's it then?"

Virgil huffed out a breath. "We'll fan out tomorrow and go over the area again, but I'm guessing we won't find anything."

"Thanks for looking." She closed the door and returned to the supplies she'd laid out earlier.

Where was Parnell? The posse couldn't find hide nor hair of him. Her men were exhausted from keeping watch day in and day out. She and Sarah Ann hadn't dared visit Everett's grave for a week, and even the guests couldn't partake of trail rides as she'd promised.

That veil of danger hanging over Rocky Point was sure to run off future guests. Was that what Parnell had intended? To keep everyone at the ranch on edge? To ruin her financially as she'd done him?

Josie drummed her fingers. What if there were too many people on the ranch for Parnell's liking?

She'd rarely been alone for long. Maybe it was time to make a change—set a trap for the man she despised.

The rattle and creak of a wagon grew closer. Josie ran to the window and looked out.

That tingling warmth spread over her, thawing some of the fear and worry that'd been gripping her. Sarah Ann sat between Gil and Eliza.

Gil angled the buckboard between the house and

Virgil. Before Gil stopped, Dwight heaved out of a rocker and ambled off the porch.

Josie frowned. Abigail sat in a rocker that looked awfully close to the one Dwight just vacated. This time she knew she wasn't imagining things. Something was going on between the cowboy and the heiress.

Gil helped his sister and Sarah Ann down, then strode over to Virgil while Dwight drove the buckboard toward the barn.

Sarah Ann ran into the house, boots clumping and dark hair flying behind her like a horse's mane. "May I go up and talk to Mrs. Cooper?"

Jealousy pinched Josie, and she kicked it a good one right back. "Yes, but knock first."

Josie waited until her daughter did as told, then she stepped out onto the porch. Abigail and Eliza were halfway to the cabin they shared.

Virgil trotted off toward the waiting posse. And Gil—

Her heart pounded as his long legs closed the distance between them. "Did you send a telegram to your pa?"

"Eliza did." He motioned to the rockers. "How about us having that talk now?"

"Might as well." Josie eased into a chair.

His creaked as he dropped into it. "Why would Parnell be wanting to get back at you?"

"I cleaned out his cash box the night I ran off."

Gil whistled. "How the hell did you manage that?"

"While Parnell was hauling a drunk out, I sneaked into his office." Josie's hands shook as she gripped the rocker arms. "Getting the money without him seeing me was the easy part."

"You said he caught you in the storeroom, but you never told me how you got away from him."

She closed her eyes, seeing every detail, hearing every curse and scream. "He had a gun. I meant to pluck it out of his hands with my whip, but he rushed toward me just as I let it fly." Her fingernails bit into the wood. "The tip caught him above his left eye and laid his cheek open. There was so much blood. He bellowed and dropped the gun. My sister and I ran and didn't stop until we got here."

Gil's hand closed over one of hers, warm and re-assuring. "What did you do with all that money?"

"Some went to the man who drove us to Wyoming in his wagon. Some was spent on medicine for my sister." She looked at him. "The rest I gave to Everett for the ranch."

"No wonder he left you a share in it."

She'd never asked for it, or expected it, but she surely treasured owning Rocky Point. "Parnell has it in for me, and if he's sneaking around, I want to draw him out into the open."

"Got any idea how to do that?"

"I suggest we proceed as planned and you and Dwight take Sarah Ann, your sisters and Ivy on a two-day trail ride."

"And leave you here with Hiram? Forget it."

She sucked in a deep breath and let it out in a rush. "I thought Virgil or one of his deputies could ride out to the camp, and you could sneak back here."

"I don't know."

"You'd be in the house with me." She turned her hand over and threaded her fingers through his, mar-veling at his gentle strength. "It's worth a try, Gil."

His fingers closed over hers. "I'll think on it."

"You do that," Josie said, rising as his sisters headed back to the house.

After a fitful night, Josie dressed before daylight, went down to the kitchen and set to work. The canned goods she'd set aside should feed her guests on their camping trip middling well, but she wanted to send them off with some freshly baked goods.

"Why are you up so early, Mama?"

She turned to Sarah Ann standing in the doorway, looking like a child in her flannel nightshirt and sleep-tousled hair. "I'm going to bake biscuits for the camping trip."

"Do I have to stay home again?"

Josie took the second tray of golden browned biscuits from the oven. She wanted her daughter far away when Parnell showed up here. As sure as the sun rose every morning, that snake from her past would strike soon.

"No, I thought you'd go with Gil and his sisters."

"You mean it?" Sarah Ann asked.

"Of course. Now, you'd best run upstairs and get a few things packed for the trip."

Her daughter skedaddled with an excited squeal.

Josie set her biscuits to cool alongside the dried peach pie she'd made last night. She was doing the right thing. Neither her hands or resolve shook one bit.

When this camping trip was over, she'd have to tell Sarah Ann a varnished version of the truth. That as unlikely as it seemed, Gil Yancy was her father. That Josie had met him at a social, and they surrendered to love one hot summer night.

If only that had been the truth.

"You're up mighty early," Gil said.

Josie glanced to the back door, surprised she hadn't heard Gil walk across the porch or open the door. "I had baking to do for your trip."

"You that sure I'm going to agree with your plan?"

"Are you?" She chanced a glance at his face, and this time she saw worry carve lines next to his eyes.

He grabbed two cups from the sideboard and filled them with coffee. "I don't like it, but I can't think of anything better to draw Parnell out."

Gil took a break from setting up the tents to stretch the kinks from his back. Dwight was off gathering a second load of wood for the fire. Near the creek, Abby and Sarah chattered away like a couple of red squirrels.

With Landon out of the picture, his little sister had loosened up her corset strings. In fact, watching her josh with Dwight put him in mind of Sarah.

Ivy perched on a boulder nearby, watching the water splash over rocks or the clouds drift by in turn.

Eliza strolled over to him and perched on a log near the fire pit. "This is real nice."

"It's right pretty here."

"I meant us being together again as a family. All that's missing is Father."

"I'm surprised he hasn't come sniffing after his wife."

"Really, Gilbert. Did you love her that much?"

Gil wanted to laugh. He'd respected and cared for Ivy, and felt proud having her on his arm. As for love, she'd never roused his passion.

"Hell, no." Gil grabbed another folded tent from the wagon, tossed it on the ground a few feet from the other one and asked the question that he had wondered about for fifteen years. "Do I have a half sister or brother?"

"Ivy lost the baby."

He looked at her. "They try for another?"

"I don't know." Eliza shook the dust from her skirt. "Their relationship is—odd."

"That don't surprise me."

"Maybe this will. Six months after they were married, Father succeeded in financially ruining Arthur Doyle, Ivy's father. Father bought Doyle's company for a song, and personally saw to it that Doyle was stripped of everything he owned. Doyle committed suicide soon after."

"The old man always did covet Doyle's company. How'd Ivy take it to watch her father ruined?"

"It didn't seem to bother her at all."

"Guess I was right. She's as cold blooded as the old man."

"Father isn't as heartless as you think."

Anything Gil said would only upset Eliza, so he kept his trap shut. "So instead of a merger between the two companies, the old man runs it all."

"No, Ivy manages her father's company now."

"The old man gave it to her?"

"Right after her father's funeral."

No doubt about it Ivy and his old man were two peas in a pod—both of them hard as rocks.

Dwight stomped from the brush carrying an armload of greasewood, and Gil pushed his curiosity about Ivy and his father from his mind. "This ought to do it for tonight."

"Yep. Once I get this tent set up, we'll eat." Then as soon as darkness fell, Gil would slip back to Rocky Point.

* * *

Josie looked out her bedroom window. A waning moon cast a muted glow over the ranch, giving enough light to make out the outbuildings.

The wind had lain by, and the night hush was both soothing and unsettling. Was Parnell watching her now?

After dinner, she'd sat on the front porch until dusk, the Navy Colt beside her and the old hound at her feet. Hiram had stood outside the bunkhouse, frowning at her.

"Damn risky poking a stick at a rattler," Hiram had said at dinner when she told him their plan. "If he's got a mind to, he could shoot you dead."

"Parnell won't do that."

"How can you be sure?"

"He wants me to suffer, and a bullet is too quick."

So she'd sat outside well past sunset, challenging Parnell to show his face. She wanted him to believe she wasn't afraid, to know she was alone in the house.

Hiram had doused the light in the bunkhouse long ago, and only she knew he was watching the house. And Gil? She'd expected him to sneak into the house an hour ago.

A chill that had nothing to do with the brisk air swept over her. Parnell had always called on her in the middle of the night. If he was coming at all, it'd be soon.

The back porch floorboards groaned. Josie held her breath, listening. Metal scraped metal, then the door creaked open.

Gil? Or Parnell?

Josie darted from the window to the bedside table

and grabbed the Navy Colt with shaky hands. The flickering light from a lone candle danced over her whip lying on the bed.

Slow, steady thuds proceeded across the kitchen and down the hall. Footsteps rang out dully on the steps. One. Two. Three. He climbed the stairs, coming closer and closer.

Josie struggled for breath and inched back into the shadows until her backside smacked against the wall. Fear threatened to choke her, the taste as bitter as it'd been years ago.

The rap on her door startled a whimper from her. "Josie?"

Gil! She put down the revolver and wrenched open the door. She drank in the sight of those long, denim-clad legs, cambric shirt hugging a broad chest and hat pulled low, casting shadows on his handsome face.

"What took you so long?"

"I left Rhubarb at my place and walked here." Gil stepped inside, then closed the door behind him. "Figured there was less chance of being seen or heard that way."

"Lillian had always said Parnell was sly as a fox."

In admiration at first, then in disgust after Parnell agreed to sell her contract to Everett for an outrageous price, but refused to put a price on Josie. They'd been nothing more than indentured servants with no hope for a better future.

Gil peered out the window. "Reckon Parnell is damn good at smelling a trap or he'd have been dead long ago."

"What do we do now?"

"We wait." He glanced at her, then blew out the candle. "You might as well get some shut-eye."

Josie had never been able to close her eyes around a man. Besides, sleep was the farthest thing from her mind. But she did crawl on the bed to rest a spell.

Moonlight filtered in the window and washed over Gil. He looked dangerous and unyielding, and she smiled into the darkness, then yawned. Parnell would be hard-pressed to get the drop on Gil.

The hand shaking Josie's shoulder jerked her out of the most delicious dream of Gil Yancy. She opened her eyes and stared at Gil standing over her. The weary set to his mouth brought reality crashing back on her.

"Is Parnell here?"

"Nope, and I got a hunch he ain't going to show. Dawn will be breaking soon, so I'd best head back to the camp."

"Don't go."

He frowned. "I know Parnell has you running scared, but I have to get back before my sisters, Ivy and Sarah wake up."

Josie glanced at the dusky light drifting in through the window. She'd dreamed of this cowboy so many times, imagined opening her arms to him because she wanted this joining of body and heart so badly, not because he'd bought her for the night or because giving this cowboy what Parnell had coveted was another means to get back at the man she'd despised.

She reached up and ran a finger down his shirt buttons, and he sucked in air like a bellows. "Stay for a while."

"Sweetheart, the last thing I wanted with you after all this time was a quick tussle."

"You turning me down, cowboy?"

"Hell, no."

Chapter 18

Instead of fear, anticipation rippled through Josie. Her breath hitched as he shrugged off vest, gunbelt and boots. She expected him to shuck his jeans and crawl atop her, but he didn't.

He sat on the bed and leaned over her, his mouth closing over hers. His kiss was light and sweet, his tongue a hot caress that stoked the fire deep within her.

She closed her eyes and sighed, imagining he cherished her. Even his touch adored her as he slipped off her bodice and skirt without breaking the kiss.

Then his hands were roaming over her shift, setting off fires in her that burned away those faded memories. How odd she'd taken his money long ago, and he'd returned to steal her heart.

She fumbled to free the buttons on his shirt, tempted to rip it open when they refused to budge.

He brushed her hands aside, breath sawing hard and fast and eyes glittering with need and laughter. "You act like you've never undressed a man before."

"It's been a spell." When Everett was too sick to

care for himself toward the end, but she saw no need to tell him that was the only time she'd done so.

Josie lounged against her pillow, excited but nervous just the same. She'd seen her share of naked men and suffered abuse, but she'd only known the pleasure of a man once. Though she'd been terrified and desperate that night, she realized now she'd fallen in love with Gil Yancy right then.

He pulled back and stared at her, and she wished she could read his thoughts. "I don't want to hurt you, but I want you too much to poke along."

Josie almost laughed. She'd waited nigh on twelve years for this moment, and the waiting was torture. And if he changed his mind— She couldn't let him do that to her, or them.

"That's all right." She smiled as she raised both arms to him. "I want you, cowboy."

Gil's blood pumped like a geyser. All he'd known were whores, though right now he had a helluva time believing Josie had been one.

Oh, those long, firm legs of hers could hang on to a man's hips and ride him all night. That saucy mouth was made for kissing. But those pale blue eyes were the oddest mixture of passion and innocence.

The thought had his pecker rearing to ride.

He stretched out beside her and worked her shift up her body, damning his callused hands that snagged the fine muslin. His mouth claimed hers as his fingers parted the opening in her drawers and drifted through the nest of tight curls.

She spread her legs and lifted to him, and her eagerness had his blood roaring like a locomotive. The bit of dew on his fingertips dragged another groan from him, proof she was as ready for this as he was.

Josie grabbed his neck and pulled him down on her, kissing him like a wild thing, gliding a hand down his chest to his crotch. He grabbed her hand to stop her from stroking his pecker, knowing if she did he'd come like a green boy.

"Easy now," he said, pushing into her slowly.

She wrapped her legs around him and arched her back, taking him in before he could blink. Her gasp was soft and throaty, vibrating through him in sultry spurts.

He groaned and broke out in a cold sweat. She was tighter than a bung in a new barrel. How in the hell long had it been since she'd had any?

Too long. Even if he hadn't felt her struggle to take him all in, her face registered a moment's discomfort. So despite his pounding need, he held himself still and closed his eyes. Just a moment. That's all it'd take to get a grip on himself.

Spasms rippled through her and into him, drawing him in deeper and milking him at the same time. He rocked his hips and her body gave one hard shiver. A sound of pure pleasure escaped her parted lips.

"Please, Gil."

She clung to him and pushed up against him. He sank all the way into her this time, the fit tight and greedy and feeling like the home he'd feared he'd never find.

Lust clouded his brain, threatening to shut down all reasoning except one—the wait had been worth it. He bucked into her on a ragged groan, staring into eyes that were wide open with surprise and passion and something he couldn't define.

For a heart-stopping moment, they stared at each other. Then she smiled and moved her hands to his hips, scoring him with her fingernails and setting off sparks that he was sure could be seen clear to Laramie.

His mouth toyed with hers and his body eased in and out slowly. He wanted to draw out the pleasure, but his own need was as much against him as Josie was.

Slipping his hands under her, he cupped her butt and rode her fast and hard. She matched him thrust for thrust through the best eight seconds of glory a cowboy could ever hope to have.

She moaned and bowed up against him, pressing her soft curves to his hard body, taking him up in the clouds with her.

"That's it, sweetheart. Let yourself go."

He fingered where they joined, pushing her to another climax before he let himself go. He wanted to give her all the pleasure he could first.

When he gave in to his release, he nearly lost his breath. He came back down, spent and smiling so wide his face ached.

He rolled to his side and tugged her close to him, gathering his thoughts again. Nothing he'd done in his life had ever felt so right, so perfect.

Her small hand splayed on his chest. One of his hands cupped her bottom, holding her in place, though she seemed in no hurry to get away from him now. Nope, she looked damned pleased with herself.

Gil stroked her soft skin and stared at the ceiling. Questions bounced in his mind like sagebrush dancing over the high plains.

It took him a spell to figure out what seemed off here. Josie wasn't an innocent, but she was mighty close to it.

"If Everett bedded you, it damn sure wasn't often." Her cheeks flushed. "What difference does it make?"

"None, so why lie?" He didn't give her time to concoct an answer. "Everett had his bedroom and you
had yours. Did you ever sleep with him?"

"No."

Just as Gil thought. Everett married Josie so the
baby wouldn't be a bastard.

He leaned over her and stared into eyes a man
could drown in. "That night at the Gilded Garter.
How many men had taken you before me?"

She looked him straight in the eye, then turned
away. "You were my first."

Gil hung his head, ashamed to meet her gaze,
unsure what to say. He'd been too drunk that night at
the Gilded Garter to realize she'd been a virgin. Too
full of himself to open his eyes and see how women
like Josie were being abused by bastards like Parnell.

No wonder she'd coshed him. He'd deserved it for
hurting her. For planting his baby in her belly. For
putting out a half-hearted effort to find his sweet thief.

"Dammit all! I'm sorry the way it all turned out for
you, Josie."

"Don't be." She drew the covers up around her
neck, proof again she wasn't the brazen hussy he'd
believed her to be all these years, convincing him
there was more that she'd suffered. "Dawn will break
before long. You'd better be on your way."

Gil didn't want to leave Josie now. Nope, he wanted
to hold her, get her to tell him whatever it was that
she hadn't had the heart or guts to tell him yet. But
he had to get back to the camp before Ivy, his sisters
and Sarah noticed he'd been gone all night.

He might be able to convince his daughter he'd
been up on the ridge, keeping watch over the camp.
But Eliza wouldn't be fooled.

Gil rolled off the bed and dressed, unsure what the morrow would bring. That lack of confidence rattled him. How could having Josie twice in twelve years have him doubting himself so?

He paused at the door. "Why'd you welcome me into your bed tonight, Josie?

"I wanted to," she said, but he knew Parnell hadn't given her a choice either.

"Do you regret it?"

She didn't answer for so long he feared he'd bust a gut holding his breath. "No."

He exhaled in a rush and smiled. That was enough for now.

Josie let out a tired sigh and hung the last of her bedsheets on the line. She should've told Gil everything last night, but even if she could've found the words, she didn't want to sully the wondrous joining she'd had with Gil by dredging up those dark memories of Ross Parnell.

The steady clomp of hooves had her whirling toward the lane, shaking with dread. She shaded her eyes and squinted at the lone rider. Not Parnell, as she'd half feared, but Sheriff Keegan.

She wiped her hands on her apron and walked around the house. Hopefully he wasn't bringing more bad news.

"Afternoon, Virgil."

He brushed two fingers over his hat brim. "Same to you. Mighty quiet on your spread today."

"Gil and Dwight took the ladies and Sarah Ann on a camping outing. What brings you by?"

Leather creaked as Virgil shifted in the saddle and

tugged a paper from his vest pocket. "Got a telegram for Mrs. Ivy Cooper. Seeing she's one of your guests, I thought I'd best bring it on out."

"That's right kind of you."

She took the telegram, feeling uncomfortable under Virgil's scrutiny. Any other time she'd invite him in, but now the notion seemed wrong.

"Any idea how Boyd Rowney ended up dead on my land?"

"Interesting about that," he said. "Talked to Dugan MacInnes yesterday. He admitted he cornered Rowney two days back about that stallion he sold him. Rowney claimed he didn't know the papers on him were bad. Said the man who sold him the horse double-crossed him."

"A likely story."

"That's what I figured." Virgil leaned forward in the saddle. "You getting on all right with Yancy?"

Was she ever. "Just fine. Why do you ask?"

"I don't like the way that Yancy fellow looks at you."

"And how is that?" she asked.

"Like a man gone too long without a woman."

She felt her cheeks warm, wondering if Gil would look as contented as she felt. "Since there are more men in these parts than women, I'd guess that Gil isn't the only man who looks at me, or any other available woman, with a degree of longing."

"Dang if that ain't the truth."

"Is something troubling you, Virgil?"

"I ain't one to talk outside of school, but I've seen cowpokes giving you the long eye when you come into Maverick."

"There's no crime in looking, Virgil. Fact remains I'm one of the hens in a land overpopulated with roosters."

He nodded. "Reckon so. You take care."

"You too, and thanks for bringing out the telegram."

Josie watched Virgil ride off until he disappeared over the hill, then she scanned the yard. Where was Hiram?

The outlaw kicked up a fuss in the corral, demanding her attention. She stepped off the porch to get a better look, shading her eyes.

A long shadow drifted over Josie a heartbeat before she realized someone had walked up on her from behind. She pulled Everett's heavy sidearm out of her pocket and spun around.

Instead of Parnell, she stared up into Reid Barclay's amused face. She lowered the Navy Colt, trembling and more than a bit miffed.

"Sneaking up on me like that nearly got you shot."

"I assure you that wasn't my intention." His gaze bored into hers, probing and intense, before shifting to the grulla. "That's a fine stallion you have there."

So was the one Reid ground-reined at the end of the porch. "That grulla is an outlaw and probably a stolen one at that."

"Why would you think that?"

"I bought him off Boyd Rowney. You know of him?"

Something dark and dangerous flashed in his eyes. "Who doesn't? He's a known gambler, rustler and con man who has gulled many astute men, myself included."

"One of those men killed him."

"So I heard."

Had Reid talked to one of her hands or the sheriff? Had gossip of Rowney's murder traveled to Reid's Crown Seven Ranch? Or was he the man who'd shot Rowney dead?

She wouldn't be surprised if he had. Reid certainly

looked dangerous, with that inky hair, midnight blue eyes and tall, imposing form dressed in black.

Josie crossed her arms over her chest, suddenly chilled. "What brings you here?"

"You, of course."

"Should I feel flattered or threatened?"

His mouth curved in a faint smile. "Neither. You know what I want from you, Josephine, and you know I'll reward you for the privilege of your company."

"I won't be your whore."

"Mistress."

That one word held a hint of an Irish brogue, and Josie wondered again if this English gentleman was who he said he was. He'd lived here a short time, yet often spoke like any other cowboy on the range.

"I don't see a difference."

"That makes you all the more desirable, my dear." Reid let out a dry chuckle when she frowned. "I regret I can't offer you a more respectable place in my life."

"It wouldn't matter if you could," she said as Hiram stepped out of the barn, no doubt wondering what business Barclay had here. "I wouldn't marry you."

"Just as well." His eyes locked with hers, and she stiffened at the lust glimmering in their dark, mysterious depths. "You know where to find me, should you change your mind."

He was in for a long wait. "Good day, Mr. Barclay."

Head high, Josie returned to the house, putting Reid Barclay and his outrageous proposition from her mind.

The sun had dipped behind the Snowy Range by the time Gil, Sarah and the women returned to the ranch. Energy shimmered off his daughter, but Ivy, Eliza and Abby looked saddle-sore. Even without the threat of Parnell, there was no way the women could tolerate another day camping.

A purple haze drifted across the sky, dusting the sagebrush a silvery gray. Instead of admiring that beauty, his gaze honed in on the breathtaking woman waiting for him on the front porch.

His chest tightened at the sight of Josie. He'd barely slept because she'd been on his mind since he left her bed.

On the ride back to camp he'd done a lot of thinking. He damn sure wasn't going to dally with her in secret. The last time he'd gotten to her he'd knocked her up. What were the chances he'd done it again?

No way to tell. Yet. But the fact it could happen made things simpler.

He'd marry her. Hell, he'd been ready to marry for weaker motives a few days back.

Gil reined up in front of the house, anxious to get Josie alone. He had plenty of reason to make her his wife. They were part owners of Rocky Point. They both had a say in Sarah's upbringing. Might as well make life easy on all of them and get hitched.

"I took an apple cobbler from the oven," Josie said to the women. "Coffee is on and I can steep tea for you."

"That sounds wonderful," Abby said as Dwight helped her down and steadied her on her feet.

"I must say I am eager for something sweet." Eliza winced as Gil lifted her off her horse.

"You all right?" he asked.

"I will be now that I'm off that animal. As I recall you were partial to Mrs. Alder's pies."

He had been, but it'd been a lifetime ago since he'd thought of the cook his family had employed.

Sarah bolted from her horse and ran to Josie, throwing her arms around her. "We had the best time, Mama."

"I'm glad."

Josie cupped Sarah's cheeks, her entire face wreathed in the most beatific expression Gil had ever seen. Looking at them robbed him of breath.

Plain to see Josie was a good, loving mother. Why, Sarah talked about her mama all the time, bragging about what all she could do.

His chest tightened with envy. Did he stand a chance of ever getting close to his nearly grown daughter?

Hard to tell. Truth was Sarah had spent most of her time with Ivy and his sisters. He'd ended up being the guide. On the outside looking in again. Wanting, but not sure how to grab a part of the happiness without ruining everything.

"I've got hot water heated for a bath as well," Josie said. "Help yourselves."

His gaze swung back to Josie as she held the door open. She looked at him and smiled, and he finally drew a decent breath.

"You're welcome to join us for dessert."

The only dessert he hungered for was her, and now wasn't the time. "Much obliged, but I believe I'll turn in after I see to our horses."

He led Rhubarb toward the barn. The screen door smacked shut behind him. Yep, Josie and him had some talking to do, but he didn't want an audience.

Gil carried his tack into the small room in back of the barn, surprised to see Hiram in there this time of night. "Josie's got cobbler at the house."

"I heard." Hiram worked saddle soap into a McClellan saddle.

Gil hefted a sidesaddle onto the wooden tree. "Any problems while we were gone?"

"Nope. Sheriff came by today."

"What for?" The second sidesaddle hit the tree with a muffled thud.

"He brought a telegram for Miz Cooper."

"Seems the sheriff comes by damned often."

"Yup. You ask me, he's sweet on Miz Josie."

His nape burned like a whiplash. "You sure?"

Hiram turned back to working the thick cream into the leather. "Yup. Right after Everett passed on, the sheriff started coming by regular. Been right friendly and all. The past couple of times, the sheriff's face had been as smooth as a cow's teat and he's smelled like he fell headlong into a barrel of Bay Rum."

Son of a bitch. The lawman was trying to court his Josie. "Sheriff stay long?"

"Long enough."

Gil shook off the jealousy nipping at him. He'd been the only lover Josie had known. She'd invited him into her bed last night. Yep, he stood a better chance of winning her over than anyone else. So why was he still fretting?

"Anyone else happen by?"

The black man smiled. "Funny you ask. Reid Barclay came by. Caught Miz Josie outside on the porch."

"What was Barclay doing here?"

Hiram chuckled. "Hell, Yancy. It's mighty plain to see that you ain't the only man with eyes for Miz Josie."

Chapter 19

The back door slammed, and six feet of hulking cowboy strode into her kitchen. Josie turned back to scrubbing her last plate, wondering what burr got under Gil's saddle.

"You look riled enough to wrestle a grizzly with one hand tied behind your back."

"I hear the sheriff came calling today."

"Virgil brought Ivy a telegram."

"What the hell did Reid Barclay want?"

Mercy, was she imagining things or did Gil sound jealous? "Really, Gil. What does it matter?"

"Plenty, if that son of a bitch propositioned you."

"What if he did? I'm not obliged to answer to you or anyone else."

A dark silence echoed between them. "How can you say that after what all we did last night?"

Josie was tempted to crack her good china plate over Gil's hard head. "One thing has nothing to do with the other."

She couldn't fault Gil for being irate over Reid's persistence, but he had no right to get his bowels in an uproar because the sheriff came calling. And if Gil was of a mind to treat her like his possession—

She dried her plate with a vengeance. If Gil thought no more of her than chattel, she'd be better off knowing it now.

"Well?" Gil asked, sounding more tyrannical by the minute.

"Look around, Gil Yancy. This isn't the place to discuss such things where Sarah Ann could overhear, or where one of your sisters could walk in."

Gil's chest expanded and his features tensed, but he gave an abrupt nod. "You're right. We'll talk it out tonight."

She had a hunch he intended to do more than talk, which part of her thought wasn't such a bad idea. Those same urges and wants were raising Cain inside her, too. And that was the problem. Beyond the wanting, how did Gil feel about her?

"Is that a fact?" Josie stowed the stack of plates in her cupboard, hating that her hands shook. "Have you figured out what you're going to do with me?"

"Yep, I thought on it."

"Well, so did I, and how we get on will depend on how you feel about me."

"I like you."

She waited for him to go on. "That's it?"

Gil scrubbed his knuckles along his jaw, looking around as if to ensure they were alone, acting jittery as a bull calf at castrating time. He opened his mouth, and Sarah Ann bound into the kitchen.

"Do you want to play Muggins?" Sarah Ann asked.

He smiled. "Get out the dominoes and we'll play one game."

Sarah Ann ran to the parlor.

"We'll talk later in my cabin." The heat in his eyes promised talk was only part of what he had in mind, and a small part at that.

Problem was, Josie had a hankering for more too. But she wasn't about to be any man's mistress for money, or for love.

Gil stood in the front yard, watching the house. An eternity seemed to pass before the light upstairs went out. Another before he caught the shadow slip out the front door, linger a moment in the swath of darkness under the porch, then walk toward him.

"I didn't think you'd ever come." He bent close and kissed her, but instead of kissing him in kind, she pulled back.

"It's nippy out tonight."

Not nearly as cold as Josie seemed. "Let's get inside."

He caught the hint of vanilla and tension riding on her slender shoulders as they walked to his cabin. Had he said something to upset her? Or was she thinking of her male callers today?

Gil ushered her into his cabin then kicked the door shut and faced her. So many things crowded his mind, foremost being what was she keeping from him?

She crossed her arms over her breasts. "What do you want to talk about?"

"Right now, I'll settle for hearing more about you and Parnell. You said he forced you to take your sister's place because she was ailing." He poured a couple of fingers of whiskey into two tin cups and handed one to her, thinking that once he got her talking, confiding in him, she'd finally shake off the demon clinging to her. "What was wrong with her?"

"She was hurt bad inside." Her shaky hands closed around the cup, but she made no move to taste it. "Lillian got in the family way, so Parnell called in this drunken doctor. He took the baby from Lillian two days before I met you, then gave her laudanum for the pain, same as he'd done for the other doves."

"A damn abortionist."

She nodded. "Lillian bled all day and that night, but Parnell forced her to pleasure a man anyway. He tore her up bad."

Gil tossed back his whiskey, wishing he could heap the same misery on Parnell. "So you took her place?"

"If I hadn't, he would've dragged Lillian to you." Josie stared into her glass. "Parnell told me what you wanted, and that I wasn't supposed to let you do more without you paying extra. But after that last time with Parnell, I couldn't stand to let a man do that to me again."

"Do what again?"

She drank the whiskey, and her swallow roared in the stillness. "Parnell said you were a butt man."

It took Gil a minute to understand what he was getting at. The memory came back in jagged pieces. He'd spouted off that he'd wanted ass for the night, so Parnell sent in the virgin. One Parnell had been abusing for years.

Gil dropped on the bed and ground the heels of his hands against his eyes. Good God! He'd had no intentions of anal sex when he'd said he wanted ass. Truth was he just liked gals with a good deal of bottom. Not so for Parnell.

No wonder Josie paled every time Gil touched

her behind. "How long had Parnell been doing that to you?"

She shrugged. "A few times."

He'd bet his share of the ranch that she knew exactly how many times Parnell had used her, where it'd happened and the exact second the abuse started and ended.

"So you robbed me and Parnell and then high-tailed it out of Caldwell. How'd you end up here, married to Everett?"

She smiled, looking like a young girl. "He'd proposed to Lillian in the fall and agreed to give me a home, but Parnell wouldn't sell my contract. So we headed here. By the time we arrived, she was too weak to sit up."

There was far more to Josie Andrews than he'd ever dreamed. She had more grit and courage than most men he'd met.

"According to her tombstone, Everett didn't marry her."

"He wanted to but Lillian refused. She died a week after we arrived, and Everett offered me a job as ranch cook." Her cheeks flushed. "Three months later, I realized I was with child."

Gil's child. He sucked in a shaky breath.

"Everett offered to marry you."

She nodded. "I don't know what I'd have done without him."

Neither did Gil. Just thinking what would've happened to her and his baby if she hadn't escaped Parnell made him right sick.

Gil owed Everett everything for making a good home for his daughter, and the women he'd come to respect. The little woman who'd humbled him and had him wanting to settle down with her.

"I married once out of necessity," she said. "I won't do that again."

He went stone still. "You aim to remain a widow?"

"It would be better than having a loveless marriage."

"You saying you don't care that way about me?"

"How I feel isn't what holds me back."

Gil broke out in a sweat. She was set on him professing some starry-eyed, devoted crap that reduced a man to lapdog.

Damn if he'd pretend something that went against his grain. He cared for Josie. He wanted her more than he'd ever wanted a woman. By damn he'd marry her.

All he had to do was convince her that what they had was more than enough to build a future on. He had an idea how he could do that. Yep, he'd show her tomorrow.

"It's getting late," he said. "Best get you back to the house. Reckon folks will get here early in the morning for the exhibition. I want Sarah to do her shooting first."

"She's excited. Why, that's all she talked about after she took her bath tonight." She lifted her chin in that no-nonsense way of hers that he'd come to appreciate, but that glimmer of pain in her eyes nearly undid him. "I'll need your help with the red balloons."

"You've got it." In fact he intended to be a big part of her show, not that he aimed to tell her beforehand. "Dwight and Hiram are ready to do their part as well."

"And you?"

Gil hooked his thumbs under his belt. "I'm riding the outlaw."

"I won't have it."

"You've no say, Josie."

"I most certainly do. That horse is mine, and if I want, I'll open the gate and chase him off."

He pulled her close, all teasing gone in a blink. "Don't! If you do, I'll lose my share in Rocky Point."

"What are you talking about?"

Dammit, he hadn't wanted to tell her like this. "I made a side bet with Dugan MacInnes. If I can hold two silver dollars in the stirrup for an eight-second ride, he'll pay me five hundred bucks."

"My God. If you lose, he'll own part of Rocky Point."

"I won't lose, Josie."

She jerked away from him and backed to the door, her eyes an odd mixture of hurt, disbelief and anger. "How could you make such a fool's bet?"

"It was an offer I couldn't pass up."

"Damn you." Then she was gone, slamming the door behind her.

Gil tipped his head back and stared at the just-patched ceiling. To a gambler like himself, the deal he made with Dugan MacInnes was a sure bet. He'd done the trick countless times and always won. Just stay in the saddle and keep those silver dollars under his boots for eight damned seconds.

He refused to dwell on the fact he'd never ridden a horse as wild as this one. Or that he'd never had this much to lose before.

At half past ten the next morning, Gil stood at the back pen and watched folks stream onto Rocky Point Ranch like a thirsty herd catching the scent of water up ahead. Hiram had done a good job getting things set up in the field where Sarah would display her shooting skills and Josie could dazzle the crowd with her whip. The corral had been raked, and would be the arena where they'd show off their cowboying stunts.

But there were still a few things that only Gil could see to. Things that might result in him walking away with a wad of money in his pocket, or see him hauled out crippled or dead.

That outlaw hadn't mellowed one damned bit, a fact Gil learned quickly as he took the grulla's measure at dawn. One thing was sure—the stallion was a widow-maker.

"Are you really gonna ride him?" Sarah asked.

He glanced down at her. She had on her new split skirt with a matching vest, and her eyes sparkled with excitement.

"Yep, I'll go last. Reckon that'll make for an exciting finale for the audience."

"Mama doesn't want you to ride that grulla. She said you could get yourself killed."

There was no mistaking the worry in Sarah's eyes— worry for him. His heart ached and his throat tightened with an odd emotion Gil couldn't name.

He wanted to tell her everything would be fine, but he couldn't find the words. Not that it'd matter now. It was too late to back out, even if he had a mind to.

Gil had to give it everything he had for his daughter and Josie. Damn if he'd let Sarah lose her land because her pa was a yellow-bellied coward.

He managed a smile. "Best fetch your gear and get this show started."

She grinned, and he pushed his doubts away as they angled behind the corral toward the field. Gil lugged the gunnysack of empty tin cans while Sarah carried his Winchester.

"Look at all the folks," she said, peering through the lodge pole pine rail fence.

"Good turnout." An understatement.

Gil counted at least a dozen buckboards clustered back from the corral. No way could he count how many people stood on the beds so they could get a good view of the corral and the field. At two bits per head, they'd made a good deal already. The side bets would only sweeten the pot.

"Go on down to the spot you'll be shooting from," he said. "I'll set up your targets. Soon as Hiram gives the word, show them what you got."

She nodded. "Wish me luck."

He smiled. "A girl with your skill don't need luck. Just do like I told you and you'll be fine."

"I will." She smiled back and took off toward the gathering.

Gil set up three pyramids of cans, holding a good dozen back to toss in the air. He scanned the crowd for Josie, but didn't see her anywhere.

"Welcome to Rocky Point Ranch," Hiram said, standing on the rail fence. "First off we have Miz Sarah Ann Andrews over here in the pasture who's going to show you all that a young lady can shoot as good as any man."

At Gil's nod, Sarah steadied the rifle against her shoulder, squinted down the barrel and squeezed the trigger. A pop split the air, then the top can on the right stack flew backward.

The clap of the crowd was drowned out by another shot. Then another. One by one, Sarah blew the cans off without missing.

When all twenty-four cans were scattered on the ground, the crowd hooted and clapped.

"Now Miz Sarah Ann will show you all she can hit a moving target," Hiram said.

Gil stepped to the end of the corral and started pitching cans in the air. Fast as he could throw them, Sarah plugged them. Not one miss.

"Ain't she something?" Hiram asked. "Give the lady a hand, won't you?"

Pride swelled Gil's chest as folks cheered. More than a few men whistled. Sarah smiled so big he thought her face would crack. Then a tall, dapper gentleman stepped from the crowd and approached her.

Gil froze, certain his eyes were playing tricks on him. Nope, it was him, all right. Harrison Cooper. He knew it before the old man removed his bowler hat to reveal a thick head of silver hair.

His father smiled at Sarah, his mustache moving as he spoke to her. Gil started toward them. There'd be hell to pay if the old man said one word about Sarah having Cooper green eyes.

Sarah backed away from his father, then ran toward the barn. Son of a bitch. What had the old man said to her?

"Next up, Dwight will show you all that he's the best bulldogger in the state," Hiram said. "Have at it, cowboy."

Hooves pounded in the corral by the time Gil bore down on the man who'd caused him nothing but grief. "What the hell did you say to that girl?"

Harrison Cooper hiked his chin up and tried to look down his nose at Gil, but he couldn't. They were eye to eye now. Equals on Gil's turf. The old man had best realize that.

"I see you haven't changed, Gilbert. Still full of misplaced anger."

"That's a matter of opinion and yours don't count in my book. What did you tell Sarah?"

"I complimented her on being an exemplary shot," Harrison said over the cheers from the crowd.

"Then why did she run?"

"Someone by the barn called for her. A woman." Harrison smirked. "I assume she was the girl's mother."

"What are you doing here?" He had a feeling when Eliza sent that telegram, she told their father that she'd found Gil.

"Now isn't the time or place to discuss this. But I do expect a full accounting at a later date." Harrison slid his bowler on and returned to the sidelines.

Hell would freeze over before Gil spilled his guts to the old man. All Gil wanted from his father was to be left alone.

He strode down the fence to where Hiram stood. Dwight was scrambling up from the steer he'd brought down. As the animal lurched up and raced away, Dwight slapped the dust from his chaps and took a bow.

"You ready?" Gil asked him.

"Ready as I'll ever be."

"Where's Josie?"

Hiram nodded to the barn. "She's waiting there with Miz Sarah."

"Reckon she's ready then," Gil said.

"Yup. I spotted a man up on the ridge this morning. Seemed to be watching the place."

"Recognize him?"

"Nope. By the time I got up there, he was gone. Left tracks though that headed toward Laramie."

"Keep an eye out. You see anything unusual, you holler."

"Sure enough."

"One more thing, don't forget to call out what I told you after Josie pops all the balloons."

Hiram grinned. "Believe me, I ain't likely to forget."

Gil slipped into the barn and searched the shadows for Josie. He found her near the back door.

"Where's Sarah?"

"She's with Eliza. You just missed them."

As long as she wasn't alone. "You about ready?"

"Of course. I always knew how to compose myself for the show that night, no matter what happened during the day."

Thinking how Parnell had used her filled him with a near-blinding rage. He shook it off best he could. The last thing he needed was another distraction beside having somebody watching the ranch from the ridge. If it was Parnell, Gil would make the son of a bitch sorry he'd ever looked Josie up.

"My father's here. I told him to stay away from Sarah."

"Surely your father wouldn't blurt out that he's her grandfather."

Gil shrugged. "No telling what he's got a mind to do. Harrison Cooper doesn't bow to any man's wishes."

Josie sighed. "I feared this day would come. Mercy, I don't even know how to explain it to Sarah Ann."

"Just tell her I'm her real pa." Gil caught her surprised look and rushed to explain. "Look, you married Everett and he raised her as his own, but I don't aim to ever take that away from her. Way I see it she has two pa's. One who watched over for her during her younger years, and one who'll be there for her for the rest of her life."

Her lips parted, and he had the sudden urge to kiss her and tell her everything was going to work out fine if she'd trust him. "Everett loved her, Gil. She deserves the same from you."

Gil tugged at the kerchief around his neck that felt like it was choking him. His mother had said much the same to his old man not long before she passed on. What was it with women and all this love talk?

"You know I care for her."

She sighed and laid a hand over his heart, and it bucked and reared like a bronco. "I don't think you know what you feel here, but I hope you figure it out."

Josie walked off toward the field, head high and whip coil slapping against her leg. Gil took the foot pump and sack of balloons, then headed out to the backside of the corral.

By the time Hiram finished up the last of his fancy roping skills for the crowd, including lassoing a couple of kids much to their giggling delight, Gil had the Rocky Point brand outlined in inflated red balloons. The wind knocked at them, making them slap against the wood.

Hiram caught his eye and Gil nodded, then stepped back to the corner of the corral out of sight.

The big black man coiled his rope and bowed. "Thank you kindly. Now folks, up next, Miz Josie Andrews will put on the finest display with a bullwhip you'll ever see."

Josie strode out into the field, wind snapping her split skirt and billowing the sleeves of her calico shirt. A flick of her wrist uncoiled the bullwhip.

"Ready when you are, Miz Josie," Hiram said.

Gil felt her excitement reach out to him as she took a stand and let loose the whip. It whistled through the air. A balloon exploded with a loud bang, followed by the firecracker pop of the whip's tail.

The crowd cheered, but Josie seemed oblivious to them as she kept snapping that whip over her head, hitting each balloon in rapid-fire order until nothing was left but bits of red rubber and a crowd yelling and whistling up a storm.

She took a bow then coiled her whip, her gaze sweeping the crowd. Her smile was slow coming, but when it did, she looked happier than Gil had ever seen her. Just as he'd hoped, someone shouted for more.

The flush of success stained her cheeks. Behind the questioning look she slid him, he caught sight of out-and-out excitement.

He nodded though he wanted to let out a whoop. Like he'd figured, she was ready to show off a bit more. If all went as planned, this wager would pay off big two ways. Josie would make more money, and she'd know damn well he trusted her.

Gil started toward the bag of balloons and hand pump, fishing out his makings and rolling a cigarette. No doubt folks would talk about Josie's prowess for months, which would have them clamoring for more exhibitions.

"And now," Hiram said, "Miz Josie will snap the lit cigarette out of Gil Yancy's mouth with her bullwhip. Five-to-one odds she can do it without the leather touching Gil."

Josie jerked her head toward Hiram, face pale and eyes too wide. "No."

"I'll take that bet." A man decked out in gambler's

duds and a black eye patch approached Hiram, and more soon gathered around the big foreman.

"You can do it, Josie." Gil smiled at her across the expanse, willing her to trust him as he trusted her.

She shook her head and looked near tears. If she kept biting her lower lip, she'd draw blood.

"Any more takers?" Hiram asked, but nobody stepped forward. "Ready?"

Gil dropped his hat on the ground, then struck a match and puffed his cigarette to life. He turned sideways, and his gaze locked with his father's narrowed one. He knew the old man thought him a fool for letting a woman have the upper hand.

"Ready when you are, Josie," Gil said.

"I can't."

"Yes, you can."

"Damn you."

A plume of smoke curled up before his eyes. He wanted to peek her way but didn't dare move.

Leather whistled through the air. A pop sounded above his head and he fought the urge to flinch. The cigarette was jerked from his mouth, leaving his lips tingling.

The crowd went wild.

Josie smiled and waved to them. Gil was so damn proud of her he could bust his buttons. He emptied the breath he'd been holding and started back toward the barn. This moment was all hers, and he wanted her to savor every second.

Besides, his act was next. He hoped to hell luck would ride with him.

Leather whistled again, followed by a louder pop. The whip coiled around his middle and brought him up short.

"Looks like Miz Josie done lassoed a cowboy that was fixing to hightail it," Hiram said.

Laughter erupted from the crowd.

Gil glanced at her, and her toothy grin had him chuckling. She wanted a show? Well, he damn sure would play along.

He raised his hands in surrender and let her reel him in. But the closer he got, he realized her grin wasn't real.

"You'd best smile, sweetheart, or folks will think you're fixing to hang me with that whip." He saw fear shadow her eyes, and his own smile vamoosed. "What's wrong?"

"I'll do anything you want, Gil. Anything as long as you don't ride that damned outlaw."

Chapter 20

"You all know what an outlaw horse is?" Hiram asked the crowd as Gil strode toward the corral where over a thousand pounds of stomping mean horseflesh waited for him. "That's one that can't be broken. A bucking machine. A widow-maker."

Grunts and gasps rippled through the crowd, punctuated by a few muttered curses. He'd done this trick more times than he could recall when it hadn't mattered. He sure as hell couldn't fail now.

"Gil Yancy is going to treat us to some bronco busting," Hiram said. "But to make the show more interesting, he bets he can ride this outlaw for eight whole seconds, all the while keeping a silver dollar pressed under each boot in the stirrup."

"I got a twenty dollar gold piece that says he can't stay on for ten seconds," a man said.

"I'll take you up on that," another spectator said.

Hiram eyed Gil. "You up for trying ten seconds?"

"Don't!" Josie's voice, though Gil couldn't see her among the men crowding around the corral.

"Hell, yes," Gil said. "I can hang on two more seconds."

Hiram raised a hand. "I got a watch right here to time him. Anyone care to take him up on his bet, just step on up."

Gil opened the gate and eased inside the corral. Dwight sat on the haze horse, keeping the saddled grulla cornered. Once Gil forked the saddle, all Dwight had to do was stay between the outlaw and the fence.

It wasn't as easy as it sounded. If the stallion edged Dwight's mount out, Gil could get crushed against a fence.

The grulla snorted and stomped. Pure meanness glittered in the outlaw's eyes and quivered in those bunched muscles.

All he had to do was hang on for ten damned seconds. More than his pride was at stake. He had to do it for Sarah and Josie. He had to show his old man he'd amounted to something.

The tension knotting Gil's gut popped like one of Josie's red balloons. He'd best this horse, by damn.

"Any more takers?" Hiram stuffed a wad of money in his vest pocket and nodded to Gil. "All righty folks. Sit back and watch how a real cowboy rides the wind."

Gil fished his last two dollars from his vest pocket and held them up for the crowd to see. He strode to the grulla, his spurs chinking loud in the sudden quiet.

The stallion tossed his head and crowded the corner. Gil grabbed the reins, ran a hand down the stallion's neck and vaulted onto the saddle.

The grulla tossed his head, seeming to settle down

instead of straining to get away. Gil knew it was the calm before the tempest.

He slipped a coin between his left boot and the stirrup, then did the same for the right, making sure Hiram and Dwight could vouch the money had been there at the start.

Gil got a tight rein on the grulla, found his seat, then nodded once to Dwight. The cowpoke reined his haze horse away and took up a post near the fence.

At the same time, Gil raked his spurs along the outlaw's flanks. Powerful muscles bunched beneath Gil a heartbeat before the outlaw leapt into the corral.

The grulla damned near bent double as he bucked and darted from side to side. Gil's heart flew up to his throat, then slammed down to his innards.

The crowd clapped and cheered him on, but Gil blocked them out. One distraction could end it all. So he focused on the grulla, trying to sense the horse's next move so he could hang on.

Not easy to do with the grulla whirling and kicking up a storm. Hell, if Gil didn't know better, he'd swear this kidney-scrambling sunfisher was switching ends on him.

"Six. Seven. Eight," Hiram said.

Gil held on. Those last two seconds felt like a lifetime.

"Ten," Hiram shouted.

Hot damn, he did it. A whoop went up from the crowd.

Dwight reined his horse close to the crazed stallion, but when he was within reach of the grulla's line, Gil's horse whirled and lunged the opposite direction.

Gil pulled leather to keep his seat, but the stallion

was akin to riding a cyclone. Worse, the damned grulla hung tight to the fence.

Just as Gil leaned forward, anticipating the grulla would rear, the stallion spun like a top. Gil lost his hat, then his seat.

Instead of hitting the ground, Gil slammed into the fence. One thought blazed in his head: he had one chance to grab hold or he'd fall under the grulla's hooves.

His hands caught most of his weight, but he slammed into the fence hard enough to drive the wind from him. A double kick to the rails from the outlaw's back legs send a breath-sucking jolt through him.

Pain skewed Gil's chest, and his sweaty, gloved hands nearly lost their grip. If he could climb to the top rail . . .

"Where's them dollars?" a man shouted as Dwight struggled to grab the outlaw's line.

Gil looked down. In the dirt below him lay two silver coins. He pointed at them and winced. "Right here."

The outlaw's haunches crowded the fence and he kicked it again. Wood splintered. The rail Gil was standing on gave way.

He dropped a good foot and banged his head. His arms and shoulders burned, his eyes damned near crossed.

Gil hooked an arm around a rail and stared through the opening, blinking the grit from his eyes, trying hard to focus. A man's face swam before him—a black patch covering the left eye and an ugly scar slicing his face from left eyebrow past his twisted smile.

Parnell? Had to be.

The outlaw let loose another double kick that

shook the whole fence. Gil's vision blurred again, turning into a rolling sea of browns and blacks.

"Got him," Dwight said, and the crowd clapped.

Gil shook his head to clear it and lunged for the top rail. He hauled himself up, desperate to get to Parnell before the bastard went after Josie.

He dropped to the ground and winced as pain jolted through him. The crowd closed in, all seeming anxious to slap his back.

Dammit all! He had to get to Sarah and Josie before Parnell did.

Someone pressed his battered hat in his hands. Another slapped him on his back and black dots swam in front of him.

Gil swiped the sweat from his brow. Why the hell was it getting so dark?

Sounds muffled, like his ears were stuffed with cotton. Voices died down to a whisper. Faces blurred before him. Then his knees buckled and he dropped into a black hole of silence.

"Don't think he busted his ribs." Doc Neely straightened from examining Gil. "But he surely bruised them more. Reckon the pain was too much and he blacked out."

Josie stared at Gil's prone body taking up all the room on the cot and thought he looked far paler than when she'd clobbered him. "You sure he'll be all right?"

The doctor snapped his leather case shut. "Yes, once he's rested. I'd advise against riding any broncos for a good long time."

Gathering his hat, Doc Neely left the cabin. Josie

glanced from Gil to his sisters, Ivy, and Harrison Cooper, all gathered at the foot of Gil's bed like mourners.

For all his bluster, the older man looked frail and sickly in the dim light. In fact, the only person who dominated him was Ivy, and Josie figured a blind man could see Ivy wore the britches in that family.

"We should leave Gilbert to rest," Ivy said. "Come, Harrison. You need to lie down now."

"I'm fine," he said, his gaze fixed on Gil.

"You should sit down," Abigail said to her father.

Harrison opened his mouth, but Ivy spoke. "I agree. After an arduous journey and undue excitement, your father must rest."

With that, Ivy took Harrison's arm and herded him toward the door. The old man glanced back once at Gil before he was dragged outside.

Abigail gripped the iron footboard. "Father said Gil staggered around, staring far off. He didn't even hear Father calling to him."

"I'm not surprised after all the jostling he took on that damned horse," Josie said.

"He'll be all right." Eliza laid a hand on Josie's cold one, and the warm arms of being on the fringe of a family wrapped around Josie. "Let's leave Gilbert to rest."

"I'll be along in a bit."

"Take your time," Eliza said. "If you'd like, I will gladly get dinner started."

"I'd appreciate the help."

As soon as the sisters left the cabin, Josie eased down on the bed beside Gil. She smoothed the coverlet over his muscled chest and dropped a kiss on his forehead.

The money Dugan MacInnes had pressed into her hand twenty minutes earlier weighted heavily on her.

"He'd bet his last cent on a game," his father had grumbled earlier. "Why the hell can't he overcome the affliction?"

Why, indeed? Every cowboy Josie had ever known was partial to gambling. But Gil had a gambler's heart. He'd wagered a kiss from her. Made a bet with her to practice the bullwhip.

Gil had risked his fool neck by taking that dangerous chance today. What would he do with his winnings?

"Your father told me to keep the money because he's convinced you'll gamble it away."

Josie slipped the wad of bills in his saddlebags and slid it under his bed. He'd put his trust in her today. She had to do the same to him.

She placed another kiss atop his stubborn head, then left him to rest. Before she ended up cornered in her house with the Coopers for the night, she had to have that talk with Sarah Ann.

Josie stepped outside to find a sun dipping low on the horizon and the crowd long gone. She saw Sarah Ann on the front porch with Deuce sprawled at her feet, both bathed in a orange glow.

She headed toward the house, her fingers curled at her sides and her heart beating too fast. Mercy, she'd almost prefer riding that outlaw horse than 'fessing up to Sarah Ann.

Josie eased into her rocker. "There's something I have to tell you, and it may be hard for you to understand. It's about your pa."

Her daughter's green eyes went misty. "What is it?"

Once she got it out, Josie could explain. But getting it out in the open was harder than she'd expected.

Josie picked at a loose thread, wondering if the

cloth would unravel as quickly as her past had done. "Everett wasn't your real father."

Sarah Ann's throat worked, and for a moment Josie wasn't sure if the girl would start bawling or bull up. "But Pa said he was."

"Yes, and he was your pa in all the ways that counted."

"Why didn't you marry my real pa?"

"For one, I didn't know what happened to him at the time."

"Why?"

"He just rode out of my life like he rode in, not knowing we'd made a baby." Josie gave her a moment to digest that. "Do you remember me telling you I had no family or nowhere to go?"

"Uh-huh."

"When Everett found out I was in the family way, he asked me to marry him. He was a good father. Sarah Ann, he loved you like you was his own flesh and blood. Always remember that."

Her daughter nodded, but that frown told Josie the hardest questions were to come. "Why'd you tell me this, Mama?"

"Your real pa is very much alive," Josie said. "You've seen him. And you like him."

"I have?" A look of pure horror crossed her daughter's face. "Where?"

"Right here. Gil Yancy is your pa."

Her eyes rounded. She glanced from Gil's cabin to Josie. "Is that why you clobbered him when he came here? Because you was mad at him for leaving you?"

Damn the lies that trapped her, but this time lying was for the best.

"Yes, that's why I clobbered him." Josie laid a hand on Sarah Ann's shoulder and was relieved when she didn't pull away. "Gil never intended to hurt me all those years ago, or hurt us by coming back into our lives. Do you understand?"

She frowned at the porch boards that needed paint. "I think so. Did Pa know about you and Gil?"

"Yes, I told Everett the truth."

And he'd asked Josie if she wanted him to find the cowboy, but she hadn't even known his name. Not that it would've mattered. Gil had been part of the past she'd wanted to escape.

Sarah Ann shook her head. "I'd like to go visit Pa." She blushed. "Up on the hill."

"Have Hiram or Dwight go with you." Though she doubted Parnell would show his face here, there was the question of who killed Boyd Rowney.

"All right." Sarah Ann waved to Dwight, and he ambled toward the house.

"Dinner will be ready shortly," Josie said, "so don't stay up there long."

"Okay." Sarah Ann rushed to Dwight with the hound trailing them.

She leaned back in her rocker and closed her eyes, waiting for relief to drown out the tension humming through her. But the drone born of worry just kept on.

Josie's dinner was as good as always, but the fried steak and gravy might as well been wood chips. The bitter taste of Parnell being here today coated Gil's tongue.

Gil had been the only one to recognize Parnell at the exhibition, though Hiram did recall the man with the eye patch. Even now, Gil's insides knotted when he reasoned how easily Parnell could've grabbed Josie or Sarah.

But nothing had happened then or while Gil had been out cold. Whatever Parnell's game was, they'd have to take turns keeping watch round the clock.

Josie hadn't said anything since Gil told her Parnell had been here, but she jumped at every noise. She hadn't balked when Gil told her he was staying in the house tonight either.

As for his family, Gil had been so riled about Parnell, he hadn't given his father much thought. Gil had rounded them up before dinner and told them he'd seen an outlaw sneaking round during the exhibition. From now on, they had to be extra careful. But sitting at the dinner table with the old man took more patience than Gil could muster.

"I suggest you enlist the services of a detective," his father told Gil.

"I aim to." *Hire a gun, that is.* "But until I do, we all have to keep watch."

"May I be excused to feed Deuce?" Sarah Ann asked Josie.

"Yes," Josie said. "Put a bowl of scraps on the front porch for him and come right back inside."

"All right."

Sarah's eyes flicked to Gil, but instead of shining with eagerness, they glinted with suspicion. Maybe a good dose of anger thrown in. No wonder.

Josie had told the girl that Gil was her pa. Though Josie said she took it well, the way Sarah eyed Gil heaped doubts on him. So much for him hoping things would go on as they had.

"For a man whose bet paid off, you look incensed,"

Harrison said to Gil as Sarah clomped from the kitchen.

Gil eyed the old man over the rim of his coffee cup. His father was mighty curious about Sarah, and the fact he kept looking from Abby to Sarah was reason why.

"Got a lot on my mind," Gil said. "You look a mite peaked. Reckon that trip was tiring on you."

"I agree with Gilbert," Ivy said. "You should rest."

Harrison snorted. "Stop mollycoddling me. I am far from needing a nursemaid."

"I worry about your health." Ivy perched to his father's right, looking more pinched than usual.

The old man harrumphed. "Health seems to be a particular worry to heirs."

"And wives," Ivy said. "I know what's troubling you, but there is ample time to discuss things tomorrow after we have recovered from today's excitement."

"I have no intention of taking to my bed any time soon," Harrison said. "If you are feeling indisposed, do not let me stop you from taking a nap."

A charged silence echoed in the kitchen as Ivy sat there gaping at her husband. Gil had the feeling the old man rarely put his young wife in her place.

Ivy got to her feet. "Very well. I believe I will retire to our cabin."

"I'll walk you there," Hiram said, and Gil knew the foreman would stand watch outside.

"Send Sarah back in," Gil said, gaining a nod from Hiram.

Ivy clip-clipped to the front door, sounding like one of those high-strung thoroughbreds trotting on bricks. The front door opened and closed with a click.

Abby stole a glance Dwight's way before looking

at her father. "Did Landon speak with you when he returned?"

Harrison frowned. "No, but after receiving Eliza's account of what happened here, he needn't bother."

"He was a perfect beast," Abby said, "and I hope to never lay eyes on him again."

"My thoughts as well." Harrison grabbed Abby's hand and smiled, looking far older. "I apologize for foisting him on you. You have my word it will never happen again."

"Since Baxter is out of the picture," Eliza said, her expression as ruthless as their father's. "I ask that you reconsider hiring Stuart. He has a good head on his shoulders concerning business."

"I am too tired to discuss this tonight," Harrison said, surprising the hell out of Gil. No doubt about it, his father wasn't the cutthroat businessman he remembered. "In fact, I believe it is time we spared our generous hostess our company for the night."

"Very well. We'll talk tomorrow." Eliza rose and turned to Gil. "How are you feeling?"

"Like I got walloped upside the head."

Harrison pushed to his feet, his expression mirroring Gil's pain. "I am sure you have done many exploits over the years, but watching you ride that horse took ten years off my life."

"It took some out of this cowboy as well," Gil said.

"Obviously." Harrison inclined his head Josie's way. "Thank you for a wonderful meal, and for stepping in when Abigail needed a champion. I will see you are recompensed for your trouble"—he glanced at Gil—"and the good care you've given my family."

"That isn't necessary," Josie said.

"I believe it is, Mrs. Andrews."

The front door banged open. Hiram staggered into the kitchen, blood streaming from a gash alongside his head.

Dread slammed into Gil. "What the hell happened?"

"Got jumped outside Miz Ivy's cabin. When I came to, she was gone."

"What?" Harrison said.

Josie leapt to her feet, sending her chair crashing back against the wall. "Where's Sarah Ann?"

"Gone, too. Here, see for yourself. Found it on the porch."

Gil grabbed the paper Hiram handed him. "Son of a bitch! Parnell has them, and he wants Josie to bring him one thousand dollars by noon tomorrow or he swears he'll kill them both."

Chapter 21

Josie huddled on a chair and watched Gil pace the living room like a caged bear, anger radiating from him. If Hiram hadn't held Gil down, he would've ridden out into the night.

As it was, Gil had fought like a madman until Hiram finally got through to him that he'd waste time looking for a trail in the dark. Dwight had ridden off right away to fetch Sheriff Keegan and send a telegram to Philadelphia on Harrison Cooper's behalf.

Now Gil paced Josie's parlor, waiting with her and his family for the sun to rise. Dwight and Sheriff Keegan should arrive near dawn with a posse.

It was the longest wait of Josie's life. If Parnell abused Sarah Ann—

Josie pressed a hand to her stomach, feeling right sick. She knew what Parnell would do to her daughter if he had a mind to. Knew firsthand the pain Sarah Ann would suffer at that sadistic bastard's hands.

"With the trains down, I fear we won't have the

ransom in hand until late tomorrow," Harrison said, his eyes bleak.

"There must be some way we can get that amount of money sooner." Eliza voiced the one thing Josie had been gnawing over for hours.

"Only one way I know of to double my money," Gil said.

"Gambling?" Harrison harrumphed. "It's too risky."

Gil scrubbed a hand over his nape. "So is hoping to hell your money gets here before Parnell makes good on his threat. Nope, my mind's made up. I'll ride over to MacInnes's at sunup and ask him for a loan."

"I'll go with you," Josie said.

Gil shook his head. "No. You stay here and I'll take the ransom to Parnell."

"You can't," Josie said. "If I don't show up with the money—" She broke off, unable to voice her worst fear.

"She's right," Harrison said. "The ransom specifies that Mrs. Andrews is to deliver a thousand dollars to some cabin near Diamondback Crossing. There will be directions there where she's to leave the money. If we deviate from that plan in any way, Parnell will kill Ivy and the girl."

"Not if I get to him first," Gil said.

"What if he sees you coming?" Harrison asked.

"He won't." Gil lifted his cup to his mouth, then frowned and set it down, empty again.

"There's no way you can be sure of that," Josie said.

The fear and determination in Josie's eyes gave Gil cause to worry. "I don't want you to leave this ranch. You hear?"

"I hear."

But Josie wasn't about to sit here on her hands. Ross Parnell had Sarah Ann, and Parnell had never played by any rules. This time was no exception.

"I'll put on more coffee."

Josie slipped into the kitchen and set to work, but her mind was miles away. Her daughter's life hung in the balance, and she knew Parnell would never keep his word, especially if Gil showed up instead of her.

She had to do this alone, but how? Gil wasn't about to let her leave without him, so she'd have to escape without him knowing. Damnation, she'd have to hoodwink this cowboy again.

An idea came to mind as she carried the fresh pot of coffee into the parlor. Gil had planted his hands on the window casing and stared out into the night. Her heart went out to him, but she couldn't let him ride into a trap, and she couldn't let him stop her from doing what she must.

"Do you know the cabin at Diamondback Crossing?" Gil asked her as she filled his cup with coffee.

"As I recall, there're about five shacks near there."

Gil scowled. "You sure?"

"Yes. They were abandoned by the tie-hacks after the railroad went through."

"Parnell must be holed up in one of them." Gil frowned into his coffee. "Any way to sneak up on the shacks?"

She shrugged. "Maybe. They squat in a row and butt up against the bluff."

But they were also near the road, and because of that Josie doubted if Parnell was hiding there. He'd want to be able to see anyone approaching. A remote spot.

Only one of those came to mind. She recalled an old cabin up the mountain above the crossing. From there Parnell would have a good view of the valley and would see a rider approach from about any direction.

And if that rider was Gil? Parnell would kill him.

Josie shivered at the thought and splashed coffee in her cup. Gil saw Parnell here today, watching the exhibition. Even if he didn't remember Gil as being the cowboy she'd given her virginity to, Parnell had seen that little show she and Gil put on. How she'd lassoed Gil with her whip.

That'd be enough for Parnell to go after Gil. No, money wasn't all Parnell wanted. Making her scramble to get it was just another means to torture her.

He'd want to take what she cared about from her. That was his game—making Josie hurt.

That's why he took Sarah Ann. Parnell wanted Josie, and he knew she'd do anything to protect her daughter.

Well, she wanted Parnell, too. Wanted him dead. By damn, she'd see to it that he breathed his last.

Josie didn't dare tell Gil about the cabin or he'd ride up there. If she was the cause of his death— Well, she couldn't live with that either.

Besides, Gil would find out about the cabin when Virgil got here and read the letter. By then she'd be up there, cutting a deal with the devil.

But first, she had to get away from Gil's watchful gaze. She jostled her cup and coffee splashed on her split skirt.

Hot liquid burned her leg. Josie sucked in a breath, jumped to her feet and shook her skirt, managing to spill more coffee on her rug.

"Oh, dear, did you burn yourself?" Eliza asked.

"It stings some," Josie said. "Mercy, I can't believe I was so clumsy."

"You have every right to be nervous," Eliza said, and Harrison nodded.

Josie eased toward the door. "Excuse me while I go upstairs and get out of this wet skirt."

Gil stepped in front of her and cupped her shoulders in his big hands, and the tenderness of his touch brought tears to her eyes. "It's going to be all right, Josie. Just trust me."

She nodded and slipped away, unable to look him in the eyes when she was fixing to trick him again. She mounted the steps and looked back, fearing she'd see him watching her.

But nobody was there.

Josie quietly descended the stairs, tiptoed down the hall and ducked out the back door. She took a jacket off the peg, grabbed her bullwhip and ran around the side of the house.

The chill night air nipped at her skin as she raced the long way to Gil's cabin, careful to stay hidden from Hiram standing guard on the front porch. As dark as it was, slipping inside the cabin was easy.

His saddlebags were where she'd left them, as was the prize money. An ache settled in her heart as she stuffed the five hundred dollars in her poke.

This was the second time she'd lied to Gil and robbed him blind. He'd never understand she was doing this as much to keep him alive as she was to save Sarah Ann.

She peeked out the cabin door. Hiram's head was turned toward the road.

Josie ran to the barn, grabbed her tack and hauled it far into the pasture. Once she was over the hill, she whistled softly. Her paint mare moseyed out of the darkness.

In no time, she had Clover saddled and was galloping away into the dark night. If only the chill air could numb her aching heart like it did her hands and face.

An eternity seemed to pass before Josie reined her mare up before the massive, stone house. Her stomach ached something fierce as she stared at the lone light shining in a lower window.

It didn't make the place look the least bit welcoming. If anything, it proved the rumors she'd heard that the mysterious man who lived here never slept.

Just as well. He'd be less apt to deny her if she didn't have to wake him out of a sound sleep.

Her legs trembled as she dismounted and tied her reins to the hitching post, careful not to let the heavy ring clang against the iron. She'd gone over all what she had to say on the way here. Still she feared she'd trip over the words when the time came.

Josie wiped her hands on her skirt and knocked on the door. Before she lowered her hand, the heavy door swung open.

She stared up into Reid Barclay's dark eyes and felt a chill ripple over her soul. He always had that dangerous air about him, but tonight he looked angry.

"Come in, Mrs. Andrews. To what do I owe the pleasure of your company?"

"I need money right now."

He stared at her so long she feared he'd laugh. Or curse her and run her off his place, like she'd done to him. But he didn't laugh. Or swear. Or smile.

"Follow me." He walked off.

Josie closed the door behind her and trailed him down a long hall lit with gas lamps that hissed like snakes. She shivered and hoped he couldn't hear her heart thunder or her knees knock. Her stomach cramped so much she was glad she hadn't eaten dinner. For sure it wouldn't have stayed down.

Reid entered a room with dark paneled walls, dark furniture and heavy dark draperies pulled shut at the windows. It felt as oppressive and obscenely wealthy as the man before her.

He stopped at a sideboard and poured an amber liquid into two glasses. "Does Gil Yancy know you're here?"

"I don't see what difference that makes."

He handed her a glass, but she shook her head. Though she'd prefer to be totally numb while she endured this bit of business, she couldn't afford to have whiskey muddle her thoughts later.

Reid took a sip of his whiskey and watched her with dark, glittering eyes. "Be honest with me. That's one thing I have always admired about you."

"I need five hundred dollars tonight, but I don't want to be your mistress. That hasn't changed."

"That's cutting straight to the heart of the matter." He surveyed her with a slow, smoldering look that did nothing but make her more nervous. "In many ways we're cut from the same cloth. For that reason alone I believed you'd suit as my paramour. In fact I was looking forward to tutoring you."

Her face heated. "Are you refusing me a loan?"

"That depends on why you need it so badly. What aren't you telling me, Josephine?"

She sniffled, hating the tears that wouldn't stop. "Sarah Ann has been kidnapped, and we couldn't scrape up enough for the ransom."

"That's a matter for the sheriff—"

"No! I know who has her, and I know if I don't bring

the money to him by sunup, he'll have his way with her." She stared into his eyes, searching for a shred of compassion and finding none. "She's just a child."

"You are playing a dangerous game, one I am sure Yancy has no clue about or he'd stop you."

Arguing only wasted time. "Please, just give me the money now. I'll make it right by you somehow."

"Very well. Let's be done with it then."

Reid walked to a massive bookcase and removed a large bust of an extremely ugly man from the shelf. He opened a small safe with a distinctive click, and to her horror, her lower lip quivered uncontrollably and tears stung her eyes.

He counted out a stack of greenbacks and looked at her. "It's yours, but I'm going with you."

"No. I have to do this alone."

"You are stubborn and proud and quite courageous." He folded his arms over his chest and she glimpsed the beginnings of a rare smile. "By damn, I should make you my wife."

A nervous laugh bubbled from her. "You deserve far better than me."

"Actually, I'm not worthy of you." He pressed the money into her hands. "Go, and be careful."

"Thank you."

Josie clutched the money to her chest and ran to the door. She stopped and looked back at Reid. Danger radiated from him.

"I'll pay you back."

This time he did smile, and the way it changed his features took her breath away. "If Yancy doesn't marry you, I may sever my promise and become your ruthless suitor. Now go."

She ran out the door, thinking she'd be lucky to survive the night, let alone live to marry Gil.

Gil glanced at the mantel clock. Josie had been upstairs a good thirty minutes. If she was the type of woman who dawdled over her clothes, he wouldn't have thought anything of it. But Josie wasn't one to primp.

He strode into the kitchen, thinking she'd slipped back and started cooking to keep her mind occupied. The kitchen was empty and so was the back porch. And her whip was gone.

Worry clung to his back as he hurried down the hall and ran up the stairs. He checked her room first, not bothering to knock. Empty, and he didn't see her wet skirt hanging to dry. He didn't find her in the other bedrooms or the bathing chamber.

Gil ran down the steps and yanked open the front door. "Josie!"

Hiram materialized out of the darkness. "She ain't out here."

"Dammit, she's not in the house either."

"I'll check the cabins and the outbuildings."

Gil wouldn't put any money on them finding her on Rocky Point. Nope, he wanted to kick his ass for not figuring that she'd go after Parnell on her own.

"What's wrong?" Eliza asked when Gil stormed into the parlor for his Winchester.

"Josie took off."

Fear like he'd never felt before knifed through Gil. If he lived to be a hundred, he'd never forget the hatred glittering in Parnell's one good eye, or the smirk that hinted he had the upper hand.

Now the son of a bitch did. If Gil didn't move fast, he could lose Sarah and Josie to Parnell.

The front door swung open and Hiram stepped inside. "Her tack is gone. Reckon her paint mare is, too."

"You stay with my family." God knew his old man would be no help if trouble sprang up. "When the sheriff gets here, send him over to the shacks near Diamondback Crossing."

"I will. Watch your back," Hiram said.

"Wouldn't it be wiser to wait for the sheriff?" his father asked.

"Not the way I see it."

"Would you risk your life if Ivy had been the only one abducted?" his father said.

Gil paused at the door and glanced at his father. The worry that'd carved new lines on his face shocked him. Hell, Gil reckoned that if he took a gander in the mirror, he'd see much the same on his own mug.

"I'd do what I could to save her," Gil said and meant it. He caught Hiram's gaze. "Are there any other shacks near the crossing?"

"There was an old line cabin up the mountain," Hiram said.

"You know a way to get up there without being seen?"

"Yup. A trail winds up the backside of the mountain." Hiram gave Gil directions.

Gil jammed on his hat and headed out into the murky night. A quick check in his cabin confirmed Josie had helped herself to his winnings.

She had half the ransom. Not that it mattered.

Even if they came up with the whole amount, Parnell wasn't likely to take the money and run. He burned with vengeance for Josie. And damn if she hadn't gone to the bastard alone.

Josie pulled back on the reins as she reached the edge of the wooded plateau above the creek. Dawn was nigh breaking. She could make out the shadow of a cabin up ahead.

In back of it, she saw two horses tethered. Had Parnell made Ivy and Sarah Ann ride double? Or had the sadistic cur forced one of them to ride with him?

Images of what he might have done to Ivy and Sarah Ann all this time tormented her mind. She wanted to thunder to the cabin and call the bastard out, but she'd play right into hands.

Her chances were better if she surprised him. That wouldn't be easy with a window on the side facing her. She reckoned its twin was on the other side.

Just like she'd thought, Parnell could see anyone approach the cabin. That left one way—stay close to the bluff and sneak up on the backside.

Josie angled her paint mare toward the trees and the swath of darkness clinging there. Thoughts of Gil played in and out of her mind like the shifting shadows.

Though Everett had told her she'd find a man deserving of her and give her heart to him, she'd never believed it. But it had happened. It was as if she and Gil were destined to be lovers. And Everett had a hand in bringing Gil back into her life and Sarah Ann's.

And what had Josie done? She winced. She'd lied to him again, stolen his money and ran off.

She wouldn't blame Gil if he didn't want to have

anything to do with her. But my, her heart would surely shatter. *Don't think about that now.*

The one man she despised had her daughter. Josie had to make a bargain with the devil to free Sarah Ann. Once she'd done that, she and Parnell would square off for the last time.

She tied her mare to a low-hanging cottonwood limb near the other horses, grabbed her whip and crept toward the cabin while her aching heart yelled at her to run. Soft sobbing carried on the air.

The painful sound slammed Josie back to a dark, mean room in the Gilded Garter. She stumbled to her knees, hugging her middle, reliving the horror of Parnell looming over her. He'd forced her to do what no young girl should know about, much less endure.

Josie shook off the memory crippling her and hurried to the back of the cabin. She pressed her back to the rough boards, afraid to breath. The sobbing was louder here. Her child or Ivy?

She slipped around the corner and crept down the side, wincing as her foot came down on a twig. Its snap seemed unnaturally loud.

Crouching, Josie waited a lifetime for Parnell to show his face. The sob came again, and there was no disguising the pain.

Josie peeked in the side window, but the shutters were closed. She hurried to the front of the cabin, shaking with anger and fear.

Again, she squatted. The door hung on one hinge. Dead sage piled up like a snowdrift in the corner.

"No!" Sarah Ann shouted. "You're hurting her!"

Josie flicked her wrist and the whip uncurled behind her like a deadly snake. A man's heavy panting echoed inside, hard and guttural as she remembered.

Josie slipped into the cabin, blinking to see. The hulking form of a man kneeled on one cot. Beneath him, the voluminous folds of a skirt spilled over the edge.

Ivy. Her sobs tore at Josie's heart.

She looked to the other cot and rage exploded in her. Sarah Ann lay on it, hands tied above her head. Even in the dim light she could make out the dark bruise on her daughter's cheek. Had the bastard raped her?

Josie narrowed her eyes on Parnell's backside. She took aim and let her whip fly. The tip flew across the room, but instead of popping above her target, it hit the man's back. His fine shirt split clean down the back, followed by a stream of bright red blood.

"Yeow!" Parnell scrambled to his feet and faced her.

Josie went cold inside. She was to blame for that scar that sliced across an eye and mouth, leaving his lips pulled into a permanent sneer. And the black eye patch? Had she blinded him?

"You crazy bitch. That's twice you've lashed me. You won't live to do it again."

She stared at the six-shooter Parnell aimed at her, then hiked her chin up. "You kill me, you'll never see your ransom."

He barked out a laugh. "Are you saying you got it?"

"Let Ivy and Sarah Ann go and the money is yours."

An evil laugh rumbled from Parnell. "What, and lose my bargaining chips? The old man will pay dearly to get his wife back."

Thank God he didn't realize Sarah Ann was part of that family. "I'm worth more to Harrison Cooper than Ivy."

"How you figure that?"

"Gil's his son, and I'm carrying Gil's child. Heir to

the Cooper fortune." Even before the lie left her lips, she wished it was true.

Sarah Ann's eyes went wide. Ivy stiffened. Just stay quiet, Josie prayed.

Parnell scowled and worked his mouth in a knot. Good, he was thinking it over, which meant he was on the verge of believing her.

"So the cowboy knocked you up." Parnell laughed and holstered his six-shooter. "All right. I'll take you up on your offer. With one change. We leave them and you and I get the hell out of here with the money."

"Fine." She was willing to do anything to put distance between Parnell and Sarah Ann, but leaving Gil—That hurt more than she'd thought possible. "Untie them and we'll go."

"They stay tied," Parnell said, aiming his revolver at Sarah Ann. "Drop the whip or I blow your brat's head off."

Josie was good, but a bullet was faster and deadlier. Hating him with every fiber of her being, she dropped her whip.

Parnell bent down, grabbed the tip and yanked the bullwhip out of Josie's reach. That old feeling of helplessness settled on her, weighing her down to the past. Down to his level.

"Outside," he said, motioning for Josie to leave.

She glanced at Sarah Ann. "I love you. Always know that."

Tears streamed down her daughter's reddened cheeks. "Mama?"

"Hush. Everything will be all right."

Josie stepped outside, weighing her chances of forcing the cabin door shut. But the door hung on one hinge.

One kick and Parnell would break it down, and then there'd be hell to pay. She didn't doubt he'd point his gun at Sarah Ann and pull the trigger, relishing Josie's agony.

She glared at the bloody welt on his back. "There was a man found shot on our ranch. You do it?"

He slid her an evil look and shrugged into his jacket. "Yeah, I plugged him."

"Why?"

"He caught me watching the place and tried to blackmail me." Parnell's laugh would curdle milk. "Damn fool."

He grabbed her arm and hauled her outside. A flash near the bluff caught her attention. She squinted, catching the silhouette of a rider amid the trees.

Her heart thudded. Gil? Had he found her already?

The boom of a rifle behind Josie deafened her, but seeing the rider topple drove a knife in her heart. My God, he'd shot Gil. The father of her daughter. The man she loved.

Parnell grabbed her by her hair and yanked her against him. "Told you to come alone."

"You killed him!" Josie slapped Parnell as hard as she could.

His head snapped to the side, and an angry flush bloomed on his scarred cheek. She staggered back, but not quick enough.

He backhanded her. Josie stumbled and fell, but caught herself from sprawling at his feet.

Josie wet her lips, tasting blood, reliving nightmares. She lunged forward and butted him in the crotch.

Parnell grabbed her arm as he staggered back. He

yanked her on her toes and pressed his ravaged face against hers. "You've still got fire in you. That's good. I like a feisty woman in my bed."

He looped an arm around her neck and dragged her toward the horses. She dug her fingernails into his arm, struggling for breath, willing the fallen man to rise.

But he lay still as death.

Parnell tossed Josie on her mare and bound her hands to the saddle horn, smiling as he untied the poke. The money meant nothing to her as long as she saved Sarah Ann.

But had she lost Gil in the process?

One thought blazed in her mind as Parnell mounted his horse and heeled him into a gallop, dragging her mare in tow. If it was the last thing she did, she'd kill Ross Parnell.

Chapter 22

The rifle's blast shattered the silence. Gil reined his gelding before the empty shacks at Diamond-back Crossing, realizing the shot came from up the mountain.

A thousand things went through his mind and none of them pleasant. Josie and Sarah were up there. Maybe hurt. Or dead.

He urged his horse up the rocky trail Hiram told him about, taking it slow when he wanted to ride hell-bent for leather. But pushing Rhubarb faster would likely get Gil a broken neck or a crippled horse.

Fifteen minutes of his life trickled by as he picked his way to the top. The morbid silence rode heavy on his heart.

Gil topped the ridge and stopped, giving his geld-ing a moment to catch his wind. He scanned the sage-riddled plain that hugged a rocky bluff.

Sunlight glinted off a tin roof in the distance. Must be the cabin.

He fisted one hand. Josie knew this was where Parnell

was holding Ivy and Sarah all along. Yet she kept it
to herself.

She hadn't trusted Gil to save his own daughter.

He squinted at the cabin, seeing something move
in back near the trees. A horse? Yep, Sarah's piebald
mare.

Gil road near the tree line and the waning shadows. If he could sneak up on Parnell, he could get the
drop on him.

A horse whickered, the sound echoing from a jut-
ting wall of rocks up ahead. He reined up, scanning
the flickering shadows.

One finger of sunlight poked through the canopy
of trees and glittered off something on the ground.
The wind carried a low groan to him. Whoever was
there was hurt.

Gil rode closer, right hand hovering over his Peacemaker. He caught sight of the sleek chestnut first,
then the man sprawled at the stallion's feet. The fine
thoroughbred tossed his head and stamped in place,
challenging Rhubarb and anyone else who dared
come closer to his fallen master.

He recognized the horse and rider right off. Reid
Barclay. The Englishman's presence didn't ease Gil's
mind one bit, especially since it was plain to see Barclay had been shot.

Gil ground-reined his gelding and slipped behind
the rocks. The stallion laid his ears back.

"Easy, boy." Gil inched toward the pair. "I ain't
gonna hurt your master." *Yet.*

The stallion snorted, but didn't challenge Gil.

He crouched by Barclay. The Englishman had a nasty
gouge on the side of his head. If whoever shot him had
better aim, Gil would be digging a grave. As it was, Bar-

clay would end up with a bitching headache and a scar that was as ugly as the nobleman's temperament.

Gil shook Barclay's shoulder, dragging another moan from him. "Wake up, damn you."

Barclay fixed hostile eyes on him, then sat up and winced. "Bloody hell."

"What're you doing here?"

"Trying to be gallant, though I fear I failed Josephine."

Anger sliced through Gil. "How'd you know where to find her?"

"I followed the lady when she left my ranch."

Barclay grabbed his horse's saddle and pulled himself to his feet. He swayed, and Gil was tempted to knock him down again for the hell of it. For not stopping Josie. For taking advantage of her when she was most vulnerable.

Gil sucked in air like he'd been gut-punched. "What was she doing at your ranch?"

"That is between me and the lady."

"You gave her the money." Bile burned Gil's throat. "You son of a bitch! What did you make her do for it?"

"Need I remind you that Josephine came to me?"

He grabbed Barclay by the collar and slammed him up against the rocks, knocking a groan from him. "I ought to plug you right here for bedding my woman."

"Don't be an ass. Though I'd like nothing better than to make love with Josephine, she refused my advances and pressed me for a loan. I debated about striking a new bargain with her, until she told me of why she needed such a large sum."

Gil gulped in air and released Barclay, though he had a mind to shoot the bastard dead. "You expect me to believe you gave her money out of the goodness of your heart?"

"Believe what you will."

"You let Josie go, knowing she was riding into danger?"

"What is your excuse for doing the same?"

Gil didn't have one. Hell, she'd outsmarted him. But where she'd escaped danger the first time, she rode headlong into it this morning.

"You should've stopped her."

"To do that, I would have had to tie up Josephine." Barclay smiled. "The thought had crossed my mind on more than one occasion, though for an entirely different pursuit."

The fingers on Gil's right hand balled into a fist. He had a mind to pound Barclay into the ground.

"Instead, I followed Josephine as discreetly as possible and planed to overtake the man she came to meet, thereby being the hero," Barclay said.

"Some hero. You ended up shot."

Gil squinted at the cabin and Sarah Ann's horse tethered in back, pushing Barclay from his mind. "Keep an eye peeled while I sneak around back and get the jump on Parnell."

"I doubt he is in there. A man and Josephine quit the cabin. The bastard obviously saw me because he fired. I heard horses ride out as I fell," Barclay said. "I'd hazard a guess that he escaped with Josephine."

Not what Gil wanted to hear. "I'll deal with you later."

"No doubt you'll try," Barclay said in a curt voice that grated on Gil's already short patience.

Gil gained his saddle in one leap and galloped

toward the cabin. Muffled sobbing carried on the wind, ripping something deep inside him in two.

He ground-reined Rhubarb and drew his revolver, pressing his back to the rough cabin walls, terrified what he'd find inside. Slipping down the side took a lifetime, each sob from inside tore at him, drawing blood.

At the front porch, Gil chanced a look inside, then rushed into the cabin. On one cot huddled a pile of silks. A reedy sob echoed from the woman. Ivy.

Sarah was tied to the other cot. His throat worked and his heart thundered as he inched toward his daughter.

Fear widened her eyes, proof she'd seen more than a girl should. If the son of a bitch abused her, he'd chase Parnell into hell and kill him with his bare hands.

One swipe of his knife severed Sarah's bonds. She jumped off the cot and swayed.

Gil steadied her, aching to pull her to him and afraid he'd cause her more distress. "You okay?"

She nodded, tears swimming in her eyes. "He hurt Mrs. Cooper."

Thank God Parnell hadn't molested the girl. By the sounds coming from Ivy, she hadn't been as lucky.

Gil couldn't find it in him to shun the woman he'd once planned to marry. He squatted beside the cot. "Ivy?"

She flinched and pulled away from him, curling into a ball as much as her bound hands would allow. Her whimper scared the shit out of him. He'd never heard that sound come out of anything but a bloodied pup he'd rescued from a beating by hooligans.

"It's me. Gil." His swallowed hard as he cut her bonds. "Gilbert. You're all right now. You hear?"

She stared at him, but Gil had a hunch she didn't see him at all. He suspected whatever Parnell had done to Ivy trapped her in some trauma from her past.

"Mama lashed Mr. Parnell with her whip and he stopped hurting Mrs. Cooper." Sarah stood close beside him and laid a hand on his shoulder. "It riled him something awful."

Josie had guts to confront the son of a bitch. He picked up her whip and curled the leather into a loop. "What happened?"

Admiration and fear churned in Gil as Sarah told him the rest. "Mama told him she was worth more than us to Mr. Cooper because of the baby."

"What baby?"

"The one you got on Mama." This time there was a touch of resentment in Sarah's voice.

Gil blew harder than a winded horse. "She said that to save you."

But it could be true. Funny how having more kids with Josie appealed to him, made him feel whole.

A scuff at the door had Gil shoving Sarah behind him and drawing his Peacemaker. Reid Barclay leaned against the doorframe, bleeding like a stuck hog.

The Englishman nodded toward Ivy. "How is the lady?"

"Don't know. Sarah said Parnell hurt her."

The two men shared a knowing look. Parnell had his way with Ivy while a young girl was in the room, watching and hearing the worst a man could inflict on a woman. Just like the son of a bitch had done to Josie's sister.

Barclay staggered inside and dropped onto an upended log that served as a chair. "Get on with you and pick up Josephine's trail before it grows cold. I'll stay with the lady and Miss Sarah."

"Sheriff should be along shortly." Gil turned to Sarah. "Did Parnell say where he was taking your mother?"

"No."

"That's all right. I'll find them. You stay here with Mr. Barclay."

Gil spared Ivy one last look, then marched to the door. Barclay's words stopped him.

"Fair warning, Yancy. After today, I'll move heaven and hell to make Josephine mine."

"Stay away from her."

"If you don't marry her, I shall." The hint of a smile touched Barclay's hard mouth. "When you find Parnell, kill him."

"It's as good as done."

Parnell set a ground-eating pace, angling south along the mountains. He hadn't stopped when he took a drink from his canteen, and he never offered her a sip either.

Josie had called him every vile name she could think of until she couldn't muster up the spit to swallow. Now she spat silent curses at him. Somehow she'd make him pay for all the hell he'd heaped on her and those she loved.

Loved? Yes, she loved Gil Yancy. And this poor excuse of a man had shot Gil, taking that from her too.

The punishing noonday sun was nothing compared to the burning hatred she felt for Parnell. Sweat slicked her body. The rope digging into her wrists had drawn blood. Her back ached and her parched throat screamed for something to drink.

Still they rode on. Even though nobody was following them.

Parnell angled off the trail that wound south, hugging the mountains to their right. They were riding toward Colorado.

"If we don't stop soon, my mare is going to drop in her tracks," Josie said.

His laugh was low and cold. "If she does, then you'll be on foot."

Parnell would enjoy it if she had to walk.

Her fingers felt raw from struggling to untie the silver concho within her reach, but she had to free it. Hiram or Dwight would recognize it came from her saddle. They'd know she'd come this way.

"If you hope to get a good price out of me, you'd better treat me right. You won't see a red cent if I lose my child."

"I've been thinking about that. It's too soon for you to know if he caught you." Parnell let out a caustic laugh. "You conned me good. I'll give you that. But I've got the money, and I've got you."

That wouldn't be for long, if she could get the drop on him. "Where are we headed?"

"Don't you get tired of yapping your mouth?" Parnell asked.

"They'll send the posse after you."

"Let 'em. They won't find me." He smirked. "Won't find you either."

Maybe, but a slice of hope bloomed as she untied the thong and the silver concho fell to the ground.

* * *

Gil pushed Rhubarb as hard as he dared, hoping he'd catch up with Parnell. Time was against him. Parnell had too good a jump, and when Gil reached the crossroads, he had no idea which way Parnell had headed.

"Dammit all. Where's he going?"

The right trail climbed into the mountains that stretched out in a dark green mass before him. Nothing much up there except logging camps and what remained of Cummings City.

Heading left took him out of the foothills to the road that passed through Virginia Dale. Gil figured that's the way Parnell would go, hightailing it to Colorado.

Something glistened on the ground up the trail on his right. Gil jumped off his horse and took a look. A concho.

He picked it up. Josie's saddle had ones like this. He'd bet it came off hers. He walked farther on, searching the ground.

Gil crouched and studied the hoofprints. Two horses passed here recently, moving fast.

His chest tightened with worry. A man like Parnell would take a woman into the mountains for one reason.

He'd never overtake them on the flats, but he had a chance of getting in front of them by taking the deer track.

Gil climbed onto the saddle and urged his horse up a rocky path running parallel to the road. Twenty minutes felt like a day. His horse blew, near exhaustion, but Gil pressed on.

The track hugged the stands of ponderosa pines and aspen on his right and rode the sheer drop off on the left. He ground-reined his horse, pulled his

Winchester from the scabbard and picked his way to the edge of the bluff.

Below lay the trail. Gil eased down the rocky slope to an outcropping of giant boulders. He settled in to wait, hoping to hell he'd gotten here first.

Sweat streaked down his back and face. The cold settling over him had nothing to do with the higher altitude. If he lost Josie—

The crunch of hooves on rocks echoed up to him. *Riders.*

Parnell rode into view on his dark horse. A rope stretched from his saddle to the paint trailing him. Josie atop her mare.

Gil raised his rifle and swore. He backhanded the sweat dripping into his eyes and sighted down the barrel again.

The loose rocks under Gil's feet broke free, sliding and bouncing down the embankment. Parnell looked up, and Gil knew he'd been seen.

He squeezed the trigger, but Parnell heeled his mount at the same time and galloped behind a wall of rocks with Josie in tow. Dammit!

Gil couldn't breathe. If he shot Josie—

Parnell disappeared behind the rocks. A gray cloud exploded along the outcropping in front of Josie's mare, right before her horse joined Parnell's.

Gil took off toward a cluster of rocks farther along the slope. He'd have a better chance to pick Parnell off there.

A gun boomed. Fire seared Gil's arm as he ducked for cover. He slammed his back against the rock wall and hissed out a breath.

His right arm burned like a prairie fire. The bullet

had sliced a wedge out of the upper part. Blood soaked his shirtsleeve and dripped on the ground.

Gil ripped off his bandanna and wrapped it around the wound, tying it tight as he could using his left hand and teeth. He flexed the fingers on his right hand. They moved all right, but he'd lost his quick reflexes.

Josie's cry drove the air from Gil. He peered around the rocks, but couldn't see a damned thing.

All the abuse Parnell had heaped on Josie tormented Gil. He wouldn't put anything past this sadistic bastard.

Gil dropped his hat on the ground and swiped the sweat off his brow. The fear of failure dumped a load on him. He had to kill Parnell before he hurt her more, but getting a clean shot at him now wouldn't be easy.

He took a stance at the edge of the outcropping, shouldered his rifle and squinted down the barrel. He spied a flash of black before it ducked behind the rocks. Parnell's arm.

Gil focused on that spot, finger poised to squeeze off a round. All he needed was one good shot. He could suffer the pain burning clear through to his back, but the stiffness settling in gave Parnell the advantage.

Josie popped into his sights, hands tied before her and barrel of a six-shooter pressed to her head. Fear slammed into Gil, leaving him struggling for air.

He lowered the Winchester, hating the helpless feeling stealing over him. He hated Parnell with a vengeance.

"What's the whore worth to you?" Parnell asked.

Everything. "She's my partner in Rocky Point."

"Is that all?" Parnell's laughter pinged off the canyon walls like bullets.

"You're boxed in, Parnell. Turn her loose and I'll let you go."

"You expect me to believe you?" Parnell let out a cold laugh. "Toss your guns down the slope or I pull the trigger."

Gil pinched his eyes shut and swore. The bastard had him by the short hairs.

"All right."

Gil dropped his rifle over the edge, gut knotting as the Winchester slid down the slope. He drew his Peacemaker and tossed it the way of his rifle.

"Let Josie go."

Parnell yanked her back behind the rocks. A horse's whicker reached up to Gil.

He pushed from his hiding place and skidded down the hill to the next outcropping. His left hand scooped up his Peacemaker.

Gil crouched behind the smaller shield of rocks, willing Parnell to make a move in the open.

Parnell led Josie's paint mare from behind the rocks, using the horse as a shield. Josie sat atop her mare, hands tied before her.

Gil's heart stampeded. Never in his life had he felt so damned helpless.

"You want her," Parnell said. "Then catch her."

Parnell cracked a quirt over the mare's rump. The horse snorted and lit out at a gallop with Josie clinging to the saddle and the reins trailing the ground.

A heartbeat later Parnell took off at a ground-eating gallop going back the way they'd come. Damn the man to hell and back.

Gil inched to his Winchester, then scrambled up the slope and leapt on his horse, his chest so tight with fear he could scarcely breathe. If Josie's mare went down or she lost her seat, she'd be killed.

He pushed his gelding as fast as he dared, leaning back in the saddle and keeping an eye peeled for Parnell. He was an easy mark as Rhubarb skidded down the slope, snorting and muscles taut. The gelding bobbed on his haunches, then lunged forward and got his legs under him.

Gil raked the gelding's flanks and the horse broke into a gallop down the winding trail. He hit the straightway and caught sight of Josie struggling to stay in the saddle as her mare slid down the next slope. Each time the mare sat back on her haunches, Gil held his breath. If the mare went down, she'd take Josie with her.

Desperation rode Gil's back. He let Rhubarb pick his way down, each second seeming like an hour.

The paint's hooves slammed the ground below, tossing Josie forward. Just as fast, the horse lunged into a gallop down the trail.

Gil didn't know how she stayed on. He was sure he'd aged ten years getting down off the damned mountain.

When his gelding's hooves hit the trail, Gil gave Rhubarb his head. Foam flew from both lathered horses. He leaned over his gelding's neck and steadily gained on the mare.

Up ahead the trail narrowed, the sides dropping off sharply. Sweat and fear stung Gil's nostrils. With his right arm weakened, he had to use his left hand to grab her mare's reins. He had one chance before they hit the narrows.

Gil leaned forward farther than he dared, missing

the lines and nearly losing his seat. He heeled Rhubarb to go faster.

Twenty feet from the narrows he reached out and snagged her horse's lines. His muscles screamed as he sat up and pulled back on his own reins. Pain exploded in his right arm, but he gritted his teeth and held on, the misery nothing compared to his choking fear he'd lose Josie.

The mare stumbled to a stop beside Rhubarb. His gelding blew and the mare stomped and snorted. Gil had a mind to bellow as he took in the red mark on Josie's cheek. He swore he'd make Parnell pay for laying a hand on her.

"You all right?"

"I am now. Mercy, I thought I was dreaming when you caught up to us." She frowned, staring at the bloody bandanna. "He did shoot you."

"Bastard winged me in the canyon."

Tears slipped from her eyes. "I thought Parnell had killed you back at the cabin."

"Your admirer is the one who took the bullet."

"What?"

"Reid Barclay. He aimed to be the hero in this stupid melodrama you cooked up."

Gil untied her hands from the saddle horn and pressed the reins in her hands, feeding on that anger to keep his edge. He couldn't risk letting his guard down now, even though he wanted to take Josie in his arms and banish all thoughts of Parnell and Reid Barclay from her mind.

Her face turned ash white. "Is he dead?"

"No, but Barclay got a new part in his hair. I left him with Sarah and Ivy, though I reckon the posse found them long ago and took them back to the house."

"Which is where we should be," she said. "Parnell will try to grab her again."

"He's going to have to go through me to get close to either of you." Gil thumbed his hat back. "Dammit, Josie, you could've been killed."

"So could you, Gil."

He'd have walked through hell to save his daughter and Josie. He still would.

"You should've asked for my help."

She shook her head. "You wouldn't have helped me. You'd have done things your way and left me behind, and Parnell would've shot you dead."

Dammit all! She was right. "Come on. Let's go home."

They headed back to the canyon at a trot, but not for long. Josie's mare pulled up lame.

"Clover's favoring her left foreleg," Josie said.

Gil swung off his gelding and checked the mare's front leg. No heat or swelling. He lifted the hoof, thinking a rock had lodged in the soft tissue. Not a one. The foot was clean, and the shoe was in tact.

"She must've twisted it when she stumbled. Let her walk a ways."

He watched the mare. Clover's strides were shorter, but she didn't favor the leg if she stayed to a walk.

He mounted his horse and caught up with her. "We'll have to take it slow."

The last thing he wanted to do with Parnell out there. He damn sure didn't look forward to going back the way they'd come. Parnell could be lying in wait for them. With Josie riding a lame horse, they couldn't outrun trouble.

Gil pointed east. "If we head that way, we'll cross the stage road."

"That's a long way from home."

Josie had gone that way when she'd come to Rocky Point twelve years ago. She prayed it'd see her home safe this time as well.

They rode for hours. The sun dropped behind the mountains fast, leaving pockets of shadows on the hilly terrain. Hiding places that had her holding her breath each time they passed.

Josie wondered if Gil's thoughts mirrored hers. Parnell could be out there waiting for them. Or had the bastard ridden back to the ranch?

She wanted to see her daughter so badly she hurt, but she was so tired she could barely stay upright in the saddle. She feared her mare would go down any time. And she was worried sick about Gil's arm.

"There's an old line cabin up ahead. We'd best hole up for the night."

Josie wasn't about to argue. "Sounds good to me."

They reached the deserted cabin just as the first stars lit the sky. The door looked solid enough to keep out predators—two- and four-legged ones.

Out back was a pen for the horses. Gil drew water from a well for them, then brought the tack inside the cabin.

She batted down cobwebs with an old broom, wishing she could sweep away her troubles as easily. In no time Gil had a fire crackling in the fireplace.

Josie looked around the sparse room. One rickety chair. One cot nailed to the wall. One daring cowboy who was favoring his right arm.

"Sit down and let me tend that wound," Josie said.

"You don't have to bother."

"I want to."

He sat, and she fussed with the wet knot in the bandanna. Her chest tightened with worry. He'd lost a lot of blood.

"Let's get you out of those dirty clothes so I can dress that wound."

Gil slid her a lopsided smile and shrugged off his vest, shirt and undershirt. She watched, waiting for the overwhelming fear to grip her, but different needs stirred within her.

As her heart warmed, heat spread up across her belly and ignited an ache she never dreamed she'd feel. She longed to touch Gil and be touched in turn. Was she wanton to long to lie with Gil at a time like this?

"Something wrong?" he asked.

"Not now."

Josie tore a strip off the leg of her drawers, then grabbed Gil's canteen. She wet the cloth and cleaned the wound as best she could, hating Parnell for hurting the man she loved. Dare she tell Gil what was in her heart?

She tore a strip of cloth off the other leg of her drawers. "If I was home, I'd stitch you up and pour whiskey on the wound before bandaging it."

"In my saddlebag. There's a pint of whiskey and a pouch with a needle and thread."

Josie rummaged in his saddlebags and found both. She soaked the needle and thread in whiskey. "This is going to hurt."

He took a sip of whiskey. "Get at it."

She did, wincing when his breath hissed through clenched teeth, feeling each stick of the needle and burn of the thread through his flesh. Her hands shook when she finished and dribbled whiskey on the wound, then bandaged it with the strip of muslin.

"I got jerked beef and canned tomatoes in my saddlebag," he said. "Not much but it'll take the edge off."

"I don't have much of an appetite," she said. "I'm worried. Parnell isn't going to go away."

"Didn't reckon he would. That scar on his face— Every time he looks in a mirror, he remembers you lashing him."

She nodded. "And no doubt dreams of torturing me for it."

"Shame you didn't kill the son of a bitch."

Or that someone hadn't spared them the trouble. To think her advertisement for the guest ranch was what brought Parnell back into her life.

"He shot Rowney," she said.

"I ain't surprised." Gil tore off a strip of jerky and handed it to her.

She broke off a smaller piece and gave the rest back to him. If she managed to get this much down she'd be doing good.

"Here I thought you'd be hungry as a bear, what with you packing the heir to the Cooper fortune."

Her cheeks heated. "I said that so Parnell would leave Sarah Ann and Ivy and take me instead."

"It worked." He opened a can of tomatoes with his knife and held it to her.

She shook her head. "Later, Parnell realized I'd gulled him."

He spooned a chunk of tomato in his mouth, and she resisted the urge to dab the spot of juice that trickled down his chin. "Thinking of you packing my baby is mighty appealing."

Her breathing hitched. "Is it now?"

"Yep. You did a fine job on my firstborn. You want more children?"

Mercy, she'd really never thought about it with Everett, and now—"May I remind you that I'm a respectable widow lady."

"Not for long. Single that is."

"Don't josh with me like that."

"I'm not. There's no reason why we shouldn't get hitched."

Josie went still. She could think of one very good reason, just the same as she'd told him when they'd had this conversation before. She wouldn't enter into another marriage of convenience. Dare she hope he'd come to love her as much as she loved him?

"Why do you want to marry me, Gil?"

"There's Sarah for one. Two, we're partners in the guest ranch." The teasing glint in his eyes changed to something keen. Shrewd. The look she'd seen in Harrison Cooper's green eyes. "I've got some ideas how to make a good profit for us."

He hadn't changed one damned bit.

Gil went on about hosting hunting ventures. The need for more cabins. More hands. More horses. More land.

Josie's rosy glow went up the chimney in a gust of hard reality. Gil viewed Rocky Point as a business, and her as a bonus. Not a home. Not a wife and family. Not for love.

"You've given this a lot of thought," she said.

"Yep. Started mulling things over the first time I got a good look at the spread and its potential."

She waited for him to go on, to tell her what was in his heart. But willing it didn't make it so. Her heart ached. Gil Yancy wanted her as his bed partner.

Oh, he'd care for her and see she didn't want for anything. But he didn't love her. He loved the idea of owning a ranch and the chance to build a dynasty here.

She wouldn't be part of a loveless marriage, and she sure wasn't going to be his mistress. But how could she be around Gil all the time, knowing she'd never again feel his touch, his kiss?

She didn't know.

Then there was the worry of Parnell, waiting for the chance to kill her.

Josie looked into the warm eyes of the cowboy she loved. She might never have more than this night with Gil.

She couldn't fret about her future until they made it back to the ranch and Parnell was no more a threat to her. Only then could she butt heads with Gil about his ideas for the ranch. And tell him why she couldn't marry him.

Chapter 23

Josie took the bent spoon and can from Gil and set them on the hearth, glad her hands didn't shake. It must be a sign that her plan was right, that wanting to share one more night of pleasure with him would be enough to last her.

She took her time undoing the buttons on her bodice, then peeled the garment off and let it drop to the floor. His eyes rounded and she heard him suck in a sharp breath.

"I want you, Gil." She walked toward him, knowing her love for him must show in her eyes.

He stood and pulled her into his arms, wrapping her in heat and strength and wanting so keen it brought tears to her eyes. "I'm yours for the taking."

She smiled, intending to do just that. Her lips brushed his, teasing, tasting, then opened to him.

He moaned low in his throat, the sound vibrating through her in warm waves. The melding of lips and tongue was so perfect, so right that she never wanted the moment to end.

He eased down on the cot and lay back, pulling

her atop him. Her legs naturally straddled his hips, and he bucked against her once, as if letting her know his need.

His hands slid under her skirt and glided up her legs to cup her bottom. She pushed against him and moaned. The heat and power in his touch burned her through the thin muslin, making her wet with want.

She trailed kisses along his jaw and down his neck, feeling reckless and free, loving him as she'd dreamed of doing all those sleepless nights. He reached for the button at her waist.

Josie pushed his hands away, knowing if she let him have his way, he'd take charge of this coupling. She wanted to call the shots. She had to, just once.

Her body hummed with passion as she scooted down his length and flipped the buttons free on his trousers. In no time, she had his impressive length in hand.

"Josie?"

"Trust me," she said, repeating what he'd told her that night in her bed.

He pinched his eyes shut and gave a jerky nod. "Easy, sweetheart."

"I'll be gentle with you, cowboy."

And she would, pouring out her love in every touch, every kiss.

Their eyes locked for a second, then she lowered her mouth to him. She stroked him slowly, branding the touch and taste of him in her memory.

Watching calico queens do this to johns had seemed vulgar—something she'd vowed she'd never do. But loving Gil every way possible, loving him as he'd done her the last time, felt natural and right.

He groaned and arched his back, pushing against her. "I can't hold out much longer."

She trailed her tongue up his length again and scraped a fingernail over his sacs, marveling at the differences in their bodies, as well as the similarities of their need. "Then don't."

Gil growled low, and she feared he'd had enough of her play, that he'd take over and pound into her. His eyes, glinting with passion, locked with hers.

Josie read the silent battle going on in him. The aggressor forced to submit. To trust.

He threw his head back and groaned, surrendering. She took him in again, deeply, as if doing so would take him into her heart forever.

His explosive climax rocked through her, triggering her own release. Before the last shimmers left her, he pulled her up beside him. His breath sawed loud in the small cabin.

"Now take that damn skirt off."

She undid the buttons then reached up to nip his chin. "Be gentle with me."

"You're going to get what you gave, sweetheart." His wicked smile shot straight to her heart. How could she ever say no to this man?

He shucked her from her clothes and peeled the rest of his away, kissing her so thoroughly she only thought of him and this glorious moment. She opened her arms and body to him, welcoming the cool air on her heated skin.

It wasn't near enough to temper the fire in her. Nothing would douse that, just sate it for a spell.

She'd expected him to take her quickly. But he knelt between her legs and inched his hands up her inner thighs. She knew she'd die of want if he didn't make them one now.

"I dream about you," he said, the admission shocking her.

"Wet ones, I imagine."

"Sometimes." He slid a finger over the heat of her, and she bucked. "What about you?"

"Once or twi—"

The hungry press of his mouth on her there ripped a gasp from her. Stars flickered behind her closed eyes and she reached for him, desperate to hold on to him as she rode the intense pleasure for all it was worth.

Her fingers tangled in his thick hair. But like a flash fire the feelings swept over her quickly, consuming her.

She clung to him, wanting more. Wanting all Gil had to offer her. Wanting him to truly love her.

He shifted and rose over her, pushing into her in one smooth glide. His fingers threaded through hers, and that connection brought new tears to her eyes.

"Hang on, sweetheart."

She did, her heart thudding against his in perfect rhythm. Each thrust, each glide carried her higher as she moved with her cowboy.

She stared into his eyes, certain she saw stars glittering in them. One final thrust sent her spiraling into the heavens on a reedy cry, her pleasure made sweeter because he joined her with a shout.

He cuddled her against his side and dropped a kiss on her forehead. "I want us to get hitched right away."

For the moment, she basked in the glow of spending the rest of her nights with him. Of having his children. Of him loving her as much as she loved him.

"Why?"

"No sense waiting."

Not the love words she'd waited all her life to hear. "Gil, how do you think of me?"

He cupped her bare bottom and pressed her closer to his side. "Like this."

She swatted at his hand and joined him in a laugh, though hers was edged with hurt. "I'm not talking about sex. I'm talking about how you feel about me."

"You're one helluva fine woman, Josie. No doubt in my mind that you're the wife I need." He yawned, his eyelids drooping. "Yep, the best thing I ever did was take Everett up on his offer."

His breathing evened out in sleep. Tears stung her eyes and she blinked them away. Her heart ached so badly she thought it'd break in two. His feelings for her hadn't changed, and probably never would.

Josie kicked herself for being a lovesick fool. There was no way she could live on the ranch with Gil and never share this pleasure with him again. One of them would have to leave.

They reached Rocky Point the next afternoon. As soon as Gil was sure Sarah Ann and his sisters were safe, he went into his cabin to change clothes and clean the trail off him.

Josie had been too quiet on the ride back. She hadn't looked him in the eye all day either, which seemed mighty peculiar to him.

At first he'd thought she was fretting over Sarah Ann, but he knew there was more to it now. Damn if he could figure what it was. Last night they'd had sex hot enough to burn down the cabin, and today she'd given him the cold shoulder.

Women! Hell, when he told her more of his plans for the ranch on the ride home, she busted his bubble by saying he was just like his father.

Like hell he was.

Gil shrugged into a clean cambric shirt, stewing about her ridiculous claim. He damn near didn't hear the light raps on his door. Probably one of his sisters. Or Sarah.

He crossed to the door and opened it. His smile froze. Ivy stood there, head high and chin out.

"I need to talk with you, Gilbert."

"Then talk."

"In your cabin, if you please."

Gil didn't budge. "The last time you conned me into being alone with you in a room, I ended up getting blamed for getting you with child."

She sent him a tight smile. "I assure you that won't happen again. Please. It concerns Harrison."

Well, hell. Looked like the only way he could get rid of his stepmother was hear her out.

"Come on in."

Ivy breezed past him on a cloud of roses and haughty poise. She moved to the lone chair and perched on it, but she wouldn't look at him.

"Out with it." He closed the door and leaned against it.

"I regret the fact that I was the cause of the rift between you and your father."

"Do you now?"

"Yes. The estrangement has been extremely hard on Harrison. You've no idea of the sleepless nights he's had, or the amount of money he's paid the Pinkerton Agency to find you."

"The old man should've figured that'd happen when he up and married my pregnant fiancée." The old hurt and anger boiled in him. "Problem was I'd never touched you, but the old man was sure you were packing the heir to the Cooper fortune. Tell me, Ivy. Did my old man knock you up?"

She went deathly pale, and he fully expected a reprimand about him being vulgar. "No. Mine did."

Talk about taking a bucket of cold water in the kisser. Of all the possibilities that had hounded Gil during that awful time of his life, incest hadn't been one of them.

Ivy Doyle's father was from old money, a pillar of the community. A respected businessman. Hell, he'd suggested the arranged marriage between Gil and Ivy when they were children.

She looked at him then, her smile sad and melancholy. "I have shocked you."

"That's putting it mild. Dammit, why didn't you tell me? Why didn't you tell somebody what was happening?"

"Fear that you wouldn't believe me. Fear if the truth got out that my father would beat me more than he had, or worse, that the abuse would simply continue."

Gil scrubbed his knuckles along his jaw, wondering how something like this happened. When it started. "Did your pa do this to you after your ma passed on?"

"No. My mother knew what was going on for years"— she looked him dead on—"and up until the day she died, she never tried to stop my father. After she was gone, his abuse increased. That last time his precautions failed and I got in the family way."

Gil walked to the window and stared out at the open plains, trying to absorb the awful truth. "What about my father? Does he know?"

"Yes. After you broke off our engagement and stormed out of my father's study, he flew into a rage and blamed me for not being convincing. For my failure to seduce you."

"He beat you?"

"Yes. Then he proceeded to rape me in his study."

Guilt nipped Gil for causing her more pain than she'd already endured. For doubting her all these years. For thinking the worst of her.

Like he'd done Josie?

"I'm sorry, Ivy. If I'd known, I'd have stopped him."

"Like father, like son."

He glanced at her, honed in on what she'd said earlier. "How'd the old man find out what Doyle was doing?"

"Your father came to our house to formally sever all ties between you and me, and he heard me scream." She smiled. "Harrison actually broke down the door to Father's study and caught him with his pants down."

Gil fisted his hands, thinking of the abuse Josie and her sister had endured at Parnell's hands. Nobody had been there to save them.

"Harrison took me out of my father's house that night. He was the first person I had ever confided in, and I did it so you and he wouldn't be at odds anymore."

"He married you the next day," Gil said, recalling the chain of events.

When his father and Ivy had returned to the house

as husband and wife, Gil had drawn his own erroneous conclusions and ran off. He'd been too hardheaded and filled with hurt and anger to listen to reason.

He'd been looking for a way out of Cooper Enterprises for years. He'd convinced himself he'd been born a cowboy, not a businessman tied to a damned desk. So he jumped at the first excuse that came his way and did what he wanted.

"Eliza told me you lost the baby."

"It was for the best," Ivy said. "I would have killed myself if I'd brought another beast like my father into this world."

"Eliza said the old man ruined your father. Did you know he aimed to do that?"

"Yes, and I gave Harrison my blessing to destroy Father. Within a year, my father lost everything, and the devil finally claimed his soul."

Gil nodded, taking it all in. He wasn't sure he'd have believed the story first off, but after what he'd seen, he knew men like Doyle were out there. Didn't matter what station in life. A cur was a cur by any name.

Where his father ruined Doyle by legal means, Gil would've been more apt to kill the bastard. But the end results would be the same.

Damn, maybe he was like the old man after all. He aimed to hunt Parnell down and kill him, if it was the last thing he did.

"Please, talk to Harrison." Ivy crossed to him and laid a hand on his chest. "Don't let this rift between you continue. He longs to be a part of your life."

"I'll think on it."

He was willing to bridge the gap, but he damned

sure wouldn't hold with the old man sticking his nose in the ranch business.

Josie stepped out on the front porch, wondering how two people could argue as much as Eliza and Harrison Cooper and swear they were a loving family. No wonder Sarah Ann had slipped out here, except a quick glance showed she was wrong.

"Where's Sarah Ann?" Josie asked Dwight, who was sitting on the front porch with Abigail.

"In the barn. Told her Hiram was tending your mare, and she wanted to watch." He shrugged. "I kept an eye on her going down there."

"It's been real quiet," Abigail said.

"Let's hope it stays that way." But Josie couldn't shake the feeling that something bad was about to happen.

She slipped in the barn. Her mare was in a stall, but she didn't see her foreman or her daughter.

"Sarah Ann? Where are you?"

A thump on the stall boards answered her. Anxiety scraped over Josie. She reached in her pocket, cursing as she recalled leaving the Navy Colt on the kitchen table.

"Sarah Ann?" She stepped back and searched the shadows, ready to run to the house. "Hiram?"

Another thump, followed by a muffled groan. Josie inched toward the stall, terrified what she'd find. Clover tossed her head and blew softly.

Josie slipped around the mare's stall. Fear nearly brought her to her knees as her eyes locked with Hiram's.

He sat against the far side of the stall, hands and

feet bound and a bandanna stuffed in his mouth. Blood crusted the side of his head.

"Mercy, what happened?" She pulled his bandanna out, then loosened Hiram's bonds, cursing her shaking hands.

"Someone slipped up behind me while I was wrapping a cloth around your mare's foreleg. Next thing I know, I woke up trussed like a goose."

She hugged her bucking stomach and leapt to her feet. "Oh, God. Sarah Ann!"

Josie ran from stall to stall, panic clawing at her throat as she looked everywhere in the barn. She pushed through the back door, mindful to look for tracks.

Only one set. A man's came from the stand of trees and returned the same way. Had Parnell kidnapped Sarah Ann?

Josie sagged against the door, heart breaking, knowing it was true. "*No!*"

Chapter 24

Josie's anguished cry tore through the air and slammed into Gil. He shoved Ivy away from his door and bolted outside, searching for her.

Nothing but a sense of dread hung on the wind. Eliza rushed from the house with their father on her heels.

Abby leaned over the porch rail, pointing to the barn. "She went in there a bit ago."

Dwight was barreling toward the barn, his face bleached of color and his sidearm clutched in his hand.

Gil took off running to the barn too, getting there first with his Peacemaker in his hands. "Josie! Where the hell are you?"

"She's in back," Hiram said, his gait unsteady.

Gil took a gander at the knob on the foreman's head and burst out the rear door. Josie had a saddle on Sarah's piebald mare and was tightening the latigo like she was running a race. Her whip coil that he'd seen in the tack room now hung from the saddle horn.

He slid his Peacemaker back in the holster. "What the hell's wrong?"

"Parnell has Sarah Ann."

"You saw them?"

"No, but I know he took her." She dropped the stirrup, gathered the reins and climbed onto the saddle.

"I'm going with you."

"I'm not waiting."

Josie wheeled the mare around and the animal burst into a gallop. In no time she'd raced past the stand of trees, heading north.

Gil whistled for his gelding then ran to the tack room for his gear.

"What you want us to do?" Hiram asked.

"Get to the house and stand guard." Gil stared at Dwight. "You get your ass into town and fetch the sheriff."

"Yes, sir." Dwight heaved his tack over a shoulder and headed into the corral.

Gil grabbed his saddle, blanket and bridle and barged out the back door. Rhubarb stood there, ears pricked, sides heaving. Dammit, he'd nearly run the legs off his gelding already. How much more could he ask of Rhubarb?

It took no time to saddle his horse, yet eons seemed to trickle by. Didn't help that images of Parnell torturing Sarah and Josie flashed in and out of his head like lightning.

In moments he was in the saddle. He flat out flew over the pasture, following the trail Josie had blazed. How the hell could this have happened again?

As if it mattered now. Parnell would enjoy torturing Josie, and the surest way to do that was by hurting Sarah. If Parnell did, that'd be the death of him because Gil wouldn't stop hunting the son of a bitch if he took his child and woman from him.

Gil didn't even want to think about going on here at the ranch if he didn't have the two women he loved beside him. That admission came hard, but it was the truth.

His sweet thief roped him all right, and Gil didn't ever want to toss off those ties.

Before he realized it, the ground sloped sharply. He reined his gelding and scanned the incline that spilled into a creek. To his left lay the trail that led to MacInnes's ranch.

Due north was his land.

A high-pitched scream split the air and raised the hair on his nape. Sarah? Or Josie?

Didn't matter. They were across this ravine, and he didn't want to waste time finding an easy crossing.

"I ain't ever asked this much from you," Gil said, urging the horse close to the slope.

Rhubarb tossed his head and snorted. Just when Gil feared he'd have to find another way, the gelding planted his front hooves on the slope and started down.

The powerful animal's haunches bunched beneath him, scrambling for purchase on the incline. Rocks tumbled down to plop in the water, sending up sprays. The gelding faltered once, then found his feet near the bottom.

Going down the creek bank seemed tame, though the footing was as dangerous. Rhubarb hit the water with a snort and plodded across to find an easy way to climb the other side.

Gil pulled back on the reins, letting the gelding get his bearings. He scanned the ground for tracks.

Another scream took that thought from his head. Gil put his money on his instincts and followed the sound.

In a stand of cottonwoods, he found Sarah Ann's

mare. Josie was nowhere to be seen, and her whip was gone.

Gil shifted in the saddle, getting his bearings. Through the draw was a shortcut to his land, and nestled back against the foothills squatted that old lean-to.

Cold fear crawled down his spine. He and Hiram had avoided the area because of pit vipers.

Gil jumped off his horse, whispering his rifle from the scabbard while rage and fear roared in his blood. The quiet was damn near as unnerving as keeping an eye peeled for rattlers.

Two screams then nothing but dead silence.

His fingers curled around the Winchester. He'd never killed a man, but he'd gladly end Parnell's miserable life.

The shack squatted dead ahead. He caught site of Parnell's horse tied behind it, but no sign of Parnell.

He crossed to the animal and untied him, then slapped his rump to shoo him off. To his relief, the horse took off the way Gil had come.

Gil started around the lean-to. It stood to reason that Parnell had Sarah inside. His damn bad luck there were no windows and only one door.

"Let her go." Josie's voice rang with cold authority, bringing Gil up short.

"Not on your life."

Gil recognized Parnell's voice. Josie had the bastard cornered.

A small whimper reached out to Gil. Sarah. God almighty that pitiful sound clutched at his heart.

"Drop the whip or I shoot her dead."

"Only a coward hides behind a child," Josie said. "But then you never were much of a man."

Parnell bit off a vicious curse. "You wouldn't talk so big if you didn't have that whip."

"Bring back unpleasant memories for you, Parnell?"

"You always were a defiant bitch," Parnell said. "I broke your sister's spirit. I'll do the same to you."

"Not in this lifetime."

Gil couldn't have put it better. He stopped by the corner of the lean-to, lifted his rifle and squinted down his barrel.

Parnell stood fifty feet from him. The son of a bitch held Sarah at his right side in a stranglehold. The barrel of a forty-five pressed to her temple.

Her small hands clutched at Parnell's punishing arm, and her wide eyes were fixed on something in front of the shack. Josie? Gil would bet on it.

Dammit all! If not for Sarah, he could pick Parnell off right now. But if he missed, or if Parnell had enough life left in him to pull the trigger, Sarah would die.

No, his best bet for getting the jump on Parnell was with Josie. She was out there challenging Parnell to shoot her.

All Gil could do was wait for Parnell to get a belly full of her insults and take aim. In that split second when Parnell's aim moved from Sarah to Josie, Gil would take him out.

Parnell tightened his hold on Sarah. The girl cried out and jerked her head toward Gil. Her eyes went wide with relief when she spotted him, and his throat clogged with more emotion than he thought a man could feel.

He tapped a finger on his lips. If Parnell realized Gil had a bead on him, God only knew what the man would do.

"Let her go," Josie said. "It's me you want."

"Yeah, I do. But I got a hankering for the brat, too."

Over his dead body, Gil thought, anger stampeding through him. He inched closer, desperate to save his daughter and his Josie.

A hollow rattle stopped Gil in his tracks and broke him out in a sweat. Sarah stiffened and her eyes bugged, but Parnell didn't seem to have heard the snake's warning.

Gil scanned the area, desperate to spot the viper. He saw a rattler near a greasewood bush ten feet behind Parnell.

Sarah squirmed, her gaze locked on the snake as well. Parnell gave her a hard shake and stepped back.

Gil fired at the snake. A click roared in his ears.

He tossed the jammed rifle aside and pulled his Peacemaker, knowing he'd have to get much closer to kill the rattler. If he could draw the snake's attention away from his daughter, the damned viper wouldn't strike her.

"Snakes," Josie said as another rattler made himself heard.

Gil frantically searched the ground.

"Where?" Parnell asked.

"One of them is fifteen feet to your left."

Parnell swung his revolver around and fired at the snake. A puff of dust exploded a foot from the rattler.

A loud crack split the air. Gil faced Josie. Her whip plucked Parnell's revolver from his hand. The six-shooter sailed into the air, landing ten feet in front of the viper pit.

Before Gil could blink, Josie sent the whip flying toward Parnell again. The tip caught the right side of his face near his ear.

Parnell yowled, clutching his bloody face with

one hand. Sarah twisted free and ran full tilt into
Gil's arms.

Gil wrapped an arm around her and cradled her
against his thundering heart. She burrowed against
him, clinging like a burr. He'd thought to set her
aside and go after Parnell, then realized to do so
would cheat Josie out of her retribution.

God in heaven, he felt foolish for ever underesti-
mating her grit, her courage. Josie advanced on Parnell, proud and fearless. An avenging angel.

"This one is for Lillian." Her voice was as hard as
the rocky outcropping behind Parnell.

Josie let loose her whip, and Parnell backed up out of
reach. "And one for me. And for all the other women
and children you've abused."

She let the whip fly once more, forcing him out of
the whip's reach, closer to the coiled vipers, rattling,
waiting to strike. Parnell spun around and ran toward
his six-shooter.

A flash of gold and brown leapt from the ground
and struck Parnell on the hand. Parnell swore and
jerked his hand back.

Another rattler caught Parnell on his leg. He stumbled, going down on one knee near the rocky ledge,
his hand useless.

Gil saw the third viper stretch out in thin air and
hit the man's throat. Parnell let out a guttural cry and
dropped hard on all fours, breathing hard.

More snakes struck Parnell, so many Gil lost count.
The man sprawled on his back, spread-eagled, his
breath rasping loud. As quickly as the snakes attacked, the rattlers retreated back into the rocks.

"Your mare is in those trees," Gil said to Sarah,

shielding her from Parnell. "I want you to get on Daisy and ride home fast as you can."

His daughter looked up into his eyes, and the fear in them brought a giant lump to Gil's throat. "Mama?"

"I'll see to her. Go on."

Sarah took off running to the horses, away from the dying man and the snakes.

Gil crossed to Josie and grabbed her upper arms, pulling her to him. "You ever do something like that again, I'll— Hell, I don't know what I'll do, but I guarantee you won't like it."

"You've no right to boss me, Gil."

He took in the resolve shining in her eyes and knew a dark part of her past was finally behind her. But there was a sadness there too that he didn't understand.

"You're right."

"Let me go so I can see to Sarah."

"I sent her home." Dammit, why wouldn't she look him in the eyes?

"Help me," Parnell cried out, his voice a mere croak.

Gil cupped Josie's face and planted a quick, hard kiss on her mouth. "Take my horse and get back to Rocky Point. Soon as I see to Parnell, I'll be along."

"What are you going to do?"

"Nothing. He's dying. Ain't nothing I can do for him now but see he passes on to hell."

She nodded, then coiled her whip and walked past him. The distance between them grew with each step. Each breath.

Gil walked toward Parnell, careful he didn't scare up more vipers. "Reckon you got your due."

"Bastard," Parnell said, his breath a choked wheeze. "At least have the decency to shoot me."

Gil took in the glazing in Parnell's one eye and read the excruciating pain distorting his face. "Heard a rattler bite hurts like hell."

"It does." Parnell gritted his teeth. "Don't leave me to die like this."

"What did you aim to do with Sarah?"

Parnell smirked. "Break her to ride, cowboy."

Gil whipped his Peacemaker at Parnell, then stopped himself. Slowly, he released the hammer. "You ain't worth wasting a bullet on."

He turned and walked away, careful of his footing.

"Damn you to hell," Parnell said, his words slurring. "Remember I had her first. Remember—" A grunt punctuated the air, then dead silence.

Gil stopped to pick up his Winchester and looked back. Parnell's body jerked once, then sprawled. Lifeless. It was over.

Parnell's horse whickered, ears twitchy and reins dragging the ground. Gil eased to the skittish gelding, mounted and took off back toward the ranch.

His thoughts centered on Josie. Though he'd called her a shady lady more times than he cared to admit, he knew there wasn't an amoral bone in Josie's delectable body. So why the hell had she loved him with all her heart last night, yet refused to marry him?

The answer still hadn't come to Gil when he rode onto Rocky Point some twenty minutes later. The last person Gil thought would be waiting for him was his father.

"Did you kill that lying bastard?"

"Didn't have to," Gil said as he dismounted. "Pit vipers got him."

Gil led the horse through the barn to the hitching rail out back with his father pulling drag. He imagined this was the first time his old man had ever set foot near so much muck. He'd bet money it'd be the last.

Hiram was turning Sarah Ann's mare out into the pasture where Rhubarb grazed. "So you know, Miz Abigail rode to Maverick with Dwight."

"Did she now?" Gil pulled the saddle off the horse and grabbed a towel to rub the animal down.

"Against my orders," his father said. "But neither your *foreman* or your hired hand dissuaded her."

"Ain't my place." Hiram nodded to Gil and walked off.

"That's the problem," Harrison said. "Your employees don't know their place, especially the black one. In fact, neither show much gumption."

Gil shook his head. His father was being a true pain in the ass. An ill-informed one.

"Miserable country," Harrison said, like a Philadelphia lawyer presenting his case before the jury. "You need dependable workers and a trustworthy manager in place before you return home."

"I am home."

"Don't be a fool. I got the entire story from Reid Barclay how you wheedled Everett Andrews into selling you a good portion of his ranch. Then you worked some deal with Mrs. Andrews into selling you more land, thereby giving you the lion's share."

"Barclay has been sticking his nose where it don't belong."

"The man has integrity."

"The man is as ruthless as they come."

"That is not necessarily a bad trait. Look at yourself. I warrant the only reason you want to stay here is because you'll own all of this godforsaken land once you marry Mrs. Andrews."

"You're wrong," Gil said. Though that had been his

exact thought when he told Josie they should get hitched.

"Is it? I never saw you work for anything in your life if you could finagle it someway."

"People change. For the record, I'm only holding part of Josie's share until she can pay me back."

Though he didn't expect or want that from her. Not now. In fact, he figured the debt was paid in full. Hell, he owed her interest.

"Extending loans was how I began acquiring land. You had a penchant for gambling and lacked drive, but you've attained a shrewd eye for business after all."

"Now there's an ass-backwards compliment if I ever heard one."

His father grimaced. "By damn, Gilbert. Hire men to run this ranch. Raise beef or sheep. Turn this holding into a hunting park and make a sizable profit."

"Josie is set on a guest ranch that caters to women."

"There is little money in that type venture." Harrison rocked back on his heels. "Once you marry, she'll understand that her position is to care for your daughter, and assume her rightful role as your wife."

Gil smiled. Not his Josie. Nope, she'd earned independence the hard way, and nobody would ever take that from her. Especially him.

"Your place is in Philadelphia, Gilbert. You are expected to take over the reins of the company."

"Let Eliza run it."

Harrison sputtered. "She's a woman."

"You noticed that, did you?" Gil grinned. "Eliza's a shrewd businesswoman. In fact, I'd bet she and her husband are more than qualified to move Cooper Enterprises into the next century."

His father didn't comment. No surprise there. Harrison Cooper believed a woman's place was in the home. He was a dyed-in-the-wool believer in keeping them pregnant and barefoot, though he imagined the old man had his hands full keeping his young bride satisfied.

"Do you still insist on refusing your birthright?"

"I sure as hell do." Gil faced his father. "The west made a man out of me and I'm staying right here on Rocky Point."

"Very well. Perhaps it is time Cooper Enterprises expanded into ranching. I will gladly back you in your endeavor."

"Keep your money. Whether we turn a profit with the guest ranch and the beef we run on the land, or barely keep our heads above water, it'll be all ours."

"You are making a grave mistake kowtowing to a woman. Mrs. Andrews needs to get this foolish guest ranch idea for women out of her head."

Gil had had the same thoughts. But after talking with Ivy and seeing how his sisters flourished while here, he agreed that women did need a retreat.

"You forget you're in Wyoming. Out here a woman has as much say over running her land as a man."

"Idiocy," Harrison muttered. "A man has the better business head."

Harrison stormed out of the barn, a good deal of his bluster covered in dust.

Gil shook his head and went back to rubbing the horse down. Yep, he'd been betting and bullying his way through life like Harrison Cooper. It was high time he set things right, starting with one little stubborn woman who'd lassoed his heart.

Chapter 25

"Do you intend to marry Gilbert?"

Josie glanced up from peeling potatoes to find Harrison Cooper standing in the kitchen doorway. She'd been expecting a visit from him, but she hadn't realized his obvious disapproval of her would chafe so.

"No."

"You surprise me, Mrs. Andrews. I thought you fancied yourself in love with my son."

She nearly cut off her thumb. "One has nothing to do with the other, Mr. Cooper."

"I disagree, especially if you're willing for Gilbert to stay on as your trail guide and, shall we say, suitor."

"If you have something to say, then please do."

He snorted. "I understand you are indebted to Gilbert."

"He told you that?"

"It came up while we were discussing business."

Well, damn. She focused on peeling potatoes, wondering what Gil had told his father about her debt to him. Surely he wouldn't breathe a word about her stealing from him in the brothel. Though Harrison's frown wasn't reassuring.

He walked to the table and grasped a chair back with both hands, chest puffed and back as rigid as his principles. "I am prepared to give you enough money to satisfy your loan to Gilbert, with enough left over to manage your business venture."

"Why ever would you do that?"

"As a reward for saving my wife's life and for raising Sarah to be a pleasant young lady. With the proper schooling, I believe the girl will do well."

Josie reckoned that was the closest Harrison Cooper would ever come to admitting Sarah Ann was his flesh and blood. Not that Josie cared, since it was obvious she didn't measure up to his high standards.

"Thank you kindly, but we'll do fine on our own." She grabbed another potato and skinned it in a matter of seconds, wishing she could peel off her troubles as easily.

"Will you? How many people besides my family have paid to partake of your rustic guest ranch?"

"When the sheriff came by earlier, he brought out a letter from New York. A group of lady teachers have decided to come visit in August." And instead of a deposit, the banknote they sent covered half their stay at Rocky Point. "In July, I have another group of ladies coming from Chicago."

"Is that all?"

"More folks will visit once word gets out."

"Perhaps, but you certainly won't become financially solvent at the rate you're going."

A fact she couldn't ignore, though she was loath to admit it to Harrison Cooper. While Everett was alive, he'd managed all the ranch dealings. She'd never objected, and never known how poorly he'd handled things.

This was his land, and she was grateful he'd taken her and Sarah Ann in. But though she'd known times were hard, she hadn't realized they'd been living hand to mouth since the deadly blizzard of '86 until after Everett passed on.

Harrison walked to the back door and peered out. "I want my son to return to Philadelphia with me and take over my empire, but he insists his home is here."

She wasn't surprised. Gil had big plans for the ranch.

Josie couldn't run him off Rocky Point, or buy his share. And she'd decided last night that she wasn't going to be the one who sold out and moved on. But she didn't how she'd live here with him, and know all he felt for her was lust.

"Where Gil goes or stays is up to him," she said.

"A fact I'm well aware of. Once he gets his hands on money, I'm sure he'll be a frequent visitor at the local saloon." He looked at her. "You do realize he has a fondness for gambling?"

"Most cowboys do like to wager. Why are you telling me all this?"

"So you're prepared when Gilbert loses his share of the ranch."

"He'd never do that." *But Gil had already when he'd made that risky bet with Dugan MacInnes.*

He shook his head, as if he pitied her for being gullible. "At present, this ranch appeals to my son because it's the first land he's held title to, and because of some noble sense of duty to you and Sarah. But when the girl is grown and gone, he'll likely tire of this isolated place."

And her? He didn't come out and say it, but she knew that's want he meant.

"You sound mighty sure Gil will fail."

"He has numerous times before." Harrison Cooper withdrew a stack of bills and dropped them on the table. "Take it, Mrs. Andrews. Pay off your debt to my son before he loses your ranch on the turn of a card. Believe me, when he's broke, he'll return home where he belongs."

He stalked out, and Josie stared at the money. Damn Harrison Cooper for trying to buy her compliance, and damn him for planting doubts in her head.

Josie waited until all the lights went out in the guest cabins that night, then she gathered the money and went to Gil's cabin. She knocked once.

"It's open."

She slipped inside and closed the door. Low lamplight painted a seductive glow over the tall cowboy with the whiskey-tinged hair and kiss-a-girl-senseless mouth.

"Here's the money I owe you." She tossed bills and their agreement on the bed. "That covers the interest Everett owed—what you paid Dugan MacInnes."

"Reid Barclay give you that?"

The insinuation stung, but she couldn't dwell on that now. "How I got it doesn't matter."

"Like hell it doesn't."

"Are you going back on your word?"

Gil tipped his head back and stared at the ceiling. "No. You got your share back free and clear." He tore the agreement in half, and the shadow of doubt in his eyes surprised her. "Where does that leave us, Josie?"

"Right back where we started. Good night."

Josie slipped out the door and stared up at the moonlit night, expecting that misgivings would sink deep roots in her. Had she made a mistake she'd soon regret?

No. She'd never felt more sure of herself.

Smiling, she headed to the bunkhouse. She knew she could trust Hiram to carry out her wishes. She hoped Gil would understand why she'd taken this course.

Long before dawn, Josie got up and put the coffee-pot on. Then she set to preparing a huge farewell breakfast for her guests.

Harrison Cooper was the first to arrive at the table. She imagined the man tried to beat the chickens up every morning so he could retain bragging rights. A shame he couldn't see the beauty in a clear blue horizon such as this one.

He claimed the head of the table. "I trust you settled the matter we discussed last night, Mrs. Andrews."

"I did."

"Excellent," he said as his daughters and wife entered the kitchen and took their places.

Josie smiled and served up a stack of flapjacks and a platter of bacon. Though she was glad this was the last meal she'd fix for Harrison Cooper, she would miss Eliza and Abigail.

"The time to leave has come too soon," Eliza said when breakfast ended and the wagons were brought around.

"You are always welcome in my house," Josie said, gaining a grunt of disapproval from Harrison.

Abigail hugged her next. "I do plan to return soon." She glanced at Dwight and winked. "Very soon."

"We shall see," Harrison said.

Josie bit back a laugh. Oh, he'd see all right. She almost wished she could be there to witness his enlightenment.

Gil guided the one-seated buckboard into Maverick. He'd volunteered to drive his sisters to the stage station this morning. Eliza's voluminous skirt filled the space at his feet.

Up ahead Hiram drove the surrey with the old man and Ivy. Pulling drag was Dwight with the wagon loaded with Saratoga trunks and a variety of carpetbags. Riding with him was Abby, the sister he'd thought was a snob, who'd given him the slip before he knew it so she could ride with Dwight one last time.

"Did you notice Father is in a wretched mood this morning?" Eliza asked.

Gil grinned. "Nothing new about that."

"His temper is much worse than usual, like when a business deal doesn't go as he'd hoped," Eliza said. "I wonder what set him at odds?"

"Maybe he and Ivy had a spat."

"I think there's more to it than that," Eliza said. "Did Father say anything to you?"

"Nope."

Gil had stayed away from the house this morning because of Josie, so he hadn't run into the old man. He hoped his luck held out as he pulled the buckboard to a stop before the Maverick Arms Hotel and set the brake.

The stage was there already, loading up. Parting with his kin would be short and sweet.

Dwight held on to Abby far too long to be respectable, but Gil held his tongue. For damn sure his little sister would be heading back to Rocky Point soon.

Gil handed Eliza down while his father assisted Ivy from the surrey. Ivy looked regal. Untouchable.

She was a good partner for his father. For once, Gil no longer resented her, or the old man.

"This here's for you." Hiram handed Harrison a small, linen-wrapped bundle. "Miz Josie told me to give it to you when we got to town."

Harrison tore it open and glowered. "By damn."

"What is it?" Ivy asked.

"Nothing that concerns you, dear."

Harrison slapped the bundle against his palm, and a chill went through Gil as he recognized it for what it was. Money.

The questions that had kept him staring at the ceiling all night suddenly had answers. His father had given Josie that money. A helluva lot of it.

She'd paid off Gil with some of it, then slipped the rest back to Harrison. Why?

Gil aimed to find out. He herded his father into the alley.

"What the hell did you do, old man?"

His father hiked up one gray eyebrow. "My actions are not accountable to you."

"They are when they concern the woman I love or my daughter. Now spill your guts."

The beginnings of a smile teased his father's rigid mouth, then his green eyes glittered. The old man tipped his head back and guffawed.

Gil stared at him, not seeing anything to laugh about. Hell, he could count the times he'd seen the old man crack a smile. Fewer when he'd heard him laugh.

"Have you lost your mind?" Gil asked.

"Just had an enormous load lifted off it." He waved the linen-wrapped bundle before Gil. "As you have no doubt guessed, I tried to buy Mrs. Andrews off with this last night."

"Damn you! You had no call to do that."

"I needed to assure myself she wasn't a gold-digger."

Gil grabbed fistfuls of his father's fine coat and slammed him against the clapboards, ignoring Ivy's gasp. If the old man screwed up his chances with Josie, he'd stomp a mud hole in his ass.

"Mark my words, she ain't one. But even if she was, what the hell difference does it make to you?"

"Come now. You're a parent, Gilbert. To what ends would you go to ensure your daughter's well-being?"

There was no limit. "What the hell's your angle?"

"I care what happens to you. You were a miserable young man in Philadelphia." His father blinked, like he had sand in his eyes. "I want you happy, Gilbert."

"All aboard," the stagecoach driver called out.

"Harrison? Do hurry," Ivy said.

Gil released his father and stepped back, his own eyes feeling a mite gritty. "That's right good of you."

"Clearly this life agrees with you. So does that fine woman waiting at the ranch for you." His father slapped the money in Gil's hand. "Cherish her, son. She's being stubborn about marrying you, but don't take no for an answer. Let me know when you've increased your family."

"I don't want your money."

"Nonsense. Consider it a wedding gift as well as past

birthdays for my granddaughter." His father gripped Gil's shoulder. "Just don't squander it at the tables."

He walked away.

Gil couldn't force his feet to budge. He swiped his eyes on his shirtsleeve and sniffed. Distantly he heard his sisters shout their good-byes as the stage pulled out.

Dust swirled around Gil's feet, but as it died down his anger went with it. His father had tried and failed to buy off Josie. By damn, she'd defied the old man.

She'd refused to marry Gil, too, but she hadn't ordered him off her land or out of her life. Nope, she'd paid her debt, but a part of her was tied to him.

He smiled, knowing why. She loved him.

Gil stuffed the money in his vest pocket, and headed down the boardwalk. The chink-chink of his spurs was drowned out by laughter and the tinkle of piano music spilling from the saloon.

He smiled and pushed through the door.

Josie straightened from scrubbing the pine floor in the first cabin and pressed a hand to the small of her back. She'd started in cleaning as soon as the Coopers left this morning.

With the sheriff assuring her that Parnell was dead, she'd let Sarah Ann ride over to Chalmers' Ranch. Their youngest daughter turned thirteen today and Mrs. Chalmers' saw fit to throw a party for her. Josie didn't expect Sarah Ann home until suppertime.

Early afternoon, Josie heard the jingle of harness rings. She hurried out the door, smiling. Hiram and Dwight were back. But where was Gil?

Hiram stopped in front of the house. "Gave Mr. Cooper the bundle like you asked."

"What did he say?" she asked.

"Nothing to me, but him and Gil had a powwow in the alley. Cooper seemed right happy when he boarded the stage. Gil had that bundle in his hand as he headed into the saloon."

The saloon? "Oh, my."

Hiram frowned. "Anything you want me to do?"

"No. Thank you."

The money. Harrison Cooper had given it to Gil. But why? Had he bought him out when she'd refused to cave in to Harrison's wishes? Had Harrison succeeded with Gil?

Josie went back to scrubbing, working so hard sweat popped out on her brow. She'd gotten her third of the ranch back, just like she'd wanted.

And it wasn't like she'd agreed to marry Gil. Damnation, why had he gone to the saloon?

Harrison Cooper's warning needled her. Gil did have a bundle of money and his share of Rocky Point. He could gamble away all of it and come dragging home dead broke. Or worse, he might not come back at all.

If she never saw him again, she knew this awful lonely ache within her would never leave her. Maybe loving a man who didn't love you in return wouldn't be horrible. Maybe Gil would learn to love her in time. Maybe since she'd turned him down, he'd ride out of her life.

No, Gil wouldn't do that. He'd be back, if for no other reason than to fetch his horse and gear.

Josie carted her bucket of suds to the cabin door and pitched the water into the dust. The wind caught her kerchief and nearly whipped it off her head.

She grabbed the thing before it blew clean to the

house. That's when she saw the cowboy walking toward her.

The wind whipped at the sleeves of his cambric shirt and plastered his vest to his broad chest. His boots kicked up dust clouds, and the chink-chink of his spurs was sweet music to her ears.

Gil had come home. Her heart beat too fast. She laid a hand over her fluttering stomach and tried to read his expression.

My, but he seemed unnaturally tense. A thousand reasons why ran through her mind, none offering a shred of comfort.

She swallowed her panic and backed into the cabin. He followed her in and slammed the door. A pulsing hush settled around them.

"I didn't expect you back so late." She wasn't about to tell him she'd fretted the day away.

"Had a few things to tend to."

Like gambling? She grabbed the broom and swept up the leaves and dust that'd blown in, needing something to do. Needing something to hold on to.

"I hear your family got off just fine."

"They did. Had a talk with my old man. Dammit, Josie, why'd you pay me off with his money?"

"I didn't. What I gave you is the deposit I got from our next guests." She looked up into his troubled eyes. "Hiram told me Harrison gave you the money."

"Yep. Told me not to squander it."

She gripped the broom with both hands, suddenly unsure and hating every second of doubt. "Did you?"

He thumbed his hat back. "If I told you I lost it all gambling, would you take that broom to me?"

"If you don't tell me the truth I just might."

Gil laughed and grabbed the broom, pulling it and

her into his arms. "All right. I 'fess up. I've always had
a weakness for gambling. Sometimes I've won. Most
times I've lost. It never made a damned bit of difference to me. It was just a game. But as I was holding
that money, I knew the urge to take a chance was too
much to turn down. So I bet the highest stakes in my
life and put everything I owned on one play."

She gulped. "Did you win?"

"You tell me. Do you love me?"

She blew out the breath she'd been holding. "More
than I probably should."

He kissed her, hard and fast, then let her go and
tugged a paper from his vest pocket. "Here."

Josie opened the paper and read the words. Then
read it again to make sure her eyes weren't playing
tricks on her.

"I don't understand. This is the deed to Rocky
Point Ranch." Her eyes met his. "You signed over
your share to me?"

"Gambled it away, sweetheart." He took another
paper from his pocket and flicked his fingers against
it. "On this."

Her hands shook as she read it. "I don't understand. This is another deed."

"Yep." He pulled her back into his arms, his smile
a bit crooked and unsure. "I tracked down Dugan
MacInnes in the saloon and made him an offer on
half of his land that borders Rocky Point. He agreed
to sell it to us."

She read the deed, then looked at him. Her head
spun, wondering what it meant. "But this land is in
my name, too."

"That's right. All my life I've measured my worth
on whether I won my father's approval. I used to

think I had to hold title to a big ranch and have a fine herd of cattle."

"What changed your way of thinking?"

"You." He stroked a finger over her cheek and she resisted the urge to snuggle against that big, warm hand. "I won't lie to you, Josie. At first I wanted to marry you so I could get my hands on the ranch."

"And now?"

"Now I just want you." His mouth covered hers in a kiss that seared her to her soul. "I love you, sweetheart."

No one had ever said that to her before. She'd feared she'd never hear those words, especially from this cowboy who'd stolen her heart. And now that she had—

She grabbed his vest and stared into his eyes, heart galloping as she realized he'd finally spoken from his heart. "Say it again."

"I love you, and if you let me, tonight will be the start of showing you how much. Will you marry me, Josephine Mae?"

"Yes, Gil Yancy. I surely will."

Every doubt she'd had vanished in a blink. Josie planted her hands on his chest and walked him backward until he dropped onto the bed. She pushed him onto his back and sprawled atop him, happier than she'd ever been in her life.

"Now, about you showing me how much you love me— Why wait till tonight, cowboy?"

He laughed, his eyes glittering with passion and love as he pulled her down on him. "Can't think of a reason, sweetheart. Not one."